The
DANCERS
of
SYCAMORE
STREET

Books by Julie L'Enfant (non-fiction)

William Rossetti's Art Criticism: The Search for Truth in Victorian Art

The Gag Family: German-Bohemian Artists in America

Pioneer Modernists: Minnesota's First Generation of Women Artists

Other Realities: The Art of Paul Kramer

Persistence of Vision: The Art of Bettye Olson
(with Jaden Hansen)

Nicholas R. Brewer: His Art and Family

To Barbara, my dear friend, with love—

The
DANCERS
of
SYCAMORE
STREET

A Novel

Julie L'Enfant

Julie L'Enfant

**CALUMET
EDITIONS**
Minneapolis

CALUMET EDITIONS

Minneapolis

FIRST EDITION May 2019
The Dancers of Sycamore Street. Copyright © 2019 by Julie L'Enfant.
All rights reserved.

This is a work of fiction. Names, characters, places and incidents either are
the product of the author's imagination or are used
fictitiously.

Printed in the United States of America.
10 9 8 7 6 5 4 3 2 1

Cover image: Maggie Siner, *Ballet Studio*, 2015, 13 x 15 in., oil on linen
Cover design: Sue Stein
Interior design: Gary Lindberg

ISBN: 978-1-950743-03-2

BOOK ONE

THE SYLPHS

1

It all started back in 1955, the day Geoffrey Render came to Mme LeBreton's ballet school to observe our class, just to "watch," everybody said, although of course I knew that nobody of Geoffrey Render's stature ever just watched anything: a man like that would take what he liked, and do whatever he wanted to with it. Of course the school had existed for some time before that—seventeen years, in fact—and I had been going to it for more than two years, but still, that day when Geoffrey Render came to "watch" seems, in my mind the only place to start.

Of course it looks very different now, but back then the LeBreton School of Ballet looked like some lonely little cabin, situated as it was at the rear of a large gravel parking lot surrounded by a stand of pine trees that gave the impression of being the edge of a deep dark forest. The impression was false, of course: this wasn't the wilderness—it was on the edge of Collegetown and right near Middleton Community College—but you could think so, when you first saw it. I expect Mr. Render thought so, when he first saw it.

On that day, as usual, I rode my bicycle up to the studio. I remember being intensely anxious to see inside since I doubted that Mr. Render would really come. I plunged through the gravel, walking the bike, then planted the front wheel in a tangled old flower bed to peer into the dirty little set of casement windows in the side of the studio. Then, finally, I saw them: Mme LeBreton and Mr. Render!

They seemed to be getting along well, which was a big relief after what I had seen and heard the night before, so I stopped worrying about that and took a few seconds out just to gape at Mr. Render. If I hadn't already seen the great dancer and choreographer "in person," I would have been awfully surprised at his appearance. Oh I had known what he looked like from photographs, of course, though in recent years, when he was no longer performing, these were generally of his extraordinary face. He was bald except for a fringe of dark hair which looked like some kind of honorable adornment, such as a coronet or a wreath. He might have been a Middle Eastern potentate, a desert ruler. He had fine strong features—a notable mouth—but it was his eyes, I think all his public would agree, that riveted the attention. They were black and had a commanding stare, as if they had looked out over wide dominions. So it was not the face that would have surprised me if I had not seen Mr. Render before, but rather the body. To be frank, Geoffrey Render did not look like a dancer or anybody who had ever *been* a dancer.

Now, there was one full-length photograph of Geoffrey Render that I knew well. This hung with a collection of photographs in Mme LeBreton's studio, over in the corner right above the Mothers' Bench. It showed him in a classical tunic at the apex of some fantastic leap—a *ballotté*, perhaps—at least it looked fantastic, although there was no floor in the picture to show how far off the ground he was, just a line of handwriting—the words "With love to my Milly" in a bold black script. That picture showed Geoffrey Render to be of stocky build, but because of the vague perspective it did not show how short he was. He was quite short, about five feet six, I believe, and by the time I am talking about, when he was about fifty-five, he had put on some weight around the middle and looked even shorter than that.

So there he was, on my special stomping ground, the ballet studio, demonstrating some step for Mme LeBreton, who stood looking on in a worshipful posture. They seemed to be alone in the studio. Geoffrey Render, with his arms held out in second position, was gliding from side to side, humming to himself perhaps, thinking and working with his body. He wore a red plaid flannel shirt, I remember, which hung out over tiny-looking black pants. He looked more like a country grocer than a choreographer who had played a major role in the history of ballet in America. Ah, but I knew enough not to judge him by his appearance! I was separated from him by the glass of the windows, but even so I could feel the force of his concentration, and I thought I could glimpse some of the richness of his personality. In particular, I knew that he had the power to change all our lives.

***

In those days, ballet was a glamorous and cosmopolitan art form which celebrated its rites in New York and London and St. Petersburg (as I still thought of it) and other great capitals of the world, but which in Middleton, at that time a medium-sized city of about two hundred thousand people, was honored and practiced only at Mme LeBreton's school. In my mind, this school was a rustic but valiant little outpost of ballet. This is not to say that there were not other dancing schools in Middleton: there were actually three or four other studios around town but none of them carried on the universal traditions of ballet in a pure and unsullied way. Mme LeBreton had nothing to do with tap or jazz or acrobatics or any of those other tainted forms of dance: she purveyed classical ballet and classical ballet alone, as was evident at the delicate recitals she put on every year down at the Civic Auditorium.

This was the first time during the years I had been taking lessons there that something so earthshaking as the appearance of Geoffrey Render had actually taken place at the LeBreton School of Ballet, but I had always enjoyed the hope that something of the sort would happen, something unexpected and wonderful which would flow from Mme LeBreton's impressive contacts in the great world of ballet. It was widely known that Mme LeBreton had been a professional dancer before she married and settled in north Louisiana in the late 1930s and that this career had produced enduring connections with the National Dance Theatre in New York City. Indeed, Mme LeBreton went to New York every year to the NDT summer school, carrying her beautiful daughter, Cecilia, and perhaps another advanced student who was very serious about her dancing, and this annual pilgrimage to New York was a guarantee to the community that the version of ballet taught at the LeBreton School was the true one, not some provincial or personal version such as girls were likely to get at Mrs. Wright's little school over on Fairchild Avenue (among the tap dancers and the acrobats), or at Mrs. Farfel's, which was a joke.

Mme LeBreton's connection with the great world was documented and certified by the aforementioned gallery of photographs which hung above the Mothers' Bench in the front studio. I was fascinated by these pictures and often stopped to look at them on my way by. In fact, I would often straighten them, for they tended to go askew, perhaps because, deep into class, our *changements* and *jetés* would shake the very foundations of the studio. There were ten or twelve of these black-and-white photographs hanging there in black wood frames, like diplomas. The largest of the pictures was the leaping Geoffrey Render. There was another one of him in street clothes, an old-fashioned double-breasted pinstripe suit, like a gangster, where he had his arms around two girls, one of whom was, without question, "his Milly." Along with two or three others capturing her in a swan costume or some flashing dress for a character role, this picture formed my principal impression of Mme LeBreton during the time of her professional past. It showed a round, smooth face with bright eyes and what you might call a pert nose and mouth, and she had fluffy blond hair, not (I found this significant) long enough to pull back into a knot at the nape of the neck like the other women in the pictures wore. She looked like a silent film star back then. It was not a beautiful face, but it had spirit. The same sort of conclusion was to be drawn from the full-length "Milly" in the cygnet role: she did not have a good confirmation, to use the professional term—her hips looked too wide and her calves seemed too thin and weak for a rock-firm *pointe*—but her pose suggested a certain verve which would be highly attractive on stage.

It always distressed me to look at Mme LeBreton right after contemplating these photographs. I found it much more pleasing to observe her, as I did on the pivotal day I am talking about, in the company of one of these mythical colleagues who had been deteriorating along with her. Although she was not very old—I figure she was about forty at that time, an age which I myself will reach in less than a year—she had aged much more dramatically than he had; she was, to put it bluntly, a wreck. She still had those thin calves, but now her hips were two mounds and she had a paunch. She always wore a leotard. with a long tulle skirt over it, waltz-length, I think it was. The skirt always matched the leotard perfectly. They were always in a shade of red or pink, and she must have had a hundred of these sets. I imagine Bartlett the Costumer ordered them for her, or possibly Mrs. Oleander "ran up" the skirts, but anyway, the general effect was still lumpy, even decadent, somehow.

Not only that: the round smooth face of the pictures was now wrinkled and baggy, and the blond hair looked like sparse feathers, as if she were wearing some worn-out cygnet's cap. Her chest looked like a rope ladder descending into the coral or magenta or puce bodice, and her feet! Her feet deserve their own chapter, they were so knobby and misshapen in the soft old toe shoes she always wore. The shoes must have been pink at one time, but now they were gray, and they looked like two very dirty cloth bags full of ball bearings, to tell you the truth. I did not see how she could walk on them, much less dance. Nor did I see how she could stand to see herself in the mirror, and her studio, like all ballet studios, was lined with big, honest mirrors. It seemed to me that looking at herself in those old pictures would be very depressing for her. Now I think that maybe they comforted her by proving how attractive she used to be. Or, and this is more likely, she never looked at those pictures at all, and they inhabited the studio in that haphazard way everything else there did.

***

Before they noticed me outside gaping at them, I began to walk my bicycle around back to the door of the little studio. (There was a front door, by the way, but nobody ever used it except that one time I'll have to tell about.) This was an arduous effort, this walking the bike, as Mme LeBreton's parking lot was made up not of shells or small pebbles, like most driveways or parking lots, but of little rounded rocks. I pushed through these, wishing as always that I got a ride to ballet. I was always embarrassed to arrive at the studio too hot, or too cold, depending on the season, and windblown, particularly since I was the only one in the advanced class to arrive in this disheveled state. But I had to ride my bicycle, or else walk, which wasn't much better, since I lived so close to the studio, just down the street in the rather weird neighborhood called Collegetown. In any case my mother couldn't bring me, since she wasn't like the Mothers who always drove their daughters to ballet.

The parking lot was filled with cars, big cars with Mothers in them waiting for the horde of six- and seven-year-olds in the class that met before mine. This class had left the studio and some of the little girls streamed toward the cars, but I saw now that something unusual was happening. Not all the little girls were getting into the big cars and surging away in a heavy spray of rocks. In fact, some Mothers were stopping their roaring motors and getting out of their cars and actually walking around to the back of the studio. I prayed they were not going inside to see Mr. Render "in person": Madame wouldn't like this unauthorized entrance into the studio. (She strictly forbade Mothers inside, except by special invitation, and even then they were restricted to the Mothers' Bench.) But as I rounded the corner of the studio I saw that a little crowd was gathered back there where Madame parked her car and I stowed my bicycle: the attraction was something in the underbrush. Then I heard the yowls, or rather realized I had been hearing the yowls, of cats, which meant that Colette, the studio cat, was in heat again. Madame's slovenly cat was apparently in some bushes just a few feet from the back door with a male cat. I saw a cluster of shiny-haired little girls in leotards jostling for a good look at what they were doing and a complement of well-groomed Mothers crying to pull them away.

"They're fighting! They hate each other!" one little girl cried ecstatically.

"Let's go home, Susan dear," a Mother said. "That's not nice to watch."

It was a real relief to me that the commotion was not connected in any way with the presence of the famous Geoffrey Render inside the studio. And I found it very understandable, considering the nature of the Mothers. If *my* mother had been there, she too would have been more concerned with preventing me from seeing what Colette was doing than with the presence of Geoffrey Render inside. But of course my mother was not a Mother in the sense I am talking about. By "Mother" I mean something very particular: a member of the LeBreton School of Ballet

Mothers' Guild. My mother was not a member of the Mothers' Guild because she did not "stay at home" like these women: she was what they would call a career woman.

My father, you see, was an attorney in practice with a small firm that had an office up on Tates Parkway, the thoroughfare running by the college, and—this is the crucial thing—my mother was an attorney with him. I was deeply embarrassed by this. It seems incredible that I should have been so embarrassed by this fact back then, and actually I don't believe I would have been had it not been for the vision of motherhood I got at Mme LeBreton's studio. There, the lacquered and bejeweled Mothers chauffeured their daughters to lessons in Cadillacs or else station wagons with artificial wood paneling on the sides and—this is the remarkable thing—often they just sat in these great cars out in the parking lot all through their daughters' class! They might have a dog or two for company, or they might visit with each other briefly, but on the whole they simply sat there in their cars for an hour and a half. They did not read or sew or even try to see in the windows of the studio, as far as I could tell, but just stared out into the tall woods. They remind me of those painted wooden statues that are borne through crowded streets during the religious festivals of underdeveloped nations. They had that same glossy passivity while they waited for their daughters, coming to life only when they were with their daughters, or doing something to benefit their daughters, like putting on the Christmas party or the great Spring Bazaar.

My mother, in contrast, was at her office—cheerful, smart, and efficient—every day until five o'clock. I suspect that my ballet lessons four days a week from four-thirty until six appealed to her practical nature primarily as a wholesome, health-promoting activity, so conveniently located, from which I could cycle home almost every day and find her and my father there to meet me, as if that were the first time I had arrived home that day. This would mitigate wonderfully the fact that she "worked." But I do not know for sure. Lucille, our housekeeper, was always there after school, of course. Possibly I just impute a certain guilt to my mother because I suffered so at this time on account of her not being a regular Mother.

***

Hastening up the several sagging steps to the back door of the studio, I hoped this feline commotion wouldn't offend Mr. Render. I also hoped he liked the school. It wasn't impressive to look at, Lord knows: there was not even a sign out front saying what the building was, though you knew it must have some public function with all that parking. It was finally identified around by the back door by a little brass plaque which said "Mildred LeBreton School of Ballet, Dedicated September 1, 1938," which was nice and official, but the plaque was sickly green now, and the whole place was run down. As always, the back door was wide open to allow some air to pass into the otherwise suffocatingly stuffy little dressing room through a ratty screen door that screeched like a bat when I opened it, not that you could separate out that sound from the sounds of the mating.

"Oh hey, Alma," I said to the only person in the dressing room. Usually the dressing room was bulging with dozens of ballet students and all their paraphernalia, far more than it had been designed for. It was as narrow as a school cloakroom. You got the impression that the school was a much bigger success than Mme LeBreton had ever envisioned in 1938. The walls, for instance, were rough unpainted paneling: she hadn't gotten around to having them painted, as if she had thought not many people would ever see them.

"Hey, Meredith," Alma said to me. She was sitting on one of the benches that lined the room, reading a book. "I was real early today."

"Well I guess *so*," I said appreciatively, starting to peel off the jacket and slacks I had to wear to the studio on account of the dratted bicycle ride, going over to consult a little mirror that hung on a wall about my hair. Of course it looked scraggly. "I could hardly wait either. Lordy mercy, I wish those cats would hush."

"What do you mean, 'hardly wait,'" Alma asked absently, turning a page.

I thought at first that Alma might be kidding, but she looked quite serious. I saw too, as I observed Alma, that the book she had been reading was a cookbook and not a real book. Well now, possibly she *was* genuinely ignorant of who was in the front studio and what it meant that he was there.

"You *did* go see NDT last night, didn't you?" I ventured.

Alma hesitated a second or two. "Oh, the National Dance Theatre! Well, I wanted to go, but Tom doesn't really like ballet and so I didn't bring it up. It was in the middle of the week and all, and he has to get to the bank so early."

"I see!" I murmured. Alma was an oddity (the only married girl in the advanced class), and in many ways she was a mystery to me. Marriage must be terrible, I deduced, to make you omit to mention the coming of NDT.

"Was it good?" Alma asked.

"It was absolutely wonderful. I couldn't begin to tell you," I said carefully, eyeing Alma. I was only fourteen at that time and to me she was "old," that is, out of high school and apparently not in school anywhere. Actually I think she was about twenty-five. She was rather pretty, but there was a disturbing thing about her: a complexion which got very oily when she got hot, which of course she did at every lesson. I vaguely associated this unusual oiliness with the fact that she was married: it made me think of the word "lubricious." Alma had a slight and youthful figure, but she was not a good dancer. She could not do an *entrechat* three, for instance or anything else involving real control. But she had a sweet presence on stage and had had something of a success in the recital the previous year as "La Fleur," a brief solo role which exploited her poignant quality and was innocent of any turns or leaps. She was a member of the advanced class only because it was too ridiculous to put a person of her years with the beginners.

"I'd love to have gone," Alma said, with a bright little air.

"Well, you'll get to see Geoffrey Render today anyway, and for me that was the best part. I went to the cocktail party afterward. Stood quite close to him," I said nonchalantly.

"Who's Geoffrey Render?" Alma asked.

"Oh, Alma," I said. "You *are* kidding, aren't you?"

Alma stood up and yawned. "No, I'm not kidding. I've heard his name somewhere but I'm not sure who he is."

"Alma. Geoffrey Render is the Artistic Director of the National Dance Theatre and *has* been lo these many years. He *founded* it. Before that, he was a famous dancer himself and he ran Ballet Benet, the touring company that turned into NDT. Madame danced with them. They were good friends back then. Surely you've seen the pictures on the wall."

"Oh, the pictures on the wall," Alma said, stretching and smiling vacantly.

"He's in the front studio now," I said.

"Oh?" Alma said, jumping a little, looking around suspiciously.

"He's *only* one of the most famous choreographers in the world," I said. "He's *only* in every book on ballet you pick up," I added, casting an indignant glance at the cookbook on the bench.

"And Madame's an old, old friend of his, then?" Alma asked, looking impressed at last.

"Well, yes," I began. By this time I knew that the situation was far more complex than this, however. I knew, as a matter of fact, that while Mme LeBreton and Mr. Render went under the banner of "old, old friends"—at least Mme LeBreton did, witness those pictures in the front studio, which seemed to attest to a warm, continuing and permanent friendship—in fact, Mme LeBreton and Mr. Render had not, before the cocktail party that took place the night before, spoken to each other for many, many years. I knew too that Mr. Render was visiting the studio for other reasons than merely to see some classes taught by his old friend, and that there was a terrible burden upon us to impress him favorably. But at that point the other members of the advanced class started clambering and knocking into the dressing room to undress and chatter, and I abandoned the effort of communing with Alma. I am happy to say *they* had been to see NDT the night before and *they* knew who Mr. Render was, even if they did not know all the private things I knew from having hung around near Mr. Render at the party. It had been the most exciting evening of my life up to that time, and while I am sure that this was not the case for most of my classmates in the advanced class, who were mostly very fashionable and led very exciting lives, I was confident that they had a pretty good idea of just how important this class would be.

***

We had definite ideas about what to expect in the course of the class. In fact, our routine was so predictable that we functioned not as a dozen or so individuals but as a kind of multi-limbed organism. First we gathered in the dressing room, all except for Claude Bateson, that is, the only boy in our class—the only boy in the whole school—who had to dress in a little room in the back, or the back studio, as it was called.

We waited to be summoned into the front studio, which, unlike the dressing room and the back studio and the primitive little bathroom off the little hall between them, was very grand. This is what Mme LeBreton had been thinking of when she designed the building; everything else had been neglected for this. It was a long room, lined with mirrors and barres, like every ballet school. It had banks of fluorescent lights on the ceiling, but Mme LeBreton did not like these and often left them off until the room was practically dark. It also had an air conditioning unit, even back in the 1950s when very little in Middleton was air conditioned. Mme LeBreton did like this, and ran the air conditioner all the time unless it was freezing outside. So I remember the front studio as being very large and dim and cool. There was of course a piano at the end of the room nearest the dressing room, not far from the Mothers' Bench, and right before class was to begin we could hear Mrs. Fister, Madame's old accompanist, start tiddling on the piano, or we would hear the stirrings of Madame's gold-headed stick, her instrument of instruction.

The studio had a particularly fine floor, gray asphalt linoleum which Mme LeBreton took better care of than her face. It was swept and mopped at the end of every working day, but not of course ever waxed; it was a superb surface for dancing, and I do not remember a single injury attributable to the floor. Mme LeBreton would rap her stick on this admirable surface, and we would move our multi-limbed organism (loose-limbed, and with the duck-like waddle dancers have) out of the dressing room and into the front studio, where we would fan out to take our places at the barre. There we did what is called the "barre," the fifteen or so exercises, the traditional *pliés* and *battements* and *relevés*, designed to warm up every muscle in the body, and, after this, we moved out to the center floor where Madame called out combinations of steps for us to do in her gurgly and very authentic-sounding French.

When I first joined the advanced class, this portion of the class terrified me. I started ballet rather late, I should tell you: I was twelve, while most of Madame's students began at five or six. My progress through the ranks was rapid, however: I had very strong legs and, most importantly, reliable musical instincts. And so at thirteen I was promoted to the advanced class. I felt like a mere mortal among goddesses. It wasn't long before I realized that not everybody in Madame's exalted advanced class was a brilliant dancer, but until then I felt miserably inadequate. At no time was this more true than during combinations, when Mme LeBreton would screw up her haggard face to think, then start beating her stick as she intoned a string of nasal syllables—*glissade, jeté, glissade, assemblée,* or some such—walking negligently through the steps as she chanted their names. The class would already have begun sliding and twirling and lunging and I would be on the back row, hopping anxiously, trying to catch on.

I had already had certain combinations in my beginners' class, but Madame always demonstrated them full out to the smaller girls: she did not expect anything of them in the way of memory. I was twice the size of the biggest of those classmates and, of course, a great deal more advanced mentally, at least more attentive, and I had no trouble at all. But the advanced class was another matter until I caught on to the steps and discovered that these classes were just as predictable as the beginners' class, if on a grander scale. And while I was not the best in the class I was by no means the worst either, and by the time I am telling about I was perfectly calm in the face of Mme LeBreton's combinations.

I should also mention "the dances." Around October or November of each year Madame would begin teaching us the numbers we were to perform in the spring recital. These recitals were all the same, gently lyrical in tone, each of us in a lovely tutu except for Claude, who did all the vigorous bravura parts. Each class did two numbers and every student remembered every step of these dances the rest of her life because Madame taught them so carefully and thoroughly, feeding them to us phrase by phrase during the combinations. In time, say around

January, she would reveal the pattern of these combinations so that each dance would stand before us as a whole, after which the climax of each lesson would be a rehearsal of "the dance" or "the dances." The dance became an automatic response to the music: it was grooved in our brains. No one, to my knowledge, ever forgot her steps at one of Mme LeBreton's recitals.

Each member of the advanced class had a solo, which also frightened me to death my first time around. I was the Lark that first year, and even today I could do the Lark steps. In fact Mme LeBreton's pedagogical system was so measured and so patient that I believe anyone who was not actually lame could have done the Lark variation with some success. By my third year, then, I was also calm at the prospect of another solo.

***

When I think of those first lessons at Mme LeBreton's, before the day Geoffrey Render came, I think primarily of Madame's stick, an elegant black walking stick with what looked like a solid gold head. She was never without it in class: she used it to beat time and she also used it to prod her students.

She had to beat time with great force because of the vagaries of Mrs. Fister. With great enthusiasm but little accuracy, this knobby old woman played a strange mixture of songs, from commonplace ditties and Broadway show tunes to excerpts from the great ballet repertoire (Chopin, Delibes, Tchaikovsky). Now, this mix is usual with ballet accompanists, I understand, but Mrs. Fister was unique in taking *her* merry mélange of melodies and making them all do the dogtrot. This was accomplished by means of a peculiar flailing technique in the left hand. The melodies were extremely difficult to identify, and I spent a lot of mental energy as my body toiled away at the barre or in center floor trying to figure out the identity of the melody trotting through the room, with Madame vainly trying to bring it to heel with striking blows of the stick. One day, for instance, the jaunty tune to which we were doing *pirouettes* turned out to be "Flow Gently, Sweet Afton." Her way with a song was such that this, and even more common standards, almost got by me.

Sometimes, however, God granted that Mrs. Fister be sick, which meant that Madame played some old records on a record player that was behind the piano. The stick, on those days, did not need to attempt to corral Mrs. Fister (who was probably a little deaf), so it beat more gently on the immaculate linoleum. One felt it more often in its other function of correcting our mistakes, particularly in the vital matter of the turnout. Now, my main talent was an extraordinary elevation—jumping—but the strong thighs that were the basis of this talent were part of a tight musculature that prevented my ever being as limber as some of my classmates (I could never do the splits, for instance), and also prevented me from having a good turnout. Everyone knows that the object of ballet training is to realign the body, which we normally use on a front-to-back axis, into a side-to-side configuration, which promotes balance and speed. For some body types this is easy. Lola Stewart, the overweight girl who in other ways was so little like a dancer, could *sit* in the splits, for fun. She could turn her feet out in first position in a neat little line, heels together, without effort, while I grunted and strained and never achieved more than a trembly one-hundred-fifty-degree or so angle, on good days. Even now I can feel Madame's stick grinding into the ball of my foot (as if it were a pool cue and I the resin cube), as she tried to widen that stubborn angle.

Or, Madame would make a more personal appeal to excellence. Sometimes she would interject herself into our line at the barre, facing one of us. She might look like a wreck, but she could pull herself erect into the sacred positions as if there were a brilliant arrow in that lumpy leotard that could be unsheathed and put to use any time she cared to take the trouble. You might be doing *battements tendus,* for instance, those small, careful extensions of the foot forward, sideways, backwards, stretching and pointing, never lifting the toe from the ground. Mme LeBreton might come upon you and lock your eyes with hers. I always had trouble meeting her eyes, as if I were guilty of something, although I had no reason to feel guilty; and she would murmur "Look at me," like a hypnotist, while our feet slid toward each other and away from each other, mirror-like, in the timeless ritual. The stick would be in her outer hand, throbbing gently on the floor, and I was close enough to smell her breath, which was mysteriously strong and pungent.

2

The evening before the day that Geoffrey Render came to visit the LeBreton School of Ballet, the National Dance Theatre had made its first appearance in Middleton, Louisiana. Now this is not so much a comment on Middleton, which even then was a culturally active city that was visited regularly by such companies as the American Ballet Theatre, the various Ballets Russes, and even on occasion the New York City Ballet, as it was a comment on NDT, which up to that time had done very little touring and none at all in the deep South. Even so, everyone who knew anything about ballet knew about NDT, since at that time the company had a reputation comparable, in some ways superior, to those of the three companies I have just mentioned. We of the advanced class felt a special link with this renowned company because of the summer school sessions and the warmly autographed photos, as though we were, somehow, children of the company, its southern offspring. As if in acknowledgment of this, we were offered tickets in a LeBreton block so that we could sit with each other rather than with our parents. And, more importantly, we were actually going to meet the dancers! The family of Christabel Merrick, a girl in our class, was giving a party for the company after the performance, and we were invited to go.

It was considered unfortunate that the performance had to take place down at the Civic Auditorium, which landmark had been built in the 1920s in the florid baroque style so popular back then. By the mid-1950s it was considered not only too small for a city the size of Middleton but also too old-fashioned, even vulgar, and construction had already started on a new theater out in the woods on the south side of town—a project of the Merricks, the same family giving the cocktail party. In view of this, the Civic Auditorium was considered nothing more than a tacky old fossil at the time of this performance, and I joined in the complaints against it, although privately I enjoyed being there. Part of my attachment was sentimental: this is where the LeBreton recital was held every year; this is where I had been the Lark. But another part was aesthetic: I actually liked the dark red velvet and the ormolu; I thought it looked the way a theater should. The night of the NDT performance, the LeBreton students found each other beforehand in the great gilded foyer and traveled together in bands around crowded horseshoeshaped halls dim with cigarette smoke. We felt very important, and we laughed a lot as we walked with our feet turned out to show the people of Middleton that we were dancers too and were here as members of the dancing fraternity.

Unfortunately, I ended up in the particular company of my classmate Dorcas Durward: we had worked out a car pool to the cocktail party afterward, since neither her parents nor mine had been invited; and anyway I suppose Dorcas was my closest friend in the class, in spite of her uncommonly petulant personality. Actually when I first got to know Dorcas back in the sixth grade she was fairly affable; she was deeply interested in ballet, having taken lessons since she was six, and talking to her about ballet helped me decide to start taking lessons from Mme LeBreton even though I was so old to start at the beginning. Dorcas even talked about pursuing a professional career in ballet, which I thought wonderfully bold and imaginative; but then Dorcas began to grow. In fact, she shot up like a beanstalk. She had always had a rather small head, and thin hair which she pulled back in a flat ponytail like Olive Oyl; and now that she was so elongated, she looked like a pinhead. And she was not only hopelessly tall but also awkward: her little head yanked to the side when she did any steps involving turns such as *pirouettes* or *chaînés*, and I remember her looking loose and lanky, like a puppet designed by Giacometti. Naturally Dorcas was fretful the night of the NDT: it was the prospect of seeing all those petite professional dancers.

Really they had a profound effect on all our class. There were a dozen of us, ranging in age from twelve to seventeen (not counting Alma), every one of us over the age when ballet is considered a cute thing for a little girl to do. Every one of us was hooked on ballet in one way or another. But one of us was particularly hooked and would take the NDT appearance even harder than Dorcas. That was Claude Bateson, the only male student at Mme LeBreton's school. I cannot insist too much how odd it was for a boy to be taking ballet in the city of Middleton in the mid-1950s. It was *so* odd I can hardly believe in the scope of this oddness myself, and can hardly hope to have people believe it who live in cities with ballet companies that include large numbers of men. But it is true, anyway, that Claude's presence in Mme LeBreton's advanced class was virtually a scandal. It caused Claude an enormous amount of suffering, and by this time, when he was about seventeen and a senior in high school, he had cut himself off from the normal activities for a boy his age, even sports, although I believe he would have been a respectable track and field man. He was a particular failure in ROTC, I remember, where he remained, as a senior, a private of hostile mien.

Things would have been different if Claude had been handsome like John Kriza or Leon Danielian, for example, because Middleton, as I say, was a culturally active Southern city and no stranger to the species of "artist." In fact, Middleton had a high regard for artists, having produced several examples, including a classical guitar player, a piano virtuoso, an operatic baritone, and a "serious" actor, who were written up quite regularly in the *Morning Chronicle,* the fine Middleton daily newspaper. But these favorite sons were handsome, or at least photogenic, while Claude was not handsome and was thus, like Dorcas, rather cruelly frustrated by the accidents of his outward appearance. Claude had a good body—strong, lithe, and tall enough—but the problem was with his head. It was too big for his body, with very sharp features: small eyes with thick black lashes that made him look as if he was wearing mascara, a long pointed nose, and a broad mouth chock full of big teeth, some of which were pointed. His mouth stayed open when he danced, giving him a desperate sort of leer.

And then there was Claude's hair, of which I was very conscious as Dorcas and I took our seats in the first balcony.

"Oh Lord, I didn't realize *Claude* was going to sit in front of us," Dorcas wailed.

Claude had thick curls which stood out around his head in an aureole. Later this style would be dignified by the term "Afro," but then none of us had ever seen hair like that on anyone but Claude. It was complicated hair, full of whorls and swirls. From a distance it looked like a dark-brown sponge, or the photograph of a human brain.

"Well, *you* can see over him if anybody can," I said, rather unkindly, I know, but by that time I was weary of Dorcas, who had been gabbling about how she looked and what she would say to the dancers at the party afterward.

Claude appeared to be nervous too but not in the giggly hysterical way the rest of us were. Rather, he sat forward in his seat, even before the curtain was raised, and watched, motionless, although there was nothing to see but the gigantic old chandelier suspended from the ceiling and, directly below it, tiny people threading into the rows of folding chairs put out to constitute the "Orchestra" and the "Orchestra Circle" for this major occasion.

"Doesn't Madame look nice tonight," Dorcas murmured as Mme LeBreton took her place a couple of rows down, in the front row of our balcony. She had obviously been to the beauty shop because her thin hair stood out around her craggy face more buoyantly than usual. She was wearing a rose-colored bouclé suit.

"Very nice," I said, "and Cecilia is looking awfully lovely too, don't you think?" Cecilia, Mme LeBreton's daughter, had a gorgeous face with a high domed forehead which seemed to refract the light from the chandelier. "Although I'm not sure that dress is really the most flattering for her figure," I added with fine critical judgment, for Cecilia seemed to care very little about how she dressed.

Claude whirled around and looked murderously at me. Everyone knew that Claude was "in love" with Madame's beautiful daughter and that she did not even look twice at him, and so of course my comments were meant for his ears, which were small and ever so slightly pointed.

Dorcas and I tittered at each other: like everyone in the advanced class, we enjoyed torturing Claude.

Once the performance started Claude turned around from time to time and hissed furiously because we were commenting on the dancers and the sets and the costumes. It was our duty, we thought, since we were students of the art. The program was one of those *potpourris* typical of the companies that I had seen in Middleton before, Act Two of *Swan Lake,* some variations from *Coppélia,* a Western-flavored dance, and a "modern" work by their artistic director Geoffrey Render where the dancers slithered around in gray leotards and tights, looking like rolls of aluminum foil, to the music of Hovhaness. I would like to be able to record some sensitive impressions of these works, but the truth is that I was so excited I could hardly pay attention to the dances. I was very conscious of my body in the prickly red plush seat and I did not think I could keep sitting there. I kept twisting around to catch the light from the stage in order to read the program. Both Dorcas and I zeroed in on the dancers we had read about: we watched for them, and after they exited we were bored, almost asleep, until they came back on stage. My main emotion was pride, I think, that I was seeing famous dancers in the flesh and had my opportunity to judge them for myself. This was very exalting, and when it finally did become impossible for us to keep our seats, Dorcas and I threaded our way down our row and went to the bathroom during *Jesse James Rides Again.*

One of my clearest memories of that performance is how interesting the music for that ballet sounded from the corridor as Dorcas and I made our way to the Ladies' Room through the smoky yellow light. Out there, as usual at performances like this, I observed a number of men standing around, smoking meditatively, passing the time; clearly they were the husbands of women with cultural interests and had been dragged there by their wives, against their will. For a long time the word "husband" reminded me of this reluctant, half-hearted obedience.

Back in the auditorium, the performance was almost over except for the tinfoil number, *Encumbrances,* which puzzled and bored me. Nevertheless I bruised my hands clapping when Geoffrey Render came out on stage afterward. *This* was my first sight of him. He was bald, as

I have said, and short and fat, and he would not have been out of place or even particularly noticeable in the throng of husbands back in the hall. But he had a grand manner about him on stage, even in that brief appearance; and we all clapped and at the same time leaned forward to get a look at Mme LeBreton's face as *she* clapped for her old, old friend.

***

Part of the lure of the cocktail party was the opportunity to go to the home of Christabel Merrick's grandmother. The Merrick family had an oil fortune with which they had bought a number of businesses in Middleton, including the *Chronicle,* which often pictured big charitable and social functions at this house. Old Mr. Merrick was dead and old Mrs. Merrick was nearly dead. She was to die within a year or two, and I remember how dried-up and crooked she looked that night. She was a very lively woman; however, and seemed to still have plenty of energy to carry out her duties as the matriarch of a large and important family. She had had eight children, the eldest of whom was Christabel's father, an oil tycoon who had three children of his own. Obviously these people were Catholic, which in Middleton was considered almost as odd as if they had been a family of ballet dancers or tightrope walkers, since almost everyone in Middleton was Methodist or Baptist or, in some highly specialized cases, Episcopalian; and it was widely commented upon that old Mrs. Merrick went to church every morning.

There was no house in my neighborhood of Collegetown grand enough to entertain a ballet company and a good portion of a ballet school, as well as a large number of local businessmen and their wives, and I was properly awed by the Merrick mansion. Located on an eminence in Gilbert Oaks, an area of town where many of my classmates in the advanced class lived, it had all the brilliance of the White House in Washington, D.C. I was deeply impressed by the first room of the house, not a foyer and not a "living room" but a vast reception room with a circular staircase leading to the private upper reaches of the house. Here hundreds of people stood talking and drinking and waiting for the dancers to arrive under a chandelier which was far more scintillating than the one back in the Civic Auditorium. Christabel's mother, Lyda

Merrick, was clearly in charge of the party even though it was in her mother-in-law's house. She was floating around in a long billowing caftan of peach-colored silk telling the servants what to do. Lyda Merrick could have been a dancer herself, I thought as I watched her graceful movements and admired her patrician features and gleaming pulled-back hair, which was the color of gold.

At last the dancers arrived. Geoffrey Render came in first, a great relief to me since I had thought he might be too famous to come, and I was overjoyed to observe such a great man being so extremely nice. He shook old Mrs. Merrick's hand and then, after she croaked something up at him, bent down and kissed her hand. He shook Christabel's father's hand and kissed her mother on either cheek. He continued to shake hands and beam at the tycoons and wives and ballet students who crowded urgently around him until Lyda Merrick threw out an elegantly draped arm and created a path for him and his entourage to proceed toward the refreshments, which were found in the second room of the great house, lower of ceiling and darker, altogether more intimate and home-like than the blazing foyer, but still bare of any accoutrements of daily life, so far as I could see. Soon Mr. Render had a glass of champagne and something to eat, and the party dissolved into a general festive babble.

"Where is Mme LeBreton?" I asked Dorcas as we took crystal cups of lime sherbet punch, the beverage served to girls at all fashionable parties in Middleton. "It's funny she's not here."

"Maybe she had car trouble," Dorcas said, alluding to Mme LeBreton's old maroon Lincoln. It was a dignified car, with some remnants of prestige, quite suitable for Mme LeBreton, but it could no longer be counted on. Once or twice Mme LeBreton had arrived at the studio, late and cross, in a Yellow Cab.

Dorcas and I wandered around, staring at the dancers, and I do mean "stare": now that we had the opportunity, neither of us would have dared go talk to them. They stood in knots talking to each other, looking different from everyone else in the room. The women seemed very small and compact, and their heads were very sleek. They wore dramatic eye makeup, including false eyelashes like fringes. In fact they all looked very much alike, as though they had worked with their faces at their mirrors so long, applying greasepaint, then taking it off with cold cream and Kleenex, that they had brought their features into line with a dancer's ideal of beauty. Their clothes also looked different from the other women's: they wore dark filmy dresses that hugged their torsos in the same way that costumes do—small dresses with tiny straps over strong, well-shaped shoulders held back to display bony chests which, like Mme LeBreton's, looked like rope ladders. The men looked even more unusual than the women. Although Geoffrey Render had on evening clothes, as did many of the other guests, the male members of his company were dressed more casually in slacks and shirts that were open at the neck, or turtleneck shirts. They looked very suave and peculiar, although when I say "peculiar" I am not talking about homosexuality: I did not know what homosexuality *was* at that time, as incredible as that may seem today, and while this factor may have played its part in Middleton's suspicions of male dancers, it had nothing to do with my perception of them as strange. Later I found out that some people thought Claude had homosexual tendencies and that this was behind some of the jokes and jeers, but I don't know why. It certainly wouldn't have made much sense for a boy who was interested in other boys to spend most of his free time at an all-girl ballet school. Besides, everyone knew how Claude felt about Cecilia.

I saw Claude talking brashly to a couple of the dancers. I recognized them as Nils Lundgren, who had danced the role of Jesse James, and Lynette Jones, a soloist in *Coppélia.*

"Look, Dorcas, Claude is talking to Lundgren and Jones," I cried, pulling on Dorcas's arm.

"Watch it, Meredith! You're gonna make me spill this punch on the white carpet," she said crossly, gaping with me.

I also noticed that Christabel Merrick, a granddaughter of this house, and Hilary James, who was, like Christabel, quite wealthy and far more socially confident than I was, were standing very close together talking to a young man I remembered as one of the Encumbrances.

But just then Mme LeBreton entered the room.

"Oh, look," Dorcas crooned. "Here comes Mme LeBreton. Cecilia's not with her. I wonder if she went off with Charlie!" The conduct of

Cecilia with her boyfriend was a very interesting subject to me, but I shushed Dorcas so that I could concentrate on Mme LeBreton's entry into the room. She was dressed, as I have said, in a rose-colored suit. It was very unusual for us to see Mme LeBreton in street clothes, and I was disappointed that she looked even fatter around the middle and skinnier in the shank than she did in leotard and tights, although I would expect *that* to be the most revealing, unflattering costume in the world. She was smoking a cigarette and moving through the crowd without speaking to anyone, even though it was clear that many of the socialites recognized her and were trying to catch her eye. I even heard some of these people murmur "Madame," which was pronounced various ways there in north Louisiana, where there is no French influence such as that which dominates the southern half of the state, and where a word like "Madame" is distinctly foreign. Some people said "Mi *dom*" (this is how I, and most of her other students, said it); some said "muh *dam*"; some few even said *"mad'*m." But everywhere the word had a romantic sound and carried a tone of admiration, even obeisance: it was clearly regarded as a title of some kind earned somewhere in Madame's professional past.

Anyway, the guests parted respectfully for Mme LeBreton and tried to catch her eye in her progress across the room. But all was not right: her eyes, red-rimmed, had a strange light.

My first thought was that she was looking for Cecilia. I always expected her to get angry with Cecilia for how she carried on with her boyfriend Charlie Hill, as well as for how she didn't work very hard in class even though she unquestionably had greater natural gifts than any student in the school. But now I know that Cecilia was the furthest thing from Mme LeBreton's mind as she made her way through the murmuring crowd. It was Geoffrey Render she was looking for.

At that moment Geoffrey Render was standing with Mrs. August Smithers. He had an arm around Mrs. Smithers and she had an arm around him, and when he saw Mme LeBreton coming toward him his mouth fell open and his fine strong face, the face of a potentate, took on a peculiar expression of surprise and wonder. A moment later Geoffrey Render had released a bewildered-looking Mrs. Smithers in order that he might come forward toward our Mme LeBreton. He took both her outstretched hands in his and said, "Milly!" She burst into tears, whereupon he gathered her into his arms and patted her back in what appeared to be a steady and comforting rhythm.

I was flabbergasted by this scene. I had been keeping an eye on the Artistic Director of NDT ever since he had arrived, and I had observed him talking to Mrs. Smithers and Mrs. Merrick and other Middleton notables in the easy and comfortable way of an old friend. But there was nothing easy or comfortable about this meeting. The tearful embrace was followed by a staring contest. Mme LeBreton and Geoffrey Render drew back from each other and glared at each other with the kind of expression someone wears after he has been slapped or had a drink sloshed in his face. Alert for flying liquor I took Dorcas's arm and anxiously moved toward the pair to be sure we didn't miss anything. Others, I was dimly aware, did the same.

"You could have returned my call," Madame said at last.

"What call?" Geoffrey Render said, breaking into a genial smile. "I didn't know you had called."

She studied a distant corner of the room. "I called your hotel."

"Oh," he said with a negligent shrug, "the hotel. I didn't get your message. I haven't had a message from you in over fifteen years!"

Ignoring this, Madame said, "You're looking well," in an accusing way.

"You're looking well too, "he said, insincerely I am sure, since he had been looking her up and down with what appeared to be a very penetrating gaze. "The same."

"Bullshit," she said tersely, to my great shock. "I need a drink."

"Here, let's send this young lady for a drink," he said, in some way which I cannot explain forcing my eyes to meet his, beckoning to me with an imperious forefinger. "Honey, would you get this lady a drink?"

"That's my teacher," I babbled.

"That's Meredith Jackson, one of my students," Mme LeBreton said, a trifle impatiently. I successfully fought down my impulse to prostrate myself before the great man. "I would like you to get me a Manhattan, Meredith. Tell that man at the table."

It seemed to me that it took the man at the table an hour to make this strange concoction. He went off to the kitchen for a while and came ambling back with a jar of cherries, of all things. My mind was awhirl with what I had seen: a mysterious drama of reunion and, it seemed, reconciliation. I had of course assumed that Mme LeBreton had maintained her friendship with Geoffrey Render and was on good terms with him, but now I realized that she had never said one word about him, had never even mentioned his name. Mrs. Merrick had mentioned his name: it had been Christabel's mother who had handled the tickets for the students and arranged this party. While the man made the drink I began to think back to what I knew about Madame's professional past. It was very little, really: only that she had danced several seasons with Ballet Benet, a small company founded by Geoffrey Render which toured the country during the Depression, and that she had quit to get married to a man from Middleton. Her husband, Maxwell LeBreton, had died the preceding spring, but there had been no observable effects of this death upon Mme LeBreton or upon the school.

Mme LeBreton took the drink I brought her and drank it down in two or three swallows.

"You still guzzle, Milly my love, but you shouldn't, you know. It isn't good for you," Mr. Render said.

Their conversation had gone down unknowable paths while I was gone, and it progressed even further while I went back for another Manhattan for Mme LeBreton. The bartender, now equipped with his jar of cherries, made the second one much more quickly, however. When I returned and served Madame, she seemed more collected and took a full minute to empty the glass. Now they were talking about touring and Geoffrey Render was complaining about conditions on the road.

"Naturally I don't get the best out of the dancers," he said morosely. "You saw how sloppy they were in the *Swan*. Mark was working with a torn tendon and another kid had her ankle held together with tape. It was a mess."

"Oh no, hon," Madame said warmly, more in the spirit of an old, old friend.

"I *tell* Nils this. If we tour we're going to be as bad as Ballet Russe. You can't keep standards up when everybody's ragged as hell."

"We know ragged, baby," Madame said in a swaggering sort of way. "Meredith," she said, frowning and looking for me. She gave a slight jerk of her head in the direction of the bar.

"Make two this time, would you?" I asked the bartender.

The truth of the matter is that Mme LeBreton got a little drunk that night, but apparently this helped her get through something very painful for her. I could see no signs of strain in Mr. Render, however: he seemed very relaxed and contented, even with his displeasure in the evening's performance, and I believe that if the evening had ended here he would simply have talked about touring and theaters a while and then cheerfully kissed the remnants of "his Milly" good-bye.

But there was a crucial turn of events, and the harbinger of this was Claude Bateson.

"I hope I'm not intruding," Claude said boldly, bowing slightly to our teacher, then turning toward Geoffrey Render. "I am Claude Bateson, and I am wondering if there is any possibility of arranging an audition before you or a member of your staff, sir."

Dorcas and I raised our eyebrows at each other. What incredible nerve Claude had! How odd he looked! Even though the weather was still quite warm, he wore a suit of the kind of strange tweed you'd expect to be employed in a pair of knickers, what they used to call plus fours.

Mr. Render did not laugh with curt cruelty, as I would have expected, but instead looked at Madame, as if for a reference. She held her latest drink with both hands and seemed lost in her own thoughts.

"I've been studying with Mme LeBreton for ten years, sir. I would have come to New York long before now except that Madame is so determined that I graduate from high school."

Mr. Render frowned and smiled at the same time. "Very sensible, my boy! Very sensible, Milly. I commend you. I wouldn't have expected such sense from you!"

It sounded like a terrible rebuke the way he said this so genially, and I blushed for Mme LeBreton. "How old are you?"

"Seventeen, sir."

"That may not be too old," Mr. Render said skeptically.

"Claude would kill for a chance to audition for NDT," Mme LeBreton put in absently.

This amused Geoffrey Render, who put a hand on Claude's shoulder. I was struck by the total contrast between them: poor, intense, odd-looking Claude Bateson and relaxed, overfed Geoffrey Render. Neither of them looked anything like a dancer. The suave blond Nils Lundgren did: he was saying good-bye now to Lyda Merrick, who then wafted in the direction of Mr. Render. The party was beginning to break up, and Dorcas and I had to go soon.

Mr. Render said, "We'll have to see what we can arrange in the morning. Nils makes all the plans. I don't even know what time we leave tomorrow. We're going on to Dallas, I believe."

"You don't leave for Dallas until noon," Claude said promptly. Mr. Render laughed again and held out his arm for Mrs. Merrick to glide into. I believe she thought she looked like Ginger Rogers. I certainly no longer thought she looked like a dancer of the more classical type after having seen the swathed and swarthy little women of NDT.

"Thank goodness," she said to Mr. Render. "You're talking to this poor young man at last. He's been dying to have a word with you. Be an angel and take a look at his work. It's most promising. We all think so, don't we, Milly?"

Mme LeBreton nodded. She was looking sadly into her empty glass, but I was not leaving again, having, like Cinderella, so little time.

"What you ought to do," Lyda Merrick went on, "is stay over in Middleton. Stay out at *our* house, and come to Milly's studio tomorrow. It's perfectly charming. Have you been there before? No? Then you can see the school and you can see Claude. And we'll have time to discuss an idea I've just thought up."

Mrs. Merrick told Mr. Render about the new theater that her family was building on the south side of the town. She had an unusually beautiful mouth: wide, with very full lips. I watched these lips intently, as astounded by the words that now came out as if Mrs. Merrick were the sweet sister Melisande in the fairy tale, and the words were pearls and diamonds.

"The theater opens in April with a play, but you've given me an idea tonight. A gala première! We must have a gala première, and it must be ballet! Middleton went wild tonight over ballet! And you heard it, darling—Middleton went wild over Geoffrey Render!"

Mr. Render laughed delightedly, throwing his bald head back. "You come down and choreograph a ballet for Milly's little dancers, and Claude here. And Cecilia. Don't tell me you wouldn't want to work with that lovely girl?"

"Cecilia?" Mr. Render said blankly, at which point Dorcas, who had been nudging me for some minutes, grabbed my arm and began to pull on me.

"It's *after* eleven-thirty, Meredith. I'm sure Daddy's waiting outside. We've *got* to go."

And so I was dragged away from this provocative scene, although I was churning with sensations and questions and I knew I was destined to lie awake all night. I had the feeble hope that Dorcas might help me work a few things out on the way home, but this was extinguished soon enough: Dorcas was tired and jealous of the dancers, and she wouldn't even admit she had noticed anything unusual about the way Mme LeBreton and Mr. Render met.

***

Let me explain something else about why I did not attempt to talk to any of the NDT dancers at the cocktail party, since to talk to them would seem to be the most natural thing in the world for a young ballet student as enamored of the ballet and as interested in the dancers themselves as I was. In my view, there was a solidarity among the dancers that it would be rude to intrude upon, as if, even while they just stood around at the party in their honor, they were in fact dancing together and I was considering "breaking in" on their dance. Although this was not a conscious thought at the time, I sensed that these people of the NDT ballet troupe enjoyed a brotherhood of work and sweat and hardship, and that they were bored with people who did not belong, or even looked down upon them. They were laughing at us a little; I think they were even laughing at the Merricks. I also had the sense that while these dancers were distributed throughout the gathering they were acutely aware of each other at all times. They had the air of disciplined troops who, while presently at rest, are still on the *qui vive,* alert for the signal which will draw them together and send them out to their next assignment in the night. Their leader, I had no doubt, was Geoffrey Render, but he had a spirit larger than theirs, and he deigned to smile on the party and participate in it.

I had been daunted by this same sort of solidarity, at least an amateur version of it, the first time I went to the advanced class at Mme LeBreton's studio. I felt that the advanced class was a distinguished unit that had been together for years and years and had attained a level of perfection that was forever beyond my reach. This illusion was fostered by their practice costumes, which consisted of a black cotton knit Danskin leotard with the sleeves cut out, pink tights, and pink Capezio ballet slippers. Of course I too wore a properly abbreviated black Danskin leotard, pink tights and pink Capezio ballet slippers, but I wore them self-consciously, like an imposter; *theirs* seemed to have grown on them as the spontaneous excrescence of their talent. Mine were black and very pink; theirs, for the most part, were washed-out slate and weak shrimp, attesting to the many, many times they had worn them in the course of acquiring their incomparably greater experience.

I already knew every single person in the advanced class, at least by sight, either from school (some of these girls were in my grade, at that time the eighth) or from the recital of the previous spring, where, as the biggest beginner, I was quite naturally riveted by the doings of the members of this exalted class. The LeBreton School of Ballet could be diagrammed as a simple pyramid, the very broad base representing the large number of little girls of five or six in the numerous beginning classes, the narrower middle the smaller number of middle-sized girls of nine or ten or so in the intermediate classes, and the tiny apex the dozen or so "big girls" who persisted in ballet and were chosen for the glorious advanced class with the privilege of performing solos at the recital.

Most of the advanced class, on the other hand, did not know me, or know me well enough not to be surprised, or even shocked, when I showed up at their class.

"I know you," Melissa Martin said thoughtfully, glaring at me and shaking a forefinger my way. "You're in my Louisiana history class."

"English," I said.

"I didn't know *you* took," she continued suspiciously. Melissa was wonderfully cute: short and blocky, like a Madame Alexander doll. Her voice was a high little-girl singsong and she spoke in a twangy chant. This was natural to or affected by many cute girls in Middleton.

"I remember you in the recital last year," Hilary James remarked. She was a year ahead of Melissa and me in school, already a freshman at Middleton High, and notoriously intelligent. Unlike the more frivolous Melissa, she had a grasp of the facts. "You were the great big blue sylph, weren't you?"

I acknowledged this. Hilary, I should note, did not talk in the kind of singsong that Melissa used but, rather, a low and hoarse voice, which made everything she said in the idle babble of the dressing room seem not only important but definitive. She was handsome or striking rather than "cute" and, apart from Christabel Merrick, had more prestige than anyone else in the advanced class.

Taking no further notice of my presence, Hilary said to Melissa with a note of grievance, "I didn't think Madame was letting anybody else in."

"It's not as good as it used to be," Melissa returned. "There's that new married girl too. What's her name? I'm thinkin' of not takin' next year."

"If we don't get good solos," Hilary said with a certain hoarse menace.

Most of the class, in contrast, was very friendly to me. I knew Dorcas Durward and Rachel Mintz from school: they were in my Louisiana history class that year and both of them knew it. Mme LeBreton was also very friendly and helpful, in her gruff and businesslike way. But somehow Hilary James set the tone for that first class and many classes to come until I began to feel more at ease. I am sure now that this was because Hilary had more self-confidence than anyone else at the LeBreton School of Ballet, more, I believe, than Madame herself. And her self-confidence was fully justified. She was an excellent dancer, long-legged and strong; and in the wider world she had all the attributes of adolescent success: good looks, brains, wealth, even that mysterious attribute "popularity."

It did not surprise me, then, when Hilary mingled easily with the NDT dancers, free of the scruples and reserves that I felt. I overheard her say something about how she had seen several performances by the National Dance Theatre in New York the winter before; I did not doubt that Hilary had the *savoir faire* to mingle with the dancers up there too. I must add that by this time I had "made friends" with Hilary. I too chatted casually with her at the performance and later at the cocktail party. But I was still afraid of her, even though I had realized by now that she was aloof and sometimes cruel with everybody: this was her style.

I had also decided that Hilary was more complex than she had at first appeared to me. As I have said, she was very wealthy—her family's name was associated with an industrial firm having something to do, like so much in Middleton, with petroleum (you saw trucks with her family name all the time in the streets of Middleton)—and this meant to me that she could have as many new clothes as she wanted. Yet she wore the same dress to school almost every day. It was what we called a "peasant dress," with a black lace-up bodice over a white drawstring blouse and a gathered skirt in a blue provincial print. Now, this is not as bizarre a school dress as it might seem: peasant blouses and peasant dresses were actually quite fashionable in Middleton in the mid-1950s. The unusual thing was that she wore it so often, as many as three or four times a week. I thought this very odd in a girl of Hilary's high station, although it came to seem less odd as I began to spend more and more time at the studio. Further on into this year I am telling about, I went to the studio five or six, even seven times a week; it came to seem more and more important, it came to seem like the whole world. I think now that Hilary felt that way earlier, even before that particular year. With its air of remoteness, the little roughhewn studio was, to my mind, an enchanted place, along the lines of the gingerbread house belonging to the witch in *Hansel and Gretel* (though Mme LeBreton was no witch!), or the workshop in *Coppélia,* and I can see how it would be very natural for a girl with romantic inclinations anywhere in her soul to dress the part of the fresh-faced peasant maid who wanders there to find her greatest adventures.

***

I hardly slept the night of the NDT performance, which may account for my aberrant behavior at school the next day. Once up in my room, I fell upon the NDT souvenir program and studied the pictures. There were thrilling portraits of the principals in costume, also fine group pictures of the *corps*. Toward the rear, there were also some fascinating shots of the company in class or in rehearsal. Several pictures were taken in what I took to be the NDT studio. I hunkered under the covers, poring over these photographs to see what life was really like for a dancer in New York City. It was not glamorous—no, it was better than that! Even in the romantic medium of black-and-white photography you could see the scuffed floors and the peeling paint, you could practically hear the clanking of radiators and, from far away, the roar of traffic. I could see the dancers clearly as they had class up there in New York City, way upstairs in some ratty old building, with the floor shaking and the piano thumping. They were not children as we were, but adults; and they did not wear childlike matching practice clothes but rather all kinds of things: leotards and T-shirts and headbands and legwarmers and sweatshirts with the arms tied around their waists. They were sweating and working for their lives while, outside, it snowed, as in *The Nutcracker.*

I was particularly struck by the last photograph in the program. It was a picture of one of the girls in the *corps* by the name of Tamara Genovese sitting on a large trunk or packing crate, wearing a fur coat made out of some kind of spotty fur which did not look real. Her hair was slicked back in a ballet knot and her eyes looked enormous. She had dark circles under her eyes as if what had occurred on the preceding pages (the work in the studio) had worn her out, but she had to go on tour to another old foreign capital anyway, despite how worn-out she was. To think that I had just seen Miss Genovese at the Merricks' party! In reality she was tinier than she looked on the crate, and swarthier, but the enormous eyes were the same. I had seen her eat the party food in such quantities as to suggest that it was the first food she'd been able to get her hands on in many a mile. I do not think she spoke English.

Still, the most interesting figure in the program was Geoffrey Render. His picture came first, even before the premier danseur Nils Lundgren or the prima ballerina Yvonne Chausseur, and near the end he was in several of the studio pictures, in shirt sleeves, working like the devil among his dancers in New York City. Mr. Render had also been the most compelling figure at the Merricks' party. I couldn't get over it: I had thought Mme LeBreton would be perfectly at home with him, but she wasn't. Something had gone wrong years ago and she did not move back and forth between Middleton and New York City with quite the ease I had imagined. In fact, meeting Mr. Render again had been less like a happy reunion than an awful train wreck—a collision somewhere between here and there, say Memphis.

I kept seeing Mme LeBreton glaring at Mr. Render, and Mr. Render blandly eyeing her back; meanwhile, I remembered Adelaide Henderson over to the other side of them, opposite Dorcas and me, staring at them too. Adelaide had big bovine eyes, which gave her stare a special scope. It occurred to me that Adelaide, who was also a member of the advanced class, was the most likely person to understand what had happened between Mme LeBreton and Mr. Render since she was so close to the LeBretons: she taught at the school, part-time, and she had gone with Madame and her daughter up to the NDT summer school, twice now. She probably knew all about it, and sometime around three o'clock I got a wild idea: I'd go find her at school the next day; I'd get her to tell me.

3

Thursday morning I was exhausted, of course, having spent the night in New York, and Middleton High School was no place to rest. Middleton High was a big school—the biggest high school in Louisiana, I believe—with 2,500 students and a building large enough to be an airplane factory. Now that I think about it, this immense square building was probably as big as the imaginary one I put the NDT classes in. Here too people worked for their lives. Like America itself, Middleton High School was theoretically a place where hard work and virtue led to success, a meritocracy, but even then I knew that the system in force there was more complicated than this, and that just as in that NDT rehearsal hall, talent or other natural gifts played an inscrutable part in things. I won't describe the Middleton High system—it was probably much the same as that of every other large high school in the United States at that time—but I will simply say that the students there aspired to being recognized as "smart" and "popular," particularly "popular." "Athletic" was also a basis for distinction if you were a boy, and was closely aligned with "popular," though proficiency in ballet did not count toward "athletic," especially if you were a boy, and even if you were a girl, since this pursuit, regarded as feminine and rather frivolous, not to mention foreign, was so alien to the world of the school. It was really inappropriate even to *think* of ballet at school, which was dedicated to more serious public goals. Middleton High school had the best football team in the state and the best basketball team; it also had the largest number of National Merit semi-finalists in the state every year, and countless important organizations doing important things, beginning with the Student Council and going on down to the Future Farmers of America. As a freshman I was acutely conscious of the many tests to be passed and offices to be won.

That morning as I mounted the stairs on my way from one class to another I was weary and distracted, but still I smiled brightly and said "Hi!" "Hi!" "Hi!" as I met classmates and acquaintances coming down the other side. This was important in the promotion of "popularity": Middleton High School put a high value on friendliness although there were some people who were popular without being friendly at all (Hilary James was one of these), which is part of the mystery I was referring to. But I knew I was not one of these special few with a native social power and so I zealously said "Hi!" "Hi! "Hi!", even that day.

I might as well confess that I did this because I wanted to be a Booster. I imagine that every big high school has an organization comparable to the Boosters but back then I thought it was a group of unique glory, something like the seraphim and cherubim. This was the squad of girls elected to cheer on that championship football team. They appeared at football games and pep rallies and assemblies in resplendent uniforms: brilliant starched white blouses and dashing red wool skirts and white oxfords, garnished with leather belts and white gloves and red berets and important-looking insignia and, in some cases, leather straps and harnesses. Forty girls were elected to this organization at the end of the sophomore year, the forty most popular in a class of six hundred souls, and forty more girls were chosen from among the leftovers at the end of the junior year. By senior year, then, the eighty most popular girls were Boosters and could wear the uniform which signified how popular they were. The original forty became the Drum Corps in the senior year: when the squad marched, the Drum Corps lugged drums and xylophones, or maybe they were glockenspiels, to provide rhythmic accompaniment. The Drum Corps was the acme of feminine achievement at Middleton High. As a freshman, I would no sooner go up to the bass drummer of the Middleton High Boosters and speak to her than I would to the prima ballerina of the National Dance Theatre.

I mention this only to explain why I would bother to grin and say "Hi!" "Hi!" "Hi!" between classes on such a day as that Thursday, when I was terribly tired and whirling with unanswered questions about the night before and the afternoon to come. I suppressed ballet, for the nonce, and climbed the stairs, trying not to step on the heels of the person in front of me and at the same time trying to keep from having my heels stepped on by the person in back of me. This was taxing and required all my concentration, at least until I rounded a bend in the stairs and began climbing a particular flight which had a high importance for me. This was an intoxicating flight, the last before the fourth floor, where my next class was, and it was here that I met Paul Wheeless coming down every day. The traffic moved with such regularity on these stairs that it was usually on the fifth step that we met—he coming down, I going up—and he would look down into my face and I would look up into his and he, being popular as well as smart, would say "Hi!" and give a curt nod and I would say "Hi!" and smile, and almost fall down the stairs in a faint.

I was deeply in love with Paul Wheeless. I had realized this my first day at Middleton High School the preceding month, on the occasion of my first ascent of that particular flight of stairs, and the more I learned about him the more I worshipped him. He was a junior and the treasurer of the Student Council, among many other things. I was on the Council now, in the humble capacity of homeroom representative; and I had already volunteered for four or five committees, one of which was a new committee just formed to study and revise the school disciplinary code. Paul Wheeless was its chairman. It made me happy to think that he remembered my bright and eager face from the two meetings of this committee, but I also recognized that as a very popular boy who was a strong candidate for president of the Student Council the following year, it behooved him to look at every upturned face coming toward him in the stairwell and say "Hi!"

Let me point out here, at once, that I was not hoping to have a "date" with Paul Wheeless, or anyone else: my mother and father had decreed that I could not go out on dates until I was a junior, and that was far in the distance. Nor did I particularly want "dates": why, this daily intersection on the stairs was almost more excitement than I could handle! A lot of people in my class were already dating, such as the cute and fashionable girls who took ballet with me, Melissa Martin and Rachel Mintz, for example, and Dorcas was willing and able to date, just waiting for a boy tall enough to ask her. Their ease in the social world was due at least in part to their membership in Roundelay, the class social club which had been started back in the seventh grade. My mother, alarmed at this early intermingling of the sexes, had not let me join. But I had not really minded this, and even in the ninth grade still did not resent being denied close social contact with boys. I just loved Paul Wheeless from afar, hoping he would recognize in my grin and my "Hi!" the makings of a smart and popular girl.

This day, however, I was churning with feeling and I gave Paul Wheeless a look more charged with meaning than usual: a heavy-lidded look, something like the one Tamara Genovese wore on the steamer trunk. This expressed my weariness and hinted at my preoccupation with things that were romantic and far removed from the purlieus of Middleton High; and possibly it was just my overexcited imagination, but I thought that Paul Wheeless looked at me longer, and with more interest, than the custom dictated, and I climbed on, filled with Tamara's air of secret heartache.

"Hey, Meredith, you look sick," Susan Taylor said to me in geometry. "You ought to see the nurse or something."

"I'm all right!" I declared, but I doodled with the pencil in my compass all through class and afterward meandered down the hall to my next class without saying "Hi!" to half the people I always said "Hi!" to on that route.

***

I did not usually see Adelaide at school except in passing. In fact I did not regularly see anyone in the advanced class at school except Dorcas Durward and Rachel Mintz. It might be expected that the members of such a class, who spent four afternoons a week together and shared a strong interest in ballet, would seek each other out at school and hang around together, but this was not the case: groups at school were organized along different lines. Most of the advanced class were older than I was (this was the major barrier), but also they were for the most part higher in school society. Hilary James and Stephanie Sillerman were not only sophomores, for instance, but also as sure to be elected to Boosters as it was sure that the sun would rise the next day. Adelaide Henderson was a junior, and she was a Booster; in fact, she was secretary-treasurer of that organization. Adelaide was known to everyone, being one of the most outstanding girls in the junior class, and the first person I asked knew exactly where she could be found.

I had never liked Adelaide. She affected great sweetness. I've mentioned the big bovine eyes, and she also had a high little-girl singsong twang even more exaggerated than Melissa Martin's. She taught some of Mme LeBreton's baby classes in the afternoons, and she talked to everybody, at least people of high school age and under, as if they were these little beginners who had to be exhorted and cajoled. She was the kind of girl who could talk this way to a little kid and at the same time squeeze its arm until its little eyes popped out. I saw her do this one time with a hapless little ballet student who had wet her pants in class and soaked her tights down both legs. I couldn't argue with Adelaide being "smart," but I could not understand how she was so "popular." She wasn't one of those petroleum princesses like Hilary or Stephanie: in fact she was a poor girl, with a job after school. I guess she just played up to the electorate with that voice and those eyes, and said "Hi!" so often that they developed the mistaken idea that she was nice.

I did not admire Adelaide at the studio either. You had to admit she was one of the best dancers in the class because she was unfailingly competent: she was strong and flexible, and she was tireless. But she had what is, in my opinion, the worst kind of body to have. She was short and she had a small trunk with narrow hips, then thick short legs with calves as thick as the thighs. Nonetheless she was devoted to ballet and was widely suspected of having professional ambitions. She did go with Madame to New York.

Adelaide, I was informed, was in the Booster room since it was Thursday, the day the Boosters wore their uniforms to school and marched after lunch in smart kaleidoscopic patterns, to drum and glockenspiel, down on the parade grounds behind the school. I almost gave up the crazy idea of going to find Adelaide when I found out she was in the Booster room: I was only a freshman, and my going there might be seen as presumptuous, even obstreperous, but in the end I went on down there, driven by curiosity. The Booster room was in the basement, along with the band room and the cafeteria and about a thousand lockers. All these things produced clangs and clatters, so that the subterranean portion of Middleton High School was as noisy as the subway system of a great city.

"Is Adelaide Henderson in here?" I shouted at the door of the Booster room. A beautiful girl named Dixie Basham, in the full and glorious regalia of the Boosters, said, "I think so, hon," in the high voice of a five-year-old and motioned for me to come into the Booster sanctuary as if it were just an ordinary place. It was a cavernous room full of desk chairs just like the ones we sat in upstairs in the classrooms, and a panoply of percussion instruments. Ten or twelve Boosters sat around eating bag lunches or toying with the drums.

"Meredith Jackson, what are *you* doing here?" Adelaide said.

She was sitting at a desk eating a sandwich and now she dabbed at her lips with a paper napkin.

"Is it all right for me to come in here?" I asked humbly.

"Of course, darlin', just for a minute," Adelaide called out.

Once I was sitting down beside her she said, "Why, you're not well!" with the kind of fake solicitude she would use on one of the baby dancers who had just thrown up.

"Of *course* I'm well," I said. "But I've got to know, first, is Geoffrey Render really coming to the studio this afternoon? I can't wait to find out."

"Well," she said, batting her big cow eyes and looking around complacently, "I *happen* to know he spent the morning with Lyda Merrick and that he's having lunch with Milly at the Captain Frick."

Adelaide had named the city's best restaurant. She had also called Mme LeBreton "Milly," which no one our age did, not even the bold Hilary.

"Is he coming this afternoon?" I begged.

Adelaide paused a moment for drama. "Yes. Yes, he is."

A torrent of feeling washed over me; I think I lost consciousness a few seconds. Then I said, "Gosh, gosh, gosh," or something like that. "Gosh, Geoffrey Render coming to our class. I can't believe it. I couldn't go to sleep last night."

"I couldn't either," Adelaide said. "God, if Lyda Merrick can get him to come down and make a ballet for us. Godamighty."

"What's he like, Adelaide? Did you have him at the summer school? Do you know him at all?"

"Oh no," Adelaide said. "He's away in the summers. I never saw him."

"Oh," I said, deflated. "I was real surprised last night when he and Mme LeBreton met at the party," I went on anyway. "It looked like they hadn't been friends for *years*. It surprised me. Did it you?"

Adelaide exhaled a long time and then started fiddling with her harness. She carried a flag out in front of her company of Boosters, possibly a perquisite of the secretary-treasurership, and so wore an elaborate leather harness with assorted loops and buckles. Quite by coincidence another Booster, one Bitsy Hamilton, picked up some drumsticks and started to practice a drum roll on one of the Booster snares, so that it sounded as if someone were about to do a feat on the high wire.

"Tell me, Adelaide," I wheedled, seeing the room filling with Boosters, the whole regiment of them, and knowing that I'd soon have to go. *"Please."*

Adelaide spoke quickly, out of the side of her little mouth, as if against her better judgment.

"Well. Don't tell anybody. Milly'd *die*. She's never said much about it, even to Cecilia, but Celia told *me* they haven't seen each other for years and years, and haven't spoken as long as she can remember. She told me that one time she and Milly were in New York for summer school just like usual. Celia was about ten. Now, lately Geoffrey Render hasn't even been in New York in the summers—he goes to London I think—so like I said I haven't seen him there at all. But back then he still taught some of those classes for visitors, people not in the company, but Celia says her mother never ever took Geoffrey Render's class and that she, I mean Celia, never even knew who Mr. Render was."

"Maybe they'd just lost touch," I theorized.

"No, no! Celia said Milly told *her* that Geoffrey Render was a terrible man."

"Terrible?" I asked, thrilled.

"Yes. A terrible man," she said. "See, when Celia was ten, she and Milly were waiting for an elevator in the building where NDT rehearses and the doors opened, and there stood this man, and Milly and he just stood and looked at each other until the doors started to close and then he reached out and pushed the doors apart and just walked on past them without saying a word. *That* was Geoffrey Render. Celia knows because Milly told her right afterward who he was and that he was a terrible man."

"Wow!" I said softly. "I *see.* Last night you saw them meet after all that time?"

"Yes I saw," Adelaide said importantly. "I thought Celia should see too. I knew it would mean a lot to see her mother making up with Geoffrey Render."

"Just what were they making up, Adelaide?"

"Well, I don't really know," Adelaide had to confess. "Professional differences, I suppose. Celia doesn't know. Milly won't talk about it. But with creative artists like Milly and Geoffrey Render you just don't know. It could be anything. Celia thinks... Well, I'm talking too much."

"Oh *no*," I assured her over the drum roll and the throbs of a bass drum, "not at all. Tell me what Cecilia thinks! Where was Cecilia last night?"

"With Charlie of course," Adelaide said, rising from her desk chair dismissively. The Booster skirt was cut straight and Adelaide looked like a fireplug with a stout red base. "But that's none of your business, you know. None of this is. And you better not tell anybody."

Or you'll squeeze my arm, I thought, as Adelaide escorted me through chairs and percussion and popular girls to the door.

"I won't, don't worry," I said. "But tell me," I implored as I was about to be ejected from the Booster room, "did Mrs. Merrick *know* Mme LeBreton and Mr. Render hated each other when she got up that party? Did she know they hadn't spoken to each other in all those years?"

"I really don't know," Adelaide mused. "I only found out a few days ago myself. Celia just told me about the elevator thing a couple of days ago because Milly was telling her all of a sudden she couldn't go last night. That worried Celia. She was afraid Milly would hurt everybody's feelings if she didn't go."

"But she'd been *planning* to go?" I pressed. But Adelaide was smiling at the other Boosters and saying "Hi!" and "Hey!" with that effervescence so admired at Middleton High, meanwhile bundling me out of the door.

"Now run along, Meredith," Adelaide said, cocking her head in an admonitory way, the way she did with the wee little dancers. "Remember that what I've said is hush-hush. And listen, dance *good* this afternoon. Milly's counting on you. Tell everybody to dance really good for Milly this afternoon. It could just mean *everything* to her!

"And tell them no Mothers. Don't let your mother come!"

"Don't worry about that," I said.

"And Meredith, one more thing," Adelaide called out to me. "If you wore a foundation lotion and some pressed powder I really think you could hide those freckles. You could really be pretty!"

"Gee thanks, cow," I said softly as I broke into a run.

"Hey, Celia!" I heard Adelaide croon affectionately over the din of the hall. "I thought you weren't coming!"

Cecilia, I should mention, played the glockenspiel in the Drum Corps of the Boosters at Middleton High.

4

I thought of what Adelaide had said—"Hey, Celia, I thought you weren't coming"—when four-thirty came and we heard Mme LeBreton's stick whacking peremptorily on the floor and still Cecilia had not come. We all exchanged uneasy looks and began a reluctant shuffle into the front studio. The first girls stopped cold, causing the next girls to run up against them; then we all went on in, skirting shyly around the Mothers' Bench, which was in that corner right near the door. Instead of an admiring and fundamentally ignorant Mother sitting there, it was Geoffrey Render himself.

"Come in come in girls," Mme LeBreton barked. "Don't act like geese. This is Mr. Render, of course you all know Mr. Render." I blushed and tears came into my eyes as I headed for my place at the barre while the great man just sat there smiling at us.

No one had come out and said so, but I could tell that the nine other girls in the dressing room with me had also been scared to death. (And I knew Claude Bateson was too, though of course he wasn't in the dressing room with us but in the back, where we could hear him thumping and heaving in some kind of frantic private warm-up.) All the girls knew who Geoffrey Render was, now that I had filled Alma Doyle in, and even though the hortatory Adelaide had told everyone, "Milly says just relax, he's coming strictly to watch, *strictly* to watch," none of us, with the possible exception of Dorcas, was a dope. News about what Mrs. Merrick had said about a "gala première" had of course spread. In the dressing room, particularly after Christabel had arrived, every other word was "gala." Everybody had sense enough to know that our performance in this class determined whether there would be a "gala" or not; and beyond that, it was clear to some of us at least that if Geoffrey Render saw somebody he really liked, he would snatch them up and take them right back to New York City with him. This is why Claude was thumping so.

Yet I think the girls in the dressing room would expect such a discovery to be not Claude but Cecilia. Cecilia! I have mentioned Mme LeBreton's credentials as the representative of the world of ballet in Middleton: the purity of her school, her professional associations. But really the main evidence of her competence was Cecilia. Cecilia was so beautiful that she looked as if she would inevitably be "discovered" as a dancer on the strength of her beauty alone (as it is said Carla Fracci was). In fact, she looked as if Madame had built her for purposes of dancing rather than given birth to her. Well, no: the most likely thing was that the infant Cecilia had been found in a Capezio box, swaddled in lamb's wool, on the doorstep of the studio back when it was new, some seventeen years ago. Our nervousness that day in the dressing room had taken the form of exasperation that Cecilia was not there.

"Where *is* that girl?" said Lola Stewart, who was a senior like Cecilia and probably her best friend. "Why doesn't she come?"

"I saw her leaving school with Charlie Hill," Dorcas said primly.

"Of course she's with Charlie!" Lola said. "The only question is when he will get her here!"

Filing into the front studio like the multi-limbed organism, we tried to look complete, as if Cecilia were among us, but of course Mme LeBreton noticed right off that she wasn't. She didn't say anything but I noticed she kept glancing out of the casement windows for Charlie's black Chevrolet, and as we began the barre by bobbing gently through the *pliés* we were listening desperately for a crunch in the gravel. Even so, I think we must have been a beautiful sight, even to such an acute observer as Mr. Render. Arranged at the barre according to ascending height, beginning with the doll-like Melissa and going all the way around the big room to the towering Dorcas, everyone wore the regulation black and pink practice clothes, and a few of the girls had tied bright scarves around their waists or pinned silk flowers in their sleek hair in honor of the occasion. Claude Bateson, who had bounded into the room already hot and heaving, also wore festive gear: black leotard and tights and a red satin cummerbund. He looked like a stage pirate. But despite Claude, who of course did not look like anyone else and was straining for effect even in this most restrained part of the class, we were a pleasantly homogeneous sight. Our identical costumes and our synchronized movements obscured all the differences among us: here we had a real life together and it was these slow, willowy motions at the barre, matching quite exactly the fervid ump-chunk-chunk-chunk of Mrs. Fister's tinny piano as she played some mystery melody.

Meanwhile, Geoffrey Render sat on the Mothers' Bench, his hands on his knees, watching, watching.

***

Cecilia LeBreton just didn't obey the same rules I did, or most of us did. She was often late for class, or she cut class altogether, both here and at school. Cecilia missed a lot of school. Since she was apparently healthy as a horse my mother would have said, flatly, that Cecilia had no "character"; Mme LeBreton, on the other hand, didn't say much of anything about Cecilia and just went on without her.

I would have thought Cecilia would feel a positive obligation to dance since she was without dispute the most talented, and certainly the most beautiful, dancer in the school; I would have particularly expected Mme LeBreton to insist on this. Cecilia had been given every advantage a ballet student in Middleton could have: lessons from her very own mother ever since she could walk, as far as I knew, and trips to New York City every year to the NDT summer

school. I would have thought that Cecilia would have progressed, calmly and inexorably, toward the New York stage. But, unlike Dorcas, Adelaide and Claude, she had never given any indication that she considered becoming a professional dancer. In fact, she hardly seemed to want to be an amateur dancer. Still, her lack of interest in meeting Geoffrey Render, now that he and her mother were back on speaking terms, astounded me.

But Cecilia's greatest deviation from the ordinary rules of behavior was her attachment to Charlie Hill. They had been "going steady" for as long as I had been taking ballet, over two years, and this boy was, to put it bluntly, completely outside the social system. A gloomy-looking, craggy-faced boy, he had finished with Middleton High School a couple of years before—it was not firmly established at the studio whether he had graduated or just quit—and now he worked as an automobile mechanic at a filling station up on Tates Parkway. (He loved cars: you could tell by looking at the high gloss on his black Chevrolet, one of those humpy, rounded models that even then was considered an antique, and which he treated the way Mothers treat their mahogany furniture.) Actually Charlie Hill looked more like somebody from Woodpark High School, across town: they were a tougher lot over there where the heavy industry was. But strangely enough Charlie Hill was from our part of town. In an area of Middleton where ninety-five percent of the high school graduates went on to a college or university, Charlie Hill had gone on to the Gulf Station.

I tried to apprehend what Cecilia saw in Charlie Hill but I never could. He wasn't even handsome. Of course when Cecilia was with him she looked even more delicate and beautiful then ever—people called them Beauty and the Beast—but Cecilia had no need of a foil. No, it was "love," whatever that was. One time I thought I overheard Lola Stewart saying to Adelaide that Cecilia and Charlie Hill were going to get married at the end of the year, when she graduated, but I could not believe it. If Cecilia did evade her manifest destiny to become a professional dancer, then surely she would go to college. I could not conceive of Madame's tolerance extending to the divine Cecilia as a mechanic's wife. That would crush her (I could hear my mother saying this); that would just put her in her grave.

One day I had been late to class myself, and as I rounded the back corner of the studio I came upon the black Chevrolet parked in the little clearing where Madame's car usually was and where I always left my bike. I could not help seeing them because I was right there on them: Cecilia and Charlie, wrapped into one, in an immobile kiss, like a statue. They were partly screened from the studio by a big overgrown bush, but not from me. I had seen my mother and father cheerfully peck each other, but I had never seen anyone kissing in this way, except of course in the movies. I was deeply stirred by this scene, and I crept in the screen door to the dressing room, taking great care to keep it from squeaking. After that I watched Cecilia dance with even more interest than before, appalled that someone as off-brand as Charlie Hill could have this mysterious bond with her that she might consider more important than dancing.

But even with all Cecilia's disregard for the laws of society, she remained very much a part of the social system. She was even exalted by it. She was a member of the Boosters' Drum Corps, remember, and wore the fine uniform. I don't know that any other Booster could have gotten away with dating a ruffian like Charlie Hill: I imagine any other girl would have been drummed right out of the organization. Not that any of the other Boosters would have wanted to date him: I don't believe Bitsy Hamilton or Dixie Basham would even have said "Hi" to Charlie Hill in the hall.

***

Thank God, during the *ronds de jambe,* while our rows of legs swiped around, then around again, like synchronized windshield wipers, we heard the heavy crunch of gravel, and a dozen heads turned and saw the bulbous black shape of the Chevrolet hump past the windows. Soon Cecilia came tripping lightly into the front studio, taking her place down the row from me with the taller people and starting to swipe her lissome leg too. I could not help but notice that she had rose-colored lipstick ground into the blooming skin around her mouth and that her thick chestnut-colored hair was tumbling out of the attempted rigors of a chignon. She looked wildly lovely, and I glanced at Mr. Render in a kind of fever of pride to see his reaction to this most beautiful of us, and the crowning achievement of his old, old friend and colleague, but he was looking in another direction.

Mme LeBreton coughed majestically and glared at herself in a mirror, the only way she deigned to acknowledge her daughter's arrival, and the class began in earnest. The barre went very well, of course, these exercises being ingrained in our muscles, and we enjoyed displaying our gifts for the monumentally silent Mr. Render. I am sure we were all very proud of ourselves as we rounded out this first portion of the class.

"Stretches," Mme LeBreton called. Then, "*Pointe* shoes, girls, run change."

Mr. Render woke up out of his trance of attention and I heard him say, "Marvelous, Milly. You've got some wonderful little dancers here," as we filed out of the front studio into the dressing room. I felt that this was the settling of that old score between them, whatever it might be; that she, and we, had passed an important test. We walked with our feet turned out, swinging our hips and passing quite close to the Mothers' Bench. We had been comically fearful of it before!

Everyone breathed out violently back in the dressing room. "Well, y'all. That wasn't so bad," somebody said imprudently.

***

Pointe shoes, which we called our "toe shoes," were the center of the most important ritual at Mme LeBreton's school. Mme LeBreton had very firm ideas about toe shoes, unlike many American teachers who let girls as young as six or seven teeter around on *pointe* because they looked so cute. She knew—it was part of her legendary "purity"—that this sort of nonsense would do permanent harm to legs and feet. No student of Mme LeBreton could go on *pointe* until she was at least eleven years old, and even then it was not an automatic promotion. She held an audition for the top three classes of the school, and some girls were eliminated. These were only the weakest, most hopeless dancers (a girl like Dorcas could pass), but their elimination made the girls admitted to the toe classes feel talented and special. But even they did not get free run of the toe shoes: the shoes were not permitted until after the barre. No toe shoes at the end of a cold leg, lest an unwitting *relevé* ruin an unsuspecting muscle.

I adored my toe shoes. Mme LeBreton ordered them for us from Capezio in New York City through Bartlett the Costumer up on Tates Parkway. The boxes of shoes were waiting for us at the first lesson in the fall, and we took them home afterward to sew the ribbons on. They were pink satin with a toe as hard as the tip of a baseball hat. In our shoes, which were student models, this blocky wooden toe was covered with doeskin to prevent slipping. Professional shoes, on the other hand, have satin blocks which must be darned to prevent slipping, but no one was taking any chances with our young amateur limbs. Professional dancers go through nine or ten pairs of shoes a week, but we got one pair a year, although we might get another for the recital in the spring, since by that time the doeskin soles and toes of the first pair had gone black and shiny and the pink satin was discolored and rough.

Now eleven girls sat around the little dressing room of the LeBreton studio exchanging their pink ballet slippers for their toe shoes. Some sat on the benches but most sat crowded together on the floor, working quickly and silently. Dorcas was folded up next to me on the floor, where we were shredding our lamb's wool, impacted into a tight mass by yesterday's class, and shaping it into the right configuration to cushion our toes in the toe shoes. This was always a moment of some pride for me: since my toes are almost squared off at the end I could shape my lamb's wool into a nice simple oval and slip it over my toes and shove it in a shoe in a moment, whereas some others, even Cecilia, took a lot longer fashioning protection for their more irregular toes. I saw the renegade Cecilia working at her toes, which sloped precipitously from a very long and bony big toe to a small, almost gnarled little toe. The elaborate structure *she* was working on, with a frown creasing her glorious forehead and troubling her wide blue eyes, involved not only lamb's wool but wads of cotton balls, held in place by means of narrow white tape. Sometimes you could see blood on the wool and cotton when Cecilia unwrapped her feet after class.

As we were scrambling to our feet and testing our shoes, pushing first one *pointe* against the floor and then the other, a surprising thing happened. Christabel's mother, Lyda Merrick, appeared at the screen door of the dressing room. She looked as beautiful as usual: her face was smooth and tanned and, as always, her hair was pulled back into a chignon that was perfectly simple and elegant. I was surprised to see her, after what Adelaide had said about Mothers, although it was possible that she had been especially invited. But somehow I knew from

Mrs. Merrick's pretty flurry as she came in and said hello to everyone, kissing some, that she had not.

Mrs. Merrick led us back into the front studio. Geoffrey Render cried out in delight when he saw her; Mme LeBreton, on the other hand, did not, but, with one eyebrow raised, instructed Mrs. Fister to start playing something slow as we formed two interspersed lines in center floor to do our combinations. After a few pleasantries with Mrs. Merrick, Geoffrey Render resumed his position of watching.

***

During the *port de bras* (slow exercises featuring the arms), Geoffrey Render began to chafe visibly at being a mere spectator. For one thing, Mrs. Fister had begun playing "Ebb Tide," one of her favorites for *adagio* exercises in arrhythmic little surges, with a peculiar twiddling in the bass and little rushes in the treble which I imagine from her broad grins around at the class she took for a witty suggestion of waves. Sheet music and books of music were piled on the top of the piano, an ancient old thing with yellowed keys, and around its legs. The bench bulged with music, and Mrs. Fister had to sort of ride it because it would never close all the way. Mme LeBreton was always buying new sheet music, in the hope that the accompaniment would improve, I suppose, and they must have had a copy of everything that had been composed before the year 1955. Mrs. Fister prided herself upon her versatility. Mr. Render clearly did not admire it, however, and he kept sighing loudly and shooting resentful looks at her oblivious back. He also called Mme LeBreton over to him a couple of times and whispered urgently in her ear. I had taken him for a placid man the night before, when he had talked so genially about the horrors of touring, but now he looked as if he were about to jump out of his skin.

In another moment he had sprung upon Claude, who had thrust himself on the front row today although his regular spot was on the back row with the taller people. "The hand," Mr. Render muttered as he reached up to the outstretched hand of Claude *en attitude,* a pose rather splayed by tension. "You must have a beautiful hand." He seemed to massage Claude's hand, which did relax; then he ran his hands the length of Claude's arm. "You're so terribly tight in here. Think, now, of a long line. Think of this arm as a streamer going through the air!

"And keep moving, kids! *Adagio* is slow but it is inexorable. It moves. Don't crouch like that in *plié. Plié* is a movement, not a position!"

As if he had discharged an unpleasant duty Geoffrey Render sighed again and returned to his seat, crossing his efficient-looking little legs. Before he resumed watching he spared a second to press Lyda Merrick's hand and exchange brilliant smiles with her.

He also exchanged friendly smiles with Mme LeBreton, who nodded graciously to acknowledge his help. She pounded her stick in an effort to regularize Mrs. Fister's waves. Soon she put forward a new *adagio* combination featuring several different *arabesques*. This sort of movement was of course very flattering to Cecilia, Hilary, Christabel and Lola, those girls with good extension, and it was natural for Mr. Render to get up again and go help them improve what was already so good.

"Look, Mill," he said to Mme LeBreton after a few moments of this. He motioned us and Mrs. Fister to stop. It took a moment to stop Mrs. Fister. "Let me try something," he said. "Let me see how they do with something new. Let's surprise their bodies!"

I was surprised all over by this development, and I remember that from that moment I could feel sweat coming out of every pore. He stood among us, looking at us but not seeming to see us in the ordinary way. He put a finger to his lips and began to move his feet, which were encased in soft-looking shiny black street shoes, in odd little shuffles and wave his plaid arms. The studio was perfectly quiet except for our breathing. Mrs. Fister sat looking, reared to one side of the bulging bench, with her knobby old hands still suspended above the keyboard.

When he finished sketching out what he wanted to do Mr. Render turned all the way around as if he were extricating himself from some private world and rejoining us in ours. He was a shade less genial.

"'Traumerei,' Mrs. —?" He could not remember her name and as a substitute for it revolved his hand in urgent circles like a conductor anxious for a crescendo.

Mrs. Fister's music library was equal to this challenge, and after only a short search on top of the piano she began to bang out this

Schumann piece with an obliging smile. Mr. Render began to dance full out, as dancers say, and I watched him dumbfounded. He looked so middle-aged, so round and so bald, I really had not dreamed that he would dance for us, or even that he could. I glanced away once to see how Mme LeBreton took this, and she looked much the same as when I saw her through the window before class: standing to one side with her stick clutched passionately to her breast.

His *adagio* involved a marvelously slow *pirouette en dedans,* which is to say back around the supporting foot, a feat that seemed impossible in street shoes, and yet he had done it without visible effort: no trembling arm or bulging eye for him, no splayed Claudelike fingers. He was wonderfully of a piece—stocky, compact, strong. He ended *penché,* bent forward in an *arabesque* with the back leg up some eighty degrees, a feat that seemed impossible in street clothes, but there it was before us, Geoffrey Render upended in a beautiful line. He was finished. Mrs. Fister, who had jounced through "Traumerei" somewhere to the side of the true pulse of Mr. Render's creation, trailed off brokenly, and the class erupted into applause.

"Now you try it," he said grandly, quieting the applause with a lordly gesture. The blood drained out of my face. *We* try it? Now I think the *adagio* might have been very ordinary, maybe even something that the National Dance Theatre did every day of the week, but that day I thought it was the most original combination in the world, something that reached right into the heart of the dance.

Original or not, however, the combination was extremely difficult, and Mme LeBreton abandoned us to it. She leaned her stick against the windowsill of one of the casement windows overlooking the parking lot—a darkening window, I might add, for the gray afternoon was almost over—and sank down on the Mothers' Bench by Lyda Merrick to watch. For the next half hour they seemed very amicable; they appeared to enjoy watching us struggle.

For we could not "get" the *adagio composé.* It seemed to me you would have to be an eel to perform its sinuous movements. We were supposed to be both still and at the same time never still, "infinitely plastic," I think he said. I was blue in the face with trying, but I could not do the *arabesque penchée:* I threatened to snap apart and I envied the fat-thighed Lola, upended in that impossible position in a fair imitation of Mr. Render. But mostly people hopped helplessly at that point, tittering nervously as the master demonstrated again and again.

Then he wanted just Cecilia, Hilary and Christabel to do it. He also wanted to accompany them himself, and so he went over to the piano and displaced Mrs. Fister. I am sure he was only helping her up but he seemed to pick her up by her shoulders and place her to one side of the piano, where she stood a minute, looking bewildered, before wandering over to join the party on the Mothers' Bench. Mr. Render played "Traumerei," and I was dazzled by the fact that he did not even look at the keyboard but kept his eyes the whole time on the *pas de trois* he had made. He played very well, and quite sensitively, following them in a way Mrs. Fister never dreamed of, and also getting a pleasant antique quality out of the aged keyboard that it had never had before.

The combination was too difficult for Cecilia and Hilary and Christabel: they teetered too much, and swerved dangerously in places, but I thought they had the right look. Cecilia, in particular, had the complacent, almost simpering expression of the ballerina in a white tutu. Hilary was not so beautiful, being rather too long in the face, but I admired her long lean flanks and it did not detract from her dignity that she stuck her tongue out in the hardest parts. And Christabel was piquant in the extreme, so skinny and flexible! As I watched her do the *arabesques* I thought of Tinker Toys: she looked like her legs were Tinker Toy sticks she could insert in any hole of her hips she wished.

Mr. Render cleverly edited "Traumerei" to end when they did (they doing just the most delicate little skips to maintain their balance), and the rest of us again clapped helplessly. Now Lyda Merrick called out "Brava! Brava!" in a very understandable display of enthusiasm. Geoffrey Render bowed slightly and gave a small quick wave, not speaking, as if to say to everyone, "Forgive me, won't you? I couldn't help myself."

***

Yet he did not return to the Mothers' Bench and it was obvious that the class was now his. This was not universally welcomed: a lot of the girls were beginning to look tired and cross. Adelaide checked a tiny gold watch and sang out "Five fifty-five" to no one in particular. The class was supposed to be over at six. The windows were now black and I had already heard, several times, the great scrunch of gravel that announced the arrival of a Mother. Mr. Render took no notice of any of these signs, however, for he was thinking again.

"Allegro!" he shouted, clapping out a rapid beat. Mrs. Fister, who had been restored to her place at the piano, gamely jumped in with "The Hall of the Mountain King" from the *Peer Gynt Suite,* one of her favorite fast numbers. Calling out the steps, Mr. Render hurled himself into a combination; the class followed along behind. I was flooded with sudden joy: my *changements,* the jumps on one spot, switching the feet in fifth position from front to back, were higher than anyone's but Claude's. But all of us jumped, like a herd of alarmed kangaroos.

Mr. Render was down on the linoleum with his ear to the ground. "Too noisy!" he yelled. "I can hear you!" which was funny because the class, all of us except Claude in wooden-toed toe shoes, sounded like a herd of hooved animals, buffalo perhaps, rather than kangaroos. We shook the windows; we jarred the photographs.

He continued to give us combinations. None was too difficult, except that no one in our class could do the triple *pirouette* he tossed off and most everyone began to stumble and even just walk through the steps he proposed. Soon people began dropping out: I think Alma Doyle, the married girl, was the first to go. Dorcas spun wildly out of a *pirouette* and fell to the floor melodramatically, folding up over an ankle, but Mr. Render took no notice. She had to drag herself out of the way of the thundering *tours jetés* coming her way down the studio; she found sanctuary against the wall, under the barre. Not too long after this three or four others silently slunk back to join her. Red-faced and bedraggled, Cecilia and Christabel frankly walked off together toward the end of the room where their mothers sat and where Mrs. Fister was still doggedly flailing away at her egregious Grieg. Meanwhile Mr. Render was caught up in the abundance of his ideas for new and more complex combinations. How much *batterie* had we mastered? Claude and Hilary and I jumped and jumped, fluttering our feet in desperate little beats.

We were red and wet and stinking. I felt like I had a hot spike down my esophagus and might pass out at any moment. Hilary looked wildly tired too, and her gold chignon had come down to form a flopping ponytail. And Claude: well, Claude had seemed to me to be hot and exhausted from the beginning of the class, and now he stood to one side, heaving. You could see every one of Claude's ribs as they went in and out, in and out, so violently.

But Mr. Render wanted to do *tours* now: turns from one side of the room to the other, on the diagonal. As usual he did them first himself (oh, he was good, you could tell by the instantaneous whip of the head, the way he stopped on a dime), and of course everybody cheered. We followed, though not on so straight a line, and with slower whips and stops, and it was clear that this was an ordeal which everyone was enjoying very much except Hilary, Claude and me. I have already said that Claude's facial structure was such that his teeth were almost always bared, and now the pressure, the heat, and the fatigue combined to make Claude's expression look maniacal. I believe it was on *emboîtés,* the little turning jumps, that Hilary failed to stop and crashed into the Mothers' Bench. It gashed her leg and a red stain spread on her pink tights.

Mme LeBreton was very concerned, of course, and after hovering over Hilary a moment she stood up. I was doing *chaînés* around the room at the time, with Claude close on my heels (looking, I am sure, as if he were out to murder me), but I was spotting on Mme LeBreton as I whipped around and so was aware of her reasserting herself into the violent scene. I was spinning with the last ounce of my energy. I was also aware of my classmates who ringed the room, cringing and tucking up legs and feet as we came whirling by. The next moment I crashed into a corner; Claude went on, heaving audibly and shooting off sweat like a lawn sprinkler.

My mind was red and whirling and I believe I came very close to fainting. But someone pulled me up and I was on my feet as Mrs. Fister broke into the minuet from *Don Giovanni.* She played it execrably, of course, but it had a divine loveliness for me that evening because it was our traditional end-of-class music and it meant that I had survived the most grueling class of my life. Girls kept patting me on the back or squeezing my arm and I saw that they were even congratulating Claude.

"*Révérence,* class," Mme LeBreton said, "*tout de suite, mes enfants.* She looked a little bewildered and concerned (she who was always so distant and demanding) as the class, many of whom were wounded, staggered into two uneven lines for the series of elaborate curtsies (bows for Claude) with which we customarily ended class. "You've got some fine little dancers here, Milly darling," I heard Geoffrey Render repeat as we hauled ourselves out of the front studio, higgledy-piggledy. I think I hated him a little for his pleasantness. The dressing room was horribly crowded: several Mothers had quit their cars and come in to see what the delay was (it was now six-thirty). Rather than push my way in there I paused to look back into the front studio. I saw Geoffrey Render lean down and get a strange-looking tweed cap from under the Mothers' Bench and put it on. It looked like an Irish workingman's hat, squashy with a little bill, and it made him look like a lorry driver, say, rather than a ballet master. He looked rested, as if the work of running young dancers into the ground were as refreshing as a pint of stout to him.

Mme LeBreton and Mrs. Merrick were standing talking to each other. They had lit up cigarettes and stood talking and laughing and smoking, just as everyone had at the party the night before. I heard Mr. Render say, as he joined them, "God it's cold in here Milly. You've got it like a meat locker." Meanwhile poor Claude stood nearby, frowning and wringing his hands, obviously waiting to get a word in with Mr. Render.

I went on out into the dressing room then, not wanting to lurk, like Claude, and threw on my slacks and shirt and changed into ordinary shoes. Almost everyone was gone: the studio had emptied almost as quickly as an auditorium does after a performance, becoming drained, a dead thing, and I ran out into the warm darkness, snatching up my bicycle, and leapt in sharp crunches over the gravel, pulling it along beside me. Even the cats were gone; at least they were quiet.

I whizzed down Sycamore Street, pumping madly and quite unnecessarily, since it was downhill from the studio to my house. I had no more physical energy left: this was pure nerves. The only question of any importance at all was, had we impressed him?

5

My family—my mother, my father and I—had lived on Sycamore Street since I was nine years old. The neighborhood, which was called Collegetown since it was right across the parkway from the community college, was a pleasant area, quiet, with a lot of trees, but I would have preferred to live in one of the posher, more stately areas of town like Middleton Park or Gilbert Oaks. In Collegetown, the houses varied in style and size—some were very big, others practically shacks—and most of the houses had some whimsical feature or other. One house, a yellow brick "contemporary," had a tree growing right up through a hole in the roof; another house, Victorian in spirit, had elaborate gingerbread trimming which the owner had painted the color of pistachio ice cream. In one front yard there was an ironwork sculpture that looked like an early flying machine, and in another front yard around the corner was a pile of rusted machinery all covered over with vines that didn't look too different from the other people's sculpture. One house had stained glass windows; a couple of other places had no windows at all. I believe this diversity was due to the fact that so many of the residents were connected with the college and came from foreign countries, or at least from parts of the United States foreign to the more upright region of northern Louisiana which had flowered into Middleton, where people generally don't incorporate any odd ideas they have into their domestic architecture.

Our house was not one of those bizarre houses, though. It was a two-story house of dusty rose brick with black shutters that were real and could actually close, and some fine details which I now recognize as "Georgian" such as a fan light above the front door and a carriage light beside it. It looked pleasantly old-fashioned there in Collegetown. I almost said "conventional," but that would not be right since there are not that many Georgian houses in Middleton, where the antebellum plantation style is the hallmark of good taste and luxury and any house with aspirations to style has its complement of columns. But, in a neighborhood where some houses looked like power stations or trading posts, our house, which was made out of brick and faced the street and had windows and a front door, did look conventional, and of course I was glad of it.

Around where our house is, Sycamore Street reminds me of a creek bed in a canyon. This is because it is a narrow and winding street from which the lawns rise at such a steep angle there isn't room for sidewalks, then seem to rise even higher because of all the trees. Our house was up on a small hill among many trees, pecans, oaks, pines, sweet gums, magnolias, maybe even a sycamore or two, I do not really know. When I think of the house back then, it is usually the way it looked in the fall when the leaves from all the deciduous trees started falling. None of us much liked to rake leaves and so they made a fairly permanent cover to the hill, and the rose brick house seemed to have a quilt tucked around it in a quietly crazy pattern of yellows and oranges and reds, getting duller as the weather got colder, finally turning into a comfortable brown blanket.

Because it had two stories and stood on a hill I thought of our house as a "big house," although in fact it was not all that large. Downstairs, along with a dining room we rarely used, was a pleasant living room with a fireplace and enough built-in bookcases to justify my mother in calling it the "library." The kitchen, a clean white place, ran almost the width of the house in the back and had three big windows overlooking a small back yard, also chronically leafy. My parents' bedroom was down a short hall from the library and the kitchen, an addition to the original house, and my bedroom (the glory of the house!) was upstairs, along with a guest bedroom and two other rooms which my parents used as home offices, or rather *designated* as offices since they never did much work at home but spent most of their free time in the library reading or listening to chamber music. As it happened, the library was directly under my room and so except for the three or four months of really cold weather when we kept the windows closed I could usually hear the faint sounds of Boccherini or Mozart or some other such gentlemanly composer coming up through the leaves into my room.

I loved my room. I could have had any one of the four rooms upstairs, and there was a larger one in the back, but I chose this one, which looked out over Sycamore Street through the branches of an old sweet gum tree. I had the feeling of being way up high and capable of seeing for great distances out over Middleton although this was not the case on account of the trees. What I mainly saw was the sweet gum tree going through its seasonal changes. It was not the view in this particular room that I valued, anyway, but another feature: one of the windows had a window seat commodious enough for me to curl up in and read a book, or just regard the tree and, way below, the street. I did not have to debate about which room I wanted after I saw the window seat.

We had a pleasant life there, although it was rather secluded, now that I think about it. We did not have guests very often. It is not that my parents were inhospitable; it's just that they were almost entirely self-sufficient. My mother and father had both grown up in a small town about fifty miles northwest of Middleton called Ardis. Being the same age, they had known each other all their lives. Mother said one time they knew they wanted to marry as early as high school, and they did marry as soon as they graduated from the branch of the state university in Barston. After that, my father entered law school at the main campus of the state university in Baton Rouge, and I was born down there. This was in 1941 and so my father did not get to finish law school on account of the war. He was called up sometime in 1942 and went to the Philippines. Mother, meanwhile, entered law school herself (one of very few women) and finished before he did. In 1947, when they were both finished with school and ready to practice law, we moved to Middleton, where they entered into partnership with Charles Matlock and Gerald Wilson, other graduates of the LSU Law School who were from Able and Miriam, other little towns near Ardis. We rented a small house near their office on Tates Parkway for about three years before we bought what I thought of as the big house on Sycamore Street.

Anyway, as I was saying, the very thought of "company" filled my parents with innocent horror, and they were never happier than when they could be alone for the evening in the library downstairs. They did go out to plays and concerts and performances. One important reason they had settled in Middleton rather than Ardis was the cultural offerings, and they continued to take advantage of these, walking slowly arm in arm up Sycamore Street to the college theater, or driving downtown to the Civic Auditorium; but they recoiled from purely social events such as the Merricks' cocktail party. They had gone to the NDT performance, by the way; they had enjoyed it and we had talked it over at breakfast the following morning, my mother reading Clara Vere's review in the *Chronicle* aloud over the scrambled eggs. But they had not of course gone to the party afterward. Not that they were invited: the Merricks did not know them and they did not know the Merricks. They did not "know" many people at all, in fact, although I think it would have been quite easy for them, as lawyers, to know a good many people in Middleton had they wanted to.

The thing was, they did not like to spend time with people who, in my mother's phrase, "don't think like we do." My mother was a slender woman with short black hair that was even then going gray around her handsome face. She had sad, intelligent gray eyes with bags under them, and she wore glasses with black frames which she drew off just before she said this. "They don't *think* like we do," she would say thoughtfully, biting an arm of her glasses. This was a definitive statement, a damning thing, and I took it literally. Most other people, it seemed, had serious and irreconcilable differences from us in the matter of their thoughts, perhaps in the very process by which they thought, or was it *processes:* how could I know how many and complex the differences were, since I was confined to our kind of thought?

The Jacksons and the Merediths (the Merediths being my mother's people, after whom I was named) thought like we did, I suppose: at least assorted Jacksons and Merediths from Ardis or other towns in north Louisiana to which they had emigrated from Ardis came to our house and we went to theirs. But beyond that it seemed that very few people thought like we did. Even Mr. Matlock and Mr. Wilson, my parents' law partners, who presumably thought like they did in the legal sphere, did not agree with my parents on the matter of alcohol (they "drank"). How *did* we think, I often wondered. Very straight, of course, very rightly, but somewhat mysteriously. My parents did not disclose any of their underlying assumptions or premises to me, just the cryptic, definitive conclusions. In fact they never discussed anything of importance in front of me: serious conversations always took place in the library under the cover of chamber music, or back in their bedroom.

My father was slender, like my mother, but fair rather than dark and without the gray hairs and the eye bags that made her seem so melancholy. He was considered quite a philosopher in the Jackson family circle, partly because he was the only lawyer in the family (apart from my mother) and thus was the family's public man, but mostly, I think, because of his characteristic facial expression, which might be described as a wry glare. He turned this wryness upon everything, all those people who did not think like we did and also those who presumably did, including my mother and myself. Just as my mother and father kept most of their thoughts to themselves, I learned early on to keep my thoughts to myself because when they did burst out of me my father turned his twinkly gaze upon me or— and this was worse—my mother whipped off her glasses and I knew, with a terrible sinking feeling, that I had just betrayed an alien kind of thought.

I do not want to give the impression that our house on Sycamore Street was a dull or gloomy place, however. My parents might have been austere, but they were never glum or harsh: they loved to joke (they were the clowns of Ardis) and they were always interested in things. My father loved the great nineteenth-century Russian fiction; he also played bluegrass tunes on the violin. My mother loved opera and never missed the broadcasts from the Metropolitan Opera on Saturday afternoons. They bought a lot of books, which kept them busy because they both felt a duty to read every word they bought. Even as a very young girl I realized that their enthusiasms, odd as they might be, worked to my advantage: they diverted my parents and gave me the freedom to explore my own interests in ways that the junior members of more normal families did not enjoy. My friend Danna Masters, for example, had a far more normal house: she had a sister and several dogs, and her parents had company all the time. As far as *I* could see, Danna didn't have a minute to call her own.

***

Friday night, after that climactic class with Geoffrey Render on Thursday, I reclined in my window seat with the window open to the evening breeze to enjoy thinking over the events of the week. I was just beginning to recover from them. The night before I had come up to my room, wringing wet and exhausted, and flung myself across my bed, too tired to go down and eat supper, too tired even to take off my wet clothes. I had fallen asleep a little while. Later, to soothe my mother, who was upset by this demonstration of fatigue, I had taken a bath and eaten a bowl of cornflakes with trembling hands; then I had fallen in bed and slept the sleep of the dead. Even now, twenty-four hours later, I felt a certain exhilaration of the chest that comes with physical exhaustion, as if I had just recently been breathing hard; and it felt superb to drape myself in the window seat and lie there, as if I were in a canoe just drifting down a peaceful stream.

I had hoped to find out at school that day that Mr. Render had issued some kind of judgment on the class or even a proclamation about his intentions with regard to a "gala," but there hadn't been any news at school. I had accosted Adelaide before school: all *she* knew was that Mr. Render was staying out at the Merricks' estate ten miles out of town, and since Christabel and her two older brothers went to Catholic schools rather than Middleton's fine public schools, there was no direct link between the people out there and the advanced class's Protestant majority. For all Adelaide knew, Mr. Render had already flown back to New York. I saw Cecilia in the cafeteria at lunchtime and went so far as to ask *her* if anything had developed, but she only gave me a dreamy smile—I am not sure she recognized me—and said she "didn't have the slightest," I'd better ask Adelaide Henderson.

So far as I had been able to determine, there had been only one definite consequence of the class with Mr. Render, and that was Dorcas

Durward's ankle. I had completely forgotten that Dorcas had hurt her ankle in the course of the class until I saw her standing outside our homeroom before school the next day with it all taped up. Dorcas felt cross and ill-used, and she said a lot of amazing things about Geoffrey Render.

"That mean little man," Dorcas said, right there in the hall. "I tried that *pirouette* three times with him standing right in front of me. He saw me stumble but he just said, "Again! Again!' like a little emperor. He was just being cruel to me, Meredith. He knew that if I kept going on this ankle I'd injure it but he kept on making me use it, just so he could laugh at me!"

"That's silly," I told Dorcas. "I'm sure Mr. Render didn't give a thought to your particular ankle. He pushed everybody."

"No, I saw him laughing," she said. "I think Mme LeBreton had told him I wanted to go professional, and he just wanted to humiliate me. They *do* that, you know, they try to discourage you.

"He made me sick playing favorites," Dorcas went on as people rushed past us, saying "Hi!" and "Hey!" and scurrying about their appointed rounds. "You could tell he knew Cecilia and Christabel and all them. He's real thick with their mothers and they all know each other in New *York*. I don't know if he even looked at us!" Dorcas was contradicting herself, but I didn't bother to point this out. "They think if you're in the South you can't dance. *I* think we have a whole lot of talent in our class. Even Claude's good. And really, Meredith, you're not bad. You really *can* jump!

"Well thanks, Dore," I said perkily.

"Oh, why did I have to be born in the South?" Dorcas wailed as she leaned away to grapple with two incredibly long crutches which I had not noticed leaning up against a locker. "Get my books, would you?" she said.

"Your foot's not broken, is it?" I asked, trailing her into the classroom.

"No, just sprained," she said loftily. "But it's a bad sprain, and Dr. Mintz says it'll be a while before I can dance again."

More like forever, I thought, watching her swing along like the pendulum of a grandfather clock. Actually she looked more graceful this way than in her toe shoes. She looked happier too: she obviously enjoyed the flap her crutches caused among our fellow students. That is because Dorcas had no sense whatsoever. Why, she was answering questions about her ankle with the blatant statement "I got hurt at dancing. Yes, I take ballet," which showed that she was oblivious to the strict dichotomy between the two worlds of the big hollow school banging with lockers and the quaint little studio thumping with feet. I would *never* say I "took ballet" at school, and would have answered questions like those directed at Dorcas (unless they came from an old friend like Danna Masters) with something vague like "I had an accident," and let the people at school think I had fallen down some stairs.

***

That night I lay in the window seat a while, then wandered over to my dressing table, where I sat down and stared at my face. Sometimes I got fairly depressed about my face. There was nothing really wrong with it, except the freckles which bothered Adelaide, but there was nothing particularly right with it either. It was just a face. It did not even have any interesting angles. Mother had interesting cheekbones but I hadn't inherited them, or perhaps they just hadn't emerged yet. (I liked to think that maybe they would, like islands that appear in the ocean after the eruption of a submarine volcano.) I would have to do some experimenting with makeup. It was time I did; a lot of girls my age already wore makeup. Meanwhile I leaned into the mirror and pulled my hair back, looking for some signs of distinction.

I was cheered to see that I looked something like Christabel. Her eyes were so wide, her cheekbones so prominent that she always looked like her hair was pulled back too tight like this. Of course she had unusual, exotic hair: pounds and pounds of it, almost the same sandy brown as mine but very crinkly instead of only slightly wavy. (Actually Christabel looked very much like one of the "stunners" so admired by the Pre-Raphaelites, although of course Christabel was very active and mischievous and never displayed the Pre-Raphaelite languor.) Now, looking into the mirror, I decided once and for all to let my hair grow long so that I could pull it back and wear it "up" all the time. Not to emulate Christabel, though, nor anyone in particular, unless it be Tamara Genovese, sitting with such world-weariness on the packing crate.

Hair was as important in dancing, in its way, as legs. Before I started taking ballet lessons I had short hair. (Mother would take me up to the Tates Parkway House of Beauty to Alice, who gave her the efficient-looking bobs she liked.) But most dancing students had long hair, at least long enough to twist into chignon or loop into a ballet knot at the nape of the neck. I also observed that they wore it "up" at ballet and "down" at school, which seemed to recognize what I have already referred to as the dichotomy between the two places. I could hardly wait until my hair was long enough to follow this happy scheme, couldn't wait, in fact, but pinned my hair up for ballet class with a myriad of bobby pins into a rudimentary sort of chignon. It looked something like the stump on the rear of a dog who has suffered an amputation of the tail. And I could not get past it. My hair was slightly wavy, as I say, and it looked just too raggedy growing out. Before my hair could get past the awful stage between "short" and "long" Mother would pull her glasses down, peer at me across the breakfast table, and say speculatively, I'll bet Alice could work you in this afternoon if you called her." Feeling mangy, I'd go running to Alice, who cheerfully whacked off most of my hair. But now, on this Friday night, I vowed to endure the grievous intermediate stage and let my hair grow long enough for a legitimate ballet knot, one with two glossy loops. I then went to my mother's sewing box, a seldom-used receptacle that she stored in her upstairs office, got a pair of scissors, carefully cut out the picture of Tamara Genovese and wiggled it into the frame of my dressing table mirror.

Finally I got in bed and tried to go to sleep. This was always my favorite time of day, when the house was quiet and it was dark and very nearly quiet outside. All I could hear was an occasional gust of wind and the faint rattle of leaves, on the trees and on the ground, and, very rarely, a car laboring up the winding gradient of Sycamore Street toward the parkway, or else coming, more easily, down it. But that night my mind still whirled with words like "gala" and "première" and "choreographer," and other words suggesting spotlights and starlight which had never before been employed in discussions of our endeavors at the studio but which had been bandied around quite freely since Mr. Render came. I tried to imagine what it would be like to take part in a "gala" at the Merrick Theater under the guidance of Geoffrey Render. That idea was just a blaze of light, and soon my mind, wanting particularity, drifted back to images of the known. I dwelt, that last minute before falling asleep, on the picture of Geoffrey Render, Mme LeBreton, and Lyda Merrick standing in a circle, smoking cigarettes and blowing the smoke into each other's eyes.

The complexity of the arrangements among these adults for a gala première had to be staggering, but as I saw it they took such obvious pleasure in each other's company (whatever problems Mme LeBreton and Geoffrey Render might have had in the past) that I thought they could hardly keep themselves from making some kind of plans for being together, working together. The smoke: I thought of the smoke rising above their heads in a little cloud. This was something to think about: Mme LeBreton liked to smoke, I knew, but she had a rule against smoking in the front studio and no one, to my knowledge, had ever smoked in there. As I thought about it, this violation of the usual rule seemed to promise a new era in the life of the studio, one that was far more adult and sophisticated than the life we had enjoyed there in the past.

BOOK TWO

THE NUTCRACKER

6

Later on I would remember this smoke and compare it to the mushroom cloud that rose above Hiroshima, but for the next couple of months after the earthshaking visit of the National Dance Theatre to Middleton I continued to see it as a symbol of the benevolent adult guidance that had so happily been brought to bear on our little lives. I knew that something important had been set into motion. I did not know the mechanics of the arrangements. I was only fourteen and also I was not in the inner circle at the studio. But I sensed that they must be both exceedingly intricate and exceedingly grand. The idea, you see, was to bring New York, that fabled place, into conjunction with humble Middleton—more particularly, bring New York to Sycamore Street, and to my mind this seemed as much out of the course of nature as to arrange for the sun to rotate around some obscure planet for a while.

But it was going to happen. Word got around pretty quickly over the weekend that Mr. Render had been favorably impressed by our class and the school and, improbable as it seemed, something was likely to come of it. This was very exciting, and we converged on the studio Monday afternoon in a silly state of pride and selfcongratulation.

But, and I'll never forget the shock of this, like cold water coming out of a shower head when you expect the hot, what we found when we got there was a notice on the bulletin board in the little hall beyond the dressing room.

The notice said simply,

Audition
MERRICK GALA PREMIÈRE
Saturday, Dec. 5
9 a.m.

I cannot convey the horror of that word "audition." Why, we had
survived that grueling class and he had liked us! Surely that had been
the audition, we thought. Mr. Render had exhausted us, in some cases
even *injured* us, when he was only supposed to be watching us; there
was no telling what we would suffer from him at something called an
"audition."

That day Mme LeBreton told us that Geoffrey Render had accepted
Mrs. Merrick's invitation to choreograph a ballet for the Merrick Theater
when it opened in April and he was coming back in about two months
to hold an audition for it. The word "audition" had a terrible effect on
us dancers, about the same as the word "execution" would have. But
Mme LeBreton was unmoved: *her* dancers had nothing to worry about,
she said; *they* would all be chosen. This audition was just for people
in the other dancing schools around town. It was a question of money.
Wide community support was required for a production such as Mr.
Render and Mrs. Merrick had in mind, and it was politic to give the
entire community a chance to take part.

This explanation of the audition did not stop us from worrying,
however: no ballet student with an event called an "audition" in her
future can ever be relaxed and free from fear. It was too serious a subject
even to talk about: no one ever mentioned the audition, not even in the
intimacies of the dressing room. I did not like to look at that cryptic
typewritten announcement, and I noticed that the other dancers also
averted their heads as they passed by.

Mme LeBreton did not raise the subject either, after the initial
explanation, as if the audition was too unimportant to talk about, but
I knew even then that her silence on the subject had something to do
with that old trouble between her and Mr. Render, whatever it was. He

couldn't come down here and upset *her,* she might be thinking. As if to demonstrate this, Mme LeBreton simply picked up where she had left off the day NDT came to town, taking up her stick and conducting classes according to the old routine. For my part, I worked harder in class than I ever had before, trying to put into practice the things Mr. Render had said about "line" and "movement," and I thought I could see others doing so too (particularly Claude, who struggled in vain to look like a streamer); but Mme LeBreton did not refer to any of these points or mention Mr. Render. I got the impression that if he had suddenly reappeared at the door she would have run him off with her stick.

Mr. Render began to seem unreal once we got back to our regular routine: he might have been a magnificent genie who had just popped into the studio one day, larger than life and promising a magical future. I thought about him all the time. I went over and over every moment I had been in his presence, beginning with the NDT performance, every single part of which seemed to be an expression of his personality. I went over and over the cocktail party, always marveling at Mr. Render's cool gallantry toward Mme LeBreton, who had rather lost control of herself there. And of course I went over and over the class which we had had with him. Possibly I had impressed him: at least I had survived until the end of it and he had smiled upon me, along with Claude. And he had touched me during this class when he had corrected my faults. One of my wrists, also my sides right at the waist, tingled at the memory of how he had touched me when he loomed up close, watching and talking. No male had ever touched me in this sensitive, prompting way, apart from Dr. Freeman, my pediatrician, and the effect of recollecting this was exceedingly powerful. In my mind, it rivaled the effect of passing Paul Wheeless on the stairs of Middleton High.

7

But Madame did not entirely ignore Geoffrey Render and the audition and the effect all this was having on us. Right before the Thanksgiving holidays she invited the advanced class to her house for a supper party, which is something she had never done before, as far as I knew.

I was very interested in going to Mme LeBreton's house. I hadn't even known where she and Cecilia lived until she gave us the address for the party. Actually I knew practically nothing about Madame's private life apart from a few glimpses I had had of her late husband. I did know that Maxwell LeBreton had been a plate glass manufacturer and that this accounted for the first-class floor-to-ceiling mirrors in the studio with "LeB M Co., Inc." imprinted in milky block letters on each panel. I assumed that Madame and "Monsieur," as we had cleverly dubbed him, were very wealthy. Sometimes, before his death, "Monsieur" would come to the studio to pick up his wife and daughter, and he would always stand outside the screen door and wait for someone to let him in, as if he were visiting the house of a stranger. Sometimes whoever saw him standing there would just yell for Madame instead of getting up to let him in, especially if everyone was busy with shoes, and he would just stand there while his wife's students whispered about him and giggled. I don't remember whether he really had a hat, but he had the demeanor of a man with his hat in his hand. Although I had the impression that Maxwell LeBreton was a very nice man, he was, I thought, rather ugly. He had a dogged-looking gnarled face, and when he stood patiently waiting outside the screen door like that he looked like a toad in a net.

The spring prior to the time I am telling you about, Maxwell LeBreton died of a stroke or a heart attack or something else which was swift and, so far as I know, unexpected. One afternoon in April I arrived at the studio and found a note pinned to the back door which said that classes were canceled that day and the next day because of a death in the family. Rachel Mintz and Alma Doyle stood there wondering who had died, and it occurred to me that we were the only people there for class and that the other students had known not to come. This taught me a lesson: there was an inner circle at the studio and some of us were not in it. The next moment I saw Dorcas running toward us over the gravel. She had a peculiar run: like a giraffe's, her spindly calves seemed to poke forward with each step. "He must have died!" she shouted hysterically. "Hilary told me at lunch he was at the hospital!"

I did not go to Mr. LeBreton's funeral, but I know that many of my classmates did. (Dorcas, not having the sense to know about the inner circle, went to it and probably sat on the front row.) I wonder whether they were remorseful about having made fun of the dead man with the ridiculously debonair sobriquet of "Monsieur." Classes resumed the following Monday, and I looked for signs of bereavement in Madame. I had thought she might wear a black leotard and tutu for a while, but she did not. That Monday she wore carnelian, I believe. She had a grand manner which was quite suitable to the situation of recent widowhood, but then she had always been this grand. Nor could I see any change in Cecilia, who was always rather vague and subdued, although it seems to me that as time went on she was more in the company of Charlie Hill than before her father died. But actually I had no idea at all at that time about the relations between Madame and her daughter, much less how they felt about the passing of Monsieur.

The LeBretons lived in a neighborhood near Middleton High School called Inglenook. You could actually see the high school from the house: when I ran from the family Chevrolet across the front yard to the door in the cold dusk the night of the supper party, I saw the topmost story of the high school building in the distance, rising up over the trees. This was a modest neighborhood, filled with small frame houses with screen porches of the type built in Middleton in the 1920s and 1930s, the kind industrious old retired people tend so carefully, with pyracantha bushes and pots of geraniums. Mme LeBreton did not tend her house and garden so carefully, but this was not apparent in the near darkness as I approached her door. It is really turning cold in Middleton by the end of November, and I remember the front yard crackling with leaves that sounded as if they were already, even at that early hour, frozen solid.

Frankly I was surprised at the house. I had recognized the street name and knew it was in Inglenook, but there are some big houses in Inglenook, such as the one my friend Danna lived in, and naturally I thought Mme LeBreton had one of these. But this was a very small house, and as I lifted the brass knocker on the front door I thought of the small studio, roughhewn and possibly not even completely finished. Manufacturing must not have been very profitable back in the 1930s. But of course it wasn't, I thought: that was the Depression!

Adelaide let me in and bustled me back to where the party was, an informal room to the rear of the little house next to the kitchen, where Madame was still preparing the food. Just about everybody but Claude was already there, sitting around talking, just as they usually did in the dressing room, about the next dance or football game or assembly, anything, that is, except the audition. Hilary sat on the floor in a circle of girls with her peasant dress spread out around her. I said "Hi!" to everybody, restraining an impulse to go curtsy to Cecilia, who sat above the others among a heap of cushions on a long divan, like a princess.

The room looked like a back porch that had been "closed in" by means of a big bank of opaque louvers from the late Mr. LeBreton's plate glass company, and I expect Mme LeBreton called it a sun parlor. The furniture was wicker that looked as if it had once sat out on a porch and braved the elements. The decor was botanical: several macramé plant holders were suspended from the ceiling to cradle big clay pots from which trailed long stringy plants, and there were also two or three rusty-looking ferns sitting around in long-legged wicker fern stands.

And the kitchen! Well, it was hard to tell just what the kitchen looked like because it was in such disorder. When my mother had one of her rare dinner parties, she "cooked ahead" so that on the evening itself the kitchen was so white and clean it looked as though it had never been sullied by the preparation of food. Mme LeBreton, on the other hand, was doing her cooking now: she was at the stove, in the midst of a jumble of pots and pans and tools, tasting something from one of the steaming vats. She looked as hot as after a lesson: her face was fuchsia and her hair had collapsed. She pushed it off her glistening forehead with the back of a hand which held a glass with what I recognized as another Manhattan in it.

"Hi, there, Meredith! Have some punch, or a little wine. Hey kids!" she shouted amiably to the crowd out in the sun parlor. "Who wants punch, or wine?"

"Wine! Wine!" a lot of girls cried out.

"Oh please, Madam L," wheedled Christabel, who was twelve, "give me some wine. I have it all the time at home!"

Adelaide and Alma helped serve the wine and the punch (mainly wine), and later the supper, but Cecilia did not get up to help, I noticed, just sat on the divan among the cushions. Christabel sat at her feet, and Cecilia toyed with Christabel's copious hair as if Christabel was her special little pet.

The supper was an unusual gustatory adventure for me. I was used to plain food, like roast beef and brown rice and mixed vegetables, but Mme LeBreton served *ratatouille,* something I had never heard of, and a complicated casserole with artichokes, I believe. The bread had black seeds on it; the green salad glistened with fiery dressing. I found myself back in the sun parlor sitting on a creaky wicker loveseat with a pottery plate on my knees that was rough on the bottom and as big as a manhole cover, removing big forks and big knives from a red napkin the size of a tablecloth, or so it seemed. Alma Doyle came and sat down next to me.

"Isn't this the most gorgeous food you've ever *seen?"* Alma cried, already chewing. "I wonder how she did this *ratatouille?* Do you think she would give me the recipe?"

I thought of the inner circle at the studio as I looked down upon a crowd of my classmates who were sitting together on the floor, somehow managing to employ the plates like manhole covers and the utensils like garden tools with carefree grace. Hilary and Melissa and Stephanie and Lola and all them looked as if they had been to a thousand supper parties.

They certainly knew how to enjoy themselves at a supper party, whether because of constant practice or simply by superior social instincts I cannot say. Dorcas sat on the floor too, but she stepped in Hilary's plate when she got up for a second helping, and whatever Hilary said made her go sit in a chair across the room and snuffle.

During supper someone boldly brought up the gala première. "I hope it's going to be a *ballet blanc,*" Hilary said. "NDT has a beautiful production of *Les Sylphides* we saw last year in New York, and Mother thinks we ought to borrow that."

Yes, yes, I thought, *Les Sylphides* would do very well, and it required only one male dancer, which was all we had.

"No, no!" Christabel said petulantly. "Mama intends for Mr. Render to make a brand-new ballet just for us."

Without mentioning the awful audition that would intervene between then and now, the inner circle continued to munch *ratatouille* and speculate upon the gala. As usual with the leaders of our class, this was done languidly, as if they had often taken part in gala premières and were wondering whether one more might be too much trouble. Who would do the costumes, Stephanie asked a trifle crossly. She *did* hope they got somebody besides Mrs. Oleander; Mrs. Oleander was such a pain. She couldn't say she was anxious to wear anybody else's costume either, even someone in NDT. Her mother said you could catch things from other people's costumes.

There was also talk of the Merrick Theater. I knew something about it from the *Chronicle,* but Hilary and the others seemed to know a great deal about it, expounding on the size of the stage, part of which would revolve, and the ingenuity of the "fly system," which would allow all sorts of special effects. But the big thing was the dressing rooms, which were supposed to be large and luxurious. All these things would be a great relief after the nasty old Civic Auditorium, where, Melissa recalled, she had picked up a sweater last year after a recital rehearsal and a mouse ran out. Christabel screamed a short but unbelievably piercing scream at this recollection and everybody laughed.

"Well, what do you think of this audition?" Alma said brightly, after this. "Are you going to try out or what?"

How insensitive Alma Doyle was, how indelicate! We weren't mentioning the audition! "Sure," I said, trying to sound casual. "We *all* are," I added, by way of reproof.

"I just can't decide whether to try out or not," she said, buttering a bite of the bread. "It'll take up so much time—nights, weekends."

"Really?" I said hopefully.

"But then it might be fun."

"Fun?" I repeated in wonder. "Fun" did not begin to suggest the importance, the magnitude, of doing a ballet with Geoffrey Render.

"Tell me why I ought to try out," Alma said, looking at me expectantly with her shining brown eyes.

"Well," I said, poking around in my strange food and sighing, "I don't know how everybody else feels about it, but this is the biggest thing that's ever happened to me." I paused, not sure how to explain it. "Mr. Render's the most famous person I've ever seen up close," I said lamely.

Alma smiled. "Me too, I guess. Of course Tom sees famous people all the time on account of his work."

"Really!" I said, perking up.

"He's a CPA at Middleton Bank and Trust, you know, and he handles the account for Channel 13. He sees all the TV personalities. Rick McIntyre was in his office just yesterday!"

Middleton, being a progressive city, had not one but two television stations in the mid-1950s, but I did not know much about them because my family did not have a television set until after I graduated from high school. "Who is Rick McIntyre?" I asked.

"Why, the weatherman!" Alma exclaimed, drawing away to give me a merry stare. "Don't you watch the news?"

Alma got confidential over dessert, which was simple cake and ice cream, I was glad to see. "I wish Tom liked ballet," Alma said, face shining.

"If he doesn't like it, why do you take?" I inquired, since she seemed to be so in thrall to this Tom.

"I've always loved ballet and I've taken lessons all my life whenever I got the chance. It wasn't all that often. I've never had any money!" she declared cheerfully. "But now, with Tom doing so well at the bank, we can afford it. And Tom really doesn't mind! Tom thinks that when he's at work my time is my own and I can do whatever I want to. Tom says it's good for me to develop outside interests."

I pondered this, puzzled as to whether this was generous of Tom or not.

"What do you do the rest of the day?" I asked politely.

"Run my house, child!" Alma said, shocked even more than she had been about the weatherman. "Cook! Clean! Do the laundry! Do you know it takes twenty minutes to iron a dress shirt? Tom uses five dress shirts a week at the bank! What I really want," Alma went on in a lowered voice, seeming to forgive my silly question, "is a baby. We've been trying ever since we got married, five years ago, but it just hasn't happened. But I keep hoping."

I was flabbergasted. I had never heard anyone yearn for a baby before. After all, this was "pregnancy," which I understood from conversations I had overheard among my female relatives to be a highly undesirable state, and which at Middleton High School was naturally the blackest scandal. But then families had to start somewhere, I supposed. I sighed over my cake, vowing never ever to get married.

***

After supper we wandered in and out of the kitchen where some girls, bossed by Adelaide, began washing the heaps of dishes and cooking vessels. Cecilia still sat on the divan, and Christabel gamboled around the crowded little sun parlor showing off. She knocked over one of the fern stands and, while the clay pot did not break when it hit the floor, a great quantity of dirt spewed out from it, but nobody took any notice.

Suddenly Mme LeBreton ordered us into the living room. I had the impression she was finally getting down to business as she sat down in a formidable wingback chair which I imagine had belonged to Maxwell LeBreton. It seemed to occupy the chief position in the room and looked like where the man of the house would sit to read the *Chronicle* and smoke a cigar. Actually that chair was the only thing I had seen to remind me that until about six months before there had in fact been a man in this house. On my way to the bathroom after supper I had peered discreetly in the bedrooms. There were only two and they were very frilly. The bathroom was festooned with leotards and tights hung out to dry. It was hard to imagine Maxwell LeBreton having so recently lived here until you saw that leather chair.

Madame's living room was very nice. I thought it was probably one of those living rooms that isn't used very much: apart from that chair, the furniture was velvet or velveteen and looked formal and uncomfortable. I sat on the floor near the blue leather chair and a fireplace which did not have a fire in it or any signs of a fire. Above the ornate white mantelpiece was a reproduction of a pretty painting which I recognized as one of Degas's ballet rehearsal scenes.

While we were getting settled Claude arrived. As always, Claude arrived in a rush, as if he had just torn himself away from something important, although I suspected that there was nowhere else in Middleton for Claude to go and that he had come late to avoid the awkwardness of supper. I could understand that, having found it a little awkward myself, and I looked at Claude with more sympathy than usual as he settled himself cross-legged on the floor not far from me. He was wearing those peculiar tweed pants again and a turtleneck sweater, the turtleneck part of which looked like a neck brace with his big fuzzy head sticking out of it.

Possibly it was Claude who alerted me to the importance of this segment of the supper party. I do not think my classmates noticed that anything was up as they milled around and chattered, but Claude and I looked intently up at Madame. Claude usually gazed at Cecilia in a lovelorn way, but tonight I do not believe he even looked at her; he just looked at Madame. She had taken off her shoes, which were gold pixie slippers with fake gems on the tops and turned-up toes, then put her feet up on an ottoman that matched the blue chair. My God, those feet! I had never seen her bare feet before and I was horrified at how gnarled and knotty they were. Why, the soles looked like hardened lava!

With a fresh Manhattan in one hand and a cigarette in the other, Mme LeBreton spoke bluntly. "Let's talk about this idea of the Merrick production. It's something we didn't expect. Frankly it's a wonderful opportunity for all you kids and for the school. Of course we have to thank Christabel for it. Christabel's mother has done it all."

Everyone in the room was suddenly paying close attention. There was a murmur of agreement, and Christabel hung her burnished head.

"But I want you to know that you don't have to try out," Madame said baldly. "Some of the Mothers have been afraid that if their children didn't try out they would be out of the school, or that if they stayed on that most of the classes would be spent on the production, but what I want to say is that classes will go on as usual. The only difference is that we probably will not have our annual recital this year, but we might."

"I thought the production was like the recital, only bigger," Hilary James interjected. "Mother doesn't know this about maybe having the recital." This was an important point because Mrs. James was the president of the Mothers' Guild, which did so much every year to finance and promote the popular LeBreton recital.

"Don't worry about it now," Madame said, waving her cigarette. I'm just thinking out loud. The point I want to make tonight, with all due respect to your family, Christabel, great folks," she apostrophized, lifting her glass, "my point is that we are not turning over our school lock, stock and barrel to anybody else, no matter how distinguished or influential they may be."

Here Madame stopped and sucked passionately on her cigarette, frowning, and placid sighs could be heard around the room as we thought proudly of the school. Of course we knew nothing was ever going to change at the LeBreton School of Ballet!

"What I'm saying is," Madame went on, crossing the terrible feet on the ottoman, "you all don't have to try out next week. Being a LeBreton student does not mean you have to participate in this thing. It will take extra time. Your mothers might not like that."

"How often will we rehearse?" someone asked.

"Well see that's just it," Mme LeBreton said, aggrieved. "We've spent these last few weeks on the phone to New York. Christabel's mother has talked to everybody in NDT at least three times, I think. Mr. Render is still on tour and so we haven't talked to him since he left here, and besides, he wouldn't know his schedule anyway. I think they tie his shoes for him in that company. I can't tell you how long he can stay, or even exactly when he will come, apart from the audition date. He's promised on the grave of his mother to be here for *that*. All I know is that they think he can come back for a few days, maybe a week, before the performance for the final rehearsals."

"That's not much rehearsing!" cried Dorcas, our deprived provincial.

"Oh, we'll rehearse between those times. *I'll* rehearse you," Madame said grandly, "but I don't know at this point how much rehearsing you'll need. I don't know what Geoffrey will take it into his head to do with you. You can see what my position is, can't you? Everything is up in the air!"

Supportive murmurs could be heard.

"The thing is, what most people do not understand is that working with somebody like Geoffrey Render isn't as glamorous and exciting as it looks. I'm not sure you have any idea what you're in for."

"That class with him!" someone groaned.

"Oh *that* class was nothing," Madame said recklessly. "You should have class like that in the morning, then have a three-hour rehearsal in the afternoon and a performance in the evening, then ride a bus half the night to the next town and do it all over again." Now everybody groaned, except Claude, who leaned forward watching Madame with eyes that glittered like a rodent's.

"Tell us about when you were a dancer with Mr. Render's troupe," Claude called out. "You've never talked about it!"

"Oh yes! Yes!" everyone called. "Please, please, Madame."

"I'd need another drink for that," Madame declared.

"I'll do it!" cried Adelaide.

"No baby, I'll do it. My leg's asleep. I need to move. I won't be a minute."

I thought it was ominous that Mme LeBreton was dragging her feet in the great enterprise, but such feet! How battered they were! How battered *she* was! Still, Mme LeBreton was the most theatrical person in Middleton, and I had the feeling that she was staging something tonight. While she was gone I looked around at the green and azure and blue furniture and then more closely at the Degas, as if for clues as to what this might be. In the painting, an old dancing master in a gray smock and trousers leaned on his staff, lecturing a class of young ballet students.

They were wearing knee length white tutus with bright sashes around their waists, more like costumes for the stage than practice garments, and no one looked hot or tired. They looked, in fact, as if the lesson of the master were a cool and refreshing drink and they were about to quaff his cup. What a studio there was in this picture! The ceiling was so high that the dancers looked tiny, like the "ballerinas" you see inside musical jewelry boxes. And, if there were barres around the walls the dancers' bodies obscured them. The walls were a deep green that made me think of the sea, and there were no mirrors on them. Now I realized that the color scheme of the living room was cued to this picture (Mme LeBreton was too artistic for this to be coincidence). When she came back and started talking I thought she looked something like this old man talking to the young dancers: she seemed so old and so wise and she talked to us like we were the most innocent of children.

"Once there was a little girl named Mildred Frobish who lived in Albuquerque, New Mexico," Madame began. She had her new drink; she lit another cigarette and then kept shaking the match to extinguish it for a very long time. "One time when she was seventeen years old a little one-horse ballet company named Ballet Benet came to Albuquerque and so enchanted her that she ran away with them the next morning and was never heard from again."

"Oh, cut it out, Mama," Cecilia, who was not theatrical, called out from over on the green sofa.

"No, tell us really," Claude pursued, eyes aglint above the neck brace, thighs abulge in the peculiar tweed. "Was this when you met Geoffrey Render, on the road?"

"God, this was a century ago, kids," Madame proclaimed. "I was a girl out in New Mexico, the age a lot of you are now, when this little ragtag company came to town. I can't help laughing when I think about it. It was Geoffrey and about ten or twelve other dancers, and they had two or three dozen costumes that they used for everything and not more than four or five flats. They picked up musicians when they could, or if they couldn't, Geoffrey or this old gal from California played the piano."

"Were they good?" Claude asked.

"They were wonderful!" Madame shouted. "Or *I* thought they were. *God,* Geoffrey was a marvelous dancer. He'd just come back from Europe, you know. He was with Diaghilev's troupe over there for a while. You'll have to get him to talk about that. He loves to tell stories about himself. Why, he even did some of Nijinsky's numbers, the Faun, the Slave, the Rose. All that stuff. It would just knock you out to see him."

"Was he as good as Nijinsky?" Claude asked.

"Oh hell *I* don't know! I never saw Nijinsky! He was before my time. But he was good, Geoffrey was. Why, he's *still* damn good."

Oh boy, this was the profane Mme LeBreton of the cocktail party! I moved in closer. "What did they do, do you remember?" I asked.

"As a matter of fact I do. They did an act of *Sleeping Beauty* and a two-bit *Scheherazade,* both of 'em cut way down, of course, and Geoffrey did the Black Swan *pas de deux* with Gretchen Jones. *She* wfi as an old cow! And I thought, if *she* can do it so can I. I went backstage afterward to sign up."

"And they took you?" Claude asked intently.

"Well, not at first," Mme LeBreton said with gleaming eyes. "They turned me down flat when they found out I'd never had dancing lessons."

Our well-drilled class gasped.

Mme LeBreton sat laughing at herself, sipping on her drink. "I talked to Geoffrey and to Barker Jones. You know who he is: he went on with Ballet Russe after he divorced Gretchen. Well, they thought I was crazy, but they told me I had a nice face, and to get some lessons somewhere and then look them up. Well naturally I didn't take this seriously. I wanted out of the damn desert *then,* and I thought I could learn what they wanted from them better than from somebody else. I was ignorant of course. I didn't think it would take very much to run around the stage in a filmy-looking dress on my tippie-toes."

The class laughed tolerantly.

"Well, what I did was just go out the back way while they were still packing up—the dancers were mostly their own stagehands—and get on their bus. I hid in the back and waited for them to come get on. Well, they packed up the scenery and stuff, but it turned out they had found a place to stay the night in town and didn't pull out until the next morning.

God, I was stiff as a board when they found me. I think they thought they had taken on a cripple."

"So they did take you on," Claude said.

"Yes, after some argument," Madame said complacently. "They needed people to help and I was eager to learn, willing to do most anything. I guess I was Geoffrey Render's first pupil. I remember my first lesson, in the back of a Masonic hall, I think. I had a knack for it. I learned fast. Geoffrey always said I was quick."

"What did your parents say?" I asked. This had been worrying me.

"They never saw me dance, honey. I don't know *what* they would have said."

"No, I mean about you running away when you were just seventeen!"

"Oh, I don't know, hon," Madame mused, as if for the first time. "I never saw them again. I wrote them a letter telling them what I had done, and I even sent them some money when I finally got some. I was a good girl! But my parents died during the Depression and I never got back to see them before they passed on. See, neither of them were in good health, which is why they were down in New Mexico to begin with, and those were hard years for everybody. They both had TB and they had five kids who were going to have to take care of themselves soon anyway. We grew up faster back then. I just went my own way. *But,*" Madame said, slapping her thigh smartly and looking around in a bright and ingenuous way, "how'd I get off on *that,* now? Who wants to hear about this old bird, anyway?"

"Probably no one, Mama," Cecilia murmured.

"Tell us about touring," Claude said.

"That's a grim story!"

"Oh, tell us! Tell us!" we cried.

"Another time, maybe. It's getting late. That first season, though," she said, "is just a blur, but I remember the next summer we spent a month on somebody's farm in Idaho and that was nice because then we could have real, civilized classes. It's those classes that I model mine on. That was the first time Geoffrey let me on *pointe.* He was always extremely careful about pacing the new people. There were a couple of other strays like me he picked up and he always went very slowly with them. But it wasn't too long before I had some good parts. He gave me all the *soubrette* roles, the cute young things, you know. Not a lot of people know it, but Geoffrey did a *number* of roles on me, the Other Woman in *Free Time,* for instance, and Fifi in *Rodomontade."*

I had not heard of these ballets, but I was very impressed.

"Then there were the good old roles too. I was always the Glove Seller in *Gaîté Parisienne* and the Sugar Plum in *Nutcracker.* But so what? It was a dreadful life. This was the Depression, and thank God you kids don't know anything about the Depression. I guess we were crazy to tour at a time like that, but no one knew how to make a living any other way, or maybe they didn't want to try, and we did all right. It even got to where we'd schedule appearances instead of just stopping somewhere, and we'd stay two or three nights instead of just one."

"How long did you keep on with Ballet Benet?" Claude asked.

"Five long years. When I started I was a fresh-faced young girl and when I retired I looked like this."

Madame pointed to her bagged and sagging face. She laughed, although no one else did.

"You see why I can't recommend it," she said, still laughing. "But you kids don't have the remotest idea what I'm talking about. You come to ballet class four times a week and you go home and eat good food and sleep in nice beds, and you finish school and then you go to college. God, I'd give anything to have finished school!"

With this Mme LeBreton stood up and, as she did so, finished her drink. I believe she was a little unsteady on her feet, although this may have been because her leg had gone to sleep again, or because her misshapen feet hurt when she put her weight on them. She loomed above us.

"Don't get any harebrained ideas about being 'discovered,'" she said in dire tones. Then she looked slowly around the upturned faces, paying particular attention, I thought, to Claude's. "If this works out and Geoffrey comes, he will be paying a great deal of attention to each of you and it is important that you not get any wild hopes up. You see, he does this kind of thing all the time. He's worked with schools like this all over the world. I want to spare you the disappointment that would come from expecting him to discover you and take you back with him to New York."

I shook my head rapidly as if this were the last thing I would expect, and I noticed several other girls shaking their heads. Claude's woolly head was quite still, but of course he had nothing to lose.

"I've talked too long, kids. I think I've kept you too late. Go home now. Have a happy Thanksgiving but think about what I've said."

Mme LeBreton gathered herself together and walked, wavering slightly, out of the room to her bedroom, I suppose. We heard a door close before anyone said anything or moved; then we picked ourselves up and made ready to leave. If the others were like me they were trying to think about what she had said, just as she had asked. But what on earth had she said? We were accustomed to taking orders from Mme LeBreton, but this time the message was somewhat murky.

***

I had found out during supper that Alma Doyle lived in an apartment a couple of blocks on the other side of the college just off Tates Parkway, and I accepted a ride home with her rather than call my father, since it was so late and so cold. Alma had an old Dodge that chugged and banged at this low temperature, probably at all temperatures.

"Tom doesn't mind you coming out at night like this?" I asked her.

"Tonight's Tom's poker night," Alma said happily, shifting the old gears and tossing her head back and forth and back and forth to be sure no cars were coming down the bigger street Madame's little street fed into.

"Do you think Madame's an alcoholic?" I asked, "and that's why she stopped dancing professionally?"

"Oh I don't think Milly's an *alcoholic*," Alma said. She was hunched up very close to the steering wheel of the Dodge like an old lady and, as if she was so busy driving cautiously that she had to surrender other types of caution, she spoke frankly ("Milly"!) and did not seem dumb. "Some people say she's an alcoholic but I don't think so. I think she just likes her drinks. She's had a hard life. She works hard."

I thought of those feet. "Yes," I said. "What do you think she was trying to say? Why do you think she had us over? You know what I think?"

"What?" Alma said, swiveling her head frantically at the intersection of that bigger street and Tates Parkway.

"I think she was telling us *not* to try out. I guess that answers your question about whether to try out!"

"You know I *loved* hearing Mme LeBreton tell about touring," Alma said when she had lurched out onto Tates Parkway and we were chugging along in the cheerful light of its streetlamps. She spoke as if she had been too busy driving to hear what I had said; this was the regular old obtuse Alma. "It sounded like running off to join the circus."

"It did, it did," I admitted, thinking of the Ballet Benet bus sitting all night in Albuquerque, New Mexico, with Mme LeBreton hidden in it—no, Milly Frobish—then roaring off the next morning into the great unknown. I saw the desert of the West and a pink and gold Western dawn (I had not been to New Mexico but I had seen a good number of Western movies). I saw the young Milly Frobish, as memorialized in the pictures hanging in the studio, sitting expectantly on that bus, looking into the future. Just as I imagine Mme LeBreton intended that I should, I speculated on the nature of the life that in only five years could transform this clear-faced young woman into the craggy Mme LeBreton, not neglecting to consider Geoffrey Render as a possible villain in this process, wearing the black hat, as it were. I thought of those feet.

"I had a wonderful time," Alma said, letting me off at the foot of my sloping lawn on Sycamore Street. I guess Alma's train of thought during the last part of the ride had been different from mine because she said, last thing, "I'm definitely trying out on the fifth. Are you still?"

***

One of the topics of conversation before supper at Mme LeBreton's had been the Harvest Dance, a big affair to be held down at the Civic Auditorium the next Saturday night. I had not paid too much attention at the time, but the following Sunday afternoon as I lazed around the "library" at home with my parents, reading the Sunday *Chronicle* and enjoying a good fire in the fireplace I recalled some of the things my classmates had said.

The Harvest Dance was put on by Roundelay, the social club I mentioned for the freshman class at Middleton High, and the Cotillion Club, a similar organization for sophomores. They were not connected with the school in any official way: they had been started by parents back when their children were about to complete elementary school and move on to junior high—not even a formal organization of parents to begin with, just some parents who wanted to be sure their sons and daughters developed the social graces that would prepare them for the elegant intercourse of country club life. Theoretically anybody in the class could join, but the dues were high enough to limit the membership to the children of those families that had made a killing in petroleum or one of the more lucrative professions, indeed the very same families who were members of the Middleton Country Club. Doubtless everybody now in the Middleton Country Club had been in Roundelay or the Cotillion Club or one of the many other clubs just like them. Back then every class to go through the fine Middleton public school system had a club like Roundelay.

My parents hadn't liked the idea of the organization—I don't think they ever got as far as worrying about the dues—and so I had not joined. They didn't think much good could come out of it, and even then I thought they were probably right, judging by what I knew about the parties. Dorcas, Roundelay's wallflower, went to all the dances, then called me up the next morning to complain about how wild they were. Even back in the seventh grade, some boys would get drunk at every dance and "puke on the floor," in Dorcas's uncouth phrase, and some boys and some girls would go outside and "park." As far as I could tell from Dorcas's account, Roundelay parties were primarily puking and parking. Danna Masters, another friend of mine who was a more successful participant in these events, offered brighter views. But most eyewitnesses agreed that Roundelay dances were fairly depraved.

Naturally the *Chronicle* did not talk about this dark side of Roundelay, being a family newspaper. Nowadays it might—I'll have to look at the *Chronicle* more closely the next time I'm in Middleton. Nowadays it might be more like other newspapers and just tell you about all the trouble in the world, the catastrophes and disasters and calamities and disgraces. But back then, the *Chronicle,* which won national prizes and had a remarkably wide readership, had a lot more good news than bad. Whether this is because the world was actually a better place in those days or whether the *Chronicle* simply had a sunny editorial attitude I cannot say, but in either case the paper was filled with benign news about community activities. I am sure that reading the *Chronicle* made my mother and father happy they had moved to Middleton. They looked happy, sitting over by the fire reading other parts of the paper; from time to time one of them would chuckle and read something out loud. People you knew were always in the paper doing wholesome things, even if it was only going on a trip or giving away kittens. I think every man, woman and child in Middleton read the *Chronicle* first thing each morning.

Anyway, I lay on the couch over by the front windows reading the names of all the people who had gone to the Harvest Dance the night before down at the Civic Auditorium. These included Rachel and Melissa as well as Dorcas and Danna, also Hilary and Stephanie, who were sophomores. What I remembered hearing discussed at Mme LeBreton's was that Christabel's older brothers had been invited to the Harvest Dance by someone, Weedgie Scranton, I believe. The inner circle had been thrilled by this news: Christabel's brothers were supposed to be the handsomest boys in the world but no one had ever seen much of them. They went to St. Stephen's, downtown, instead of Middleton High School. They didn't even go to the country club, people said, probably because they lived on such a magnificent estate.

"Wendell Merrick, Wexler Merrick," I read on the guest list with great interest. I scanned the list anxiously for "Paul Wheeless," thinking someone might have invited him, but they hadn't. I stretched out on the couch, musing on the Harvest Dance, trying to picture the decorations of autumn leaves and *cornucopiae* down at the old auditorium among the gilt and the red velvet and wondering whether Hilary and them had realized their ambition to meet the Merrick scions. There were some photos of the party, and I was looking for my classmates among the scarecrows and the sheaves when suddenly my father said, "Why, here's something about your audition, Meredith. Look! A picture, and an article!"

My heart constricted and I tumbled off the couch, stumbling across the room to where my father sat in an armchair surrounded by sections of the paper. Looking into Mr. Render's bold fixed eyes in the picture, I heard my father say to my mother, "I didn't know the auditions were city-wide. Why, this must be a big operation, Caroline. This is going to cost a pretty penny!"

"I hope it won't take too much of Meredith Louise's time," my mother said worriedly. "Meredith, sweet, you look *so* bedraggled. I'll bet Alice could work you in Tuesday afternoon if you called her. "

But I hardly heard them as I read the article about the audition in a kind of fever, then crumbled it to my chest and walked around with it this way, dazed, panicked, recalled from the mental lapse during which I had wasted valuable time thinking about the trivialities of Roundelay. Later Dorcas called to fulminate about the Harvest Dance but I didn't have time to talk to her: I was busy up at my mirror, applying cheekbones.

8

The day of the audition was cloudy and cold. Indeed clouds hung heavy and low, and there was some talk of snow in the *Chronicle*. Possibly the weather had something to do with the chattering my teeth were doing on the way over to the gym at Middleton High.

"You sure you don't want me to stay?" my father asked from the wheel of the family Chevrolet.

"No! No!" I shouted. "It would make me nervous!"

The audition was going to be in the gym at school, of all places, and I was shocked and even offended at this. It wasn't right! It violated decorum, and I was afraid somebody would see us in our ballet clothes in the gym and shout rudely, or, worse, laugh. I had assumed when I read the cryptic notice of the audition that it would be held down at the Civic Auditorium, since the Merrick Theater wasn't finished yet; and, even while deeply alarmed about the audition, I had formed a picturesque vision of it where we performed nobly in a golden patch of light on the shabby old stage while Mr. Render called out things for us to do in that high sweet voice of his from somewhere in the dark old house—unreasonable things that we did anyway, rising to the occasion as New York collided with Middleton on a wintry Sunday morning.

Instead, my father let me off at the Middleton High gym. This was a separate building down on the plain behind the big main building, which was built into one of the city's hills. It wasn't really a "plain," of course: it was the football field and also the parade grounds where the ROTC and the Boosters did their marching. But I thought of it that way because it was so vast and, well, so "plain" compared to the leafy rolling neighborhoods surrounding it. The gym, which was to one side of this plain, was only two or three years old at that time. It had been built for the Fighting Woodcocks, the basketball team that was forever and always the state Triple A champion. I did not go there for gym class as a freshman—our gym classes met in an old gym up in the main building—but I had been in the new gym a number of times for pep rallies and basketball games. It seemed the locus of school spirit, much as Mount Olympus was popularly supposed to house the pantheon of gods. I really didn't see how we could *dance* in it.

The gym that morning could not have been much more unlike my vision of the Saturday morning theater. Instead of being provocatively dark and cloistered in atmosphere it was glaringly bright and open. It was also shockingly noisy. I got there a half hour early but there were already hordes of girls there, with their Mothers; and the smaller girls were amusing themselves by scampering all over the bleachers like a herd of hysterical mountain goats. Their every step and every shout resounded round and round the gym. Mothers shouted at daughters not to walk on the shiny gym floor with street shoes and these shouts reverberated too. Certain things looked downright dangerous from a ballet point of view: this floor, for instance. It was highly varnished and, despite the markings for basketball, looked like ice, or glass. You might be able to see your face in it I thought, yearning for the comfortable old gray boards of the auditorium.

But someone, probably the Mothers, had gone to a lot of trouble to fit up the gym for the audition. As I peered nervously into the gym from the lobby, I could see our Mrs. Fister down at the other end of the court getting herself settled at a piano which had been placed behind the basketball goal, under a panoramic banner which proclaimed this the home of the Fighting Woodcocks and listed the years of their championships. Portable barres had been placed along the sidelines, and way down by the door to the locker rooms I noticed the resin box we used at recitals down at the auditorium, or perhaps it was another one. In any case, even at that distance I knew what it was because two little girls, both in bulky plush coats with mufflers flying around them, were stamping around in the box and then leaping out onto the shiny floor to spread the resin around; and on that brilliant surface, in that temperature, the powdery resin looked like snow.

The lobby was filling up with dancers and their mothers in heavy coats and hats and mufflers, and you could see everyone's breath as they chattered and jumped up and down to get warm.

"Don't they have heat in this place?" I said to Rachel Mintz, who stood in front of me in the line where you waited your turn to register for the audition and get a big, ominous-looking number. "I wish I was dead," Rachel said. "Where is He? Is He here yet?" she asked, looking around fearfully. We could not see Mr. Render yet.

Mothers stood guard everywhere like umpires or referees, shuttling us through this line, delving down under our coats to pin on the numbers with cold, fumbling knuckles, then, back in the locker rooms, directing us to remove our outer garments (like nurses at a doctor's office here), pushing us out onto the great slippery floor. Feeling stripped and lost and cold, I looked around for my classmates in the advanced class among a growing crowd and found them, one by one. There was Stephanie, there were Lola and Cecilia (Cecilia looking gorgeous), over there was Dorcas, whom I skillfully avoided; there even was Alma, whose face reflected the glare in the gym and whose eyes shone like a possum's in the headlights. "Tom loves basketball," she said nervously. "We come to all the Woodcocks' home games!" We were all here, except for Claude.

You certainly wouldn't have any trouble picking Mme LeBreton's students out of the crowd. I had grown so used to her regulation practice costume of black leotard and pink tights and pink ballet shoes that it came as a real shock to me to see what other people brought out by the city-wide audition had on. I have already said that in my mind Mme LeBreton's school was "pure" and her rivals' were not: well, this distinction was vividly illustrated by the differences in the costumes. There *we* were, slim and supple and discreet in slate and shrimp; there *they* were in all kinds of apparel that made you gulp and gawk. Those that had leotards had them, mostly, in that adult style Mme LeBreton wore, those clingy nylon leotards with scooped-out necks and long sleeves, but in weird colors, electric blue, or purple; and if they had tights, the tights were likely to be in a violent color too. I turned away in horror from two girls, both rather lumpy, who wore purple leotards and no tights on their long legs with wayward thighs, and toe shoes (now! before the barre!) with little white ankle socks! "Mrs. Farfel!" Melissa whispered loudly in my ear in reference to these girls and I nodded sagely: I had heard about Mrs. Farfel, who put on a "revue" out at the Fair Grounds every year instead of a recital, but I hadn't realized it was quite this bad. Other girls, even more irregular, wore shorts instead of leotards, or even old costumes from bygone recitals. Two little girls—but these were whisked away by vigilant Mothers—appeared in tap shoes.

Some of the members of the crowd milling around on the basketball court waiting for the audition to start had apparently not recognized the supreme authority of the Mothers and had left on "outer garments" like coats or sweaters. Among these was possibly the most remarkable group of auditioners, about half a dozen people who were older than everybody else, save Alma, and not dressed like real dancers at all. I recognized them as students over at Middleton Community College, not that I recognized them as individuals, just that I was familiar with the type. They made a merry group: laughing and punching each other and even singing snatches of song while everybody else, even the Farfel girls, stood ashen-faced, quietly trembling. Most remarkably, three of them were boys, wearing blue jeans and sweaters and white tennis shoes; the girls wore leotards with long droopy skirts over them. They had the sort of careless atmosphere about them which at that time was called "Bohemian." Now I would recognize this little group right off as a group of drama students, nascent "theater people," who smell out theatrical events and show up, enlivened by the thought of an audition and invigorated by the pressures and the hubbub that make other people sick at their stomachs; but then I was puzzled by them, and as I watched them horse around I was confident that Mr. Render would throw them out on their ears into the cold morning.

Mrs. Fister had begun to grind out "Shall We Dance" on the piano, giving a droll emphasis to the triplet on the fifth that follows those first three words, flailing away with her elbows flying in a jolly way, the notes ricocheting wildly around the rafters of the big gym. She was dressed for a blizzard in an old gray coat, a fur hat, and rubber boots, and I was noticing how the boots squished when she pumped the pedal when suddenly there fell a remarkable silence except for the pumping piano and I looked wildly around to see the entrance of Geoffrey Render. He seemed to sail in, and in his wake was an entourage of people. Mrs. Merrick was with him but I had never seen the others. I stiffened; everyone stiffened, and my face flamed for Mrs. Fister, who kept on bobbing along on the hollow sounding piano. Then a little girl tiptoed over and laid a hand on Mrs. Fister's arm. Mrs. Fister looked around and she too froze.

"Good morning, ladies and gentlemen! It's much too cold to dance in here and so we'll have to make it quick! Let's take off all wraps, if you please, that includes hats and sweaters. It's barbaric, I know, but I have to see your bodies!"

Mr. Render's voice broke upon me like a familiar and muchloved voice; nevertheless I acted, and I observed the other people acting, as if he had just cracked an exceedingly large and ugly bullwhip. I checked my body for wraps; everyone else disrobed instantaneously, except for the male college students, who apparently had no leotards and could only frantically remove their tennis shoes. "To the barres. By height, if you can, big ones down there, little ones over there. Don't worry if you're not exact," he went on, his breath shooting out in front of him. "That's right. Oh this is splendid. Fine turnout today. I didn't think Middleton had so many dancers! Even some young men! Oh that's fine, very fine!"

Mr. Render was dressed in much the same casual way he had been at the studio two months before, including the same odd workman's cap, but now he also had on a tan suede aviator jacket that puffed out around his middle and looked rumpled, as if it had been balled up in a suitcase and only just taken out. He removed the cap and stuffed it into a pocket of the jacket where it made another bulge. Mrs. Merrick was standing slightly behind him, slim and blond in a full-length fur coat, mink, I suppose, that glistened all the way across the gym. She was carrying a clipboard which, it struck me, would have a list of our numbers and names. Her expression, which was knowing and rather sad, suggested that it was too bad, but some of us would have to die.

The audition began. First Mr. Render, who had miraculously halved the auditioners, directed just the smaller ones to do *pliés* while he darted up and down the line with that swiftness that always surprised me, straightening backs and poking bellies and aligning heads. Mrs. Fister provided a jaunty "Tea for Two," for some incomprehensible reason. Meanwhile most of us bigger dancers started on *pliés* too, in an attempt to get warm.

The Mothers and other spectators were walking around and talking up in the bleachers, and while glaring up at them I caught sight of Mme LeBreton. Why, I had forgotten all about her! Of course she was not officially involved in this audition—it belonged to the choreographer and it was "city-wide"—and perhaps her coming late and sitting, quite literally, on the sidelines instead of at the coach's table where Mrs. Merrick had gracefully arranged herself was a deliberate strategy to show Middleton that the audition was not biased in favor of the LeBreton school but really was a democratic affair. This made sense. Mme LeBreton wore slacks and an old short coat, the kind we called a "topper," and, with her head wrapped in a plum-colored scarf, she looked as if she had dressed to go out in her backyard and prune bushes. She sat smoking and staring glumly out across the floor at the little girls bobbing at the barre.

Suddenly she came to life and gave a fluttery little wave. Turning, I saw that it was only Claude, coming out of the locker room on the far side of the court where the Mothers had sent the boys. He was red-faced and out of breath—he could not seem to make his lips cover his teeth and I knew he had been pushing himself through one of his secret preparatory warm-ups. I wondered where: surely not in the locker room, the very same locker room where the Fighting Woodcocks engaged in their manly rites! Claude's peculiar role as a male dancer in Middleton was especially dramatic here in this temple to virile athleticism. I could not imagine Claude putting on his tights in the boys' locker room. At that time I did not know about "dance belts," but if I had, I would have had even more trouble imagining Claude making his private arrangements with that particular device in the locker room. Here we were in the gym; stretching out beyond us was the "plain" where the football team scrimmaged and the ROTC marched, where, farther on, the tennis team lobbed and the track team sprinted. To me it had the same hallowed spirit as the battlefields we were always reading about in Latin I, the sites of sacred combat. I do not know whether Claude was thinking of these things as he took a place at a barre and flung a leg out furiously in a series of *grands battements*—Claude did not warm up his body so much as set it on fire—but I think it must have had something to do with the haunted, even wounded expression on his face.

Poor Claude! He had asked for an audition and look what he had started! During the past few days, when the audition had become an undeniable reality, we had begged Madame to tell us what it was going to be like. "Oh it's nothing," she would say every time, "absolutely nothing!" Well, nobody had believed her and I knew, watching Claude, that he certainly didn't believe her. It was really enough to make you mistrust everything she said.

***

Not too long after this Geoffrey Render herded the little girls onto a section of bleachers and turned to us.

"Some *pliés,* kids, nothing hard. I see you've already warmed up some. Fine, great. Just want to see how you can move and whether you have some rhythm."

"I have those things!" I inwardly screamed as I performed the exasperatingly slow *pliés*. Not everyone had them, however: with first my left hand on the barre, then my right, I saw both halves of my competitors do this most basic of ballet movements in a rather jerky and unsynchronized fashion. I felt like two legs in the middle of a poorly coordinated millipede.

"Turnout! Turnout!" Geoffrey Render implored, running up and down this undulating line.

We did *frappés,* and I carefully curled my foot around my ankle; *développés,* where I conscientiously dragged my toes up my tights. I gave myself brush burns with my superb technique, but I was miserable because this was all much too easy for me to show Mr. Render how much I cared about ballet, how much I cared about *him*. What good material I was, and all I could do was hold my spine like a flagpole and use my thighs like pistons! Mrs. Fister was playing "Stars and Stripes Forever" and I wondered how she could make a piano drone so.

"Not too bad, kids," Mr. Render said charitably to the millipede after the easy barre. "Now what I want to see you do is some easy little combinations. Come on out here," he said from center court. "How about a little *pas tombé–pas de bourrée–pas de chat–pas de bourrée* routine," he said rhythmically, starting to do the little steps himself.

We did several such easy combinations, taking turns in small groups. These proved further that many of *them,* the non-LeBreton dancers, could not dance at all. The college boys, for instance, and the lumpy girls in purple could not do the simplest things, a *changement,* for instance, where you stand in fifth position, each heel pressed against the ball of the other foot, then jump up and land with feet reversed, that is, with the other foot in front. This may sound difficult, but it is easy if you have had any training whatsoever. I watched one of the college boys, a handsome boy with very clean-cut features, try to do this and stumble all over his own feet, which made his confederates mime overpowering laughter and simulate stomping on the floor. Claude looked awfully good in comparison, all his muscles flashing while he did *changements* like a pair of very sharp scissors. If only he could have switched heads with that handsome boy!

During this part I also became interested in one of the smaller girls who was wearing a costume. She was about eight or nine and had on a bright orange satin suit styled like a bathing suit, with tiny straps. I believe it was supposed to be a lion costume: it had a front panel of some white furry material and, incredibly, a tail sewn onto the seat. The costume had probably had other parts, paws perhaps, or whiskers, or even a head, but now the poor child was wearing just *this* part as a sort of deranged leotard, with no tights, and toe shoes of an even stranger shade of orange. Other people were watching her too: they would laugh when she did a *glissade* or a small *jeté* because the tail would waggle as if it were a live thing. But the girl seemed oblivious to the effect she was having: she was a very serious-looking girl, with a little pinched face and chopped-off blond hair, as fine as cornsilk, which also flopped and whipped in a funny way. Actually this little girl was surprisingly competent, and I began to watch her for the pleasure of watching her move as well as the humor of her regalia.

Meanwhile Mr. Render was working very hard, as he had at our class, moving from one person to another, to touch or straighten, or place. He came to me from time to time: I would *feel* his approach as he were a magnet (the squatty horseshoe type) and I were a scattering of nervous iron filings that rose to attention and pranced about in the irresistible electromagnetic field of his presence. But really the most accurate analogy for what was going on in the gym that day is much less fanciful: the fact is that Geoffrey Render looked like a very ordinary basketball coach striding around, shouting. He exerted such authority and exuded so much spirit that you would not even be troubled by the fact that he was much too short for that game: he was competent and confident; he looked like he was conducting a practice session before a championship game and all his will was bent on winning. He did not seem to be taking particular notice of any individual, from the best— and this was unquestionably Cecilia—to the worst, which I took to be the Farfel girls. Instead he seemed determined to teach everyone to do things right and, as I say, *win* this thing. I would not have been at all surprised if he had pulled a silver whistle out of his aviator jacket and tweeted on it, but he used no mechanical aids to instruction such as Mme LeBreton's stick, just his entire being.

Then he began to arrange smaller groups which were clearly based on size and level of competence, little squads, you might say, as if he were trying out different game plans. Here came Cecilia, Hilary and Christabel again, the predictable glamour group, doing a charming *allegro,* later the little lion in the company of some of our intermediate dancers. I was put in a small group with Lola and Claude and we were asked to do a combination which included a nice *cabriole* or two. Finally Mr. Render tested the four males asking them to do some leaps and then some lifts. Claude did these things with his usual intensity, very well; the other three, including the clean-cut boy, were laughably bad. Mr. Render asked Christabel and two other game, featherweight girls to be their partners (Claude got Cecilia, of course) and we all laughed quite openly as these horrorstruck maidens teetered up onto the boys' shoulders and the boys staggered around under them, frowning desperately.

"That's enough, kids," Mr. Render said, laughing too and shaking his head hopelessly. "I've seen enough. Men, thank you. You're good sports. You can take a seat, or go on home if you need to leave. We'll be in touch. But before we break up I want you ladies to put on toe shoes if you have them and let me get a look at you on *pointe*. No dancing, I just want a look at you. This floor is like one big banana peel!"

Mrs. Merrick came out, the tiny spike heels of her pumps clicking deliciously on the gym floor, and murmured something into Mr. Render's ear.

"Sure! Great! Good idea!" he shouted. "Girls, put on your shoes and let's do this out in the lobby. The floor's linoleum out there; you *might* not break your necks!"

Since most of "them" who had toe shoes were already in them, it was primarily the girls of the LeBreton advanced class who skittered quickly back to the locker room and frantically shredded the lamb's wool and tied the ribbons. By the time we raced to the lobby the crowd of Mothers and other onlookers, including Mr. Render's mysterious entourage, the smaller girls, the males, and any other auditioners excluded from the special world of *pointe* had formed a packed circle around the edges of the lobby. The crowd looked as if it might crush the glass cases which held the Woodcocks' trophies. In the center of this circle were Mr. Render and the offbrand girls in toe shoes.

"Relevé! Relevé!" he sang out, holding us up on *pointe* with outstretched hands like a conductor sustaining the last chord of a finale. He ran around from dancer to dancer looking at her feet, and I saw that he stopped a long while at Adelaide, who had those unattractively flexible feet that seem about to double over backward on *pointe*. Mine looked much better, I thought; I was confident of their good strong arch. While Mr. Render inspected our feet, and other parts as well—he seemed to size us up as if we were horses and he was thinking of buying us—I felt happy and relieved. The audition was over and I was still alive.

But Mr. Render went on to have us do a few little steps in our toe shoes—*piqués* and such. "That was marvelous, girls," he finally said, holding up his hands to stop the applause. "But before we go home there's this little stunt I'd like you to do." He pressed a thoughtful finger to his lips and bored his great eyes into the floor. "I just want you to do this for me *if you can,* and if you *can't* don't worry about it. It won't by itself determine whether you take part in this little adventure of ours. I want to see of course whether you can do *fouettés,"* he told the rapt assembly. Then he raised his eyes, as if he had come back from a trance, and performed one of the little whipping turns himself. "It's just a trick step. It's not as hard to do as a good *battement tendu* if you know how to balance yourself, but it's something that audiences gobble up."

As if to prove this, Mr. Render then did five *fouettés* in a row, ending with a double for good measure. Dancers and spectators gasped, then clapped wildly; I heard a "bravo" from Mrs. Merrick.

"All together now, ladies. Preparation in fourth *and—"*

He lunged deeply to start us off. We bravely began, rising and whipping with one leg and sinking down onto one bent leg, rising and whipping again, up, around, down, up, around, down; then a couple of girls in the back fell and screamed softly, but we continued, most of us up to the heady number of eight or even nine. I for one had never done more than six before, though Hilary and Cecilia could do ten and they went on to do twelve, I think, before they, as the rest of us already had, toppled and ran aground.

The amazing thing was that with everyone fallen away, some sunk all the way to the floor, there remained one dancer serenely whipping around and around. This was the little girl in the orange lion costume. Round and round she went, the tail whipping grandly after her. The crowd began to count, or rather began to shout out loud the count that at least some had been keeping in their heads since the spectacle began. No real ballet lover can see a series of *fouettés* without counting them. Think of the *fouetté* contest in *Graduation Ball,* or the thirty-two *fouettés* which Odile does in *Swan Lake.* Now, I had read that one dancer, a Russian ballerina, I believe, always did sixty-four *fouettés* at that point in *Swan Lake,* and it was this sort of legendary spectacle that came into my mind as the little girl in orange satin continued whipping around in the high twenties. This was a prodigious feat since she was too young to be in toe shoes at all, even more so since she showed no signs of strain or even effort, such as frowning or putting her tongue out. Her little face, rather, had a businesslike look such as I have seen in very young performers, little show biz whizzes. She looked like the kind of little kid you see wearing a little tuxedo and carrying a little walking stick, doing an unspeakably complicated tap dance.

But this couldn't go on: she lost her balance at thirty-three and, in response to the audience's applause and cheers, gave a funny little bow and scooted backward into the crowd. This *had* been extraordinary: dancers and spectators, who had mingled and become one while it was going on, continued to clap and laugh. The child had not been perfect, you understand: ideally the dancer doing *fouettés* stays right in one spot, as if she were actually attached to it like those little revolving dolls in the musical jewel boxes, and this girl had, it must be admitted, "traveled." "Traveling" was a technical fault, just as it was back on the basketball court. She had not traveled far, maybe two or three feet in the course of thirty-three whirls, and I mention it only to show that her success was due less to technical perfection than to her high entertainment value, at least part of which came from the incongruity of her serious expression and her funny costume. It was, in short, a stunt, but I loved it. It *gladdened* me, as such stunts always do.

***

If it had been up to me I would have taken all the LeBreton students, plus the little kid in the lion costume, and told just about all the others to go away and never come back again, but of course it was not up to me. There was no such prompt and satisfying judgment. After the *fouetté* exhibition Mrs. Merrick simply hugged the clipboard and called out, "Thank you! Thank you all for coming! You'll get letters!"

Now the crowd pressed around Mr. Render, who was very nice, just as he had been at the cocktail party.

"Sorry you had to work in a gym, Mr. Render!" one lady, a Mother, shouted out. "Middleton has better facilities than this, you know!"

"Oh, I like a gym for auditions!" he replied gaily, scratching an eyebrow. "You can see and hear so well! I *asked* for a gym! I asked for the biggest gym in town!"

"Did you like what you saw, Mr. Render?" a sharp-eyed young man with a pad and a pencil asked. He had the look of a crack *Chronicle* reporter.

"Of course I liked what I saw!" he sang out. "There's no more beautiful sight to a choreographer than a gym full of young, energetic bodies. Ballet is for the young, you know!"

"Do you have any ideas what you're going to do with them?" another voice asked.

"As a matter of fact I do, but that," Mr. Render said as he pulled his flat tweed cap out of the pocket of the aviator jacket and wiggled it into place on his bald head, "is top secret. Not discussible. I'll tell you people all about it later but not now," he said, patting his stomach. "Forgive me, but I really must have my lunch."

Mr. Render continued to hold court for a while, though, as the crowd thinned out. He did this easily and naturally and without any signs of self-consciousness, even when photographers sprang out and took his picture. Part of the grandeur of his face, I now observed, was an openness of expression that is characteristic of very young children but not adults. He saw what he looked at and he said what he felt, which may sound simple and common enough but which is not in fact simple or common. He spoke to those strangers with the same ease, the same practiced gallantry that he used later with his friends Mme LeBreton and Mrs. Merrick. I thought this imperviousness, this wonderful, bland unflappability, was part of his greatness, and I imagined him in New York in a dressing room full of people asking things of him, all the while he put on his makeup and did those things I could not imagine Claude doing. He looked to me as if he had cameras on him at all times; I could not imagine him alone.

Later, after I had run back to the locker room to change my shoes and put my outer garments back on, I found the lobby of the gym empty except for Mr. Render and Mrs. Merrick and Mme LeBreton and a few of the most important Mothers. They were talking in a more private way now: all the interviewers and photographers and spectators were gone, and almost all the dancers, except Christabel and Cecilia, who were back on the court playing with a basketball they had found in the locker room, had gone home. I was supposed to go home too (I was supposed to call my father), but I resisted this: it would be too much of an anticlimax to a day I had dreaded so long; it would be a kind of exile. So I stayed there at the door, looking out it anxiously as if watching for someone who was going to pick me up. I scanned the parking lot; I checked the snow clouds.

"Before I forget, Lyda darling," Mr. Render was saying, "some of these kids are hopeless. Cross out 8, 20, 53, 109, 142 and, let's see, 32, 33 and 34. There are some more that I'm not completely decided about. I'll tell you in a little while."

My heart did a *tour jeté* in my chest.

"None of *my* students, I hope," Mme LeBreton said, without apparent concern.

"Of course not, my darling, don't be absurd," Mr. Render answered. "Your students are splendid. Why, even the very tall child did well today and I think she'll work out fine after all. But some of the children from the other schools are disasters."

Cheered, I managed to look around.

"Lyda, get a letter out right away to all these kids," he went on, turning to Mrs. Merrick, who was busy over her clipboard. "'Pleased to have you aboard,' to most of them, then a good firm letter to those others. Explain there aren't enough parts but thank them for their interest blah blah blah. Make it firm, now. You'd be surprised how many people will come back when you've told them no."

"How many parts are there?" Mrs. Merrick asked.

"Oh as many as there are dancers," he replied cheerfully. Mme LeBreton was scrounging down in her handbag for a cigarette; when she found her pack he reached for it and helped himself to a cigarette, also securing one for Mrs. Merrick. Soon the trio was smoking together just as they had at the studio.

"We've got one problem," Mr. Render said meditatively. "None of the men will do, except for Claude, of course. That's a limitation. I *need* some men. Hasn't Middleton got *any* male dancers? Oh well, you have some beautiful little dancers, Milly," Mr. Render said again, in a more cheerful mood. "That one *there* is interesting." He looked at me, which made me whirl back to look out of the glass door to keep up my charade of obedient waiting; I knocked my forehead against the icy, sweating glass and almost fainted. Of course I was not supposed to hear this and so I did not acknowledge it but simply stared out of the door in silent rapture. This is what I mean by Mr. Render's public nature, which did not take into account ordinary notions of privacy and personal boundaries.

"She's a real jumper. And you've got some good little actresses too, I'm sure of it. There's Claude, who is a strong personality, and you've got that daughter! *Both* your daughters! *Can* I make a dance for them, I ask myself in the night? *Am* I worthy of them?"

That's the spirit, I thought, banging my head against the glass in my joy.

He went on. "We've got a lot of work to do. I need a month to crystallize my ideas and then we have to squeeze out three or four days in January to set the dances. Then it's up to you until April to carry the flags."

They murmured something.

"There's just one thing my dear Milly. I have to have a new accompanist. If I walk in next month and see your Mrs. — Mrs. —"

"Fister," Mme LeBreton said, on a low, appalled note.

"Mrs. Fister, I shall simply walk out again. The woman is wooden-headed, I can't think why you put up with her. I need to nod my head and have the pianist respond, but I have to practically jump up and down on her wooden head to get her to stop." This was said in Mr. Render's most genial voice.

"Now Geoffrey," Madame said cautiously, "we have to talk about this. I can't fire Ellie. She's been with me since the school opened. I think it would kill her to miss out on the production."

"I didn't say *fire* her. You can have a rotten musician at your school if you want to, that's your business. I just won't work with her. I can't do this kind of quickie production without certain conveniences. Why, I'd rather ride a donkey back and forth to New York!"

"Geoffrey's right, Milly," Mrs. Merrick said in a dulcet voice. "The production is going to be of professional quality. Geoffrey must have the power to set the standards."

"Oh yes! Oh yes!" Madame said, a little wildly. I looked around at them.

"She's Max's aunt, you know," Mme LeBreton said, dropping her cigarette and grinding it out on the linoleum floor. "I know that won't change your mind. I'm only telling you so that you'll know why I've had her with me all these years."

"That's one of our differences, darling," he said. "We mustn't let it be a problem. Now someone really must get me some lunch. I'm starving."

I danced out into the cold noontime, exalted: I was "interesting!" I was "quite a jumper!" I would have jumped across the parking lot but, remembering where I was, I walked instead: well, I floated. I would not call my father: I felt too accomplished and professional to call my father. I would ride the bus. It was nothing, I'd say when they asked me how the audition was, oh it was nothing much, just a barre and a few combinations, some turns. Nothing much, I thought proudly, floating down to the bus stop with my toe shoes slung over a shoulder.

9

On certain bright mornings when it is very cold I hear a sort of whining rumble in the far distance which, I suppose, is actually nothing more than the sound of traffic on the nearest busy street (back then, Tates Parkway), but which I used to imagine was coming from steam shovels and bulldozers painted with brilliant yellow lacquer. I imagined that these engines were busily breaking ground at the edge of nowhere, digging and wheeling and rearing. I have always called this exciting sound "trucks on the horizon," which seems a little crazy and which I mention only because it seems to me that I heard trucks on the horizon almost every morning of December after that day of the audition.

Of course we all made it—all of us in the advanced class, that is. Mr. Render had axed one smaller girl in the LeBreton School, a fat child, one of those children whose mother had enrolled her in dancing class in the hope that she would become sylph-like and graceful. But this did not make us feel bad because it proved that Mr. Render had not automatically taken every LeBreton student. Despite the ease of it, it had been a genuine audition after all! Privately, I thought over further proof of this: what Mr. Render had said in regard to Mrs. Fister. He had axed Mrs. Fister as well as the little fat girl and the others, and I approved of that. Now, I was as fond of Mrs. Fister as the next LeBreton student—she was a nice old thing and she called us her "chirren," which was sweet—but I recognized that the affections should not rule in matters of art. No, I could see a great gap between Mr. Render and Mme LeBreton in this matter of the affections. Mme LeBreton stood revealed as sentimental, Mr. Render as realistic. Possibly this was a clue to the nature of the disagreement that had interrupted their friendship for nearly twenty years. In the days following the audition, by the way, Mrs. Fister played for our classes in her usual knockabout way, and I was sure that Mme LeBreton had not told her the bad news.

After the audition Mr. Render had flown back out into the world; we would not see him again until he returned to, as they say, "set the dances" on January the fifth. There was nothing we could do in the meantime except take class and not backslide; *he* was the one who had to do the work of thinking up what to do with us. I did not understand how he would have the time: I had heard that he had engagements all over the globe during that month. There was something in Finland, and then he always spent Christmas in England with Lady Something-or-Other. "He's just a genius," Mrs. Merrick remarked at the studio one day when she dropped in to tell Mme LeBreton about a telephone call she had had from him. "He's flying all over the world, yet he's finding time to create our little show. He's too amazing."

She also said, "He says he's going to have his manager send a packet down around the turn of the year to give us the information we'll need before he arrives on the fifth. They'll let us know the exact time of arrival later on."

"Damned good of 'em," Madame said, bending over to stroke Colette, who was going to have kittens sometime soon and who spent these days lolling around on a sweater somebody had left on the floor.

***

The projected gala cast a glow over the Christmas season of that year, and I was grateful for this since my Christmases in the past had sadly lacked glamour, to my way of thinking. For one thing, I had a serious divergence of opinion with my parents on the matter of Christmas decorations. Middleton always went in for outdoor Christmas decorations in a big way, and most of the houses on the big fine streets, especially in Middleton Park and Gilbert Oaks, had brilliant displays of lights, and scenery on the lawn depicting the Nativity or, in a more lighthearted, secular vein, Santa and his reindeer or Frosty the Snowman. Even weird old Collegetown had its share of lights and scenes in yards. But *my* parents would never go further than to put a small electric candle in each window of our house. This same lamentable austerity governed our Christmas tree, which was never one of the big flocked trees I admired at the Y's Men's lot up on Tates Parkway but a scrubby free tree which we went and got off some land my Uncle Louis owned out to the west of town. My parents did not intend it to be "scrubby," of course: they intended it to be natural and meaningful, although they did not actually use these words, which did not come into vogue until fifteen or twenty years later. We decorated this tree with red plaid bows and ancient gold balls, no lights.

This year I did not really mind my deprivations as much as usual because once Christmas was over we were going to start in earnest on the gala; besides, I had already established strong personal links with what was most festive in our city. Old Mrs. Merrick had the most famous Christmas tree in Middleton, possibly in all of the South. Of course it was pictured from every angle in her family's paper, the *Chronicle,* but even without that coverage I believe it would have been famous because it was a truly remarkable tree. First, it was as tall as their house, or looked like it. I don't know where they got it, but it wasn't at the Y's Men's lot or Uncle Louis's land. Then, it had a million lights and miles of tinsel and—this was the special part—hundreds of decorations that members of the family had brought back from their travels around the world. Every time any member of the clan went somewhere he or she would bring back something to put on the tree. We had little red plaid bows and they had beaded artifacts from Uganda and feathers from Hawaii and little silver spoons from Austria and tiny baskets from Finland: the *Chronicle* went on and on about the tree, which had a decoration from almost every country in the world; but the difference this year was that I had stood in the very spot where it stood, right under the scintillating chandelier in the reception room of old Mrs. Merrick's house, and I felt that now its brilliant international glow shone over me too.

It was a busy season, and I did many things that had nothing to do with ballet, such as help put on a Christmas party at Trinity Methodist, our church, and go caroling with the Latin Club ("Adeste

Fidelis," we sang, up and down a Gilbert Oaks Drive that was lit up like Broadway). But because of the projected gala I felt different about these activities: I felt—how shall I say it?—like a dancer going out among the non-dancers, the civilians; I want to say "pedestrians." Now I felt like a dancer a lot more of the time than when I was at the studio or preparing to go there or coming from there; now I felt like a dancer most of the time. As if in recognition of this my hair seemed to grow faster than it ordinarily did. Every day, it seemed like, I could get it "up" with fewer bobby pins, and the knot at the nape of my neck looked less like the stump of a dog's tail and more like something an NDT dancer would wear.

***

The *Chronicle* had a lot to do with this too, with my feeling like a dancer more of the time, I mean. Along with pictures of the Merricks' Christmas tree it had feature after feature on the theater, which of course was still a building, and the gala première that was to take place there in the spring. A photographer came to the studio and took all our pictures, and my picture was in the paper some time in December. I was doing *battements tendus* at the barre, between Hilary and Stephanie. Not too long after that picture was in the paper, my friend Danna Masters asked me to spend the night at her house. Now, Danna and I were not as close as we had been at one time back in elementary school, when we were best friends and practically inseparable, and so I suspected that Danna invited me because of the interesting publicity, although it may be that her parents prompted her to have me over after they had seen the papers. I knew that Danna's mother and father thought I was a good influence over Danna, who was very sweet and pretty but not what is called smart. This was rather embarrassing to me at the time, especially in the presence of Evelyn, Danna's older sister, who thought I was peculiar.

In any case, I was very pleased to go over to the Masters' house, where I was sure of experiencing a deepening of that festive glow I've been talking about. They had a big rambling house over in Inglenook, not far from Mme LeBreton's but on a street with much bigger houses. The Masters' house was surrounded by trees and distinguished by a veranda that ran around the entire house. The veranda always seemed to have company sitting around on it, and did always have dogs because Mr. Masters, an exceptionally nice man with the substantial-sounding vocation of "banker," loved golden retrievers and had several. I had long admired the Masters' Christmas decorations. The screens of the veranda were strung with thousands of tiny white lights, as were some of the trees on the front lawn, and there was a scene there, too (the Three Wise Men). Inside, they always had a huge tree, fifteen feet high or so, which they decorated the old-fashioned way with strings of cranberries and popcorn, or perhaps I should say which Coralee decorated. The Masters had the distinction of a live-in maid and cook named Coralee. The night I spent there happened to be the night they put up the tree. Danna and I worked on it a while with Coralee (Danna's sister, Evelyn, was out, and Mr. and Mrs. Masters had other company in another part of the house), but pretty soon Danna and I gave it up, the stringing of popcorn not being anywhere near as much fun as it looks, and Coralee finished the chore by herself, I believe.

We did not get around to talking about the gala première until about midnight. Actually Danna did not have much interest in ballet itself. She must have taken ballet at Mme LeBreton's at one time (every well-brought-up little girl in Middleton took at least one year—even Evelyn must have taken on this limited basis back before she got so sophisticated), but I did not know for sure, Danna never having mentioned it. Danna did not seem to have any interests of this kind, which is doubtless one of the reasons we had drifted apart over the years. I was always off to some kind of lesson or other, and she was a girl of leisure, who naturally found other friends to fill the gap. Danna was in the fashionable set now; she was in Roundelay, as I have said, and she was as sure to be a Booster as Hilary and Stephanie and Melissa, perhaps even more sure since her sister Evelyn was immensely popular and had in a sense blazed a trail of popularity for her younger sister. (There were other dynasties like this at Middleton High.) Evelyn was much honored: she was Vice-President of Boosters; she played a snare drum in the Drum Corps.

Anyway, about midnight Danna and I were settled back in the big room she shared with Evelyn with bowls of popcorn Coralee had just popped for us. We might have had a good talk, despite having drifted apart, but unfortunately Evelyn got home from her date about that time.

"Does that Claude Bateson really take with y'all?" Danna asked. "I can't believe that boy really takes ballet. Evelyn knows him, don't you, Evelyn? Isn't he in one of your classes?"

Evelyn had just undressed; now she was hanging up petticoats. The fashion of wearing a large number of ruffled petticoats or crinolines was just beginning to take hold at Middleton High School, the idea being to make your skirts stand out, of course, but also to produce the impression of a fluffy paper carnation upon whoever was behind you when you climbed the stairs saying "Hi!" "Hi!" "Hi!" I did not have any petticoats yet, though I was hoping to get some for Christmas, but naturally Danna and Evelyn already had heaps and mounds of petticoats.

"Claude Bateson's so queer," Evelyn observed.

"Not really," I murmured, even though Evelyn *was* such an outstanding senior.

"Cecilia LeBreton's beautiful, isn't she?" Danna said, munching on popcorn. Danna herself had lovely black hair and violet eyes. "I think she's the prettiest *thing.*"

"She *is* pretty," I said possessively, "and she's a wonderful dancer. She's the best in the school. *We* think she ought to go professional when she graduates. She really is good enough. You read about Geoffrey Render coming down from New York? Well, having him come down here for this production might be just the right break! We think he might discover her and take her back to New York."

Evelyn disagreed. "Don't count on it. Everybody knows she's going to marry that mechanic. She's just throwing herself away—it's really kind of tacky. But," Evelyn said airily, "I don't think she's all that pretty anyway. That kind of looks will fade. She came to school yesterday without her eye makeup on and she looked mousy."

"Evelyn!" Danna cried, delighted to be told Cecilia wasn't all that pretty. "Not *mousy!*"

"If you ask me," Evelyn went on, though no one had, "it's more likely that the ballet dancer from New York—what's his name?—will fall in love with Claude Bateson and take *him* back to New York!"

"He's very nice," I said about Mr. Render. I was deeply disappointed that they were not impressed with Mr. Render. Of course I recognized Evelyn's authority to pronounce on her classmates Claude and Cecilia, but still, her harsh opinions ("queer"! "tacky"!) were disconcerting. Danna appeared to believe everything she said, but then Danna was just a sweet girl of no particular convictions and I knew she would believe the very opposite about Claude and Cecilia ("manly"! "romantic"!) if I took the trouble to try to convince her. I worried about whether I should do this and whether I was disloyal if I didn't.

In fact, I lay awake a long time that night feeling lonely and misunderstood among these fashionable girls who did not dance. But the next morning there were trucks on the horizon (I could hear them from the veranda), and I felt excited and happy again. We girls joined Mr. and Mrs. Masters for breakfast. Like every other man in Middleton Mr. Masters was reading the *Chronicle.* Coralee served oatmeal, which sounds like an unattractive Saturday morning breakfast but which was, at the Masters', the greatest treat in the world. It had a big pat of butter on it, then a gob of brown sugar, then heavy cream. They had a special set of red Christmas dishes! The bowls had a festive design of holly around the rim and a Christmas tree on the bottom, under the oatmeal.

"Our little dancer has quite an appetite," Mr. Masters remarked approvingly, and Mrs. Masters smiled upon me. Mr. and Mrs. Masters were very glamorous parents, I thought (only Christabel's parents being more glamorous, in my experience). Mrs. Masters was pretty like Danna, only she was something of an invalid (I never knew exactly what was wrong with her) and consequently rather wan and slow. She wore a beautiful ruffly white organdy dressing gown to breakfast. Mr. Masters, on the other hand, was outstandingly healthy looking. He had the fresh face of a young athlete, with rosy cheeks, although possibly this high color was simply the result of going out in the cold to get the paper. "Ballet dancing must be very good for you. See, ladies," he said instructively, "Meredith gets prettier every day."

I blushed and Evelyn snorted.

"Oh it's grand you've stayed with your dancing," Mrs. Masters said, beaming at me. "Grand" was her favorite adjective. "It's simply *grand.*"

"This Madame LeBreton must be quite a teacher," Mr. Masters pursued. "People have been talking about this project of hers with the National Dance Theatre man. It's good for the city. The very elegant Lyda Merrick was in the bank about it a few days ago. I told her our little Meredith was one of the dancers. We're just as proud of you as we can be!"

Evelyn snorted again, and I suffered the kind of embarrassment I was talking about.

After the oatmeal Coralee served *café au lait* in Christmas cups. This was one of my favorite parts of spending the night at the Masters': they drank *café au lait,* all of them, according to an old French custom which was practically unknown in north Louisiana, although I later found out that it was quite common in the southern part of the state. This was strong black coffee with an admixture of chicory, poured together with boiled milk. The maid poured the coffee and then the milk into the cups right at the table, holding the coffee pot and the milk pot way up high but never spilling a drop on the tablecloth. She poured a lot more milk than coffee for us girls, then we ladled sugar into the cups.

"No, ladies," Mr. Masters went on over his *Chronicle,* "I'm just observing the effects of ballet on our Meredith. She used to be such a shy little thing. Now she's looking quite the ballerina." Mr. Masters was a great *gallant.*

"It's bringing her out, it's *grand* how it's bringing her out," Mrs. Masters said. "I bet she'll be a lawyer, just like her smart mamma," she added irrelevantly.

"It's her eyes," Mr. Masters decided. "Ballerinas' eyes are larger than other women's."

"Are you lettin' your hair grow?" Danna asked me suspiciously as we all drank the sweet coffee.

***

Everywhere I went that Christmas, people asked me about ballet, which was very strange, because I had hardly ever mentioned the subject in public before. Possibly the most striking instance of this took place in Ardis. The following weekend, about a week before Christmas, my parents and I loaded up the Chevrolet with presents and drove the fifty miles over to Ardis to see our relatives. (For several years now, since the death of my fourth and last grandparent, we had spent Christmas day itself at our own house.) There, in Ardis, we went from house to house that had been primed, like the Masters', by the Middleton *Chronicle* for rounds of questions and joking allusions to ballet.

The appearance of Ardis was such that I never expected anyone in it to have the slightest idea of what was going on in the larger world, including Middleton, the nearest city. It was a town on a major highway connecting Middleton to similar boom towns in Texas—eventually Dallas—but it was still in that area of rolling piney woods of which Middleton was the center of civilization. Actually it was in a valley between two of these hills, so that you plummeted into Ardis and then, if you maintained your momentum, just as quickly rose out of it again. Ardis was very small at this time, with a population of around five hundred (of which I suppose half were relatives of mine either on the Meredith side or the Jackson side); but it had been much larger in the past, in the heyday of the railroads. The Depression seemed to be the cause of its death: my parents were both born in 1918 and so lived through their adolescence during the Great Depression of the 1930s. They talked of it often: all the Merediths and Jacksons did. It was a very important shaper of their lives, but I got the idea that Ardis got so depressed in the 1930s it simply died.

There was nothing to do in Ardis except go from house to house and play with whatever cousins happened to be there, then go out into the pastures or back to a pond or walk through some woods, although these latter activities had an element of danger since there were snakes and wild pigs back there. Other than that the Ardis experience was always very blank, to my mind, not nearly as interesting as the experience of going to the Masters', for instance, and I usually ended up on some bed in a guest room or out on some lawn chair on a porch (no "verandas" like the Masters' in Ardis), supine and rather resentfully daydreaming until such time as my parents could pull themselves away from their many brothers and sisters (those people whom I understood to "think like we do"), get in the Chevrolet, mount the Middleton-ward hill, and head back across the cotton fields and the oil fields to our more interesting home.

Oh, there *was* the Methodist church, in which all the Merediths and all the Jacksons had worked faithfully since that time, several generations ago, when one of the Meredith forebears had come to this place from North Carolina and founded the settlement of Ardis; and if we should happen to be in Ardis on a Sunday or other holiday I enjoyed going to that church, which was a white saltbox structure on the edge of a vast cotton field way back of the town (the rest of which hugged the highway). Hymn-singing was an art here, as was preaching; and there were intriguing special events like picnics ("dinner on the ground") or slide shows by a visiting missionary. An uncle of mine was a missionary to China, and one time I experienced a sense of pleasant desolation looking at his slides of the East in that church on the edge of the fields at dusk.

"I see you're going into show business, Meredith Louise," another uncle of mine said on this particular visit right before Christmas. "Do somethin' for us! Do a dance! One a them fancy leaps," he specified humorously. People in the Jackson and Meredith families, who put a high value on education and every single one of whom had or would get a college degree, often used incorrect grammar for the humor of it. Even my parents slipped into this Ardis-talk in jocular moments. "You can do it from there to here."

We were in the kitchen of my Aunt Lucy's and Uncle James's house, which had been the house of my Jackson grandparents and was now the eldest son's house and the central meeting place for the family. The kitchen was full of aunts, uncles and cousins who now fell silent and turned wry, expectant looks my way.

"Oh Uncle James!" I cried, embarrassed.

"Says *here,*" he continued, examining the Saturday *Chronicle* through the bottom halves of wire-rimmed spectacles, "that you folks over there in Middleton are going to be spending five hundred thousand dollars on this theater."

A whistle went up around the room, where ideas about the dollar had been established during the Depression.

"*Merrick* money," another uncle said.

"I saw where *Lyda* Merrick was really runnin' the whole thing," Aunt Lucy said. "Do y'all remember her? She was a Miller from Natchitoches. Her people owned Miller Feed over there for years and years."

"Old man Miller went bankrupt didn't he?" "Depression wiped 'em out," someone said, inevitably.

"I can't imagine Mrs. Merrick being from Natchitoches, Mother," I said in an aside to my mother, who sat happily in a straightback chair sipping Ardis coffee. This was poor stuff, nothing like *café au lait;* it "perked" constantly in a pot on the stove and I never even tried to get any. It was thin and just barely brown: you could see the grounds in the bottom of the cup. I was irritated by the turn of the conversation, even if I was spared from performing: I was unable to place Mrs. Merrick in Natchitoches (pronounced "Nak-a-tish"). It was not dead like Ardis, but still it was just a little old town to me.

"You didn't know that?" Mother said, frowning and smiling at the same time. "Why, Lyda Miller was at school in Barston with Lucy. She didn't get her degree, I don't think, but she was there when Lucy was."

"Lordy mercy," I said, using the only oath besides "durn" permitted a Meredith or a Jackson. This was always happening: everyone important in the state of Louisiana had some connection to someone in Ardis, from the governor on down; but it never failed to surprise me. It shouldn't have, knowing as I did that people moved away from Ardis in droves but always left relatives behind, as if for markers.

"She used to be a pretty little thing," a great-aunt remarked pessimistically. "Course now she's a good thirty-nine, forty. "

Aunt Lucy, Lyda Merrick's schoolmate and exact contemporary, was offended by this. Uncle James withdrew to comfort her. Spirited debate followed on the nature and worth of the Merricks as well as their personal attractiveness. It was disclosed that they had extensive land holdings in these parts, something I had not known before: any number of the oil wells, both the derricks and the little pumping machines that looked like ever-toiling grasshoppers that we saw in the fields between Middleton and Ardis, could be pumping incalculably huge sums of money into the coffers of the Merricks.

"Can't you even do one a them pie-roots?" Uncle James inquired darkly, having done all he could for Aunt Lucy. He imitated a *pirouette* with his fingers. "Meredith Louise is lyin' out at the ballet studio every day and she can't even do a pie-root!" he shouted triumphantly, as I escaped out the back door.

10

During this time my heart was at the studio, where all my ideas about Christmas got their most satisfying expression. Mme LeBreton had always decorated her studio as gaudily as I could wish, with strings of blue lights around the outside, a big tree inside, but this year she decorated every square inch of it, just about. However careless and shabby she was, Mme LeBreton was always alert to the theatrical possibilities of a situation, and I got the idea that she, like me, wanted to celebrate Christmas in a heightened manner this year.

I had my own small part to play in this. It came on a Saturday about two weeks before Christmas, as a matter of fact on my way home from spending the night at the Masters' house. My father had picked me up there at about eleven o'clock and we were now going down Sycamore Street toward our house. As we passed the studio I noticed Mme LeBreton's maroon Lincoln sitting in the parking lot with all four doors open and its trunk up; then I saw Madame herself up on a ladder by the studio, fiddling with a tangle of those blue lights. Even from the street she looked frustrated and cross. "Stop, Dad," I said urgently. "See Madame on that ladder? I might help her with her decorations." It occurred to me as I got out of the car and skipped across the gravel that this was the first Christmas since Mme LeBreton's husband had died and that she might really be missing him now. (He might have been the one who had put up the lights in the past.) In that moment she looked like a poor helpless widow to me, but only for that one moment, as it turned out.

"Hi Meredith!" she boomed cheerfully from aloft. "Whacha need?"

"Oh nothing, Mme LeBreton," I said sympathetically, shading my eyes from the sun and peering up at her. She wore a big-brimmed straw hat, her topper, and some dreadful fuchsia pedal pushers. Her calves looked like chopsticks, and I saw that she wore the same sad pixie shoes she had worn at the supper party. "I was just on my way home when I saw you. I thought maybe you could use some help."

"Well that was mighty nice of you," she said. "I could use an extra pair of hands."

I inferred a rebuke to Cecilia in this. Cecilia wasn't helpful! Cecilia was probably on that divan at home! "Lordy mercy," I said in alarm when I took a better look at the Lincoln. It was stuffed with bulging cardboard boxes and lots of loose things too, like wreaths and swags and tinsel. A length of tinsel dribbled out onto the gravel. I got the idea that the car was so full it had burst open.

"Tree's already inside," Madame said proudly. "Go look at it! It's a good one this year. Hey!" she called out after me, "Colette had her kittens in the night. They're in the back room. Look in the closet!"

"Great!" I exclaimed, going around to the back door of the studio. Here, in the erotic zone where I had seen Cecilia and Charlie Hill kissing in that blind, mutually absorbed way, and also where poor Maxwell LeBreton had used to stand and wait so humbly, I felt again how alone dear old Mme LeBreton was now, and I was glad I had come. I pulled open the screen door, which screamed, and went inside. It was strange to go inside the empty studio, and I realized that this was the first time I had ever been in there alone. It was still and littered and a little sad, like a parade route after the parade has passed. I ducked into the front studio to see the tree, an eight- or nine-footer, flocked white, the pick of the Y's Men's lot, I imagined, then darted into the back studio to see the kittens. Colette had given birth in the closet back there on somebody's pea coat. There were four of them: they looked like rats, scrambling all over each other and struggling blindly for Colette's nipples. They were not cute, but I knew they would be terribly cute once they dried out and got some eyes!

Once we had brought all the boxes in, Mme LeBreton collapsed on the piano bench in the front studio, saying, "Let's rest a minute.

"Well, how are you liking ballet?" she asked me as she rooted noisily around in the jumble of her purse, extracted a cigarette, and lit it. "Do you really like it? Really?" she urged, directing smoke upward with her lower lip.

"Oh yes!" I said. "Yes!"

"I thought so, yes," she said. "I thought so." She now unscrewed the top of a thermos bottle she had brought and poured herself something to drink. I sank down on the floor near Mme LeBreton, and from where I sat I caught the pungent and now familiar smell of bourbon. Mme LeBreton had sounded very happy about my liking ballet so much; very probably, however, she was just happy to get at one of her drinks.

"Oh, Meredith! Meredith!" she cried rhapsodically in this sudden new mood. "The dance! The dance! It gets in your blood! Do you think you have it in your blood?"

"Oh yes'm, I do," I said solemnly, aware even at the time that I sounded like some pious little pickaninny ("sho'ly I do, sho'ly"). "Yes'm."

Mme LeBreton sucked passionately on her cigarette, looking around at the walls and the ceiling of the studio. "And how do you feel about this Merrick Theater thing coming up? Are you looking forward to it? Do you think it's a good idea?"

"Oh yes'm I do, I really do," I answered earnestly. "I'm really excited about working with Mr. Render. I think he's just wonderful!"

Mme LeBreton did not respond to this, merely tossed off that pungent cupful and poured another, while I worried that I had committed a terrible *faux pas* since she and Mr. Render were really antagonists, deep down and from way back, whatever the reason was. Actually, until I said it and saw the effect his name had on her I had forgotten about the long estrangement: I had only meant to be supportive.

"You're so damned young," she said finally, with an awful sigh. Then she said, *"Well,"* nodding as if I had answered a question that had been bothering her. "Well! He'll be an experience for you. He'll be an experience for all of us. He's not like anyone you've ever known before. I expect he'll drive us all crazy before he's through," she said, with a stoic suck on the cigarette.

She cocked her head and squinted at me. "You really like Geoffrey? Mr. Render, I mean?"

I nodded. "Yes'm I do," I said. I had gotten myself into this; I'd have to be brave.

"In that case I'll show you something. But first I'll have to find it."

Feeling somewhat agitated I watched Mme LeBreton open the boxes we had brought in and take great quantities of things out of them. It reminded me of the day my family moved from the house we had rented near the office to the house on Sycamore Street, although I am sure my parents had organized our belongings and labeled the boxes, while Mme LeBreton had no idea where anything was. She took out enough Christmas decorations for five or six trees.

"God above. Here it is," Mme LeBreton said at last, standing knee-deep in yellowed tissue paper. She held out a wooden figure eight or ten inches high. I recognized it as a nutcracker, indeed as the nutcracker prince, having seen the ballet on the subject. "Isn't that nice!" I said, taking it from her. It had once been painted boldly in red and black, but now the paint was dull and flaky. It still wore a festive stare.

"Geoffrey sent that to me," Madame said, looking askance at the gift.

"How beautiful!" I exclaimed.

"*I* don't think it's beautiful. I think it's kind of wacky-looking. Look at those eyes! I have half a dozen better nutcrackers in here. But—this one has some history behind it. Geoffrey bought it at the big theater in Leningrad where they did the first *Nutcracker*—"

"The Maryinsky!" I cried.

"That's right," Madame said. "He went over there in the late thirties, when Russia wasn't all closed up like it is now."

I stared enraptured into the eyes of the Communist nutcracker.

"And *that's* the last I heard from him for almost seventeen years!" Mme LeBreton burst out bitterly, leaning over and pushing some of the tissue paper around her into a heap, thrashing around in it, really.

"Well, it's a fine souvenir," I said witlessly, wishing to show her I was not embarrassed by her sudden explosion and that I wanted her to go on speaking indiscreetly. But she was now absorbed in her own thoughts and busy with another cigarette and another cupful of bourbon from the thermos. Meanwhile I clutched the nutcracker, studying its every detail: why, this historic object was a direct link with the Maryinsky Theatre in St. Petersburg. This marvelous city was not, in my mind, "Leningrad" but "Petersburg," which city, for people who loved ballet, made New York as bare and empty of interest as the oil fields of Ardis: Petersburg, where it was always snowing a gentle powdery snow through which tiny golden lights shone, and where everyone danced through the great houses and the great streets to the luscious melodies of Tchaikovsky. I heard a waltz.

"Do you have a boyfriend?" Madame called out jarringly from the piano bench, where she had sat down again.

"Ah no, ma'am," I said, taken aback.

"Good! Keep it that way!" she enjoined briskly, taking a good long sip from the thermos cup. "Here. Put that old thing on the top of the piano. In honor of Geoffrey. Even though the old boy isn't here I feel like he's watching us. Clear a space in that crap up there. Make it stand up, would you? I don't think it'll stand up by itself."

Sure enough the historic nutcracker would not stand alone: the flaking boots seemed to have warped. I braced it up against a stack of Mrs. Fister's music books, then stepped back and regarded it with awe. The nutcracker was a powerful thing! Not only was it a souvenir from the Maryinsky but it was also, in some obscure way, a soldier in the private war between Mr. Render and Mme LeBreton. This war appeared to be settled now, or at least in a state of cease-fire, but it acquired new vividness for me as I looked at the nutcracker. I thought vaguely of the drama and misery of war on the Russian front as described in *War and Peace*—even then I had read *War and Peace,* the lively parts, anyway— and I saw this venerable decoration as a crippled veteran of the siege of Moscow. It stared blankly out over the studio.

Mme LeBreton stood up so that she was beside me, staring at the nutcracker too.

"You wouldn't think it of an old lady like me, would you? But once Geoffrey Render was in love with me, and I was in love with him!"

"Of course I believe it!" I said earnestly. "I knew that!"

"*Did* you?" she said, turning to face me, smiting me with her breath, staring at me with what appeared to be great interest.

"That is, I guessed," I said, retreating. I didn't want to talk about how I had arrived at this guess so I did not pause but went on to say, imprudently, "and I've been wanting to ask you something."

Now this something was, of course, "Why did you part from your old, old friend?" But Mme LeBreton was standing right in front of me, looking me full in the face with even more than her usual force. I have said how she sometimes did this to us during the barre and how it always made me squirm. Well, it made me feel even more uncomfortable now: I wasn't used to asking adults to come forth with the truth.

"Well? What is it?" she said sternly.

Daunted, suddenly shy, I said, "Why do you wear red or pink all the time to class? Even away from the studio," I tacked on wildly, "red, or pink?"

Mme LeBreton glared at me a second more, then laughed a big laugh that went on into a wheeze. She had a little coughing fit and had to drink some bourbon to get over it. She was still laughing when she said, "You're the first person who's ever asked me that. I thought nobody noticed. "Well," she said in a different mood, beginning to fool with the decorations again, "I just have a *penchant* for the rosy colors." She said *penchant* with a fine pair of nasal syllables. "Years ago I admitted to myself that my complexion was sallow and needed rosy tones. Rosy makeup, rosy clothes. It was Geoffrey who put me onto that, as a matter of fact," she said, busy in the boxes. "He's good for that kind of thing. He's full of tricks."

"Yes," I said, busy too, *"that* was what I meant about it being wonderful to work with him. I know we could learn so much."

But Mme LeBreton did not seem to pay attention to this, and I helped her decorate the big white tree without further reference to the dangerous topics of Mr. Render or the nutcracker. This took a while: with regard to Christmas tree decorations, Mme LeBreton had a *penchant* for the copious and the multicolored. First we clipped on five or six strings of lights of all colors, then we hung hundreds of balls and other types of decorations. Last came the tortuous tinsel and the icicles, which had been stored in clumps more cohesive than my lamb's wool.

"It's beautiful!" I cried when Mme LeBreton plugged the lights in.

"It'll do," she admitted, lighting another cigarette and appraising the tree.

"You were a real little trouper, Meredith," Mme LeBreton said to me a while later when she escorted me out of the front studio that shimmered with the tree. She put an arm around my shoulders and let me carry some of her weight. "Every year I tell myself, Milly ole girl, this year you won't drag out all that Christmas crap. But I end up doin' it. Then I wrestle with this stuff two, three days before I get anything half up. But this time it's all done. Thanks to *you!"*

"Can't I help you get the lights up outside, or pick up some of that paper and stack the boxes?" I asked, worried by the mess. My mother, I recalled, had had all the boxes out on the curb of Sycamore Street by nightfall on moving day.

"Hell no, baby, it's way past your lunchtime. Don't you ever skip meals, now. That's a very important rule, don't forget it. I'll just stick around a little while, have to look at some music anyway. Maybe straighten up a bit later.

"Meredith!" Mme LeBreton shouted suddenly when we reached the back door, although we were still walking in tandem like that and it made me jump. "Just thought of something. Do you have a cat?"

"No ma'am," I said, peering up at her. "I used to have a cat but he ran away."

"Maybe you'd like a kitten. Just thinkin' what I could do to thank you for being such a sweet girl this afternoon and I thought maybe you'd like a kitten."

"Oh yes!" I cried. "Oh yes!"

"You'd have the pick of the litter!" she said with a fine gaiety. "No matter *who* else begged for one."

"I have to ask my parents. Yes. Good-bye!" I called, making my way down the little steps beyond the screen door and around the corner. Passing the casement windows on my way across the rocks I saw the lights of the Christmas tree inside. While I had been in there the sky had clouded over and the day had turned dull and even colder. As I ran by, the tree looked like jewels hidden back in a cave. What a fine tree it was!

It was so much finer than ours at home, even finer, in my opinion, than the Masters' tree, or even the Merricks' giant, much-publicized tree. The Merricks' tree was just a show tree, I decided, as much a show tree as the Christmas tree that grew on stage in the production of *The Nutcracker* I had seen here in Middleton as a very young girl of nine. *The Nutcracker!* All the way home I thought of Mme LeBreton, rather drunk I feared, going back into the front studio with the tree all lit up and that nutcracker staring at her.

***

According to the custom at the LeBreton School of Ballet, the last class before Christmas was a party with the Mothers as our guests. Since it was one of the few times in the year they were allowed inside the studio, the Mothers always made a big fuss about the Christmas class, bringing refreshments which they had made themselves: cookies and cakes and candies shaped or decorated to carry out the ballet motif. But this Christmas class was even more elaborate than usual, and it revealed something I had not realized before, since my mother was not a regular Mother: that the Mothers' love for us, their solicitude, their enormous desire to develop our talent and promote the school's fortunes with a really good "gala," had been building up and building up during the past two months like water behind a dam. Now that the flood gates were opened, these good intentions practically inundated the studio. The place was awash with Mothers. The back studio was crammed with folding tables bearing not only the most imaginative sweets but champagne, in addition to the regular lime sherbet punch—*champagne!* Mme LeBreton's decorations provided a glittering backdrop for the occasion: no patch of wall was without its wreath or swag, no available surface without its angel or wise man. She had even wound tinsel around and around the barres. To add to the festive atmosphere, the day was cold, damp, and so overcast that it was quite dark even at four-thirty, when the Christmas class began. It had not snowed that December and so naturally we hoped for snow.

"You've got to see the kittens!" I cried, hanging onto the arm of my mother, who had left the offices of Matlock, Wilson, Jackson, and

Jackson early to come to the Christmas class. She looked very nice, if a trifle too businesslike, in her best tweed suit. I dragged her through the dressing room to the back studio, where Mothers and dancers were jostling around the refreshment tables and Mme LeBreton stood in a long carnelian tutu of holiday frothiness, already drinking champagne and shouting to the dancers, "Don't eat that! You'll get sick at your stomach in class!"

Colette still had the kittens, which were now about ten days old, on the pea coat back there in the closet. They had had to endure a great deal of attention and handling, even in this remote spot. Our class had rushed back there before and after every class to adore them and comment upon their development. (This worked a great hardship on Claude, whose dressing room this was, forcing him to dress in dancing gear at home and wear an overcoat to the studio.) In fact, the girls in my class paid so much attention to the kittens—so much more than they had ever paid to one of Colette's litters before—that I worried that there would be a terrible competition for the honor of taking them home, that I might not get one after all, *if* my parents said I could, and this was still in issue.

But there was nothing to worry about after all: apparently no one really wanted a kitten; everybody was simply enjoying herself by making a fuss over them, like people do when they come upon a baby in a stroller on the street and go on and on about how darling it is. This was probably just an outlet for the strong current of excitement in the school about the gala première. Besides, most of these girls already had pets, pets of a much higher order than these kittens. I always thought of Colette as the "studio cat," but in fact she was just an alley cat if you stripped her of her sentimental associations: a plain old calico cat. If my classmates had cats, they undoubtedly had genuine pug-nosed Persians or bony-looking narrowfaced Siamese, not alley cats. I knew they had dogs. Sometimes you could see a dog, either a little yipping dog that looked like it was made out of yarn or a huge stern dog that was all taut muscle, jumping from window to window of a Cadillac or a station wagon with a Mother as she kept her vigil in the parking lot during class. It was obvious that these dogs belonged to select and very expensive breeds. On rare occasions a Mother would actually get out of her car to accompany one of these priceless dogs into the pine trees at the edge of the gravel.

"Aren't they adorable, Mother?" I said, flinging open the closet door to expose Colette and the four kittens to the light and the noise. The kittens had opened their eyes and were now able to rove over the inert body of Colette, who was obviously worn out by this episode.

"Why, look how different they are!" Mother said, bending down. "All four are different. There's a black one, a white one, a gray striped one and a little yellow calico. How interesting! Mendel would like these kittens!"

"Ah yes," I said. I was taking biology that year and could appreciate Mother's little joke. "Brother Mendel." I was happy to see Mother taking an interest in the kittens because she and my father had been none too keen on a cat. We had had a cat a few years before—Andrew Jackson, best remembered for spraying the furniture and marauding the neighborhood. I had never admitted it, but even I was glad when Andrew Jackson ran away.

"I have this cute idea about naming them," I told Mother, with an eye to insinuating them more deeply into her affections. "It occurred to me that since they were born in a ballet studio and there are four of them, they ought to be named for the first famous ballerinas—you know, Marie Taglioni, Carlotta Grisi, Fanny Ellsler and Lucille, ah—Lucille Grahn, that's it. They did a famous *pas de quatre* together in London sometime around the middle of the nineteenth century, and I think of them when I see the four little studio kittens." I did not know anything about pronouncing Italian in those days and so I said "Taglioni" with a hard "g," but I believe I brought the other names, which I had read in library books late at night up in my room, out into the daylight in proper form. I had been thinking about this for several days, but I had not said anything to my classmates about it: they were not, of course, scholars of the dance.

"Why, how *clever,* Meredith Louise. That's the sweetest thing!" Mother said, getting up, frowning and shaking her head. Somebody looking over at Mother who didn't know her would probably think she was fussing at me, but Mother was actually showing her most emphatic approval.

"I like the white one best," I went on. "See how her little nose and paws are turning brown. I think she's turning into a Siamese."

"Can they do that?" Mother cried. "The others don't look Siamese!"

"Certainly," I asserted. "Just a latent strain. Check Mendel!"

"Just look at that coat," Mother said as we took our leave of the cats. "Somebody's nice winter coat."

"Oh that's Stephanie Sillerman's," I said carelessly. "She doesn't care—she has *ten* winter coats." I was proud that day of the bounty we enjoyed as dancers at the LeBreton School of Ballet.

***

In the front studio folding chairs had been set out near the piano to supplement the meager seating provided by the Mothers' Bench. The Mothers noisily settled themselves in these chairs, and I was proud to see that my mother, smart in her tweed suit, actually bore up rather well in comparison with Mrs. Merrick, who, looking slim and golden in her furs, was of course the most elegant Mother.

Old Mrs. Fister was already playing a jouncy version of "Rudolph the Red-Nosed Reindeer," and for the next hour she would play a mangled medley of Christmas carols. We did *pliés* to "Silent Night," *frappés* to "I Saw Three Ships," and so on. I knew for sure from the way she played these carols that Mrs. Fister (Aunt Ellie!) had never been told that she would not be allowed to play for Mr. Render and the gala ballet. Sporting a red dress and a sprig of mistletoe in her old gray bob, Mrs. Fister appeared to be in the highest holiday spirits of anybody as she knocked out the Christmas carols.

The Mothers raised their usual hullabaloo as we went through the age-old motions of the class, and it was easy to see why Mme LeBreton barred them from the studio except on such rare occasions as this. Although the individual Mothers were a civilized, even refined lot they had a group personality that was just plain barbaric. They couldn't keep from talking, laughing, clapping, even shouting encouragements (whatever came into their heads); in fact, as a group they acted like a crowd of spectators at a boxing match. This had happened at the audition and Mr. Render hadn't seemed to mind, but Mme LeBreton minded. She glared and whacked her stick repeatedly, but even at her most magisterial she could not quell the Mothers.

Anyway, they loved the class. Our *pointe* work evoked the most noise, of course: nothing is quite so pretty as a dozen healthy young girls delicately clopping across a floor on *pointe*. They liked Claude too, who leapt and turned with even more than his usual ferocity. I wondered whether his mother had come, and what on earth kind of person she could be, but I forgot to ask anybody and even forgot to scan the faces of the Mothers for someone unusual enough to have had Claude.

The class ended cleverly. With a flourish Mme LeBreton turned the fluorescent lights off, leaving only the lights of the tree, and in this festive gloom we danced the tarantella which had been the finale of the previous year's recital. We had not rehearsed this, but we did it very well nonetheless. As I have said, Madame's pedagogical methods were so thorough that her students absorbed her dances for all time. (I could do that tarantella now!) I expect the Mothers thought this was a brand-new dance that had been concocted just for them: first, the light was so dim, and then the music was different. Originally the tarantella had been done to the music of Chopin, while now Mrs. Fister romped out a speeded-up version of "White Christmas." Actually the music probably seemed original and new too: I think that only the most musically astute of the Mothers could have recognized "White Christmas" the way Mrs. Fister played it. I doubt if even Bing Crosby could have recognized it.

***

During the refreshments afterward all the talk was of the gala. I observed that Mme LeBreton listened rather than talked and that she drank a good deal of the champagne, while Mrs. Fister was what is called the life of the party. She hugged girls, reminisced about past Christmases, and gave expression to everyone's hopes about the future.

"Iddn she dawlin," Mrs. Fister said to Christabel's mother in reference to Christabel, whom she was pressing ferociously against her broad old bosom. "Purtiest lil ballerina! Gone be so purty on that new stage!"

Christabel freed herself and Mrs. Fister passed on to others. It amazed me that my mother, who did not usually go to parties and who did not approve of drinking intoxicants, entered into the spirit of this party, even going so far as to accept a glass of champagne, which she wantonly sipped. She chatted briefly with Mme LeBreton telling her how much she (Mme LeBreton) had done for me—I had no idea what this might mean—and she also talked with Mrs. James, Hilary's mother, the president of the Mothers' Guild. Mrs. James was a formidable woman, shaped like a cube of granite, and to my mind she was the Mothers incarnate. More precisely, she was their logical extreme. I could easily imagine her at the head of a battalion of Mothers marching upon some enemy of the advancement and glorification of their children. I cringed around Mrs. James, feeling guilty because my mother was not in the Mothers' Guild, which met in the morning hours when she was at the office or down at the courthouse. Now I blushed as Mrs. James accosted my mother, a stranger to the selfless rites of the Guild, and demanded to know her name.

"Caroline Jackson," my mother said, smiling. "We met at the recital last year."

"But of course," Mrs. James boomed.

I teetered unsteadily nearby as Mother said, quite openly, that she "practiced law." Then she tempered this by offering to help with the gala in any way she could. "I can't sew or bake very well," Mother said, without apparent shame, "but let me know if anything comes up that's more in my line."

Mrs. James seemed pleased with this limited offer. Meanwhile I did manage to enjoy myself. I had some lime sherbet punch and some cookies shaped like tutus in the classical length; I also circulated some on my own. All the talk was of the gala. Mme LeBreton could be heard to say "It's going to cost, ladies, it's going to cost a lot more than you think!" and Mrs. Fister kept saying how "dawlin" it would all be. I reveled in the collective sense of pleasure and anticipation. Now *this* is what I had hoped the cocktail party would be like (that first explosion of Render), and the foregoing class had been what I had hoped the class he had "watched" would be like. Those occasions had been mixed, difficult, provocative, unsettling, while this day, in contrast, was a simple, thoroughgoing celebration of ourselves and our future. Even my mother was drawn into it! All together we enjoyed our vision of the future, which was irradiated by the invisible, silent, ineffable presence of the great Geoffrey Render. We were his chosen ones.

***

Right before my mother and I left the Christmas party at the studio, I got the idea of showing her the nutcracker as the *pièce de résistance* of the afternoon. Although she was by now quite ready to go home, I dragged her into the front studio and over to the piano where the staring, peeling nutcracker lay against the scores.

"See, Mother! She said he went over to Russia to work on something—he's so well known, everywhere—and he sent it to her from the Maryinsky, where they did the first *Nutcracker*. See how old it is!"

I took the wondrous thing up and offered it to Mother, but she was drawing her car keys out of her clutch bag and could not take it. "Yes, yes! How interesting!" she said.

"Hey, Meredith! Hand me my nutcracker a minute," Cecilia called out to me. It was rather dark in the front studio with the lights still off, and I had not seen Cecilia sitting on the floor near the foot of the tree. Hilary and Adelaide were sitting down there with her, and I now saw that they were drinking champagne. "Have I shown y'all my nutcracker?

"This is a real Russian nutcracker," Cecilia went on when she got it in her hands. "Y'all won't believe it but little old Geoffrey Render sent me this when I was just a baby. Mama still has the card. It says something about me being a little Sugar Plum Fairy, or something like that."

"How quaint," said Hilary in her hoarse and disrespectful voice.

"Well see," Adelaide inserted. "That proves it! This is your destiny, just like I've been saying."

"I wondered why the madam put that old thing out," Hilary said.

"I think she brought out everything she owns this Christmas," Cecilia mused, fingering the nutcracker and flaking some loose patches of paint off with what I knew to be a rosy and almondshaped thumbnail. "I've never seen her like this. She's actually been cleaning house. She's taken everything out of the closets and stacked it everywhere. I don't know what's gotten into her."

"Let's go, dear," Mother said briskly.

"Wait, wait! I want to hear this!" I pleaded baldly, cocking my head discreetly toward my classmates on the floor.

"Well, one minute," Mother said, "just while I tell the ladies bye and thank you."

"—never cracked nuts anyway," Cecilia was saying when I could hear again. "It just kinda gnawed 'em."

"Oh Cecilia, you are *so dumb,*" Hilary exclaimed, beginning to laugh very hard, leaning back on her elbows and rapidly beating the floor with her toe shoes. Unfortunately this display of mirth upset her glass of champagne.

"Hilary! How *rude!*" Adelaide said sharply, leaping to her feet, running out of the room.

Hilary laughed even harder. "Nobody but you would try to crack nuts with this thing. God, look at this old fossil. Really look at it, Cecilia," she intoned, "for it is your destiny."

Hilary grabbed the nutcracker and started tossing it from hand to hand, like a juggler. Adelaide ran back in the room with several streamers of toilet tissue behind her and fell to cleaning the floor. After a few furious dabs, Adelaide snatched the nutcracker away from the laughing Hilary and thrust it up on the piano before going back to her drubbing of what was now seen to be a very sticky and decadent beverage. They seemed to have forgotten the nutcracker, which I picked up and leaned tenderly against the stack of scores again.

"I *had* to hear something, Mother," I explained excitedly as we trudged across the parking lot. It was dark, and so cold and damp I could hardly breathe. "See, Mme LeBreton was telling me about the nutcracker the other day like it was hers, but just then Cecilia was saying it was *hers.* Mr. Render sent it to *one* of them, but now I don't know which!"

"Do calm down, dear," Mother said. "That's *their* business, isn't it?"

The car would not start on account of the cold, and we sat there a few minutes while the engine churned and failed, churned and failed. At last it leapt into action. We sat there chugging up and down a minute or two while it warmed up.

"It's a nice group of people," Mother said during this. "Mrs. LeBreton is a *nice* woman. She seems very fond of you."

"I hope you didn't call her 'Mrs.,' Mother," I said despondently. *"Nobody* calls her 'Mrs.'"

"And I *enjoyed* talking to the other mothers!" she went on as if surprised at herself. "I met a Mrs. Bateson who was awfully nice."

"You *did?"* I bawled.

As we drove away, I was excited by the party, by the gala and by the nutcracker, but all these things went clean out of my head when I saw what I saw now. It was beginning to snow!

"Look, snow!" I cried. "Can you see it, Mother?"

Mother looked earnestly for the snow as she drove down Sycamore Street. It was snow all right: big fat snowflakes dancing through the beams of the headlights and up around the streetlights. All the way home we discussed the all-absorbing question of whether the snow would "stick."

***

Even though the winters are very cold in Middleton, which is in the highlands of Louisiana, it rarely snows. This snow was only the second of my life—the second that "stuck," that is. I woke up the next morning to a brilliant glare. I saw, first thing that the sweet gum tree held a load of snow on its black branches, and from the window I saw our lawn sloping down to the street like a ski run. The snow was so deep that only a few points of the dead leaves that still covered the lawn were sticking out. The street looked like a toboggan trail, and I did not think any cars had passed over it. A real snow immobilized Middleton and, except for the faint shrieks of children from somewhere down the street (probably the brown and numerous children of our neighbor who was an engineering professor from India), I could not hear a thing. There was a vast frozen silence and an air of tremendous expectancy. Even the trucks on the horizon were still.

Snow continued to fall at intervals over the next few days and amounted in the end to fourteen inches. My father and I built a snowlady and put one of Mother's hats on her; we made toboggans out of cardboard boxes and careened down the lawn to Sycamore Street on them; and, before the snow got too dirty, Mother had me collect enough of it to make that rare delicacy "snow ice cream," a mysterious concoction combining the snow with eggs, sugar, and vanilla, I believe, which she froze in an ice tray.

During this time I had a holiday from ballet class as well as from school, and I found that this year, for the first time, I missed ballet more than school. (I had always missed school during the holidays: that's the way it is when you have a lot of time to yourself, without any brothers and sisters, without much company or any friends that live nearby and are in and out of the house all the time.) I found myself wishing that the circumstances could have been different: that the Merrick Theater was already finished and we were putting on something now instead of way off in the spring, which seemed so distant, a kind of never-never land. I wished we were putting on something like *The Nutcracker*. Then instead of idling around in the snow and reading a new book every day I could have somewhere exciting to go. I pictured myself getting ready for rehearsals, pulling on long leather boots, buttoning my floor-length coat, pulling a fur hat down over my ears, stuffing my hands in a plump fur muff. I did not actually have any clothing, but it made a nice picture of these articles.

I thought a lot about this mythical *Nutcracker* production. Everybody was wondering what Mr. Reader's ballet for us would be like, and I hoped it would be like *The Nutcracker*. We had just about everything a good *Nutcracker* would take, I thought. It was a fact that Geoffrey Render could have staged as fine a *Nutcracker* as anybody around: he was a great man of the dance and he had been to the source, in snowbound Petersburg. He himself would of course dance Herr Drosselmeyer, just the role for a character dancer of his distinction. I dreamed sometimes that they would ask me to be Clara. Perhaps Madame would even insist that I be Clara as a small repayment for my help in putting up the Christmas decorations. But other times I had to admit that Christabel was a better choice, and I knew that Mr. Render would make an impartial decision on artistic criteria. Christabel had that gamin charm, and I could just see the white nightdress of Clara swirling around her spindly, gazelle-like limbs.

I do not need to say that the beautiful Cecilia was the Sugar Plum Fairy. Geoffrey Render had prophesied it or perhaps even willed it on that card. The other roles were harder to cast, except of course the remaining male roles, all of which would have to be Claude's. He would have to be the Nutcracker Prince. (It was easy to associate Claude with a mechanism meant to crack nuts with its teeth while glaring in a wooden and martial way.) He would also have to be the Snow King and the Sugar Plum Fairy's Cavalier. This would entail some quick changes, but anyone who had ever seen Claude strip out of his overcoat for class would know he could do a quick change. There was also Clara's brother, Fritz, but that would be entirely too much Claude. The audience would start thinking it was hallucinating with so much Claude; they would go home and have nightmares! Well, then, Fritz could be a trouser role. I didn't want it: I was willing to take most any part but I didn't want to be a boy. Since Fritz's main feature was bossiness colored by selfishness, I gave the role to Adelaide, with Hilary as an understudy.

I gave myself various parts in these daydreams, but whatever I danced, I played a major role in decorating that thrilling Act One Christmas tree. In my fur-lined boots I climbed a very tall ladder to hang diamonds and pearls on this Christmas tree before descending to change into satin *pointe* shoes for my dazzling variations in Act Two.

But central to this daydream was the nutcracker, and when the daydream wore thin and wasn't absorbing anymore, I still thought about that nutcracker on the piano up in the studio, which lay dark and locked for the holidays. (I was pretty sure neither Madame nor Cecilia had bothered to take it home.) As a matter of fact, I even had a dream about that nutcracker one night while the snow was still on the ground. Clearly it was derived from the story of *The Nutcracker*. It had to do with Clara and Fritz fighting over the gift of the soldier with the commanding eyes; yet in my dream Clara looked a lot like Cecilia in the swirling nightdress and Fritz, the bad-tempered brother, was a dead ringer for Mme LeBreton. Clara-Cecilia danced around with the nutcracker and Madame-Fritz snatched it away from her; Clara-Cecilia grabbed it back and Madame-Fritz slapped her face. In a fit Clara-Cecilia dashed the nutcracker to the floor, where it burst into a million pieces! I woke up and sat straight up in bed at this juncture, breathing hard and feeling perfectly awful.

It took a minute to realize why. It was because that nutcracker was Mr. Render himself: small, stout, and with eyes so much bolder than eyes usually are. Fortunately the dream wasn't really over: it was one of those dreams that keep on going once you sink back on the pillows and close your eyes. The nutcracker lay shattered on the floor but it did not stay shattered. It restored itself, by some process that is perfectly logical in the realm of dreams, because it was (I really can't explain how) essentially whole and of a piece. No matter how much "Clara" and "Fritz" fought over it neither one owned it. Nobody owned it; it owned itself, somehow. It had a blank emblematic quality that made it seem to belong to all times and all places. It did the owning, if any owning was done.

The next day, I thought of something which someone who was a little older than I was at that time, or someone less innocent, would probably have thought of long before. After I thought of it I could not believe that it had *not* occurred to me before. It was this: that Geoffrey Render was Cecilia's father. This idea came to me when I was thinking for the umpteenth time about how Mr. Render had sent that nutcracker to the baby Cecilia from Russia with that cryptic message. Possibly this was an innocent everyday baby gift, but on the other hand it might be a gift that was fraught with a terrible significance. That is how I chose to see the gift (as "fraught"), and I spent a lot of time up in my window seat figuring out the ramifications of this view. It certainly cleared a lot of things up. It accounted for why Milly Frobish quit Ballet Benet. (She would have been that most scandalous of things, *pregnant.*) It accounted for why she would marry a toad and settle under a rock, as it were, also for why she had a sublime daughter who did not look anything like a toad. It would certainly account for all those years of rancor.

Well, now, I thought, sitting up in the window seat and looking out at the snow, waiting for school and the studio to open up again, this is going to be interesting.

BOOK THREE

COPPÉLIA

11

I rode my bicycle up to the studio for the first class of the new year in a cutting wind. The snow was almost gone now, except for a few fingers at the edges of the sloping lawns, but it was even colder than it had been during that exciting time of the snow. Actually this was not a regular meeting of the advanced class but a general muster of all the dancers who had been accepted into the production. We were supposed to find out something today about the ballet Mr. Render had made for us. Sycamore Street was unusually congested. It is a narrow and winding street, as I have said, and cars were creeping along it, looking for parking places; then people were walking up the street toward the studio from these cars. Of course they were wrapped in coats and mufflers and scarves like I was, but I thought there were Mothers among these figures as well as dancers, and I did not recognize anyone. No one spoke: they just leaned silently into the wind, climbing purposefully toward the studio.

Then I rounded the last curve and saw the parking lot. I had never seen it so packed with cars! The cars did not simply line the edges of the lot in polite diagonals as usual but were wedged together in a tight pattern, as cars are in a field next to a fair or a revival. I noticed a lot of unfamiliar cars: in addition to the regular station wagons with false wood on the sides and the Cadillacs I saw Buicks and Fords and Plymouths, new and old. Dancers and Mothers converging from all directions picked their way over the gravel and through the cars while the high wind whipped and churned the branches of the pine trees against the wintry sky.

All the movement was toward the studio. Through the casement windows, which looked yellow, as if it were warm and sunny inside, I could see a bustling mob already assembled. I was wondering whether the studio could hold all of the people anxious to be in it or whether it might burst when I saw Hilary James and her mother rounding the back corner of the studio, coming *out* of it, as if perhaps it had reached capacity and someone had suggested they leave. I thought for an instant this had in fact happened: as I have said, Mrs. James was a massive woman, not tall but very chunky and her departure would create room for two or three people my size. Then, also, Mrs. James looked very unhappy, as if she had just been insulted, and Hilary was actually crying. Then I realized that it was Hilary who had suffered the blow. Mrs. James was hovering over her protectively, with an arm around her as if to support her as she walked. Oh my God, I thought, someone is dead: Geoffrey Render has had a heart attack and is dying, or perhaps he was already dead. Even worse, my thoughts ran on, maybe he had not been able to match any of his marvelous ideas to our puny abilities, maybe we had been pronounced hopeless; maybe he had canceled.

"What is it?" I cried out into the wind.

Hilary tried to say something to me but, unlikely as it was for someone so world-weary and blasé, she seemed to be stifled by her emotion and could not speak. Mrs. James spoke for her.

"It's an *affront,*" she said sharply to me, without preamble.

"It's a perfect outrage!"

"Has he canceled?" I asked in terror. "Is he never coming back?"

"I wish to heaven he *wouldn't* come back. It is my position that *we* should cancel!"

"What *is* it? What *is* it?" I implored.

Mrs. James straightened herself and stared frostily up into the flagellating pine branches.

"Mr. Geoffrey Render has sent us his plan for the production and it is something called *Mother Goose. That* is what's wrong," she said indignantly. *"That* is what's wrong."

"Oh!" I said. That did sound remote from the Land of the Snow and the Land of the Sweets.

"But Hilary, angel, you have some good parts," Mrs. James said soothingly. "You *are* Curly Locks as well as those horse parts. Just think how Adelaide must feel, and Melissa! And that Dorcas. You have some good things too, I believe, my dear," she said to me.

"What? *What?*"

"You're a dog, mainly," Hilary managed to say.

"A dog?" I said.

"That's right," Mrs. James snapped. "I believe you're the dog in Old Mother Hubbard—you know 'went to the cupboard / To get her poor dog—'"

"That's you, the poor dog!" Hilary said.

"I remember," I said morosely.

"And you're another dog too," Mrs. James mused. "Was it in 'Hey Diddle Diddle'?"

"The one who laughed, to see such sport?"

"Yes, that's it. Well, there you are," Mrs. James said.

"And Adelaide and Dorcas?"

"They're terrible little animals too, my dear," said Mrs. James. "There are really precious few humans in this production."

"Adelaide's a cow and Dorcas is a spider," Hilary specified.

"The thing that bothers a lot of girls—even those who don't *mind* being blackbirds and mice and beggars and such," Mrs. James said, "is the number of parts Mrs. Fister has!"

"Mrs. Fister?" I shouted. *"What?"*

Both Mrs. James and Hilary looked triumphant, and Mrs. James said, "She plays the Old Woman in a number of selections. You couldn't possibly realize how many Old Women there are in *Mother Goose*—the Old Woman in a Shoe, the Old Woman in a Basket—"

"And your old woman, Meredith, the one who gets you the bone," added Hilary.

"Do you think it might really be canceled?" I asked, looking over into the casement windows at all the people in the studio, expecting now to see them brawling over whether to withdraw Geoffrey Render's commission, or even whether to go further than that and issue some sort of reprimand.

"Of course not," Mrs. James said stiffly. "Not with *Lyda* playing the queen roles. I think the world of Lyda Merrick, please don't misunderstand me, but I cannot imagine her being objective enough to cancel a commission for a ballet in which she is the Queen of Hearts and the famous Geoffrey Render is the King."

"Oh my! Well," I said, remembering someone so far not mentioned, "what does Madame think about all this?"

Mrs. James gave a sort of "harrumph" sound. The sardonic and elegant Hilary said, "Tell her, Mommy. Tell her the *best* part."

"*She,*" Mrs. James said, "is not likely to offer any objection either. She has the title role. *She* is Mother Goose!"

***

The Christmas decorations were all gone from the studio, and full of people as it was, it looked very bare without them. It no longer looked better than a set for *The Nutcracker;* now it looked like a spare weather-beaten mountain cabin. The mood inside the studio that day when we were told about *Mother Goose* might be compared with the mood inside such a mountain cabin where a large party of climbers has stopped to rest and take stock just after one of their number has fallen off the mountain into a deep and craggy ravine. The wind is howling outside and the cabin seems terminally bleak; the party clings together for warmth and reassurance. Some of the members of the party are deeply shaken; they cry and hover together. Others are angry at the fates who could allow such a monstrous thing to happen, while still others seem untouched by the tragedy and talk and laugh as if nothing had happened.

There was just this kind of variation in mood inside the studio. Some girls were crying, some girls were angry, and most of the Mothers smoked and talked together in such a way as to suggest that they were hurt and angry too, although no one seemed as dramatically hurt and angry as Hilary and Mrs. James, and no one seemed to have any intention of leaving. Then there were other girls and Mothers who were talking and laughing as if this were any old gathering at the studio. I also noticed some dancers from other schools who were in the studio for the first time looking around themselves curiously, even appraisingly, and possibly with some contempt, since the studio looked, as I say, so much like a mountain cabin and not at all fancy or posh, as they probably expected it to be.

Mme LeBreton was in the front studio, standing by the piano with Mrs. Merrick. They were not talking, just looking gloomily at the crush of people in there.

"Hi, Madame!" I went up and said. "Did you have a nice Christmas? Say, my parents said I could have a kitten!"

This fell rather flat.

"Oh good, baby, fine," Mme LeBreton said in a moment. "The kittens'll be weaned in a few weeks. By the way, they're back there in the bookcase behind the piano. Colette moved 'em over the holidays. I expect she'll want to move 'em again after *today.*"

I went and claimed the little Siamese: this is the one I wanted, I said to myself agitatedly, holding on to her; her name would be Marie Taggly-onie.

I soon realized that the crowd was roiling around a particular point in the front studio: a cast list which was tacked to the front door, the one down at the other end of the studio that we never used. Notices and messages were usually on the bulletin board in the little hall joining the dressing room and the front and back studios, but this crowd would have knocked down the walls of that tiny hall and someone had had the foresight to pin the cast list to a spot that could accommodate a large and fractious crowd of readers. (Martin Luther had the same kind of foresight in the placement of his ninety-five theses on the door of the castle church.) Occasionally you'd hear a short scream or a curse as a girl or her mother would discover her part ("A mouse!" they'd scream, or "A sheep!"); then they would plunge out of the crowd, stamping angrily or dragging disconsolate feet.

Mme LeBreton and Mrs. Merrick stood close together and murmured just as if they were at a funeral or—to revive that climbing expedition analog—as if they were the leaders of the expedition and must decide whether to press on with a now dangerously nervous and even rebellious crew to the unknown heights or turn back to the lowlands to certain safety. Just by chance I had met up with the most rebellious members of the party, Hilary and her mother. Now I imagined them out loose in the lowlands of Middleton denouncing the expedition to anyone who would listen. I was really relieved to hear that Mme LeBreton and Mrs. Merrick had much more positive outlooks: they were not talking about turning back—the heinous, the fatal idea of "cancellation"—but only about how to deal with this surging, unpleasant crowd, how to turn it around so that it would be willing to go onward and upward.

Mrs. Merrick was speaking to Mme LeBreton in her low, melodious voice. "Naturally Christabel is pleased with her solos, even if they *are* unpleasant little characters, but this is hard on Melissa and Stephanie and Lola. They're such *cute* girls to be dancing nothing but men."

"Melissa *is* Jill," Mme LeBreton said, as if grasping at straws. "Hilary's the one. I was a little surprised at that explosion."

"It's Julianna," Mrs. Merrick said, referring, I guessed, to the granite-like Mother. "But it'll blow over. Julianna enjoys throwing her weight around. She'll change her mind by tomorrow. They won't want to miss anything. But you know," Mrs. Merrick said with sudden warmth, "he did Cecilia justice, didn't he? She'll be marvelous as the little wren."

"Well. She has the choice roles all right," Mme LeBreton said, looking haggard.

"And of course that's just as it should be. Don't let anyone say otherwise, especially Julianna. Now I think the *world* of Julianna. She's done miracles with the Guild, but she can't see straight when it comes to Hilary. She's a regular stage mother, Milly."

"So much for our white ballet! I'm a spider, I guess you heard," Dorcas said bitterly at my elbow.

For the first time I felt like smiling, but my lips and cheeks were still very raw and cold from the bicycle ride and so I did not actually produce a smile.

"You're *dogs,* Meredith," Dorcas said with merry spite. "How do you like that?"

Mrs. Fister came past us, grabbing on to our arms as if they were railings or banisters the way old people do, and collapsing onto her seat at the piano.

"She's in it," Dorcas hissed. "Have you ever heard of anything so *gross?*"

Although she was proscribed from playing for the gala première by the choreographer (Madame and Mrs. Merrick and I knew this if no one else did), Mrs. Fister now lit into the piano. She played "Here We Go Round the Mulberry Bush," and this, plus the insistent rapping of Madame's stick, loosened up the angry knot around the cast list and somehow the crowd arranged itself in the front studio in some kind of order. Dancers sat on the floor (I sat down, still holding on to my kitten), Mothers stood around the barres, and everyone stared balefully at Mme LeBreton and Mrs. Merrick, who took their place in front of the crowd over by the casement windows.

Mme LeBreton spoke first.

"First, let me welcome you new people who've come to take part in this special production," she said. "We've set up a schedule of rehearsal classes to meet twice a week under the direction of Miss Adelaide Henderson. Stand up, Adelaide. I'll pass around a sheet on these in just a minute.

"Now!" Madame barked after these niceties, whacking her stick hard against the floor. "I know you're disappointed! This ballet is unusual, by our standards, it's not what you're used to, but there's a lot more to ballet than pretty costumes. You'll find Mr. Render's work fascinating when you see it. He's a clever man!"

"Why, he's a genius!" Mrs. Merrick cried, stepping forward. "I do not doubt a minute that *Mother Goose* will be a work of genius."

Some people groaned.

"Why, *I* imagine from what we got in the mail that *Mother Goose* is funny—I mean witty—and just right for our abilities. Mme LeBreton here, who is one of Geoffrey Render's oldest and dearest friends, tells me he has a perfect genius for bringing out the personality of a dancer."

Here I glanced over at Dorcas the spider, who was squalling silently.

"Now listen, girls," Mrs. Merrick said, stepping closer to the crowd and obscuring Mme LeBreton, from my angle of vision, "and of course Claude," she added, looking toward Claude, who had as usual come in late and now skulked over behind the piano, probably scaring the cats.

"I'm going to read out the solos." Mrs. Merrick stood before us, slender and small but brave and true, holding the controversial cast list gingerly, as if it were a dangerous document, say a ransom note. All the time she was reading it I was conscious of an extraordinarily large diamond on her left hand, which reflected light from the fluorescent ceiling lights and flickered it all over the room. The fluorescent lights also flickered, ever so gently, on her smooth golden hair.

"We're still working on a couple of solos, doing some recruiting, but this is essentially it," she confided. "Mme LeBreton will be Mother Goose in addition to her duties as Ballet Mistress. Mr. Render is of course Artistic Director and takes the roles of the King and Humpty Dumpty."

A few people snickered at this.

"I will serve as Executive Director of the production," she said humbly. "I'll also do my best with the role of the Queen. Our own Mrs. Fister will play the Old Woman, although of course she is much too young for the part."

We laughed again to be polite, and Mrs. Fister grinned and clasped her knobby old hands above her head and bowed. Mrs. Merrick did not go on to say either that Mrs. Fister would be the official accompanist or that she would not.

"And Colette and the four kittens!" Here Mrs. Merrick had to pause to bring a pretty laugh under control. "They have parts too! When I told Mr. Render about the kittens he said he'd have to work them in. Here they are, as the kits and cats in the St. Ives number! Isn't that just adorable? You see how clever!"

People near me reached out to touch Marie, but I held her close and concentrated on the reading of the cast list. I heard *my* name! I was dogs all right, in "Old Mother Hubbard" and "Hey Diddle Diddle"; I was also "Jack" of "Jack Be Nimble." This was a blow. A boy! I wanted to be a boy even less than I wanted to be a dog, but I'd been half-expecting it after the trouble I had had casting that mythical *Nutcracker* over Christmas; well, even before that, after the audition, where Mr. Render had put Claude and Lola and me in a group for combinations and made us jump like Tartars. My strongest point was jumping, and I knew enough about Mr. Render to expect him to spot that right off and exploit it: it was pretty inevitable that I be a boy, if not a dog.

Others were not so philosophical. The *least* philosophical was of course the absent Hilary, who was named the Horse in "Banbury Cross" and other equine nursery rhymes, but Christabel sniffed dangerously when she was named the Horrid Little Girl (the one with the curl in the middle of her forehead); and Adelaide hugged herself and blinked rapidly as she was named the farmer's wife in "Three Blind Mice," "Mary Mary Quite Contrary," and, worst of all, the cow in "Hey Diddle Diddle." Dorcas was already squalling before she was designated the Crooked Man, and the Spoon in "Hey Diddle Diddle." Stephanie wept openly when she was named a member of the Trio, with Melissa and Lola, the Trio being a team of three "men" that jumped throughout the ballet as "The Three Wise Men of Gotham," "The Three Blind Mice" and the "fiddlers three" in "Old King Cole." I was gratified by this, considering my Jack and my dogs to be more important roles than the parts for the Trio; I began to feel happier about *Mother Goose,* and to smile in support of Mrs. Merrick as she continued to read.

It began to be apparent that there were others who were not insulted or at least who, like me, decided not to feel insulted. Alma Doyle was the man in "Going to St. Ives" and the maid in "Sing a Song of Sixpence"; Rachel Mintz was the little boy in "Baa Baa Black Sheep" and the dish in "Hey Diddle Diddle", all nondescript parts. Yet both these girls sat looking respectfully at Mrs. Merrick as she read the list and did not appear to be upset at all. And there were two people who had cause to feel triumphant because although no fuss was made on this point it was clear that Mr. Render had singled out Cecilia LeBreton and Claude Bateson as the stars of *Mother Goose.* And I had been so foolish as to doubt that he had noticed Cecilia! Cecilia was Little Bo-Peep, Jenny Wren, and the wife of Peter Peter Pumpkin Eater; Claude was her cavalier as Little Boy Blue, Robin Redbreast, and Peter. He was also Georgy Porgy, and Jack to Melissa's Jill. Cecilia sat over in the corner of the studio playing with Christabel's hair and looking distracted, as if unaware of the honor done to her by Mr. Render; Claude, on the other hand, paced up and down behind the piano, eyes aglint, looking as if he were thinking about jumping Cecilia first, then New York City.

Then Mrs. Merrick read a second document which listed the numbers in the ballet and everyone who danced in them. There were thirty, each based on a nursery rhyme, and they called for not only the solos I have named but also other smaller solos and numerous parts for the *corps de ballet* in the form of herds of sheep and horses, crowds of townspeople, packs of children, a flock of blackbirds, a garden of flowers and a gathering of beggars. There was also a group of demi-soloists called "a crowd": they would be the wives coming from St. Ives carrying Colette and the kittens; later they would be the girls terrorized by Georgy Porgy. The list took a long time to read and sounded unbelievably complicated. I looked at the crowd in the studio and tried to imagine how they could possibly be deployed in so many directions. It sounded like a thousand characters in a million costumes; and how many sets would the telling of thirty nursery tales require? I thought of the unfinished theater, swept by the wind.

"Ambitious, isn't it?" Mme LeBreton said, reasserting herself. "That's Geoffrey Render for you! It's going to take a lot of work, probably a lot more than you want to do!"

"It will put this studio on the map," some Mother called out from a barre.

"Exactly," Mrs. Merrick cried dramatically. "Someone sees! Thank you, Polly! You will *all* see if you just think about it for just a minute. I do not want to *hear*," she said slowly with her beautiful lips, "any more complaining about this ballet. I've listened to some very silly complaints this afternoon and they ignore the obvious point that getting this ballet by Geoffrey Render will do a lot of good for this studio, and for the new theater, *and* for the whole community. Why, I imagine that for some of you this production will make a difference in your entire lives," she finished, rattling the lists a little in her emotion, flashing that ring.

"You're not a traitor if you don't participate," Mme LeBreton put in, vitiating the effect of Mrs. Merrick's fine speech. "It's not a sin not to like one of Geoffrey Render's ballets, but of course Mrs. Merrick's right. We can't have a lot of griping because you aren't all princesses.

"Mr. Render did all the casting," she added, as if feeling accused about Cecilia's glamorous parts.

"Well listen, y'all," Adelaide Henderson said, rising suddenly from among the dancers. "I think we ought to let Mrs. Merrick and Milly know whether we're going to be in it or not. It's not what we expected and everything, but gosh, y'all, I'm thinkin' it's going to be real cute. Think about how cute the costumes are going to be."

I thought about Adelaide in a cow suit and smiled.

"So come on, y'all, let's have a show of hands of who's going to be in it."

Of course Adelaide did not have the authority to call for a vote: we had not met to *vote* on whether to participate in the gala première or not, and I looked anxiously at Mme LeBreton to see what she thought of this presumptuous procedure. She was just looking at the hands, though; there were so many of them, hundreds, it looked like. My own hand was up, waving passionately.

"Who's *not* going to be in it?" Adelaide sang out. The room was still and there were no hands.

"Yea! Yea!" the room said, in unison, dancers and Mothers alike, like a regiment of Boosters following Adelaide's flag. It was as if they had been marching one way down the field and then suddenly turned on their heels and marched the other way. They were just suddenly resigned to *Mother Goose,* even enthusiastic about it. I expected the fickle crowd to swoop up Mrs. Merrick and Mme LeBreton and bear them triumphantly on down the field and up the mountain, but the demonstration of support and affection did not go this far. After a time the emotion was brought under control by Mme LeBreton's stick. Then Mrs. Merrick could announce the schedule for the following weekend, when Mr. Render would set the dances; and everyone was so pleased by the prospect of the weekend of the choreography, even if it *was* going to turn them into terrible little animals, that no one seemed to take any notice of Mme LeBreton's accompanying warnings, such as that once he got started, Mr. Render would quite likely work us to death, and that he was famous for cutting people from a cast who would not work as hard as he liked.

12

One of the things that Mrs. Merrick talked about before the end of that highly charged meeting about *Mother Goose* was the publicity. She wanted to know if there was anybody on the school newspaper at Middleton High, and before I knew it my hand was up again, waving, and I asserted with my heart in my mouth that I worked on the *Merrymaker.* I said I would write a story about *Mother Goose,* and I even agreed to see that the *Merrymaker* kept on featuring *Mother Goose* throughout the spring. I was sorry right away: as I have said, I thought of the studio and my school as distinctly and irretrievably separate, and this responsibility to publicize the ballet at Middleton High confused and upset me, but I had spoken up in the heat of the moment and I couldn't take back what I had said.

As a matter of fact, I did not really even work on the *Merrymaker:* I just aspired to work on it. The *Merrymaker,* which won national awards all the time and which was, in its own league, quite as good a paper as the *Chronicle,* did not take freshmen on its staff. Like the Boosters, its members were chosen at the end of sophomore year, after two years of anxiety. But since there was real merit at issue here, you did not merely sit and hope, or say "Hi!" "Hi!" "Hi!" for those two years; you actually worked to show your talent for writing and your devotion to the *Merrymaker.* To this end I often went up to the *Merrymaker* office at my lunch hour to help with typing or layout; I even swept the floor if that looked like it needed doing. But I had not yet been brave enough to submit an article, and surely it was the desirability of doing an article for the *Merrymaker* that helped shoot my arm up in that impulsive way. The next day at lunchtime I trudged up to the *Merrymaker* office with this idea and humbly told it to Anne Markham, the outstanding senior woman who was the Editor-in-Chief that year.

"Sure," she said broad-mindedly. "Why not?"

One day toward the end of that week I was scurrying to the *Merrymaker* office at the beginning of lunch period when, rounding a corner and entering a stairwell, I found myself face to face with Claude Bateson.

"Claude!" I said in lieu of screaming. "You scared me!"

Claude laughed in a wily way. "Just the girl I wanted to see!"

"You were looking for *me?*" I was amazed, since I had never before had a conversation of any kind with Claude, not at the studio and certainly not at school.

Claude smirked importantly. "Yes, I just came from the newspaper room. Do you think we could talk up there for a few minutes? We can't stay *here,*" he said, indicating the empty stairwell.

"Mm, no, I mean yes," I said, continuing on up the stairs with Claude, trying to think of something light and social to say. How embarrassing, being with Claude in the building at lunch! It was naturally against school rules, which (like my mother's rules) were aimed at prohibiting any private conversations between boys and girls. No one was allowed in the classrooms during the lunch period, and no one could stay in the halls unless it was storming outside, preferably with lightning bolts hitting the school grounds. In effect, the rules turned the building inside out. Outside now the school grounds were teeming with boys and girls trying to find privacy around the corners of the building or behind the trunks of large trees. Inside, there was no one but Claude and me, and, up on the top floor, the boys and girls who were on the *Merrymaker* staff. They enjoyed an exception to the general rule, as did the Boosters and I believe the band way below in the subterranean portion of the great building. But these were the ruling class of the school, and to my mind as a freshman they were types of gods. As far as I knew they had no rules.

But Claude and I definitely had rules and we were breaking them. Claude took my arm as we went up the stairs, and I had the peculiar sensation as we went along that we were fugitives from justice. Possibly this was because Claude walked so fast and kept throwing glances behind us as if we were being pursued by dogs and men with guns. When we got to the hall we were going to, I noticed that Claude wore shoes that made a very loud click on the marble floor. I associate this sound with characters who wear sinister hats and sunglasses they call "shades" and who slouch when they walk: it is a sound you can make with your tongue, a kind of loose cluck. Claude did not look like this: he was very tight everywhere rather than loose, but he *did* have a sort of criminal flavor to him, particularly in this jurisdiction.

Then we entered the *Merrymaker* office, and the members of the staff and possibly a few other aspirants to the staff like myself looked up and saw me, without detectable interest, then Claude. It must have been Thursday, because all of the female staff members had on their Booster uniforms, and most of the boys had on their ROTC uniforms. In contrast to this martial splendor, Claude had on a pullover sweater with deer heads printed in rows all over it and the familiar tight tweed pants, and then the heavy brogues that clucked. I was embarrassed—it is not to my credit to describe the depth of my embarrassment and I will not dwell on this—but I am pleased to say that the Boosters and the officers did not even look startled when they saw Claude. Possibly some eyes widened, and there was a lull in all movement and conversation, similar to that pause in the party for the princess in *Sleeping Beauty* when the uninvited fairy comes in; but in an instant people were moving and talking again. The uninvited fairy followed me over to an empty corner of the room, where we sat down in a couple of desk chairs.

Claude took a big breath, expanding the rows of deer running around his chest, then deflated himself with a big sigh. "What I wanted was to ask you to keep my name out of the *Merrymaker*," he said. "When you write your article about *Mother Goose,* just don't mention my name."

"I don't know if I could do that," I said uneasily, thinking there was probably some rule about this. "Besides, hasn't your name been in the *Chronicle* over and over? Why would this be different?"

"For one thing, that was before we knew what the ballet was. Now we know it's *Mother Goose.* Imagine being a boy who's going to dance 'Little Boy Blue' and 'Georgy Porgy' and having it trumpeted in the school paper. I know it's going to be in the big paper but I thought I could get you to keep it out of the *school* paper. Maybe the goons around here won't see it in the big paper. You see," Claude said, "they throw you in the shower and do things I can't even tell you about when you do something they think is sissy. I just can't have that about Georgy Porgy in the paper, Meredith."

"I understand how you feel," I said, "but right now I don't see how I can get around mentioning your name since you're all the boys—"

"No, you're some of 'em," Claude said slyly.

"Ah yes," I said, laughing a little, "but you're most of them." I shrugged. "They probably won't print it anyway. I'm just an apprentice around here, you know."

"Oh they'll print it," Claude said gloomily. "Look," he said with sudden fierceness, "don't get me wrong. I don't give a shit about this school, or what anybody thinks."

I, who did, looked desperately around to see if anybody had heard this, but no one was looking our way.

"Excuse the language," he said, "but I hate the place. The only reason I'm still here is that Milly made me promise. I've wanted to go to New York for years, but I had to promise Milly I'd graduate from high school first."

"I heard you tell Mr. Render that, at the cocktail party," I mused.

"It's because I've never paid Milly a dime for lessons, you know. She's taught me free since I was eight—my mother couldn't afford it. I feel obligated. I suppose I could go without her permission, but frankly I need her help."

"And Mr. Render's," I observed.

"You bet," Claude said, shifting around in his desk chair with some violence. "NDT's my only chance. All the big companies take people from their own schools, or try to hire from the academies overseas. I'll go on up there and audition in June, regardless, but I don't have any real chance in that league without somebody behind me. I need Milly, I need Render. I have to wiggle out of the Army, too.

"Hey," Claude said suddenly, "is that your lunch?" pointing to a brown sack I had on top of my stack of books. "Please, go ahead and eat. I'm sorry. Don't let me interfere with your lunch."

"Well," I said, pleased with this gentlemanliness, "if you'll take half. Unless you've eaten. Have you eaten?"

"Oh no! I never eat at school. The cafeteria's just too horrible," he said, accepting half of my sandwich and chomping off half of it. He said this as if he were criticizing the food, the way everybody criticizes the fare in school cafeterias, but I got the idea that his remark had social implications. Maybe they threw food at Claude in the cafeteria.

Claude seemed to relax as he munched the sandwich. "Don't get me wrong about *Mother Goose*—I'm not ashamed of it. I think it's a great idea. And it could be very important for me. I'll be a lot better off going to New York in June with Little Boy Blue under my belt. I'll have had Geoffrey Render make a role on me."

"Then you *do* like *Mother Goose?*" I pressed. "So many people didn't like it at the meeting Tuesday, the idea of it, I mean. Like Hilary! Well, I guess she changed her mind, I didn't hear her say anything at class yesterday."

"Hilary! That snot!" Claude cried. Now, this did attract attention. A Booster looked our way with a royal stare (there was only one "Hilary" in the school and she was highly regarded), and I indicated to Claude that he should keep his voice down.

"That snot," he said a little more softly. "Hilary and her friends, all snots—"

I prayed Claude would stop using this terrible word "snot."

"Those snots don't think anything about ballet, they just think about their snotty selves."

"Claude," I implored.

"They were raising a big ruckus about *Mother Goose* because they weren't principals. Hilary wanted to be the principal dancer," Claude said mockingly. "They hate Cecilia!"

"Oh no, I don't think so," I said, offering Claude an apple from my lunch. He took it and began to gnaw on it absently, taking several bites before chewing it, like a raccoon or a beaver would. I was sorry I had given it to him because I could hardly stand the way he ate it.

"They do," he said, crunching the apple, "because she's so much better than any of them."

"She's very beautiful," I said reverently. While Claude pulverized the apple I looked away. We were sitting back by the windows, and from the fifth floor all you could see from the desks was the sky. It was cloudy today and the sky looked perfectly blank and white, like a piece of tissue paper.

"She's more than that," Claude said darkly, alluding, I thought, to his well-known hopeless love for her.

Claude glinted his eyes at me like a hungry rodent. Still, I liked Claude better after that conversation than I had ever thought possible. I had never talked with a boy so long before, although of course Claude was no ordinary boy and did not really count in the development of my understanding of and ease with the opposite sex. But in any case I felt a new rapport with Claude, and before he left the *Merrymaker* office I agreed not to mention his name in the publicity.

13

The following weekend Geoffrey Render set the dances for *Mother Goose* at the LeBreton School of Ballet. I wish I could convey the excitement and the disorder of those days. In talking about the day we learned that the ballet was going to be *Mother Goose,* I compared us to a band of mountain climbers suffering from all kinds of mixed emotions. Well, if I could continue that analogy I might propose that this weekend when the dances were set was something like rounding a bend in the trail and coming upon a gigantic waterfall. Even if the little band of adventurers was expecting this waterfall, the reality of it would be so much more powerful than any advance knowledge could have prepared them for. It would be thunderous, and it would be wet! A fine spray would wet their faces and they would be deafened by the noise, and they would huddle together and shiver and laugh, almost overpowered by the force and also the beauty of the waterfall. They would not be able to hear themselves think! Well, on this visit Geoffrey Render was like that waterfall: we thought we knew what he was like but he was so much *more* than that. It was frightening as well as exhilarating to be there while the ideas for *Mother Goose* flowed out of him in overwhelming torrents and the ballet took shape.

He was unquestionably in charge: I saw this right off on Saturday morning. I guess I had expected Mr. Render, Mme LeBreton and Mrs. Merrick to continue to stand around smoking together and talking out the decisions. After all, each of them, as Artistic Director, Ballet Mistress, and Executive Director, had an important title, which suggested that they were a triumvirate in this enterprise. But that just shows I didn't know Mr. Render yet. When I walked in the front studio Saturday morning he was standing in the middle of the room in another plaid shirt and his little shiny black pants and they—Mme LeBreton and Mrs. Merrick—were at the barre, doing *pliés* in leotards and tights. I couldn't believe it! Mme LeBreton, looking ahead with stony dignity, had on her shrimp-colored leotard and tights but no tulle skirt, so that you could see her bulbous middle and skinny legs without the amelioration of the tulle. Well, I knew from the audition how determined Mr. Render was to "see the body," but this seemed to be going too far! Behind her, Lyda Merrick *pliéd* too, wearing a dove-gray leotard and dove-gray tights. Mrs. Merrick in practice clothes too! She looked even more mercilessly exposed than Mme LeBreton. She was thinner, of course, in fact she was slim as a silver ball-point pen, but she was slack, and as she did the *pliés* so carefully, tendons stood out on her neck. Mr. Render did not of course have a whip; but—and this was not the first time I had thought this, and it was not going to be the last—he might as well have had a whip as he stood in the middle of the floor counting out the time for Mme LeBreton and Mrs. Merrick and the other dancers who hastily joined them at the barre. Now, of course Mme LeBreton and Mrs. Merrick had solos of sorts in *Mother Goose* that Mr. Render would set later in the day, but I really think it is open to question whether they had to warm up in so public a manner, first thing; but Mr. Render would have it so, and this was a sign of how things were going to be.

Something else dramatized Mr. Render's ascendancy right off. When I first stepped up to the screen door that morning I had heard Chopin being played on the old piano, obviously by fingers other than Mrs. Fister's. Ah, yes! I had forgotten about Mr. Render's edict on Mrs. Fister! At first I thought Mr. Render himself was playing the Chopin, but when I went in I saw—after the shocking sight of Mr. Render cracking the whip over the two women toiling away at the barre like oxen under the yoke—the back of a stranger, a male in strange clothes who had a great deal of dark curly hair that was not unlike Claude's. This turned out to be Nathan Feldman, whom Mr. Render had brought with him from New York City, who seemed in fact to be an extension of Mr.

Render himself. Nathan was a marvelous pianist (of course he was a great deal more than that!), but during these days of creation it seemed as if Geoffrey Render were playing the piano, just using Nathan's long skinny fingers to do it with.

How I wish I knew how Mr. Render's genius worked! All I know is that it worked, that weekend, with the glory of that hypothetical waterfall, producing movements of such variety and complexity that they delighted everyone, including those skeptics and critics and nay-sayers like Hilary. He presented us with more steps than I knew existed. He had not planned them all out before this time but rather had arranged the music, which was a clever medley of the most famous music for the ballet by Delibes, Tchaikovsky, Ravel, Chopin, Mendelssohn, and even Gottschalk, who was not very well known at that time, and it was this music, as rendered by Nathan Feldman, in conjunction with our eager young bodies, that produced in the maelstrom of his mind the steps we were to do. For three days (it ended up taking until late Monday night) he worked with us in crowds and he worked with each of us in the advanced class alone, and for my part I can say that working with Mr. Render all alone in the middle of the studio floor was very much like climbing into a barrel at the top of the falls and—with a cry of abandon—going over the edge.

****

Actually this hair-raising experience did not come until later in the morning that Saturday. The ballet was to open with Claude as Little Boy Blue waking up in a meadow at dawn and, after a bravura solo, encountering Little Bo-Peep (Cecilia of course) and her flock of sheep, which a person in the form of Rachel would soon shear ("BaaBaa Black Sheep"). The action would then move indoors, where Curly Locks, the three blind mice, Miss Muffet and others would dance out their domestic dramas. As one of these, Old Mother Hubbard's dog, I was down the list. In the meantime, I watched the others and roamed around the studio holding Marie Taglioni and helping to keep Mothers and reporters and other interested parties out.

We had the surprise of another newcomer besides the piano player from New York that morning: that little nine- or ten-year-old who had done the *fouettés* at the audition in the lion costume. She appeared wearing the required LeBreton practice clothes instead of her sad and bizarre recital costume, but she did not look like one of us any more than she had before because everything was so pathetically new—an inky leotard, stiff-looking tights. Clearly someone had told her what she had to buy to come here and dance. This included a hairnet, since her cornsilk hair was too short for a ballet knot. She was standing in the dressing room looking lost when I first saw her. Melissa Martin and Stephanie Sillerman were sitting on the floor.

"Hey, I'm Melissa. What's your name?" Melissa called out in her fashionable twang, as if to a very small child.

"Dotty Winkle," the girl said furtively.

"You did *so good* at the audition. Will you be takin' here now?" Melissa pursued, affecting friendliness.

"The lady *said* I would."

"Where do you live, Dotty Winkle?" Stephanie asked.

"Over to Park Ridge."

"Where do you go to school?"

"Valley Park."

Melissa and Stephanie raised their eyebrows at each other and pressed their lips tightly to express their amusement over this little girl, whose answers showed her to be a barbarian. It was clear that she lived beyond the pale of the Middleton High School district, somewhere out in that hinterland where the plants and factories were, and that she had been called up and suited out to dance with her betters because she had a unique specialty which could be very valuable. Her position was something like that of a Central American place kicker on a professional football team.

It did not help her stock around the studio, especially with Hilary, when Geoffrey Render greeted her as she went out on the floor that Saturday for her first session as Miss Muffet with a big hug and a kiss and said joyously, "Oh, my darling little lion! You know," he then remarked, holding her out from him to display her to everyone in the studio, "here is the inspiration for our gala. I knew the moment I saw her at the audition in that little orange costume that we must have something whimsical, something fantastic! I knew we had to have nothing less than *Mother Goose.*"

***

Another new dancer appeared at the studio that first eventful day, one we had never seen anywhere before. And it was a *boy*—that was the astounding thing. We first saw him when we came back from lunch: he was sitting on a bench in the dressing room in a position resembling Rodin's "Thinker," but dressed in a T-shirt and black tights; and no one spoke to him, as he looked as if he was absorbed in thinking about the superb dancing he was about to do. He looked like a very fine dancer. Unlike the nervous and taut Claude, this boy had an aggressive mesomorphic build. He looked like a football player, if not "The Thinker," with a big blocky head, a barrel-like chest, firm rounded biceps, and fine thick legs. As he sat forward, twiddling thick fingers, I noticed his forearms, how strong they looked and how the veins seemed about to pop out of the skin. He had thick lips pushed out in a contemplative-looking pout and this, taken with rather narrow eyes and prominent cheekbones, gave him a Slavic sullenness not usually found on the local scene which I considered an additional point of interest. I was dying to know where he came from and whether he would push Claude right out of the production.

These questions were obviously on Claude's mind too, right after he careened through the screen door—back late, as usual—and stopped dead still. Claude's little raisin eyes stared, and his body seemed to contract with the shock. A rival! he must have been thinking; and how rude a rival too! He appeared to look at the new boy with a certain distaste as well as shock, as if he were dreadfully out of place, like, say, a rat on a dining table. I realized at that moment that I had never seen Claude sitting on the bench where the strange boy sat because he always tore in at the last minute and did whatever he had to do privately, in the back studio. I could see, for the first time, that this way of going about things showed great delicacy on Claude's part, leaving the dressing room as it did to the girls as a kind of *boudoir*. He saw the boy as much as an insensitive intruder, I believe, as a rival. But whatever his thoughts, Claude stood there a few seconds more looking down at the other male with high emotion. We all saw, with Claude, this other male's flagrant muscles, his bull-like neck. Claude suddenly looked like a matchstick boy.

But in the next moment Claude was over by the bench shaking hands with this boy, who had risen to meet him.

"Claude Bateson," Claude said during the hearty masculine handshake.

"Albert Wasserman."

"You're not at Middleton High?"

"No, St. Stephen's. I just enrolled. I'm from Biloxi."

"Will you be studying here with us?"

"Yes, I hope to."

Claude had ended the handshake with a hand under this Albert Wasserman's elbow and while they talked had guided him politely out of the dressing room and into the back studio, shutting the door behind them. I thought this very civilized of Claude, particularly after the jolt he had had.

As it turned out, however, Albert Wasserman was no threat to Claude at all. It was only about a minute after they appeared in the front studio that this Albert showed himself to be a disastrous dancer, or rather no dancer at all. Claude was doing some quick combinations involving small jumps and turns, and Albert scrambled breathlessly behind him. You could tell right away that he was the rankest beginner: he had something of a turnout, insofar as his overdeveloped muscles would permit, but he did not seem to know the easy steps Claude was doing, and I will never forget the light, skittering way he brushed his feet out to the side during the *jetés,* hunching his body over each time as if he had just gotten a blow to the stomach.

"My God, where'd they get *him?"* I heard Hilary say behind me. "He looks like something the *cat* drug in."

"No, Mrs. Merrick got him," someone else said. "Why I don't know. He's from St. Stephen's, though. Maybe he knows Wendell or Wexler."

"Not likely," said Hilary.

As a dancer, then, Albert Wasserman was ridiculous, though I do not think he knew it, at least not until the very end. But he performed an invaluable service to Claude. Claude showed to much better advantage with Albert lumbering around: it was seen and appreciated for the first time how cleanly Claude moved, how accurate he was rhythmically, and how steady and gallant a partner he was. Suddenly Claude looked very purposeful and legitimate.

Claude also seemed more of a gentleman. Part of this might have had to do with the fact that Claude went to school at Middleton High with the rest of us. Even though he did not fit in there we *saw* him there and knew, or thought we knew, what he was up to. Albert Wasserman, on the other hand, went to St. Stephen's, a boarding school in downtown Middleton run by the Catholic Church, which was considered a very mysterious institution in north Louisiana. In Middleton, where most all of the important families sent their sons and daughters to the public schools (except the Merricks, perhaps because they were so very Catholic), this private school, St. Stephen's, had a rather shady reputation, the idea being that the boys who went there, particularly the boarders, had been sent there because they were troublesome. This may not be true, but people thought this because sometimes local boys with problems were withdrawn from Middleton's fine public school system and sent to St. Stephen's as if that institution could make a bad boy good. Perhaps it was the "Saint" part which held out this promise of reform. Anyway, Albert Wasserman had the air of an inmate at St. Stephen's who had been a problem in Biloxi: the dancing, which he worked on so doggedly, seemed to be part of his rehabilitation. To me it suggested a big clumsy convict who takes up the art of calligraphy.

***

The dances for *Mother Goose,* which were pouring cataract-like out of Mr. Render during this time, might be divided into the dances he made for dancers and those he made for non-dancers, and I suppose it is another proof of his genius that the latter were just as interesting to watch as the former. There was Mrs. Fister, for example, who had arrived even before I did on Saturday morning and proudly taken up a station on

the Mothers' Bench to await her instructions as the production's official
Old Woman. I could not see any signs of resentment on her part about
the presence of Nathan Feldman, and I do not know whether she even
realized how decisively she had been dismissed and replaced. Possibly
Mr. Render, with his years and years of handling difficult situations at
NDT, had managed it so genially that she did not even know. In any case
she spread herself out comfortably to watch her "chirren." She looked
very happy and, I don't know, maybe she was glad not to have to pump
the piano.

Mrs. Fister was first called onto the floor at the same time I was (we
were Old Mother Hubbard and her poor dog, remember); so naturally
my observations of her are clouded by my own high emotion. But I
remember very clearly how Mr. Render went and fetched her from the
Mothers' Bench as if this were a ball and it was now time for the particular
dance he had been waiting for, and how she took short rapturous steps in
her chunky black shoes out onto the linoleum holding his hand, as if she
were about to be swept away in a waltz. Of course Mrs. Fister was not
capable of really dancing: she was a stocky old thing, with heavy legs
falling in folds over her ankles; and her part in "Old Mother Hubbard"
consisted of her going, heavily, to get things—bread, a dish, a wig, some
fruit, and so on—while I engaged in diverting and incongruous canine
antics.

Much later, Sunday afternoon, Mrs. Fister was taught her part as
the old woman who lived in a shoe with too many children, and once
again her part consisted of coming and going and striking some artful
poses while, this time, a crowd of smaller girls did the real work. On
this occasion I was freer to observe Mr. Render and Mrs. Fister; and
from the sidelines I could see that his main problem in instructing her
was not in the simple steps but the acting. This is what I mean: when
Mr. Render went through the steps with Mrs. Fister *he* looked more
like an old woman than she did. *She* looked like a young girl, due to
the expression of childish delight that never left her wrinkled old face.
Actually her part called for a rather querulous astonishment, tinged with
some dismay. I mean the kind of thing a big old colored woman—what
used to be called a "mammy" in the South—indicates by rolling up her

eyes and throwing up her white apron and shouting "Oh Lawdy!" *This* I think is what Mr. Render was trying to coax out of her but he never did, on this weekend, I suppose because she was so excited to be "dancing" herself after all those years of watching dancing from the piano bench.

The other main non-dancer was of course Albert Wasserman. I had wondered from his first frowning *jeté* what on earth Mr. Render would have him do, if he did not simply run him off. Actually Mr. Render took Albert Wasserman, just as he took everything, with a jolly urbane ease: there was no trace of astonishment tinged with dismay when his powerful searching gaze first came to rest on Albert's thick body, even though Albert, at the time, was attempting a *sissonne*—a little sideways leap that leaves one leg pointed out to the side in the air—and displaying that skittering quality, as if he had not leapt on purpose but had just slipped on a banana peel.

Albert was cast as Jack in "Jack and Jill" and the knave in "The Tarts," parts which had originally been assigned to Claude and Lola respectively. Everyone was overjoyed at the new arrangement. Albert as Jack looked quite good with Melissa as Jill: his chunky build complemented her doll-like blockiness. And Mr. Render created a Jack whose main job, aside from one problematical lift, was to stride up a hill, with Melissa doing *piqué* turns around him, then fall down it. The only other challenge was for him to exit "as fast as he could caper," for with his muscle-bound build went an impressively large *gluteus maximus* that seemed to keep him huffing and chuffing much too long over the same spot. As for the knave in "The Tarts," the thrust of the action was to snatch imaginary tarts and then, when nabbed, submit to being beaten "full sore" by Mr. Render's King of Hearts. I do not know whether Mr. Render had to use his acting ability in order to beat Albert Wasserman with as much vigor as he did on Sunday afternoon, or whether he really enjoyed it. In any case, Albert's role in *Mother Goose* was to fall down and to be beaten. He *did* seem equal to that.

***

Claude and Cecilia were of course the best dancers Mr. Render had to work with, and the price they paid for this superiority was five or six muscle-wrenching, bone-crushing parts, each with a set of variations which challenged them and displayed them to a degree never approached by Mme LeBreton's safer choreography for the annual recitals. As Little Boy Blue, for example, Claude was required to do a triple *tour en l'air,* then land from this turn *agenouillement,* which is to say on one knee. He had done double *tours* as long as I had been watching him, but the triple was beyond him. Of course, Claude would have killed himself to do what Mr. Render asked of him: I believe he would have jumped off the roof of Middleton High, five stories up, and landed *agenouillement,* if so instructed, even if Mr. Render had not remarked to him, rather casually, that "the boys in the *corps,*" meaning of course the NDT *corps de ballet,* could all do "triples." This remark left me with a vision of the NDT men as I had seen them at the cocktail party, dressed in their turtleneck shirts and slacks, rising swiftly into the air and swirling around three times, landing, without having spilled a drop of cocktail, to resume a languid conversation. The contrast between this presumed insouciance of the NDT men and poor Claude—rib cage heaving as he hurled himself through the *tours,* the *cabrioles,* the *revoltas* Mr. Render programmed for him—increased my new affection for Claude; I felt almost tender toward him and had vague impulses to bathe his reddened face with a cool washcloth. "He'll kill himself, poor bastard," I heard Mme LeBreton remark after a Robin Redbreast session.

The rest of us lined up to watch Mr. Render work with Claude, and of course everyone wanted to watch Cecilia too. You had to make allowances for Claude because he was so homely and because his effort showed too much: there was a certain charity required for watching Claude, but watching Cecilia was pure pleasure. I admired her with all my heart, and never more than this weekend when Mr. Render created Little Bo-Peep, Jenny Wren and the Pumpkin Eater's Wife on her. She had a marvelous extension: she could kick backward in a *grand battement* and touch the back of her head with her foot. She was also wonderfully strong and quick so that she was capable of the most dazzling *batterie,* or little beats of the feet, during her leaps. Mr. Render murmured to her and she did the most wonderful things like turns on one point while holding the other leg straight above her ear, or an *entrechat* five, which is just about the most difficult of the several varieties of these little jumps with feet beating against each other in rapid alternation. Cecilia did these things so well—the *grand jeté* with which she entered the floor for the first time, for instance, anxious about her sheep—that I expected Mr. Render to shout "Halt!" to the piano player, take Cecilia by the arm and whisk her away to New York, where he would get her on the stage as Giselle or Odette-Odile at once: it was clear to me that she was meant for New York, not Sycamore Street, that she was too lovely for this modest meridian. But he did not do this: he simply twirled her and jumped her and, in time, wore her out as he did us more ordinary dancers.

The biggest crowds were drawn by the *pas de deux,* though. Sometimes during that weekend there were a hundred dancers or even more in the studio: this included the cadres of smaller girls whom I have not yet mentioned, there to learn their jolly little dances as sheep, townspeople, horses, blackbirds and flowers which formed the background for our more sophisticated solos. These little girls in particular gaped at the *pas de deux* which joined Claude and Cecilia as Little Bo-Peep and Little Boy Blue in a meadow, as the ailing Jenny Wren and her suitor Robin Redbreast in her bedchamber, and as Mr. and Mrs. Peter in a pumpkin; the advanced class gaped too, in its more blasé way. The truth is that these *pas de deux* were, like most *pas de deux,* so erotic as to be downright inflammatory: Claude pursued Cecilia, Cecilia melted into Claude, Claude held Cecilia in places we did not touch on ourselves, at least *I* didn't. There were thrilling lift—Claude strutting smartly around with Cecilia on his shoulders—and thrilling catches, one fish dive with Claude catching Cecilia just one second before her lovely face smashed against the floor. And at the very end, before the lights went down to total darkness, Claude pushing against Cecilia in the *cambré* position (bent back gracefully), or anyway that was the choreographic plan until Mme LeBreton whacked her stick sharply on the linoleum and said, "Really, Geoffrey! This is Middleton, Louisiana!" whereupon a tender embrace, with Cecilia's face chastely averted, was put in instead.

As for the rest of us in the advanced class, we were, each in our own way, turned inside out and exposed to the world for what we were. Christabel, for example, looked fey and practically bodiless as the Little

Girl with the Curl and the Baby in "Hush-a-Bye Baby"; Melissa and
Stephanie and Lola, in contrast, looked businesslike and competent
in their compact fleshiness as they went about being mice and men. It
was shamefully amusing to see Adelaide as a cow: her thickness and
her moony batting eyes were magnificently bovine. Dorcas was at her
spindliest, her gangliest as Miss Muffet's spider and later as a spoon (an
iced-tea spoon, Hilary remarked); and Hilary herself, well, you only
had to see Hilary doing the grand series of *pas de chevals*—that gay
stamping step—to know that Mr. Render was right to see this girl with
the long strong legs with the thin thighs and the high rounded buttocks
as a real thoroughbred.

I do not know whether everyone found this weekend as fascinating
as I did: perhaps some, like Alma and Rachel, were too frightened to be
amused by Mr. Render's powers. (Their dances were timid and, to my
mind, uninspired.) Naturally I watched Hilary to see how she reacted to
the choreography since she and her mother had been so devastated by
the announcement of the ballet's theme, but I could not see any signs of
rebellion on her handsome flushed face as she danced with her gleaming
blond hair shaking out with all those bouncy *pas de chevals* into a
ponytail. I did notice, though, that she watched Cecilia's dances very
carefully and even shadowed her, back near the barre in the penumbra
of the front studio, as Cecilia practiced them. When Hilary did this she
looked very slim and graceful and not the least like a horse, which I
suppose suggests that some of these essences I have been talking about
existed more in the dances than the dancers, although I cannot separate
these things any better than Yeats could.

This is particularly true in the case of my own two solos. As I have
said, working with Mr. Render alone was like going over the falls in a
barrel: I was terrified but exhilarated too. The first one as Old Mother
Hubbard's dog was comparatively simple, a series of pantomimes—
laughing, smoking a pipe, standing on my head, dancing a jig, playing
a flute and so forth—which involved a lot of bounding around Mrs.
Fister. The music for this was a waltz from *Les Sylphides,* which Nathan
Feldman played so well that I was literally energized by it and could do
a lot more than I thought I could do. But the second solo was much more

challenging: I was Jack Be Nimble and my music was one of Ravel's glorious waltzes from *Adelaide*. I did not know this music before that time: it was not in our calm collection at home. *Adelaide* is high-powered stuff, even in a piano transcription, and *this* music, taken together with Mr. Render right on me saying "More! More!" "Again! Again!"—well, it was like being incited to riot, on an individual basis. In this variation as Jack I had every leap a female can do, the principal one, the thematic one, being the *écarté,* which is a "split" in the air. Jack of course leaps over a candlestick, and you must picture me leaping up over our candle and spreading my legs to the snapping point, landing behind the candle in *plié,* then jumping up again, this time drawing my legs up during the leap *au raccourci* with feet together, then landing in front of the candle. Picture me alternating these two kinds of leaps over and over and over again, with Render-Feldman-Ravel pumping adrenaline through me. I see Mr. Render standing below me, boring his eyes into me and, in a crouch, rotating *his* hand like a conductor calling urgently for a crescendo because he wanted me to do more and more, although I could not, that first day, and I shook my head helplessly but continued to bob up and down in *pliés* to maintain the beat of the music, which went on, tirelessly, without me.

When I say "our candle," by the way, I am referring to little Dotty Winkle, who hunched patiently under all my *écartés.* Then she did her solo as Little Nanny Etticoat ("The longer she stands / The shorter she grows"). Naturally Mr. Render had her do thirty-two *fouettés* here: they make such a nice climax, especially to more Ravel.

14

On Tuesday afternoon as I once again rode my bicycle up Sycamore Street to the studio the insides of my thighs were sore from *écartés*. My head was still spinning with Mr. Render and Ravel, whom I had left only at eleven o'clock the night before when the whole weary ensemble had finally learned the finale. I was besotted with ballet, in body and in spirit, and I jerked along on my bicycle that day without really looking where I was going. I hopped off at the parking lot and slogged halfway across it, humming a waltz from *Adelaide* before I noticed that there were no cars there as usual before class, rather that there was only one car there, an extraordinarily long black Cadillac, with a Negro man in a uniform standing to one side of it. He was looking way up into the pine trees, which were still flailing themselves in the cold wind, according to the January custom in these parts.

Just then Mrs. Merrick came out of the studio with Mr. Render (Mr. Render! I had assumed he would be gone by now!), followed by Mme LeBreton. I saw that all three of them were carrying champagne glasses and Mr. Render was also carrying a big green champagne bottle.

"Why Meredith honey! What are you doing here?" Mme LeBreton exclaimed. "We don't have class, baby! Didn't a Mother call your mother?"

"Maybe our housekeeper," I mumbled, blushing on account of my mother not being at home to get the message, like a regular Mother, also on account of Lucille, who was a good housekeeper as far as cleaning went but who was not so dependable at taking phone messages.

"We're going to take a ride out to the new theater now. Mr. Render wants to see it. Why don't you come along," Mme LeBreton said kindly. "We'll be back by six. I don't think your mom'd mind."

Thrilled, I ran and stowed my bicycle in the underbrush behind the studio, then scurried to the side of the limousine. There was a good deal of polite scuffling as the three adults tried to decide how to arrange themselves in the car, each seeming to be more polite and self-effacing than the others. Then at last they got in the back seat, Mr. Render in the middle, the green champagne bottle sticking up between his chubby legs. I got in the front seat and the chauffeur shut us in and walked slowly around to his seat and we were ready to go. I was in a billow of gray leather facing a set of dials and knobs that suggested a larger vehicle, like a plane, or at least a yacht.

We were easing out of the parking lot before I even realized that the motor of the stupendous vehicle was on: I remember being deeply impressed by how this car rolled so smoothly over the deep gravel that made lesser cars spit and churn. We cruised up Sycamore Street and down Tates Parkway, away from downtown. All the familiar landmarks—the college, the restaurants, the stores—looked new and somehow more interesting than usual when seen from the window of this limousine, almost as if I were seeing them on a movie screen rather than through the window of an automobile. I was not of course forgetting for an instant that Mr. Render himself was behind me, and that at any second he might say something important. Anything he had to say would be interesting.

For the first time in several days I thought about Mr. Render as a person instead of something in the nature of a waterfall. Now I remembered the things I had been mulling over during the Christmas holidays, that business about the love affair between Mr. Render and Mme LeBreton (Milly Frobish, rather) and even the wild idea that Cecilia might be his daughter. I had not had time to think about that, and nothing had prompted me to. Mr. Render had treated Mme LeBreton and Cecilia in a businesslike manner with nothing recognizably familial about it and they had reacted to him in the same humble, even subservient manner everybody else did. If he had treated anybody like an old, old friend or a lover or even a father, it was not either of the LeBretons but rather Mrs.

Merrick. Now that I thought back on it, I could see that he had treated Mrs. Merrick very kindly during the long grueling sessions, you might even say "petted" her, in the same way that some of the older members of the advanced class "petted" Christabel.

Possibly this was because of the way Mrs. Merrick had exposed herself. She had looked terrible in a leotard ("flaccid" is the word), as I suppose most elegant women would have in those days before the vogue of calisthenics and jogging and tennis. She also could not dance. I think Mr. Render had probably assumed that a woman such as Mrs. Merrick had taken ballet when she was a girl and just needed to brush up on her technique, but it was pretty obvious that Mrs. Merrick, like Mrs. Fister, was actually dancing for the first time, although no one said a word about this, as far as I know, and certainly she was not a figure of fun like Albert Wasserman. Clearly she had not danced in Natchitoches, and this failure to have danced as a girl is just about the only thing I ever observed about her that was consonant with having grown up around a country feed store.

I remember her trying a single *pirouette,* which is something the smallest sheep or beggar could do, in a tense fourth position in the middle of the floor in the front studio, alone (everybody else taking a break, drinking Cokes), frowning in concentration, jerking up on *demi-pointe,* hurling herself around in an attempted circle that collapsed in a convulsive little spasm. I was sitting down by the piano, holding Marie Taglioni and drinking my warm Coke, looking up at her. The fluorescent light shone down on her golden hair, hair so thick and smooth that Rapunzel would have been proud of it, making it gleam, but also throwing the hollows under her eyes into a new prominence and highlighting the otherwise almost invisible horizontal lines on her forehead. In this light her neck looked especially gaunt and ugly. Now she looked as if she were so thin not because she was so fashionable but because she never had enough to eat, like a poor farm woman. Perhaps it was this unexpected betrayal of her true age, which was the same as my Aunt Lucy's, thirty-nine or forty (the same, too, as Mme LeBreton's!), that led Mr. Render to be so tender toward her, just as he was courtly toward Mrs. Fister. I did not like to think, now that Mrs. Merrick was back in her glistening furs and a pencil-slim suit and looking smooth-faced and lovely and twenty-nine at the oldest, that it was because of this car and the theater we were on our way to see.

He had been comparatively curt with Mme LeBreton, on the other hand. She had her vulnerabilities too, perhaps even more of them than Mrs. Merrick. She appeared Saturday, Sunday, and Monday in the leotard and the tights alone, with the belly. She also worked very hard: if she appeared to work less hard than Mrs. Merrick it was because she did not work so futilely. She not only learned her steps as Mother Goose but also everyone else's so that as Ballet Mistress she could conduct rehearsals for the next three months. To this end she sat watching and taking notes in a spiral notebook, never resting, finally exhausting herself. She learned so much she became haggard with learning. She caught a cold and started coughing a lot: she had always coughed because of her smoking, but now during the marathon weekend she had begun to cough that long, rattly kind of cough that starts low in the chest and ends with a prolonged wheeze.

Now, zipping along Tates Parkway in the limousine, I was disappointed that Mme LeBreton had not bounced back from the ordeal of the weekend as well as Mrs. Merrick. She was looking old and tired, and instead of being elegantly dressed she was wearing an ancient moss-colored raincoat and some rain boots, with a stretch of magenta tights showing. They had not been so dissimilar over the weekend: more than once I had seen them sitting together on the Mothers' Bench, blasted by the unwonted exercise, with towels around their red and dripping necks, both, I think, reduced to nothing, but now they were themselves again and it dawned on me for the first time—although an older, wiser person would have realized this long before—that there was a high tension between these two women which could be summed up, in crude terms, as a breakneck competition for Geoffrey Render.

"Well, Geoffrey darling, it's a masterpiece," Mrs. Merrick said. "And this has been the most interesting three days of my life."

"My dear lady, I hope not," Mr. Render replied, and then I heard the sound of a kiss. "I cannot believe that. Why, you've worked like a stevedore. You'll be thrilled to see me gone!"

"How can you say that? I don't know how I can go back home tonight without you. It will be desolate. Thank God I'm flying to Aspen in the morning."

"Your house is a paradise, Lyda. You don't need *me!* Your cook, now I know your cook will be glad to see me gone!"

"My house is a circus, Geoffrey," Mrs. Merrick complained. "You're just being gallant, as always. You've had such a marvelous effect on the children. I think if you would stay you really would civilize them, even Wendell! I might as well tell you, darling, Christabel's in love with you. This morning I found a whole collection of wineglasses in her room. She finally admitted that they were yours, from our meals—"

"And the other times!" he added gaily.

"Yes, the other times too! And she says she won't give them back."

"How *piquant,*" Madame said, sounding bored. The final nasal syllable dissolved into a sneeze and one of the spasms of loud coughing.

"Really, my dear, you're going to have to see a doctor," Mrs. Merrick shouted.

"Take a few days off!" Mr. Render recommended. "Stay in bed a while. You smoke too much, drink too much! Do you want some more champagne to soothe your throat? That might help."

"Yes, and a cigarette too, if you have one," Mme LeBreton said, as soon as she could talk again.

"You see! Smoking! Drinking! You don't take care of yourself!" Mrs. Merrick chided comfortably.

"It's *not* a masterpiece," Mr. Render mused when they all had more champagne and fresh cigarettes. We were past the commercial portion of Tates Parkway; now it had turned into a state highway, and I looked out onto the beginnings of the pine-crested countryside to the south of Middleton. There was only an occasional filling station or house to break the monotony. Each of these seemed to have a flourishing specialty for sale: eggs, honey, purebred pups, or worms. I studied these signs diligently to show the chauffeur I was not listening to the grown-ups.

"I don't want even you saying that it is a masterpiece, darling Lyda," Mr. Render went on, savoring the word "masterpiece." "It's just some steps thrown together. Though there is some nice work for Cecilia, and Claude, and of course my sweetheart Christabel."

"It's too damn hard for them, Geoffrey," Mme LeBreton rasped. "I wouldn't have been surprised if mothers had called me this morning and told me their daughters had died in their sleep."

While Mr. Render laughed at this, Mrs. Merrick said, "It's brilliant, darling. It's stunning. It will be a great success."

"You push like a steam engine, Geoffrey," Mme LeBreton resumed. "You haven't changed one iota in all these years. If it's a performance, you think everybody has to beat their brains out. You think they have to spill their guts all over the stage."

"You haven't changed either, darling," Mr. Render said cheerfully. "You still don't have the first idea about what it takes to be first class. You want to be comfortable. You don't want to take the trouble to extend yourself."

"That's shit, Geoffrey, but we don't want to argue about that now in front of our benefactress, do we?"

"Well, *I* don't like to argue at any time, Milly, as you ought to know, but I think we had better follow up this one point before I leave. I don't want anything changed when I come back in April, you see. I don't want things simplified or prettified. I very particularly don't want things slowed down. Any charm in this little nonsense will come from its lightness and its speed. Its *youth*. That is why I'm leaving Nathan with you."

Leaving Nathan! This was the first I had heard about that!

"Your guard dog," Mme LeBreton said in disgust.

"Well, more than that. I am sure you recognize, Milly, that your job will be easier with a good musician rather than your poor Mrs. What's-her-name. Whatever his other faults Nathan is a superb musician. You'll have to watch him of course."

"What do you mean? Does he bite? Does he chase cars?"

Mr. Render was unflappable. "Watch him around the girls, you know the kind of thing I mean. I think he will be lonely."

"Oh delightful," Madame said, clearly not delighted. "All right, Geoffrey. He's not necessary, though. I could have gotten somebody from the college. We wouldn't have had to find him somewhere to live and worry about feeding him. We wouldn't, for God's sake, have had to *watch* him."

"I think you leave here doubting that I can carry this through," she added, after a moment of heavy breathing. "But I took very careful notes."

"Your notes! Ah, yes, I leafed through your notebook this morning! Now that you bring it up I'll confess I do have some doubts, Milly my love. Your notes are rather, spotty, shall I say? And of course the *children* won't remember everything. They were hanging on by their fingernails this weekend."

I blushed. Mme LeBreton said, "Don't worry," very slowly, very distinctly. "I'll remember the dances. *They'll* remember the dances. Every blasted step!"

"I'm sure we'll all remember what you have worked so hard to teach us," Mrs. Merrick put in diplomatically.

"You're an angel, darling," Mr. Render said toward her in an automatic sort of way. "But I do wonder," he continued, with remarkable good humor. "We covered so very much ground in such a short time. I don't remember you being such a quick study as all that in the old days, Milly. What we *should* have had," he said thoughtfully, "is someone taking real notation. There's something new called Benesch that they were talking about in London at Christmas. It was just introduced over there. Something like that is really the one thing we could have done for the little production that we haven't done. It's not hard to read. I wonder if I can't hire someone in New York to do it when I get back, if anyone there knows it yet. I wonder if I could dictate the dances."

"Lovely, lovely," said Lyda Merrick. "What do you think it would cost?"

I was alarmed to hear a vast heaving and rustling from Mme LeBreton's side of the car: she sounded like she was coming over the seat into the front but she did not; she seemed instead to have wrenched herself around to confront her colleagues.

"It is well you should ask that, Lyda. Yes, *do* ask! He will do what he pleases and then present you with the bill. If *you* won't pay it then he will find another lady who will. That's why I voted for the set designer from Middleton. He might not be as good as your precious NDT designers, but he won't rob us blind either."

"Milly, Milly," Mr. Render murmured soothingly. "I do believe you're hysterical. Here, my dear, take this last sip of champagne. Now, now. Sit back, breathe deeply."

I breathed deeply too, to keep from moaning in terror at the adults fighting in the back seat, saying those insulting things to each other. I had never been so close to a grown-up argument before, and I believe that if my hair had not been slicked back and pinned up in its hopeful little ballet knot it would have been standing on end. I almost wished I hadn't come: I could have been safe in my room now, instead of down a country road in what looked like the middle of the wilderness, where the limousine had stopped at last.

***

By this time we had heard so much about the Merrick Theater that I guess I had begun to think of it as already finished. Just that weekend, for example, I had heard Hilary and Stephanie talking about how they were going to share a dressing room, and the way they talked it sounded as if that dressing room were already there and waiting for them to take their high-handed and hilarious possession of it.

It was something of a shock, then, to see the construction site for the first time. We were about three miles outside the city limits in a dismal-looking clearing a short distance from the highway. The first things I saw were piles of lumber and piles of brick all loosely wrapped in plastic, then a number of bulldozers and steam shovels. "The trucks on the horizon," I thought foolishly. But they were not painted with shiny yellow lacquer, rather with duller, more somber colors; nor were they moving and burrowing and rearing, but standing stock still. It seemed ominous that there were no workmen around even though it was a Tuesday: the woods were as still as death and the limousine might have been a hearse sitting there. The theater, what there was of it, reared up at the top of a sharp rise in the landscape like the ruin of a temple to some alien religion. It was only half finished. Actually, you could not tell just by looking whether it was undergoing construction or falling into ruins—moving toward magnificence or away from it—only that it was about halfway there.

I was afraid the adults would be embarrassed or even angry when they remembered I was there and realized I had heard all the things they had said, but in fact nobody took any particular notice of me at all. Mr. Render sprang from the car and looked eagerly around the desolate woods before he strode off across the wet soggy ground and then up the hill toward the potential theater. He walked very rapidly, as if delivering himself from the tiresome argument in the car, and we followed along behind, Mrs. Merrick picking her way over the leaves and boards and mud and rubble in her delicate way, Mme LeBreton slogging carelessly along beside her, duck-footed.

Mr. Render had picked up a stick which was just the right size for a walking stick and, after we had reached the top of the hill, he used this stick to poke around with. He poked and pointed while Mrs. Merrick picked her way around behind him, answering his questions. Although the outside of the theater, which was to have several levels with balconies and terraces and fountains, had looked grand and significant, like some sort of temple, the inside looked more like an airplane hangar, or perhaps a warehouse used for the storage of construction materials. It was not grand-looking, only confused and junky. It looked irredeemably unfinished to me, but it must not have appeared so to Mr. Render, who looked around with the same interested, animated expression I have seen since on the faces of tourists at places like Versailles and the Alhambra, even St. Peter's. He inspected the "lobby" and the "auditorium," then we all walked down the sloping concrete floor to the "stage." There was no stage yet, and so this was the lowest point of the cavernous chamber.

Mr. Render stood in the middle of this desolate space, next to a rusty oil drum filled to overflowing with empty beer cans, and spoke of the sets for the production. "Bring Beldinsky out here, often," he said, referring to the artist at Middleton College that Mrs. Merrick had chosen to design the sets. "Make sure he has the ambience, the scope of this theater. The sets have to be charming but not cloying. Do you think Beldinsky's too sweet, Milly?" he said to Mme LeBreton, as if they had not just recently been at each other's throats in the car. Mme LeBreton shrugged and smoked as he went on to proclaim that the focus of the set must be the London Bridge, which must be lit from behind to get the right dreamy look; perhaps the moon should actually glow. Now, the other things—the roads, the houses, the vistas—these were entirely up to Beldinsky, but the bridge and the moon had to be just precisely right because Mrs. Fister and Adelaide had to be catapulted over the moon and, at the end, the bridge had to fall down. Oh, and the wall had to be just right too: the one that Humpty Dumpty falls off of, and which turns like so—here Mr. Render swept rapidly around the stage space in mincing balletic steps to show how—to expose Humpty's broken shards.

They discussed costumes that day too, and the lights, and I had the impression that they had been over all this before and that this was simply a way of saying farewell, like a prudent householder walking around a house checking and rechecking the locks on the windows and doors before he leaves. Mr. Render was on his way to the airport—I had learned that the limousine would take him and Mrs. Merrick out there after dropping Mme LeBreton and me back at the studio—and he would not be coming back to Middleton until one week before the performance in April. I suddenly felt like crying as I listened to the adults talk so calmly about the gala première of *Mother Goose* in this chaotic setting; I began to wish I had not seen it. If only I could be like these adults and be sure the theater would be finished, be sure that April would come! I did not see how it could. All along Mr. Render and everything connected with him had seemed fantastic and unreal, utterly out of the course of nature—far, far greater than a mountain or a waterfall; and now Mr. Render strode around this shell of a building with a confidence that looked insane.

I realized suddenly that Mme LeBreton was no longer standing there; then I heard her cough, somewhere outside. I ran up the "aisle" toward this comforting sound.

"Oh Madame," I said, when I found her outside on what might someday be a balcony. "Do you think this place can be finished by April?"

Mme LeBreton honked her nose into an old Kleenex. "They think it will be, but I don't see how."

"I'll *die* if it doesn't get finished and we don't have *Mother Goose,*" I declared passionately.

Mme LeBreton stared moodily out over the woods around the construction site. Although it had looked as though the theater was on the top of a very high hill, you discovered, once you were up on it, that it was only a small rise and that there was no "view," no vista, only the depressing sight of the scrubby winter woods such as could be found on all sides of Middleton. I could not hear anything but the occasional swish of a car over on the highway.

"They know what they're doing, I guess," Madame said. "Of course Geoffrey would plan a production with everybody south of the Mason-Dixon line in it, if somebody would pay for it. They make a good pair. And," she said, with a mighty sigh, "they're having a hell of a good time doing it."

Mme LeBreton seemed like the wretchedest grown-up alive, standing on that parapet in those rubber rain boots with her head tied up in a purple flowered scarf, blowing her nose into a little wet ball of Kleenex. But soon, thank goodness, Mr. Render and Mrs. Merrick came out of the "theater" talking and laughing, he swinging his stick as if it were a stylish accessory. They were discussing whether "theater" should be spelled with an "e-r" or an "r-e."

"You spell it with an 'r-e' when it costs over a million dollars," he said waggishly.

"It will, any moment now, the way things are going," she retorted.

"It's so peaceful here," Mr. Render observed, having come up to where Mme LeBreton and I stood. "I miss it already, darlings. Write me now, send me pictures. Call me! You must take pity on me, going back to New York!"

Then the party tottered down the slippery hill toward the car.

"Well little lady," Mr. Render said to me suddenly as we reached level ground. "And where's your little cat? This is the first time I've seen you without it, except when you were working."

"Oh!" I said, thunderstruck at being addressed directly in this way by the great man, for he had never before said a single sentence to me that was not in the imperative voice. Branches clattered; the forest floor seemed to shift. "She's back at the studio," I managed to say. "But I can take her home in February."

"Well she has to be back for rehearsals in April. You will let her come back to us, won't you, my dear?"

Now he was helping me into the front seat. "Of *course,* sir," I said earnestly. "She'd die if she couldn't be in the performance! I named her for a dancer, you know," I went on recklessly. "I named her Marie Taggly-onie."

He smiled and gently shoved the door shut. From the back seat, where Mme LeBreton and Mrs. Merrick were settling in, I heard low, rich laughter.

"Meredith darling," said Mrs. Merrick, "that's Tal-*yo*-nie. Italian is so *gauche* when it's mispronounced. I'm sure you'd want to know!"

"Oh I'm sure!" said Mme LeBreton, with a honk into a Kleenex.

My face was blazing as the car glided away, and from this moment I was wary of Mrs. Merrick. Why, she wasn't very nice at all! Such a pronunciation expert! Maybe this was one of the advantages of coming from a place with a name like Natchitoches! I searched my memory for other instances of Mrs. Merrick's arrogance and complacency; I thought protectively of Mme LeBreton, coughing back there in a corner.

"Cats!" Mr. Render mused. "They'll be effective in the St. Ives number, won't they? Audiences love animals, every time. I never cared for cats, though. Some of my colleagues adore cats. You know who I mean! But I'm afraid they leave me cold. Dancers aren't feline to me. More like, let's see, more like—"

"Cogs!" Mme LeBreton said curtly. "Or pawns."

15

The next day Mme LeBreton collapsed. I did not see this, as it happened during a class for the little girls an hour or so before our class at four-thirty. When we got to the studio she was gone to the hospital and Nathan Feldman was left holding her stick. He looked sick when he delivered the news, as if he were responsible, somehow. "You guys don't worry," he said in a strange accent. "Your teacher just fainted. They don't think it's bad. She said she didn't want you missing rehearsal and to carry on just like she was here."

I recall that Nathan held the stick gingerly, rather as though it were some kind of weapon that might go off in his hands. I couldn't get over seeing him with it—why yesterday Madame hadn't even wanted him here and today he was in charge! I could not imagine how this had come about. Later, when I got to know him a little, Nathan filled me in on that awful afternoon. He had just been playing along on the old upright piano, happy as a lark, when he heard a thud. He did not look around right away—you hear thuds all the time in a ballet studio, he said—but a little girl screamed and *then* he looked around and saw "Milly laying on the floor like a dishrag." He thought at first that she was dead, but when he found out she was still breathing he ran looking for a phone. There was no phone in the studio, and once poor Nathan realized this he ran out the back door in search of help. Fortunately some Mothers were keeping the vigil in the parking lot and they took over from there. One of them summoned an ambulance, and by the time it arrived Madame had regained consciousness enough to say a few words to Nathan and the distraught little girls. It was then, in what I thought a particularly fine gesture, that Madame gave Nathan her stick.

Everyone in our class just stared at Nathan as he delivered his shocking news—more shocked by Nathan, I believe, than the news itself. No one really knew him from the weekend, when he had just been a strange back with ten brilliant fingers, and it may have been that nobody but me knew that he was going to stay behind when Mr. Render left, apart from Mme LeBreton and Mrs. Merrick, that is, who may or may not have confided in their daughters. He was very strange to our eyes. He was a tall, shambling figure wearing old khaki pants that were too big for him and several other layers of clothing that did not appear to touch his body—vest, cardigan sweater, jacket, even a muffler. As I have said, his hair was bushy like Claude's, and he dropped his head back in a peculiar way, I suppose to see out of his horn-rimmed glasses at the most advantageous angle. This gave his Adam's apple an extraordinary prominence. Of course his accent, the big-city kind that clips words and twists their vowels around, was also a major factor in his peculiar presence. I observed him with respect because he was from New York City where the professional dancers danced, also because he was Mr. Render's lieutenant ("guard dog"!), but I was afraid some of my classmates wouldn't care two straws about these things, and refuse to cooperate.

But the class took Nathan seriously, I am glad to say. Hilary and Christabel, the main ones I was worrying about, stared at him but did not laugh. Claude went up to Nathan Feldman and shook hands with him (causing me to reflect, once again, how it improved Claude to have these new people around: why, he looked almost like a normal boy next to Nathan!). After a few minutes of agitation, during which we wrung our hands about Madame and wondered whether all was lost, Adelaide marched up to Nathan Feldman and he bent down over her for a conference. Soon Adelaide came away with the stick, saying, "All right, people. Let's get started. Milly wants us to carry on, so let's carry on."

Carry on we did. Nathan seemed relieved to be able to get back to the piano, and Adelaide bossed us through the barre and the combinations.

This class followed the routine of our ordinary classes and yet it seemed like an entirely new type. I had noticed how Mme LeBreton, even in her extremity, had called this a "rehearsal" instead of a "class," at least that is the word the piano player had quoted, and I think this is a clue to the new quality the session had. *Mother Goose* existed now, and even when we weren't actually dancing it, everything we did as dancers was dedicated to it. Even this first class, a good three months away from the date of the performance, had a rushed and nervous quality, an air of emergency that I do not think can be fully accounted for by the fact that Madame had collapsed.

***

"Daddy went and saw her last night. She just has bronchitis," Rachel Mintz announced the next morning to Dorcas and me before the first bell at school. "It's not serious but they want her to stay in the hospital a week so she can rest."

"A week!" I cried.

"Mr. Render practically worked her to death," Dorcas said, sounding pleased. "People'll be dropping like flies."

"She smokes too much," I said, thinking about the "drinking" too but not wanting to mention this. "She's *been* having that horrible cough."

By class time that afternoon everyone had word of the bronchitis, which is a common ailment and something everybody had heard of and many had even had, and so no one was worried about Mme LeBreton anymore. Cecilia was not there, but we assumed she was at the hospital with her mother and so no one was worried about Cecilia either. Our only concern was getting along with our temporary master, Nathan Feldman. Other adults were there—Mrs. Fister appeared as a kind of *duenna* and some Mothers also came in to watch—but it was this peculiar figure from New York who was in charge of the studio, whether he wanted to be or not. Nathan was not so comical-looking once he sat down at the piano. Once he sat down there, he did not look goofy and vague anymore but astute, as if he knew everything. He was still tall, even sitting down, and as he played and swung his head around to look at us through his glasses, he seemed to be regarding us from the top of some pillar of wisdom. He looked very critical, as if he were comparing us unfavorably with his memories of the NDT classes. Actually, as I came to realize, it was not the dancing he was studying and appraising so much as the girls in the form-fitting leotards, but in those first days I always thought he was about to make some scathing remark.

Yet it was really Nathan's musical ability that established his control over the advanced class, which could have been so cocky and wayward—would have been, I believe, if left in the charge of Mrs. Fister. His playing was the perfect mixture of precision and fire. Where Mrs. Fister had a ratty old ragbag of music for class, Nathan had a simple and serene repertoire centering upon two composers, Bach and Chopin. Even on that old upright, he played these with a masterly flair that thrilled me. I think he thrilled himself sometimes: I remember seeing him clean his glasses and surreptitiously wipe his eyes after an especially lyrical Chopin *port de bras.*

Sometimes, too, Nathan would use what I took to be his own original melodies and improvise on them. This fascinated me, and as I watched Nathan at it I noticed that he would pull a small canteen or flask out of one of his pockets from time to time and take a quick swig. I also noticed that the improvisation increased in steady proportion to these swigs, until by the end of long sessions the results would sound quite grandiloquent, along the lines of Mahler.

After he got over his first shyness Nathan was very friendly, especially after a lot of improvisation. I found out before too long that he had been born in Teaneck, New Jersey, and wanted to be a conductor someday and compose what he called "his own stuff" during his spare time. He had been going to the Juilliard School of Music but had left there the previous spring. He never said why exactly, although it seemed to have to do with his belief that it was not necessary for him to practice the piano. (Was he a genius, or just a facile ne'er-do-well? I could not decide for a while.) Anyway, after withdrawing from or flunking out of Juilliard, Nathan had taken a job as a rehearsal pianist at NDT—although that seems a poor choice of jobs for somebody who does not like to practice since there's so much repetition in it ("All right kids, one more time now!")—and Mr. Render had taken an interest in him.

As Nathan told it, he became Mr. Render's most valued accompanist and would have been the chief accompanist for NDT had it not been for Pierre Metz, a dirty old Frenchman who had once played for Diaghilev. New York was full of old relics like this, Nathan said.

Nathan himself was probably not more than twenty at that time, but he did not seem that young when he played the piano: as I've said, he exerted a powerful musical authority. He would look around at us with the critical look I've described and I would quiver thinking he was about to unfurl himself from the piano bench and shout, "Mr. Render wouldn't stand for that! Bach wouldn't like it either!" Later, as we practiced parts of *Mother Goose,* Delibes and Ravel also seemed about to shout out through the lips of Nathan Feldman. And always, when Nathan played, I had the not unpleasant fear that Mr. Render himself would come leaping through the casement windows and land in our midst, shouting corrections and moving these rehearsals along on an even faster beat.

***

"Where *is* Cecilia?" Adelaide demanded on Friday. It had been three days since Mme LeBreton had collapsed, and Cecilia had not appeared at the studio at all. We were in the dressing room after class, mopping off with towels, changing our shoes, putting on coats. "I'm afraid she's sick. She hasn't been at school."

Maybe she collapsed too, I thought. But where Madame's collapse suggested something hot and disorderly, Cecilia's collapse brought to my mind the final pose of the Dying Swan, that last cool feathery flutter down over the extended foot, exquisitely arched. Actually it was hard to think of Mme LeBreton and Cecilia as mother and daughter at all. I guess this was because they did not speak to each other during class or even look at each other in any special way; they did not, of course, look alike.

"I don't think she's sick," Rachel said. "Daddy would have seen her."

"Have you called, Adelaide? Have you gone over? What does Mme LeBreton say? Have you asked *her?"* Dorcas said, working up a panic. "Maybe we ought to call the police!"

"Drop dead Dorcas," Hilary said, bored.

"Milly says Celia's resting at home, but she doesn't answer the phone and she doesn't answer the door," said Adelaide, batting her eyelashes. "I'm really worried, y'all."

"Well *don't* worry, Addie-puss," Lola said. I remember that Lola was standing in the middle of the dressing room when she said this with her arms folded under her big bosom. She was a short girl, and with her short curly black hair she would have looked like a gypsy boy had it not been for this big bosom. I was struck at the time by the mocking defiance of her pose as she repeated, "Don't worry. Cecilia just needs a rest. She's the star of this show, you know! It's taken a lot out of her!"

A murmur of agreement arose in the dressing room. "She did *so* good for Mr. Render, y'all," I heard Melissa say.

"Well I think I ought to take a casserole over there this weekend. I'll bet Celia isn't eating right. They're all alone in the world," Adelaide went on ineluctably. "Milly's in the hospital and Celia's there at home, all alone—"

"Not *quite* alone!" Hilary said in a playful voice, with a quick little clipped "quite" that made Adelaide look at her sharply and then, very slowly, turn red.

"Shut up, Hilary," Lola said crossly, although she was still standing in that defiant way and I thought she looked more amused than cross.

Nothing more was said on this topic—the conversation shifted quickly—but I was thunderstruck. I plucked at the knot of ribbon behind my ankle, unable to untie it for staring at Adelaide, who looked like she was about to cry. Even I knew that Hilary, who was now laughing with Christabel, had alluded to Charlie Hill: "not *quite* alone," plus a knowing leer, taken with the fact of Cecilia's sequestration, could mean only one thing: that Charlie Hill was staying with Cecilia at her motherless house, that they were, in the rustic but richly connotative phrase, "shacking up." I also knew from looking at her now that Hilary would have been happy to discuss this situation openly and joke about it, and that she probably would have done so just for the pleasure of further upsetting Adelaide if Lola, who was Cecilia's best friend and who was, I now saw, standing guard over her reputation, had not looked ready to stomp her flat with her wooden-toed toe shoes.

I had been dimly aware that Cecilia's relationship with Charlie Hill had been growing more and more intense: for several months now he had delivered her to each class and picked her up again afterward, and all during the previous weekend when Mr. Render was exploiting Cecilia's gifts inside the studio Charlie Hill was waiting in the Chevrolet outside. I believe he did not go home all the time Cecilia was there, nor did he ever try to come in, as far as I know. Charlie Hill did not appear to me to have any special qualities, but he did have the good sense to attend Cecilia during this historic occasion. Sitting idle in his car, he showed as much consciousness of the need to nurture beauty as any Mother, and as much selflessness. Suddenly I imagined that the feeling Charlie Hill and Cecilia had for each other had flared during this weekend and become some kind of ungovernable passion (this would have something to do with the heat of Cecilia's achievements at the hands of Mr. Render). Naturally during that time there were things standing between the two of them—quite literally, the walls of the studio, then also all the adults inside, Mr. Render, her mother—but this week all that was over for Cecilia, at least for the time being, and the two of them stood alone together, rather, "not *quite* alone"; and I imagined them, insofar as my rudimentary knowledge of such things permitted, as one.

But then everyone was leaving the studio, and soon I was on my bicycle heading home. The cold air cleared my head and now, pumping along, I decided I'd read too much into that remark of Hilary's. Oh, Hilary meant Cecilia was "shacked up," all right—that is what she wanted everyone to think—but they were just being sly about Cecilia, "catty" is the word, I think. Probably what was happening was that Charlie Hill was coming over in the evenings to keep Cecilia company, or coming into the house with her after he drove her to the hospital to visit her mother: they just weren't properly chaperoned. But talk of this kind bothered me. Even before I got home I started to worry about my mother and father somehow hearing such talk. My mother, particularly, would disapprove of it and start talking to my father, privately of course, about what kind of people the LeBretons really were and whether it was good for me to spend my afternoons in the LeBreton studio. Later, I worried too about such talk getting around school. It was just the sort of thing that gave rise to the terrible pregnancy rumors that swept Middleton High School from time to time. "So-and-so is pregnant," everyone would say. These rumors were often false; in fact, they usually were false, and most people knew they were just the products of envy and malice. But even innocent girls were damaged irrevocably—tainted, stained—and I could not stand the thought of Cecilia, who was so beautiful, being marred by a rumor of that kind.

***

I have not mentioned that my part in keeping the studio going while Mme LeBreton was in the hospital was to take care of Colette and the kittens. Mrs. Fister had given me a key on Friday so that I could get in the studio on Saturday and Sunday to feed Colette and check the litter, and I felt very responsible and official as I pedaled up there Saturday morning to do my job. But I found the studio wide open and Nathan Feldman sitting on the back steps in the sun playing with the kittens, who were falling off the steps, then teetering away and disappearing into the underbrush. Poor little Marie Taglioni, or just plain Marie, as I now called her, was embroiled in the gravel.

Nathan talked to me as I scurried around collecting the kittens and searching for Colette. "I'm supposed to meet Claude here later to rehearse his solos, but I came on over. There's nuttin to do! I'm sick of my apartment. And I can't find anybody to talk to. Everybody stays inside in this town all the time!

"Where's a bar around here anyway? Last night I walked up and down this street up here—what's the name of it?"

"Tates Parkway."

"Tates Parkway, and I never *could* find a bar."

"Oh, we don't have any bars in Middleton. Middleton's dry," I declared.

"Jesus H. Christ I hate the South!" Nathan shouted. "It hasn't even been warm until today!"

"That's true," I said apologetically, not wanting to tell Nathan that this was just a warm spell and that it would be cold again in two or three days.

"Is the whole county dry, or what?" he said in a minute.

"We don't *have* counties in Louisiana, we have parishes."

"Oh Bejeesus, parish then." Nathan sighed elaborately. "Then how did Milly get all that booze we drank last weekend?"

"That I don't know. I never thought about it."

"You guys don't have any Scotch at your house, do you?" Nathan asked with a sudden flare of interest.

"Oh no, my parents don't believe in drinking."

"I thought not," Nathan said gloomily. "Old Jiffy didn't tell me *this*. Guess he was afraid to. He was building this place up, telling me how idyllic it was. I suppose I'd have come anyway, though. I need the dough for school next fall. Jiff insists I go back to school."

"Jiff?"

"Render. That's what they call Render in the company. Because he works so fast, I imagine. Maybe it's short for Geoffrey."

"Old Jiffy," I mused, delighted with this inside view of the famous man. Somehow it made me feel really grown up to know that they called Mr. Render "Old Jiffy" in New York. "But really, I don't think he would even know there weren't any bars in Middleton," I said. "He stayed out at the Merricks' place. He probably didn't have a chance to learn anything about local customs out there."

"Of course not! He lives up in the clouds somewhere. He gets what *he* wants, no matter where he is," Nathan said fretfully, snatching up one of the kittens and rubbing her fur the wrong way with violence. "If he went to a strange city and *he* wanted a neighborhood bar someone would build it for him. 'Geoffrey darling, let me build you a tavern,'" Nathan said in falsetto, perhaps in imitation of Mrs. Merrick. "'Shall I get the mayor to rescind the foolish puritanical ordinance that is causing you undue thirst and loneliness? Shall we have your favorite bar torn down in New York and shipped down here? Oh it's a pub in London? That's no problem, darling.'"

"You'll have a lot in common with Mme LeBreton," I said, after considering this a moment. "When she comes back she can tell you where to buy alcohol. She seems to be able to get a lot," I said, hoping I was not saying too much about Madame's drinking.

"Let's hope," Nathan said, standing up to stretch. I looked up at him there on the steps and thought of the Empire State Building. He was rumpled, as if he slept in his clothes. I thought about another feature of New York City I knew about, the Bowery, which I associated with ragged clothes and a preoccupation with alcoholic beverages. I thought Nathan looked as if he might have come from the Bowery.

"Oh Nathan, I know it's hard for you!" I burst out. "But we're glad you stayed! You play so well! I love to dance to your playing. It's going to make a big difference."

"Really? You think so? Nobody's said a word this week," he said pathetically.

"They're just shy. You're so—different," I said, deciding to say "different" instead of "weird."

Nathan sat down again; I think I had pleased him. This is when he told me something about his life, most of which had been spent in New York City. He had hardly been out of New York: in fact he had never been farther south than Philadelphia. "It's not so bad down here, really," Nathan conceded after this. "I didn't wanna come, though, I can tell ya. Jiffy had to talk me into it; he had to keep talkin' all the way down here on the plane. Jesus, it's a long way."

"Is he nice, Nathan?" I asked earnestly.

"'Nice'?" Nathan scratched his head. "I don't think I'd say Jiff is *nice* exactly. He's a perfectionist, of course, yells and screams a lot. But he's always right. I don't know much about ballet, but I know he's a good musician. He's got perfect pitch. He can sight read anything and he plays better than me—"

"Oh no he doesn't!" I protested.

"He's got a great piano at home. It's a Chickering."

"You've been to his *house?"*

"His apartment, yeah, sure," Nathan said, sort of twitching his shoulders and pushing up his glasses. "He gives a big party every fall, and I went this year. He cooks dinner for the whole company, stagehands and everything. Jesus, what a mob."

"*That* sounds nice," I said. "What's his apartment like?"

"It's nice," Nathan said. "Fit for a king, of course. He's got a wonderful piano."

"What else besides the *piano*?"

"Pictures. A ton of pictures. Place looks like a friggin' museum. I think his wife had money."

"Wife?" I shouted. "What wife?"

Nathan pulled a long face and shrugged. "Excuse me. I thought he had a wife. Somebody said that, I thought."

"No, I really don't think so, Nathan," I exclaimed, my mind suddenly all atumble with the romantic troubles of Mr. Render and Mme LeBreton. "No no, there was no wife!"

"Okay, there was no wife," Nathan said agreeably. "I just thought somebody said there was. It's always good to have a wife when you're in the ballet business.

"*Not* that there's anything wrong with Jiffy," Nathan went on companionably. "Not the way *he* likes girls, the old goat."

"Girls?"

"I don't believe it," Nathan said, looking around at the trees. "I've never seen any evidence of it, but they say he sleeps with every girl in the *corps* to help him decide who to promote to soloist."

"Do they now, do they?" I murmured, trying to look blasé.

"I wouldn't blame him if it *is* true," Nathan said impartially. "There are some beautiful chicks in that company. That's one of the fringe benefits of working for a ballet company, the beautiful chicks.

"But there are some mighty cute little chicks around here too," Nathan said in a magnanimous way. "There's one in particular I like. I wish you'd tell me her name. A gorgeous little girl with a brown ponytail—"

"You must mean Melissa Martin."

"No, no, that's the one with the awful accent. No, this girl is gorgeous, like a peach."

"Oh," I said, understanding. "I think you mean Rachel Mintz."

"Rachel Mintz," Nathan said dreamily.

"She doesn't date much, though, Nathan," I cautioned. This was not true, but I wanted to prepare Nathan for being turned down. Rachel would surely turn him down, but it was not Rachel I was thinking about so much as her father. Knowing Dr. Mintz, I was positive he would not let Rachel date such a one as Nathan Feldman the piano player.

Nathan pronounced himself "starved" about this time, and as I finished rounding up the cats and doing the things I had come to do I had an impulse to invite him down to my house for lunch. But I decided I had better not. It would upset my mother to see this large, shambling boy, particularly when she realized that he was a regular at the studio these days and was actually on the premises when I went up to feed the cats. I knew it was very important to my mother's peace of mind to see the studio as an exclusively feminine place. (Claude was the exception that proved the rule, I expect she thought; and she seemed to think that Mr. Render, being bald and middle-aged, was harmless. I hoped she did not somehow hear the gossip about Mr. Render and the girls in the *corps.*)

Nathan and I left the studio at the same time, walking across the parking lot together. Nathan had a peculiar walk. At the same time as he tilted his head back, leading with the Adam's apple, he also pitched his upper body forward, swinging his right arm stiffly forward with each loping step in a way that looked military. Nathan was very serious about his walking: he frowned, he loped, he swung his arm; and I remember scampering along beside him over the rocks like the *obbligato* to a theme by Bruckner.

Once Nathan strode up toward the College Grill and I mounted my bike for home, I felt unsettled and depressed. I was upset at the idea of Mr. Render liking girls in the manner Nathan had described. I guess I felt rejected somehow, on my own behalf and that of Mme LeBreton, who still lay collapsed in the hospital. (I somehow knew that "girls" were a decorative and beguiling type which did not include either me or Mme LeBreton.) I was also bothered at the thought of Mr. Render living like a king in New York City. He had the manner of a king—I had seen this the preceding weekend in his imperious but waggish Old King Cole and his self-satisfied monarch of the counting house. Now I saw him surrounded by a harem of dancing girls drawn from the *corps de ballet* of NDT. All of a sudden it seemed foolish for us plain and simple dancers here on Sycamore Street to pin our hopes on such a man. Even such a weird specimen as Nathan Feldman thought we were plain: the only one of us he had found to admire was Rachel Mintz, and that was undoubtedly because she was Jewish like he was. She was the only Jewish girl in our class: to be Jewish in Middleton was even odder than to be Catholic, or a dancer.

***

The following week Mme LeBreton returned to the studio from her stay in the hospital looking pale and noticeably thinner. She had to sit down a lot, but she was clearly ready to get back to work. She was in a vibrant puce leotard with the matching skirt, the costume in which she looked best; she also had her stick back and, shouting sternly that we had a job to do, used it to brush away inquiries about her health.

Hawk-eyed, Mme LeBreton inspected the barre and some of the dances from *Mother Goose* and found all kinds of little laxities and even errors that had sprouted in the short space of one week, like weeds. She rooted these out with her stick. Meanwhile, Nathan played Bach and Chopin, Chopin and Bach, with serene elegance, and Mme LeBreton must have appreciated not having to whack the floor to bring Mrs. Fister in line.

I was not so sure that Nathan would appreciate Mme LeBreton, however. Probably because of the ironic and critical expression he always wore when he played the piano, I was afraid all through that first class that Madame was back he would break off mid-phrase, whirl around, and shout, "Hey lady, whaddya think you're doin'? Jiff doesn't do it like that!" But nothing like that happened. Nathan treated Mme LeBreton with great respect. For her part, Mme LeBreton was surprisingly friendly toward Nathan. The first day she was back I heard her invite him to come to her house for supper, and it was not long before they were regular cronies, talking and laughing with each other in just the way I had once expected her to do with her old, old friend Geoffrey Render. I got the idea that they spent quite a few evenings together, drinking and talking. I certainly never heard Nathan complain again about being lonely or thirsty.

By the way, Cecilia did not show up at the studio until the day after Mme LeBreton came back, and although it did not seem right, Cecilia's return was a lot more dramatic than her mother's. I came into the dressing room and there was Cecilia down on the floor, sitting with her face in her hands, sobbing without restraint. Several of her particular friends—Lola, Stephanie and of course Adelaide—were gathered around her. Adelaide was trying to get at her face with a wet washrag and they were all talking to her at once, and I couldn't understand what anybody was saying.

At first I thought this was remorse for shacking up with Charlie Hill: it was the broken, penitent, disheveled look I associated with the loss of virtue and reputation. But one of the girls down around Cecilia, one of her handmaidens, was saying, "He'll be back, he'll have a leave," which indicated that the problem was something else.

"What's happened?" I asked Rachel Mintz, who was part of a second tier of dancers gathered around Cecilia.

"Haven't you heard? Charlie Hill was inducted into the Army yesterday and he's already gone. It's going to *kill* Cecilia," she said, not taking her eyes off the tragic figure.

"Oh!" I said reverently. This was grief, not remorse! It was so much more respectable! I observed it with sympathetic interest. So Charlie Hill was gone. That was a surprise. He and his Chevrolet had become such fixtures in the parking lot I had come to think of them as permanent, like a large piece of statuary. I imagined Mme LeBreton must be glad, though: surely a mother, even one who seemed so unconscious of things, must be glad to have a boy like Charlie Hill removed from her daughter. And Claude! I wondered vaguely whether this was the working out of a curse by Claude. Charlie Hill off in the Army and Claude himself intertwined with Cecilia in all those *pas de deux:* this would have to work to Claude's advantage, I thought.

But there was a question for a while whether Cecilia would dance at all, and it was not until Mme LeBreton came and bent over her (I believe applying some pressure to Cecilia's shoulder or arm, perhaps even her ear—I could not see for the swirl of carmine net in Madame's skirt) that she consented to get up and go into the front studio. Then her handmaidens had to walk along with her, supporting her as if she were a young widow, or as if *she* were the one who had just gotten out of the hospital rather than her mother. In fact, Mme LeBreton seemed very spry compared to Cecilia those first few days, during which Cecilia looked stiff and haggard.

But I knew Cecilia would mend: all she had to do to be happy, in my view, was stop crying and look in the mirror. She did brighten day by day; she did dance, and Claude beamed at her, inhaling grandly and flaring his nostrils, looking deeply sensible of, and extravagantly grateful for, the extraordinary opportunity he had of being this beauty's cavalier. It was strange at first not to have Charlie Hill waiting outside in his black Chevrolet, but from then on Cecilia rode either with her mother or a handmaiden, and this seemed to me a much seemlier and more wholesome arrangement anyway.

16

Almost as soon as Mme LeBreton and Cecilia came back, the studio was plunged into a period that I was pleased to think of as much more "professional" than our life there in the past. This was never more true than on Saturdays—right away Mme LeBreton instituted Saturday rehearsals—when the whole cast of *Mother Goose* came together for day-long rehearsals. This included those twenty or thirty girls from rival dancing schools who were segregated into remedial classes with Adelaide during the week. Those Saturday rehearsals, with everybody toiling away, hurtling up and down the studio with fervent concentration, had a pell-mell, knockabout quality more like New York, in my mind, than anything Middleton had ever seen.

They also had a new kind of tension, which could be mistaken for plain old crossness anyplace but the studio. I discovered this one Saturday morning late in January, I believe, when I went up to my room after breakfast to dress for one of those taxing sessions. I opened the drawer where my clean leotards and tights were put away and shrieked, "Now she's done it!"

I ran down the steps with two pairs of leotards and tights. "They're ruined, positively ruined!" I shouted, unfurling them for my father, who sat in the library reading the *Chronicle.*

My mother was in the kitchen washing the breakfast dishes. "What are you shouting about, Meredith Louise?"

"Look what Lucille's done to my things," I said, heaving, presenting my beloved practice clothes to my mother. The leotards, which had been a well-seasoned slate, were now several shades lighter, about the color of weathered wood, and the tights, once a shell pink of great delicacy, were now very close to that same decayed color, with the added horror of some dribbly stains of a darker gray.

"I've told her and told her to wash them separately, in cool water," I ranted.

"It looks like she washed them together, in hot water," Mother observed.

"Exactly! Exactly! That's just what she did!" I said, hopping up and down.

"She probably thought they were already so faded they wouldn't fade anymore," Mother said, turning back to her dishes. "Poor old thing. She's so faithful. I'm glad she can't hear you raving like this."

"I might just call her up!"

Mother frowned at me. "Wear your others, Meredith!"

"My *others* are wet and stinky in the laundry bin! I wore my others yesterday! I'll have to wear shorts," I said wildly.

"Shorts?" Mother said, now showing some alarm. "Why, you can't wear shorts to your lesson. What would Mrs. LeBreton say?"

"Oh she won't care," I said, knocking crossly around the kitchen. I was thinking about other garments Lucille had ruined too: a favorite blouse with an umber scorch in the shape of an iron on the back, some miniaturized shorts. "Mme LeBreton wore pedal pushers to class yesterday. People are wearing different things now. We have people coming to the rehearsals who aren't in our school. Everybody doesn't dress alike all the time anymore." This was true. It had probably started on Saturdays with the Farfel girls in purple nylon, but already it had spread into our class. Just the other day Lola had worn a low-cut electric blue leotard to the advanced class; Christabel had appeared in something flimsy and pink. Neither had attracted the notice of Mme LeBreton.

"Really!" Mother said, stopping her dish-washing and coming over to the kitchen table, pulling out a chair and sitting down. "Is Mrs. LeBreton relaxing her standards, Meredith? I don't like to hear this. I've admired her discipline. It's so good for you girls. Is she going to get lax with all this new pressure?"

This postponement of dishes, this sitting down at the kitchen table by my mother was not a good sign. I knew right away that the fit of temper on my part had been a mistake: My mother and father were wary of *Mother Goose* and what it might do to me. They had not come out and said this, of course—all they had actually said was that it mustn't interfere with school. But I knew that they were concerned with my body, mind, and soul. They didn't want me to get too tired and possibly fall ill; they didn't want me to neglect my schoolwork; above all, they did not want me exposed to what might be called Bohemian attitudes and ways of life that might cause me to "grow up too fast." Somehow "discipline" retarded the dangerous growing-up process, and I could tell that my mother saw wearing shorts to the studio as much too loose.

"Naturally she's not getting lax," I said stoutly, with a light and wholesome laugh. "It's just that people are running out of clothes, especially at the end of the week, now that we're going more times. *Madame's* standards are higher than ever," I said, stressing the word "Madame" as if it were a rank, like Colonel. "You know," I said divertingly, "she rehearses us a lot more thoroughly than Mr. Render did. She drills us and drills us. We're going to know it so well!"

Mother evaluated this testimony while studying the leotards and tights sprawled out between us on the white kitchen table. "You can get some more wear out of these, can't you?" Mother said, thriftily fingering the dulled garments.

"Mother! I'd really be embarrassed to wear these now," I said, showing my high standards. "They don't look clean!"

"This gray knit would be useful for polishing silver," Mother said, brightening. "It's just the color of tarnish. And let's see, I could use these tights to strain things, or something. But you mustn't wear shorts, even today. I don't think Mrs. LeBreton would like it, even if she doesn't say anything. If you hurry, you could run up to Bartlett's and get new things before ten o'clock."

An hour later I came out of Bartlett's, looking guiltily up and down Tates Parkway carrying a parcel wrapped in brown paper that had something in it I was afraid Mme LeBreton might like even less than shorts. Four things in it, really: two pairs of tights and two leotards.

The leotards were a brand-new style, a simple little nylon tank with thin straps that looked more like a bathing suit than a leotard, more like underwear! And they were not black but new colors—jonquil and celadon, to be precise. The tights were *white*. I felt very daring. No one, not even the Farfel girls, had sported these leotards, which had just come in from New York, though Mr. Bartlett had told me that "the girls" would buy them up in a snap and I'd better grab the colors I wanted now.

I enjoyed my errand at Bartlett's. I had not had much occasion to go into Bartlett the Costumer (this is the quaint name Mr. Bartlett gave his shop, which was the only place to get costumes in Middleton). Ordinarily Mme LeBreton did all the ordering of leotards and shoes and so forth, and Mrs. Oleander, the school seamstress, handled the purchase of all the materials for our recital outfits. Besides, it wasn't the kind of place you browse. There was a cowbell on the inside of the door, and when you went in the little shop Mr. Bartlett would instantly pop out from behind some curtains which separated his showroom from his stockroom, like a cuckoo in a Swiss clock. Anyway, I did not stop in Bartlett's very often but I had been there enough to have an impression of a dusty place where a lot of costumes and the makings of costumes—bolts of rich theatrical fabrics and cards of luxurious theatrical "notions"—had not been moved in years and years, Middleton's theatrical needs being very modest. That day, though, things were hopping in Bartlett's. No other customer was in the store at the time, but I had a sense of brisk business and quick turnover. Mr. Bartlett rubbed his hands together when he described the other girls coming in to buy up the new style of leotard "in a snap." He had been thinking about retiring, he told me as he wrote out the ticket and made up the parcel, but *Mother Goose* was bringing in a great deal of business. Now, with the Merrick Theater opening up, he thought it might be "a whole new ballgame" in Middleton. Now, he said, he was thinking about opening up another store. I felt like a fellow professional engaging in this kind of show-business talk with Mr. Bartlett.

***

Down at the studio everything was all atumble, with dancers everywhere and a din of music and shouted directions. Our old leisurely surely routine at the barre and then in the center floor had been drastically foreshortened: now, it was just a warm-up. Where we used to do "the dance," the stately preparation for our numbers in the recital, we now hurled through the multifarious numbers for *Mother Goose*. What a difference! Where "the dance" had been a small and simple thing, easy to manage, something that you could practically hold in your hands, *Mother Goose* was huge and sprawling and unwieldy: we could only see small parts of it at one time. The main thing at first was to remember what Mr. Render had made up out of thin air (*"Croisé* here?" "No, *ouvert! Ouvert!"*), then to make our bodies do it all. Each of us had our own particular *bête noire* of a step—Claude's triple *tour en l'air, my multiple écartés,* the Trio's hurtling *pas de ciseaux.* Unlike Mr. Render, Mme LeBreton did not have the power to make us do more than we could do, but she was patient and methodical and, most important, optimistic. I thought she was a very capable stand-in for Mr. Render, and I was telling my mother the truth when I said her standards were as high as his.

I hoped Mr. Render was getting good reports. That day out at the theater he had asked Mrs. Merrick and Mme LeBreton to call him often in New York, but somehow I was sure that it was Mrs. Merrick who did this calling rather than Madame. I did not see Mrs. Merrick at the studio as often as I had thought I would, but when she did come she swept through, usually in furs, looking around and chatting and cosseting and *checking,* I thought, in a way that suggested that when she left the studio she was driven in that limousine to the nearest telephone, where she dialed New York. I did not like this drop-in approach. I thought she ought to keep reporting humbly to the studio in her leotard, as she had when Mr. Render was there; I thought she ought to sweat. But then I was still smarting from "Marie Taggly-onie" and for all I knew she was doing what the "Executive Director" was supposed to do.

There were some problems during this time: for one thing, people started getting hurt more often than usual. I think this was because we got a little obsessed with our dances, a little out of our heads about them: we talked about them a lot and, if I can regard myself as typical, we thought about them all the time, not just at the studio but at home too, or school, or church, or the few other places we had time to go. I think we dreamed about them; our arms and legs probably twitched like the paws of dreaming cats and dogs. When we actually came to *do* the steps and the movements, then we possibly tried too hard or got ahead of ourselves or were too careless with ourselves: in any case, people started getting hurt. Dorcas ripped a tendon doing a gangly *pas de chat,* Adelaide sprained an ankle during some bovine maneuver, and Albert Wasserman pulled a groin muscle, something I didn't even like to think about. Fortunately Dr. Stanley Mintz, Rachel's father, thought this studio full of pulled muscles and broken bones was an interesting professional opportunity, and he started coming to the Saturday rehearsals to hold a sort of informal bone and joint clinic in the back studio. He would also come over other times, late in the day, when there had been a particularly spectacular injury that left someone bent over on the Mothers' Bench or crumpled in a corner. Dr. Mintz was a remarkable presence in the studio. He was a well-known orthopedic surgeon; he was also as notable a civic leader as Mrs. Merrick, and often had his picture in the *Chronicle* in connection with some event in the medical community or some arcane activity at the synagogue. But primarily he was a former football player: that is what he talked about all the time, shouted about, rather, since he had the loudest voice I had ever heard. He had been a linebacker at Tulane University years before, which seemed to be the origin of his interest in torn-up limbs. He had no use for you if you were not in some kind of hurly-burly that tore up your bones and muscles, and I could not help but notice that Dr. Mintz had no use for Nathan, who had obviously never taken any exercise, except that funny loping walk, and Dr. Mintz did not even acknowledge his presence. I expect Nathan gave up on Rachel the first moment he saw Dr. Mintz.

The day I bought the leotards I pedaled furiously down to the studio, where hordes of dancers were already quick-stepping through the barre. Mrs. Merrick was strolling around the front studio with a stenographic pad while Mme LeBreton did the work; Dr. Mintz was in the back studio, thundering over some wound, with a line of other wounded dancers waiting to see him. I broke through these to get in the little bathroom, where I took off my clothes and put on my new white tights and celadon leotard with Claude-like speed. I came out nervous that everyone would stare at me in this irregular garb, afraid that all activity would stop and silence would fall, but of course this didn't happen and I just slipped into the fracas. There were too many people in the studio for me to get a good long look at myself in the mirror, but I got a shock of pleasure every time I flashed by a mirror, looking slim and muscular and even "professional" in the celadon. The outfit was a big success: a lot of girls told me they liked it. In fact, a lot of girls went up to Bartlett's and bought outfits like it, just as Mr. Bartlett had said they would; and in the end I felt grateful to Lucille, rather than angry. This, I know, was a relief to my mother.

***

I had on my new jonquil leotard not too long after that when something very nearly fatal happened. I had just reached the parking lot of the studio one afternoon in February. I must have been tired and distracted: I lived in dreams then, not the here-and-now, and I was probably thinking about Mr. Render, or the performance. In any case, I was not paying attention to what was going on around me, and I was frightened out of my wits when a yellow car zoomed backward out of the parking lot and very nearly hit me. I actually felt the wind from that car; it might even have grazed me. I'd had to do a little *soubresaut* to get out of its way, yanking my bike with me. I stood there trembling, watching the car. It did not seem to pause when it got to the street, it just reversed direction and shot like a bullet down toward my house.

The car was a Pontiac convertible, and it was jonquil-colored—the same color as my leotard, I'd tell the police, if the car did any hit-and-run damage. That's all I knew! But inside the studio I found out that the occupants of the mysterious car were well known. They were Wendell and Wexler Merrick, the legendary brothers of Christabel, and they had just brought Hilary James and Stephanie Sillerman to the studio. I should have guessed. I had been hearing about Wendell and Wexler for some time in dressing-room talk. Hilary and Stephanie had met them back around Thanksgiving at the Harvest Dance; then these bold girls had invited them to the Cotillion Club's Christmas dance; and I gathered that they often went out together now. After *Mother Goose* had been announced in early January I had worried about Hilary's pride, and Stephanie's too. But I needn't have: whatever damage Mr. Render had done to them, Wendell and Wexler had made up for it. Neither of them was the prima ballerina of *Mother Goose* but they were apparently the chosen ones of Wendell and Wexler Merrick. In contrast, Cecilia, who *was* the prima ballerina, was living like a nun because Charlie Hill was now in the Army somewhere in Germany. I thought rather longingly of Charlie Hill posted outside the studio in his black Chevrolet: *he* had never tried to run me down!

Anyway, Hilary and Stephanie had been dating Wendell and Wexler for about two months now, but this was the first time that those boys had delivered them to the studio. I was tremendously sorry I had not gotten a better look at them since they were supposed to be so handsome, also more than a little wild. It was quite extraordinary that these famous St. Stephen's boys had done something so tame as to bring Hilary and Stephanie to ballet—this was almost domestic of them—and Hilary and Stephanie were flushed and triumphant.

But I had the terrible feeling that Hilary and Stephanie were "growing up too fast." They seemed to have suddenly become a lot older than I was, not merely one year; and that phrase of my mother's seemed particularly apt because of the way their boyfriends drove. I could see that the situation was full of peril. That same day the yellow Pontiac was waiting outside in the parking lot when class was over. Hilary and Stephanie ripped off their toe shoes and, while I was still pulling on my slacks, they debouched into the cold night air. The banging of car doors was heard, then the same kind of helter-skelter departure as before. I listened anxiously: yes, the car once again plummeted down Sycamore Street and would pass my house. I imagined my mother and father inside, cocking their ears and identifying what they heard quite correctly as "reckless teenagers." They would go on to rue the conduct of young people these days and resolve to be more strict with me. Perhaps they would even go to the window, look out and see the fast car with dancers in it, and vow right then and there to take me out of the school. No, that was silly: it was dark, they would not be able to see who was in the car; besides, the car would be long gone before they could get to the window. But still, it could fail to make a curve and there could be a fiery accident that would be written up in the *Chronicle* next morning.

But that was really silly, I decided as I finished dressing and started home in my slower and more innocent fashion, following the smoking trail of the jonquil Pontiac on my bicycle. The *Chronicle* would never feature anything so discreditable to the Merrick scions as such an accident. As a matter of fact, I didn't think the *Chronicle* would print anything that would reflect unfavorably on any of our dancers. We were in the paper all the time these days—if not us, then Geoffrey Render. Mr. Render had just presented a new ballet in New York called *Transformations,* for instance, and the *Chronicle* had run a Sunday feature on it. We felt as if this feature was about us.

Such prominence in the community—fame, if you like—gave me a sense of confidence, even a sense of invulnerability. This smoothed my path at school. Almost imperceptibly during this time, the ballet studio had come to seem like my real life and Middleton High School my sideline, the tacked-on extracurricular obligation. Every day I went to ballet and also "took" school. As a result, where I used to creep through the halls of Middleton High like the lowliest worm, hardly daring to meet the eyes of my idol Paul Wheeless or my mentor Anne Markham, Editor-in-Chief of the *Merrymaker,* now I strode about more purposefully, less self-consciously, probably duck-footed, with my mind on *Mother Goose.* Sometime in February, I do not even remember exactly when, I attended a meeting of that Student Council committee to study and revise our school disciplinary code. Paul Wheeless was there, and I found myself talking with him face to face on some point in a perfectly calm and forthright way.

17

Ever since the trip out to the theater I had worried about Mme LeBreton and Mrs. Merrick and Mr. Render and how they were getting along. Specifically, I worried about Mrs. Merrick and Mr. Render pushing Mme LeBreton around. It was her school and we were her students, after all: this gala première business was just something added on, from the outside. Very occasionally Mme LeBreton's temper flared up, and I was afraid she would rear back and throw it off, so to speak, and restore the school to its quiet old routine.

I am thinking about one Saturday later on in February when the studio was bulging with about a hundred and fifty dancers—the whole cast—and Mme LeBreton was flailing away in the middle of them to organize the chaos and perfect the dances. I remember it very clearly: Adelaide was doing "Mary Mary Quite Contrary," backed up by a large number of little flowers, and I was marveling, as I always did, at the irony of Adelaide having such a good technique and yet looking so much like a fireplug, when there came a loud and constant knocking on the front door. I mean that door in the front corner of the studio which opened out onto the parking lot but which nobody ever used.

Nathan stopped playing and scowled down at the racket and Mme LeBreton said, "Get that, somebody," without looking up from a small blond flower, whose shoulders she was lowering as the little flower reached up for the sun with her arms in second position. I started for the door but Lola got there first. It was locked, of course, and while Lola fiddled with the lock, a little knob, the pounding went on. "I'm coming, I'm coming!" Lola shouted crossly. "Cut it out, will ya!" she added, which I thought was very sassy. It might be the police coming to accuse all or some of us of something. I thought vaguely it might have something to do with bills Mme LeBreton had forgotten to pay, or the way the Merrick boys drove.

"Postman!" a cheerful voice announced when Lola finally got the door open. We were anxiously crowding around the door but people began to fall away when they saw that it was just the postman with something too big to fit in the mailbox out front. "Something for the Madam!"

"God, I thought it was the big bad wolf," Lola grumbled after she re-locked the door. She was holding a firmly packed manila envelope with a lot of stamps and postmarks on it.

"I thought it was the police," I contributed.

Lola put the bundle in Mme LeBreton's hands and Mme LeBreton wandered over by the windows with it, not paying much attention to it but still watching and correcting the flowers. Casually, I stood behind her so I could see what it was. I already knew it was from Mr. Render because I recognized the handwriting: it was black and bold, just like the autograph on the picture of himself on the wall. Already stirred by the knocking, I felt very excited as Mme LeBreton ripped open the envelope and pulled out the thick stack of paper inside (shouting at the flowers all the while), and I tried to peer around her arm to read just what it was without attracting her attention. Like Lola, she was rather cross: these rehearsals were noisy, tiring things. On top was a letter from Mr. Render, in his handwriting, but Madame flipped that over before she had had time to read it, and then flipped rapidly through some more of the sheets. They were covered with unusual signs or symbols in more black ink. I knew what this was! Possibly I was the only one in the studio, apart from Madame herself, who would recognize this as the "notation" Mr. Render had been talking about on the way out to the theater. He *had* dictated *Mother Goose* to a scribe in New York! It *was* down on paper. This was a precious document, I thought, moving in closer. It was a record of all the work Mr. Render had done in this studio. Simply because of who he was it was already a historical document of some importance. I could imagine it in a glass case at a museum in New York City—no, right here in Middleton, out at the Merrick Theater, when it was finished. I could imagine Mrs. Merrick having a special display case set up in the lobby for it, since it was the record of her "gala première"; I could imagine her hiring a guard with nothing to do but stand beside it.

But as I was thinking of the glories of the document Mme LeBreton was trying to tear it in half. She didn't make a big show of this and, with everything else that was going on in the studio at the time, I don't think anyone besides me even noticed, but she was holding the thick stack of papers crosswise and trying to rip them. I was horrified, of course, and I actually moved toward the papers to try to save them, but I stopped myself. They were hers, at least they were for her use; besides, she couldn't tear them that way anyway. The paper was creamy and heavy—it looked thicker than ordinary typing paper—and she couldn't tear the whole stack any more than she could rip the Middleton telephone directory. This idea came as a great relief. I had been quite sympathetic to Mme LeBreton since that limousine ride where Mr. Render had said, flat out, that he didn't think she could remember *Mother Goose.* Since then she had worked so valiantly on it and, as far as I could tell, had remembered it so well in every particular that I could understand how insulted she felt by this notation. On the other hand, Mr. Render was a world-renowned genius, "the dean of American choreographers," as someone once called him, and this was the record of his new work, which would go in his canon along with *Encumbrances* and *Transformations* and the other ballets he had done recently for professional dancers. It was quite valuable for this reason alone.

But the next thing I knew Mme LeBreton was leaving the room. I trailed along behind as she went and shut herself up in the little bathroom. From the other side of the door I heard the ripping of paper, even over the noise of the piano and the feet in the front studio. I could have wept as I heard this ripping—she was clearly tearing each precious page into small pieces, then flushing them down the rusty old toilet. I was in despair about the notation; I was worried, too, about the plumbing. It was all I could do not to pound on the door as the postman had done. But I had to just stand there, with dancers pushing past me in their never-ending exchange between the front studio and the dressing room while Mme LeBreton flushed away the crisp and orderly diagrams of *Mother Goose*.

***

Mostly, though, the rehearsals just catapulted along to the enjoyment of all, I think, even unlikely people like Alma Doyle. I found this out the day I was able at last to take Marie home, the day that Marie and the others, Lucille Grahn, Fanny Ellsler and Carlotta Grisi, were observed to be eating cat food alongside Colette. I could not of course take Marie home on my bicycle, and Alma, who happened to be standing nearby, offered to give us a ride.

Alma thought Marie was just darling and went on and on about her as she moved some bags of groceries from the passenger seat of her old Dodge to the back seat.

"Why don't you get one of the kittens? I don't think they're all given away yet," I said, thinking of Alma and Tom and no baby. "Oh no, Tom's allergic to cats," Alma said proudly, heaving the last sack into the back.

"I wish Milly wouldn't keep us overtime like this," Alma said on the way down Sycamore Street, while I struggled not to yell: Marie had dug her claws into my leg and I could not pull them out. "I have to fix supper beforehand and let it cook while I'm at class, and Tom doesn't like it when it's overdone."

"He wouldn't," I gasped.

"I *like* my dances, though. I never dreamed I'd have a solo like the maid," Alma said, alluding to her minor part in "Sing a Song of Sixpence." "An old married lady like me. It's just the *cutest* thing I've ever had a chance to do. I *hope* I don't have to drop out."

Marie was still terrified after I got her into the house, by the way. As soon as I put her down she ran under the couch in the library and would not come out. And that's where she stayed, most of the time, in spite of my devoted efforts (cheek to floor, one hand groping around in the dark crevice) to get her out. She was, I had to admit, a strangely timid cat. "Neurotic," my father said. "Only cat I ever saw with agoraphobia."

I could not understand this. Marie had been born and bred in that studio with all those people stomping around in wooden-toed shoes that could probably kill a kitten if they stepped on it. I had handled her a lot, practically from birth. But now that she was in our house, which was always quiet, except for chamber music, and certainly always safe, she was scared out of her wits. I suppose she missed her mother and her sisters; maybe she even missed all the people. In any case, she meowed a lot from under the couch. She was a little cat, but she had a big reverberating meow, suggestive of the most horrible desolation. Like her coloring, this too was a good imitation of a real Siamese.

18

Mrs. Oleander, the school seamstress, paid her first visit to the studio that year sometime in February. When I saw her bulbous old Plymouth in the parking lot I felt a certain twirling in the bowels, which for me is the first symptom of stage fright because her first appearance each year indicated that a performance was imminent, sort of the way a robin is supposed to be the first sign of spring. When we saw Mrs. Oleander we knew we were really going to have costumes made and go out on a stage in them before the public.

Mrs. Oleander always came to *us* for the several measurings and fittings necessary to the construction of the costumes, by the way; we never went to *her,* probably because her house was way across town in the other high school district. The day I am talking about, Mrs. Oleander was waiting for us in the back studio with her tape measure. She still had the same outmoded crimped hairstyle she had had the year before, and the year before that, and she still wore the same little black slacks with the knees practically worn out, and white nurse's oxfords, which gave this garb the air of a uniform. As usual, she had brought one of her little tow-headed daughters with her.

I sighed at the sight of Mrs. Oleander. At one time I had hoped for a more elegant seamstress for the gala premier—possibly a French lady from New York or some Russian ancient who had sewed for Diaghilev; but Mrs. Oleander was one of the local people we were using to save time and money. Frankly I was afraid the costumes for a production the scale of *Mother Goose* were beyond her ability. Her methods were so slapdash and irregular! They had worked well enough for the tutus and tunics of recitals past, though sometimes bodices did not stay attached to skirts, sleeves did not stay in armholes, but here Mrs. Oleander was called upon to make a bewildering variety of costumes—animal costumes, plant costumes, and costumes for people of every type. Mr. Render had had the costumes designed in New York and they had not sent Mrs. Oleander any patterns, just a stack of watercolor drawings. I looked through these that first day she came, wondering how on earth they would be a sufficient guide for measuring, cutting and sewing: they were just impressionistic sketches by a New York designer, not the firmly delineated art of the Simplicity or Butterick staff. I *did* hope she wasn't going to get frustrated—or offended, like Mme LeBreton—and tear them up.

"Now, this dawg costume is going to be a pain in the neck," Mrs. Oleander said when she did the first measuring on me. She was scooting around on her knees, with a row of pins in her mouth. She had a monotonous, droning voice which never stopped. "That dawggone fur is hard to work with. It's not like your satin or your muslin. It sheds like a real dawg does in the summer and I just know I'm going to be takin' my machine apart ever whipstitch to pull the durn lint out. I'd just as liefer work with bathmats. I told Mizriz Merrick them mice was going to look like bathmats runnin' acrost the stage.

"Course," Mrs. Oleander added, "maybe they will look more like mice with them *masks* on."

Mrs. Oleander's tone in reference to the masks was suspicious and a little resentful. Her skill definitely did not extend to making animal masks; these had been ordered from Dallas.

"Says here you have to have plenty of room," Mrs. Oleander said, squinting skeptically at some of Mr. Render's handwriting under the sketch of the dog costume.

"I jump a lot," I explained.

"Well let's make sure you have plenty of room in the crouch," Mrs. Oleander said, running the tape measure swiftly between my legs.

"How can you sew all these costumes?" I said nervously during this assault. There were three or four hundred costumes and she only had two months. I knew Mrs. Oleander had a family to take care of: a husband, who worked at some factory (I had seen him once—a tall, thin man with a surprisingly distinguished face), also four or possibly even five daughters, it was hard to tell since they all looked alike except for their varying sizes and I had never seen all of them at once. Right now the one who had come with her (a fairly big one—nine or ten years old) had squatted down on the floor and was alternately running her fingers through Colette's litter box and picking her nose.

"Now don't do that, Altona," Mrs. Oleander said at the same speed and pitch as usual. (Never a pause! Never an inflection!) I could imagine her old Plymouth operating just like her voice, climbing up Sycamore Street to the parkway, going down the parkway past the high school and farther and farther into town all the way over to that unknown and, to my mind, uncharted industrial sector where she lived, without stopping and without ever going higher than second gear. Now with "Altona" doing what she was doing I could barely keep myself from running over to her and yanking her out into the little bathroom to run hot water on her hand (try to boil it!), but after this single remark Mrs. Oleander turned her attention back to me and continued talking.

"I can finish this thing easy as pie. I sew all night lots of the time when Otto has the night shift. I don't need much sleep so sometimes I sew all day and all night. Sometimes I think I might just go off my head from hearing that sewing machine day and night. But these here things'll run up real fast if it wasn't for the lint. Now your satin is faster than your fur. Your satin runs up real clean."

From then on Mrs. Oleander came to the studio frequently, bearing bolts of material which she whacked into pieces and pinned on all of us in turn. One day I watched her do Claude up in blue velvet flaps that would be his Little Boy Blue tunic. Claude couldn't abide Mrs. Oleander, and any time she did fittings on him he stood in an openly belligerent stance with his arms folded and his torso swelled, like an old boxing print.

"Could you possibly hurry?" he said through clenched teeth as she whipsawed him with the tape measure. "I need to get back to work. I'm getting cold."

"You sure don't feel cold, son, you feel hot as a pistol. I'm afraid y'all are bigger than usual when you're that hot. It's like tryin' on shoes at the end of the day. They tell you not to try on shoes at the end of the day because your feet are all spread out."

"I *assure* you, Mrs. Oleander, I'll be hot when I dance Mr. Render's choreography. We all will," Claude said frigidly.

"Yes sir I am sure you will," Mrs. Oleander said. She looked around at me and winked. "And them mice in the bathmats is going to be the hottest of all."

At last Mrs. Oleander finished pinning the flaps on Claude. She ran a hand over his posterior, and although I was all the way across the room I could see him shudder. Then she began unpinning the flaps and throwing them in a crude heap on the floor; Claude helped impatiently, springing away from her and bounding out of the room at the first possible moment.

Mrs. Oleander droned on. "Why, that young'un smells like a skunk, don't he? My husband Otto smelled like that wunst, after they had an explosion out to the plant and he had to work all night to get somebody's head out of a machine. I made him take off his uniform the minute he come in the front door so I could put it in the warsh even though it was five o'clock in the morning. I caint stand the smell a sweat, it makes me feel faint. I wouldn't want any a my girls to take dayncin because of it. I'd have to warsh them leotars the minute they come in the front door."

Mrs. Oleander went on for some time in this delicate vein. Meanwhile Altona stood in the corner sucking her thumb and meditatively scratching her "crouch."

***

Gradually the costumes began to take shape. Mrs. Oleander trudged in from time to time with a load of their vivid fragments heaped across her arm or loaded onto the back of one of the towheaded daughters. She didn't seem to think these pieces were anything out of the ordinary—they might as well have been a load of Otto's uniforms for the "warsh" for all the notice she took of them—but I thought they were most intriguing. The materials alone were fantastic: furs and feathers and jewels and chiffon and lace. There were rough fabrics like kettlecloth and hopsacking for the beggars and smooth fabrics like satin and panne velvet for the royalty. Indeed it looked as though Mrs. Oleander had been instructed to buy out the entire stock of Bartlett the Costumer. I thought I might just love the costumes for *Mother Goose,* even though they were not the kind of ballet finery we had wanted when we dreamed of a *ballet blanc.* I even liked my dog suit, though the fur was obviously fake and did not glisten the way Mrs. Merrick's coats did; and there was a certain reckless gaiety about the Jack Be Nimble costume, a jumpsuit-type garment made of red and white satin strips sewn together in the manner of a flag.

Some of the costumes were a little worrisome, however. Cecilia's Peter Pumpkin's wife's costume, for example, seemed too provocative for the Middleton stage. My mother wouldn't approve of it, I knew. It was not a tutu but a little dress, a skimpy thing, just slightly longer than a leotard. The material was a soft clinging nylon just like underwear is made out of. And it was red, or a kind of reddish orange, no doubt to provide a fiery, willful-looking complement to the duller, domestic orange of the pumpkin. I watched Mrs. Oleander mindlessly drape Cecilia's curves with this fabric, and I noticed that after all the flaps were pinned on, a great deal of Cecilia's scoop-neck leotard was still visible across the front, which suggested that a great deal of Cecilia would be visible when she danced in this costume. I guess the designer in New York thought this would help show why Peter was having such a tough time keeping her; and I blushed when I thought of Claude staring at her, lovestruck, as she climbed on out of the pumpkin despite his best efforts.

I was also a little concerned about one of Claude's costumes. This, the one for Robin Redbreast, consisted only of a pair of brown tights and a red sash with a rosette on it. I happened to be in the back studio when Mrs. Oleander brought the sash for Claude to try on. He flexed his arms very quickly and his T-shirt was off. Mrs. Oleander looked horrified as he put on the red sash and the rosette, and I could tell she didn't like it that his chest and back were sweaty.

"Don't worry, Mrs. Oleander, I'm going to shave my chest and underarms," Claude said, adjusting the sash. Mrs. Oleander looked sick, as if she was going to lose her lunch.

***

During this time the sets for *Mother Goose* were being built somewhere up at the college, though we did not know much about them until the day Mr. Beldinsky, the set designer, visited the studio. Mr. Beldinsky taught art at the college and was also a very popular artist on the local scene. I was familiar with his work, which hung in various public buildings around town, including our bank, also in numerous private collections, so I was told. Thinking back, I remembered seeing one at old Mrs. Merrick's house. His work was very distinctive and stood out clearly even in crowded places like that: it was always birds—not real looking birds or even idealized birds (nothing like the work of John James Audubon, that other famous painter of birds in Louisiana), but stark staring stylized birds in brash colors like fuchsia and turquoise and lime.

Mr. Beldinsky was a startling contrast to his wild-looking work. I had seen his picture in the *Chronicle* and would have recognized him anywhere with that sweet, almost cherubic face, that head as big and bald as Mr. Render's, but I did not know until I saw him in person how totally devoid of living color he was. He looked like a very sweet boy who had lost his hair, except for a small silvery fringe, and all his color, possibly on account of some illness. He stared intently at everything, and this too spoke of some nervous uncertainty or illness of the nerves, though I took into account that this might just be the artistic vision.

When Mr. Beldinsky came to our class, bringing with him a small plywood model of the Merrick Theater stage and little sets and props he had designed to go in it, Mme LeBreton and Nathan dragged the Mothers' Bench out of the corner for him to display this on and we all sank to the floor around it like children at a puppet show.

I had been concerned about what kind of sets Mr. Beldinsky would dream up since his pictures were so garish, to my taste, but I thought the little model was perfectly charming. It was carefully and vividly (but not too vividly) painted and featured two basic sets, one for the meadow and humble house of Act One, and one for the King's apartments and his vast garden of Act Two. The Act One scene was dominated by the meadow with a river running "through" it (actually painted in peacock blue on the backdrop) and a big London bridge suspended over it. The bridge was to be made of large Styrofoam blocks, Mr. Beldinsky explained in his sweet voice, staring at the model of it. There was a road across this meadow, slightly elevated so that it would be visible to the audience in the theater, and Mr. Beldinsky pulled little wooden trees and bushes out of his pockets for the meadow, and a little clock, stool, cupboard, bed, and even a cute little tuffet for the interior of the humble house. Separate backdrops, which he reeled out by means of a tiny pulley, would supply the town skyline and the hill as they were required. For Act Two there was a palace and its environs, with more little wooden props in the form of a wall, which Humpty Dumpty would fall off of and which would then rotate to expose Humpty Dumpty's shards; a pumpkin; a clothesline; a giant shoe; and more backdrops to represent the blaze of noon and then the dark of night, illuminated only by a great glowing moon. Mr. Beldinsky tinkered with these things, showing their wonderful ingenuity, now leaning down to pull little wires to show how the fly system would whisk Mother Goose on stage and then hurl both the Old Woman in the Basket and the cow up and over the moon, separately of course.

"That's brilliant, Bob, but it looks like it would cost about five million and take ten years," Madame remarked from behind us.

"Nonsense, Milly," Mr. Beldinsky said sweetly, staring at her, then tinkering with the little pieces of the set some more. It was curious to see a grown-up take so much pleasure in these little toys. "We've already started on it, and we're using the cheapest materials," he said, '*papier-mâché,* gold foil paper, crepe paper. Gaudy stuff, a lot of it, but we'll give the illusion of something very rich. Geoffrey used the word 'profusion' to me," he said pedantically, removing the fluttery little cloth that had the picture of the moon on it and folding it into a tiny square, putting it into his pocket.

I looked skeptically at his model, which looked like a fairy tale to me. Of course it was in fact intended to represent the rhymes in *Mother Goose,* fairy tales of a sort, but what I mean is that it looked like a fantasy that would never exist in reality. It reminded me of something.

I couldn't think what, right at first, then it came to me: Dr. Coppélius's workshop! One of the ballets I had seen performed by a touring company in Middleton was *Coppélia,* about the old magician Dr. Coppélius and his workshop where he made dolls or puppets, including his waxen "daughter" Coppélia. He had the insane idea of conjuring these creations into real life. Mr. Beldinsky's plans for the sets reminded me of that mad scheme. In fact, the whole studio, what with the costumes and the feverish work and now the little model, reminded me of Dr. Coppélius's dark fantastical workshop, so far removed from ordinary life. Of course Mr. Render was the Dr. Coppélius in the case, not this colorless gentleman Mr. Beldinsky—Mr. Render, the mad dreamer! The slave driver!

"Oh, there's one more thing!" Mr. Beldinsky said joyously. We sat staring at the colorful little set as raptly as he did: no one had said a word or moved a muscle. Mr. Beldinsky leaned down over the model and pulled something within its wings, a string I suppose, whereupon the components of the London Bridge arching over the stage came apart and fell clattering down, knocking down other little wooden props and skittering with them all over the stage and even out on the Mothers' Bench and onto the floor. Everyone burst into applause; and Mr. Beldinsky warmed into a flesh tone by blushing as he laughed and bowed.

BOOK FOUR

THE RITE OF SPRING

19

"Do it again!" Madame shouted to the dancers. "If you don't get those *pas de chevals* exactly together, Mr. Render's going to throw every one of you out of the show. It's in five weeks, people. Thirty-five days from now."

All the king's horses and all the king's men skulked into place again in the center of the studio. Everybody else just sighed and sipped a Coke or opened a new piece of gum (though in the old days Madame would never have tolerated the presence of Cokes or gum in the studio); nobody really paid any attention to the tirade. It was a Saturday rehearsal with the studio jammed to the rafters, no different from a hundred rehearsals that went before it except that it was the day of the Mothers' Spring Bazaar and everybody would have preferred to be over there rather than here doing the same old thing, over and over and over again.

The annual bazaar was always at Trinity Episcopal Church in Gilbert Oaks. Trinity is one of the few Gothic-style buildings in Middleton, and I always thought I was in England when I went over there and stood on the green, green lawn beyond the quaint spires of the church. Despite the fact that it is usually windy and cold in March, the Mothers always set up tables under the trees to display their famous homemade candies and cookies and handicrafts with a ballet theme. They even served punch to the customers. Unfortunately an aggressive breed of stinging caterpillars came out every year about that time, and sometimes the caterpillars would drop out of the trees onto the fancy wares or even into the punchbowl, which made everyone, Mothers and customers alike, run screaming across the greensward. But I always enjoyed stopping by the bazaar: it was one of those fashionable Middleton gatherings with lime sherbet punch that I probably would not have attended had I not taken ballet at the LeBreton School.

This year the Mothers' Bazaar was a great deal bigger than it had been in the past because there was a crying need for money. I mean this quite literally because by the middle of March Mrs. Merrick was crying about money every time she came to the studio. It seems that costs always get out of hand when you build a theater and try to put on something impressive in it, and this enterprise was no exception. Mrs. Merrick did not complain directly to the dancers, but I gathered that she thought Mrs. Oleander and Mr. Beldinsky were spendthrifts without a shred of conscience between them; she also complained that the construction crew out at the theater (not yet finished!) wanted too much money for too little work. Anyway, the Mothers, ever resourceful, had vowed to help meet the unexpected expenses. This year there would be raffles to give away a Cadillac and a television set donated by local merchants, also a brace of Mr. Beldinsky's birds.

But when the day came, bright and clear, and everybody in Middleton was strolling around the green grounds of the Episcopal Church, we were immured in the studio, rehearsing. The dancers were cross. That was the day Hilary kicked Adelaide in the shin for coming out in center floor to begin "Three Blind Mice" before she, Hilary, had finished her elaborate curtsy for "Curly Locks"; it was also the day— one of the days, rather—that Albert Wasserman dropped Melissa in the course of the shoulder-sit in "Jack and Jill," and she burst into tears.

I had my own problems. That morning Mme LeBreton had come up to me to say that Alma Doyle had dropped out of the production and I was going to have to take her solo as the maid in "Sing a Song of Sixpence." I had noticed that Alma had missed several rehearsals before that but hadn't thought much about it; I had just vaguely attributed her absence to the exigencies of Tom. But in fact Alma had resigned from the school. "This was just too much for her," Madame said, indicating the chaos of the studio, and I nodded. It could be too much for anybody after a while, particularly the quiet, domestic Alma.

Well, Alma gone! I thought, without too much regret, since she was "old" and not very good company. Besides, I was delighted to have the part, which was that of a girl and carried with it a costume that was a dress. Later in the day I learned the maid's dance in five minutes. It was very simple, as befitted Alma, mainly the miming of hanging out clothes. But I had this annoyance: the dance ended with one of the four-and-twenty blackbirds *chasséing* over and snapping off my nose. This blackbird was Melanie Richfield, a sixth grader who tweaked my nose a lot harder than she had to, then laughed about it, which got me pretty mad. Madame made us go over and over this, which did not make the day any more pleasant.

If the dancers were cross, though, Mme LeBreton was the crossest of us all. Nothing was right, nothing pleased her, and she kept reminding us that Mr. Render was coming back in just three weeks and would probably throw us all out of the show. What's he going to do when he finds out about his notation, I wondered grimly, dancing my heart out for Madame. Mr. Render loomed over the rehearsal, just as he had loomed over all the rehearsals for the past three months. During this time he had come to seem like a vindictive spirit in the vague shape of a genie. From the first I had thought of Mr. Render as a genie, but now the genie seemed threatening—an enormous personage with a bald head and an earring, his arms folded, at present confined in a jar up in New York but soon to be released so that he would swell out over the horizon and blot out our prospects for a bright future in the ballet.

***

It was so sunny and beautiful some days in March that year that going to rehearsals at the studio was like going down into the mines. "The children need a break," Mrs. Merrick said to Mme LeBreton a few days after the Spring Bazaar we had not been let out for. She was making one of her sporadic inspections of the studio. "I want them to come out to the house Saturday and spend the day. Just this class, none of the little children. None of the mothers. We'll swim all day."

"Good God, Lyda, they'll all catch pneumonia," Madame said. Sure enough, through the casement windows behind her you could see the branches of the pine trees flailing in the March wind.

"That's no problem. The back pool's heated," Mrs. Merrick said. I was thrilled ("back pool"! was there more than one?) and also surprised. I had gotten used to thinking of Mrs. Merrick as selfish and calculating, but this was very nice of her! She sounded very nice making this invitation, much nicer than Madame.

"No, they need to rehearse Saturday," Madame said peremptorily. "I can't call off a rehearsal three weeks before performance."

"Let us go, let us go, oh *please* let us go," a lot of dancers wailed, myself among them. I felt caged all of a sudden and Mrs. Merrick seemed to be opening the door. It would be wonderful to go out in the sun: we had been shut up so long in that dark little studio with the flickering fluorescent lights our skins were white and soft, like the undersides of mushrooms grown in the deepest part of the forest. It would also be wonderful to have a change of scenery, and I could not think of better scenery than that place which Mr. Render had called a paradise. It was very kind of Mrs. Merrick to offer the warm waters of the "back pool" to the dancers, many of whom had been injured in the strenuous rehearsals of the last three months and all of whom were chronically sore. I had landed awkwardly from one of my écartés recently and bruised my foot, and I yearned to sink into the warm and soothing water of the heated pool, which no doubt had curative powers.

"Well, I guess we can go," Mme LeBreton, said grudgingly. "Take plenty of wraps, though," she shouted over the cheers that broke out.

20

That Saturday morning, then, this most unusual thing happened: instead of gearing up for yet another rehearsal at the studio I was riding out to the fabled Merrick place. Because it was so far out, a good ten miles southeast of the edge of town, I had worked out a car pool with Dorcas and Rachel. My father was driving us out there. It was a clear morning, still very cold even though it was ten o'clock, and the three of us sat in the back seat under the big bags of clothing and towels and other equipment our mothers thought we needed for this day in the country.

We had to go down all kinds of twisting and turning back roads before we got to the entrance of the Merrick estate, marked by a great wrought iron gate which spelled "Merrick" in big arching letters across the top. We then went down another long road, much too long to be called a "driveway," through wooded grounds which looked perfectly natural but which I knew must be landscaped and tended by experts (*our* scraggly yard was perfectly natural!). Finally, with the turning of a curve, the house hove into view and Dorcas, who had been hanging over the front seat, panting, shouted, "Gol! That's her *house?*" It was a mansion of gray stone with a lawn even more lush and green than that of the Trinity Episcopal Church. Certainly the house was larger than that church: it had three stories and a thousand windows, some of which had balconies or terraces with blue-and-white striped awnings over them. The other windows glinted in the morning sun, like Mrs. Merrick's diamond.

"Is that a house or a hotel?" Dorcas asked querulously.

I felt very humble in the Chevrolet as we approached this magnificent dwelling. It might have been better if Dorcas's parents had driven, or Rachel's: they both had Cadillacs. But it was our Chevrolet, which was plain and three years old, that rolled up to the front. By now the road had turned into a gravel drive, and a Negro man, not the chauffeur I knew but another Negro, was working over this gravel with a rake. I had never seen gravel receive this kind of attention, nor had the others, I think. Dorcas gave me a painful rabbit punch on the arm.

My father rolled down his window and said, "Excuse me, sir. I have some girls for the swimming party. Do I let them off here?" It didn't seem likely. There was a porte-cochère at the front entrance which looked formal, even ceremonial. It looked like a bride and groom might come running through it, laughing in the rice, followed by hundreds of guests; it didn't look like an entrance for casual ingress and egress, particularly by three teenagers with bags of clothes, like hoboes.

"Nawsir, nawsir," the man said thoughtfully, leaning on his rake, "you want de back pool. Jes drive on round back there, you'll see it down at the foot of that hill yonder."

Around to the back of the house we saw a stretch of velvety green lawn before a gentle hill or declivity, then another incredible stretch of flowering grounds which, way in the distance, turned into a heavy forest, but no pool.

"That must be it," I said, pointing to a brick structure at the foot of the hill some distance away. It had high brick walls espaliered with delicate little trees or bushes; it did not appear to have a roof. It looked more like some kind of fortification than a swimming pool, but then I saw the turquoise flashes of the therapeutic waters as the car eased up to the big iron gate.

"Thank you, Mr. Jackson!" Rachel and Dorcas said, clambering out of the car.

"Thank you, Daddy," I said.

"Now, you remember what your mother said," my father reminded me. "Don't get chilled and don't swim for half an hour after you eat. Don't eat all day long either," he said.

"Yes, yes, Daddy," I said, waving the Chevrolet away.

"He's in there," Dorcas said, coming upon me and grabbing my arm. "He's *in* there," she said balefully.

"Who, Wendell, or Wexler?" I said, smiling, anxious to join in the fun. I still had never actually seen Wendell and Wexler Merrick. I moved to go in the elaborate gate. Rachel was hanging on it; she had dropped her hobo pack on the sidewalk.

"Mr. Render," Dorcas said, her eyes bugging out.

This news hit me like a sandbag. I gasped. I too ran up to the gate and hung there, letting my gear fall where it might, and stared inside. Oh my Lord yes: there was Mr. Render, sitting at one of the tables next to the gigantic pool, looking as though he had just finished a swim. He had a dark beach robe on, with his little white legs sticking out of it, and a towel hung around his neck. His face was turned up to the sun and he was smiling a smile of perfect contentment. He looked asleep.

"Jesus," Dorcas said, joining me and Rachel at the gate, "there he is."

Possibly Mr. Render heard this, because he opened his eyes and turned them upon us.

"Mr. Render!" I called out recklessly through the gate. "Gosh! We didn't think you would be here!"

Geoffrey Render lifted up an arm in salute; he kept it there as he spoke. "The little girl with the cat! Hello! Where's your cat? Doesn't it swim?"

***

We spent the morning in the pool—the class did, at any rate. The adults—Mr. Render, Mme LeBreton, Nathan, and of course our hostess Mrs. Merrick—spent their time beyond the deep end of the pool in the rich shade of another blue and white-striped awning—what they called the cabana—sharing a pitcher of drinks. It was clear that no one had expected Mr. Render to be here: he had just popped up the night before, it seemed. Mrs. Merrick looked flustered; Mme LeBreton, on the other hand, seemed quite calm, even bored. Where Mrs. Merrick, who was wearing a flattering black swimsuit and a white eyelet beach coat, fluttered around the cabana telling the several servants what to do about food and drink, Mme LeBreton lay languidly on a chaise longue. She was wearing a long caftan in one of her shades of red, also sunglasses and a floppy straw hat, even though she was in the shade; and she appeared not to have the slightest intention of swimming, though swimming was clearly the order of the day. Nathan sat in attendance upon Mr. Render and Mme LeBreton. He obviously did not intend to go swimming either, as he had on his usual conglomeration of khakis.

For a while we girls played Marco Polo, a rude and noisy water game that is similar to blindman's buff. I tried to take an interest in it, though I thought at the time that the game was just a mask for the extreme tension everybody felt on account of Mr. Render. Running true to form, none of the dancers said much about his astounding presence, just acted very silly. It is possible that Hilary and Stephanie were the silliest of them all. I noticed they kept their eyes on the entrance gate rather than the person who was "it," even when the silly game was at its climax. By that time everybody in our class had arrived except for Claude, who was always late, and the new boy, Albert Wasserman, and I knew that Hilary and Stephanie weren't waiting for either of *them*. It wasn't hard to figure out that they were expecting Wendell and Wexler Merrick, who ought to be home from school of a weekend and who might well be expected to drop in on such a festive occasion as this. But before too long Hilary and Stephanie got tired of waiting. They jumped on Christabel and shouted something in her ear.

"Mama, Mama," Christabel yelled, her hair all bedraggled like seaweed and her nose running unchecked in the excitement of the game, "where are the monsters?"

Mrs. Merrick came out of the gloom of the cabana and stood in her white beach coat with a hand shading her eyes. "What, darling?"

"Where are Wen and Wex?" Christabel yelled impatiently. "They want to know," she added, pointing at Hilary and Stephanie, who gave little cries of horror and sank beneath the water.

"Oh darling!" Mrs. Merrick said helplessly. "I couldn't have the boys here! You know that! They flew with Daddy to Longview. Tell the girls they'll have to see Wendell and Wexler another time," she said, since the girls were still embarrassed under the water.

"Well where *are* they?" Hilary demanded of Christabel when she resurfaced.

"Gone to London, to visit the queen," Christabel retorted, treading water and laughing, very pleased with herself. Hilary and Stephanie jumped her and pulled her under the water, making a maelstrom out of that part of the pool.

***

Mr. Render was taking great delight in the pleasures of the day. In that dark beach coat—a heavy-looking brown-and-white striped robe that seemed inspired by the burnoose—he made me think of some desert chieftain who has been on a long hard journey over the sands but has now reached an oasis. I sat on the edge of the pool down by the cabana, which was not unlike a sumptuous tent, and listened to Mr. Render behind me.

"Try these fabulous shrimp," Mr. Render exclaimed to someone in the cabana as I dangled my feet in the water. The pool was dark turquoise here and appeared to be bottomless, like some volcanic lake. "I've never eaten shrimp so large and tender. Why, this one's the size of a horseshoe."

"You're such a hog, Geoffrey," Madame murmured.

"No I swear it is. Just look at it. She knows what will please me," he said complacently. "Last night when we got in from the airport she had that wonderful cook waiting up with softshell crabs for me. I ate six! Can you imagine that? They were glorious. Of course I had perfectly dreadful dreams all night long. I dreamed about my board of directors. Mainly Anthony, Nathan."

"Anthony. Ha ha!" Nathan said appreciatively. I had noticed earlier how he sat looking at Mr. Render adoringly, as a dog looks at his master.

"But Anthony is so far away," Mr. Render went on luxuriously. "Here I'm surrounded by beautiful women and a whole pack of mermaids. Look at those lovely girls, they could be mermaids. I love the way young dancers look in bathing suits. Such fine long muscles. Cecilia looks glorious, Milly. I'm glad to see Cecilia looking so well."

The party was in full swing now. Claude arrived, along with Albert, and after greeting Mr. Render (they were bowled over, of course) they disappeared into the bathhouse to change. I forgot about them until Dorcas dropped down beside me in a jackknife position and whispered desperately, "Look at Albert! Will you look at that *suit?* That's the most embarrassing suit I've ever *seen,* I can't *believe* he's wearing that suit out here in broad daylight!"

Albert Wasserman was walking the length of the pool, opposite from where we sat, in a slow prance. His suit *was* astounding: not trunks but briefs in a clinging material of incandescent blue. His thick body, chunky with useless muscles, narrowed down to these tiny, lumpy briefs.

"You can see his thing, you can really *see* it, if he'd just turn around," Dorcas said urgently. Howls went up from the mermaids, who dunked each other and turned flips in the water in their amusement at Albert. Albert seemed oblivious to this, which was not, after all, so different from the commotion caused by Marco Polo. He took a seat at the glass-topped table where I had first seen Mr. Render and began applying suntan lotion to his thighs.

"See! See!" Dorcas said, giving me rabbit punches on the upper arm. "Oh Lord, here comes Claude!"

As Dorcas scuttled away there was a tremendous wrenching noise to my right caused by Claude on the diving board. Claude made several mighty leaps on the board with his feet together and his toes pointed, his chest expanded to its manliest maximum, every rib showing—leaps which, if performed at the studio, we would have called *soubresauts.* After five or six of these leaps Claude sprang from the board like an arrow shot from a crossbow and cut into the water. He did not come anywhere near the mermaids, who were down the pool a way in water not more than seven or eight feet deep; nevertheless they all screamed prolonged, thrilling screams with heavy vibratos which lasted a long time after he had disappeared into the water. At first I could not see where he had gone; then gradually he waggled into view, growing larger and larger and finally popping out of the water with a crash, grinning horribly. The mermaids screamed again as he paddled around the deep end, spewing water and laughing.

"It is good to be here," Mr. Render pronounced. "Isn't this splendid, Nathan? Nathan my boy, where's your suit? Aren't you going to swim?"

"I've never been swimming in my life, Mr. Render," Nathan said humbly.

***

On toward lunchtime everybody gravitated expectantly toward the cabana. I noticed with interest that Mrs. Merrick was getting into quite a flurry over the preparations for lunch. In fact, she reminded me of my mother, who always got frantic before her rare dinner parties and gnawed the inside of her mouth. But in my mother's case this was because she got so harried with all the work she had to do, while Mrs. Merrick had several Negro servants doing the actual work. Maids were fixing Cokes from a soda fountain—a real soda fountain, just like in a drugstore!—and Willis, the chauffeur whom I knew from that trip out to the theater, stood out in the sun by a barbecue pit devotedly turning frankfurters and hamburger patties.

"Well, I'm awfully glad to be here," Mr. Render said, while we milled around. "I couldn't wait to see you all another minute. I just decided to fly down yesterday, you know. I think I gave Lyda a turn when I called and said I was coming!"

"*I* answered the phone," cried Christabel from near his chair, and I looked curiously at the fey Christabel, remembering that she was supposed to be "in love" with Mr. Render.

"I had to get out of New York," he said. "I simply *had* to get away."

"Tell us about New York!" Dorcas cried out yearningly. Most everybody had sat down on the floor of the cabana and Dorcas's head waved above everyone else's like a dandelion in a lawn. "Does a professional dancer really have to be trained in New York?"

"Well, no," he said, laughing, "I wasn't trained in New York. I don't emphasize this, you understand. I try to skip over it lightly, just do a little *bourrée* to the next subject—"

Everyone laughed as he wafted his arms to his left and wiggled his toes in imitation of a female dancer doing *bourrées*. It struck me that his bare feet were very fair and white, hardly even calloused on the bottom.

"But I'll confess to you, since you are my collaborators, my colleagues, that I was born and got my first training in Toledo, Ohio."

"What's so bad about that?" Melissa called out in her twang.

"Nothing really, my dear. But once upon a time there was. There were several things wrong. First of all I had to go through Hades to get trained, but that's another story. The main thing is that when I went to London right after the war, in 1919, I was regarded as a lower form of life than the other aspirants because I wasn't Russian. I wasn't even French. I was an American of the most insipid variety, a Midwesterner. Diaghilev was always suspicious of me—he called me 'the farmer'—I think he thought corn was going to sprout out of my ears."

"How did you start dancing, Geoffrey darling? You've never told me!" Mrs. Merrick said as if he and she were alone somewhere.

"The key word in any American male dancer's biography is 'sister'. I had a sister who was taking ballie from a Mrs. Rubenstein in Toledo," Mr. Render said to everybody. I loved the way he said "ballet" with the stress on the first syllable. "Oh, Mrs. Rubenstein! My mother had my sister Catherine in Mrs. Rubenstein's class to learn the social graces. Mrs. Rubenstein conducted her classes in a long black dress and white kid gloves, and the girls wore long tutus. But Catherine was quite taken with ballie, even in this form, so when Nijinsky toured the United States during the war, 1916, I think, she *had* to go see him. Mrs. Rubenstein claimed to know Nijinsky's sister. She said she had danced at the Paris Opera before she married and moved to Toledo and that she had known Nijinska in Paris. She offered to take any of the girls who wanted to go with her to Chicago to see Nijinsky perform. But my mother wouldn't *hear* of Catherine going with Mrs. Rubenstein. She never would say why—she just disapproved of Mrs. Rubenstein for one reason or another. But since Catherine just had to go, the whole family went.

"My father was a doctor. He had to hand his patients over to a young partner of his for three or four days and the four of us went to Chicago so Catherine could see Nijinsky. I don't remember my father ever taking another trip."

Mr. Render stopped, apparently thinking about his father.

Someone called out, "What happened, Mr. Render?"

"This was at the old opera house," he said, rousing himself. "That's a grand old place! Well, if I'm going to tell this, you have to understand what kind of boy I was. I was sixteen years old and I was a linebacker on my high school football team. They called me 'Stump' because I was so squat and strong nobody could knock me over. I was going to medical school to be a doctor like my father."

"A rough tough All-American kind of guy, huh, sir?" Nathan interjected. I looked at him sharply for signs of sarcasm ("Old Jiffy"), but he looked perfectly serious and, as I said, adoring.

"That's right," Mr. Render said serenely.

"'Stump.' Well I was more or less pulled into that theater by my mother, God rest her sweet soul. She was always making me do things for Catherine's sake—poor Catherine, such a dreary girl. Now, this next part sounds incredible, but it's true. The first ballie at that Chicago performance was *Le Spectre de la Rose.* How many of you kids know that ballie?"

"I've read about it," I said, raising my hand only halfway since I had not actually seen it. Claude, standing at the edge of the crowd, indicated that he also knew about it, but no one else could lay any claim to knowing the work.

"It was one of Nijinsky's best roles. He played the spirit of the rose, you see. The curtain goes up on a lovely young girl fondling the rose her lover has given her"—Mr. Render humorously mimed this—"and when she falls asleep, she dreams of the rose, whereupon the real rose, the *true* rose bursts through the window behind her and takes her into his arms."

Mr. Render pantomimed this burst too, which was very funny and reminded me of Claude exploding from the depths of the pool.

"You kids *do* know who Nijinsky was, don't you?"

"Sure we do," I called, so that he would not be displeased with us. Happily I was joined by other voices.

"We *think* he was the best dancer we've ever had, but who can know for sure? There aren't any films of him and the stills don't capture anything of his—his exuberance. He leapt through that window with the force of a cannonball; then he landed on the stage like a feather.

Of course the audience went wild. They actually made him repeat that entrance! Of course we'd never allow that today. We certainly don't allow that kind of thing at NDT. But in those days, particularly here in America, ballie was still a sort of toney vaudeville and Nijinsky could do the best tricks in the world.

"The point of this is that I was lost," Mr. Render said. "Catherine sat down the row snuffling and carrying on. I sat hypnotized. I've often thought about whether I would have been so captivated right then, on that spot, if Nijinsky had looked different."

"How come?" someone who did not know what Nijinsky looked like sang out.

"To put it bluntly, he was a stump too," Mr. Render said grandly. "He was short, you see, and stocky. Strong as a bull. Graceful as a hawk. Sinuous as a snake. Fast as a cheetah. "

"Crazy as a loon," put in Mme LeBreton.

"That too," Mr. Render said good-humoredly. "Oh I *am* thirsty again. Do I have time for another drink before lunch, Lyda?"

A servant refilled Mr. Render's glass and he drank freely from it, smacking his lips.

"Well, what happened then?" Claude demanded. "Did you join Nijinsky's troupe, like Mme LeBreton ran away to join yours?"

Mr. Render laughed again, this time long and hard. "No, no dear boy," he said finally. "No, it never occurred to me to do that. I've never even thought of that! Milly was a spunky thing, weren't you, Milly? I wonder what you would have done if you had seen Nijinsky instead of me?"

"Same thing, I imagine," she said carelessly, from behind the sunglasses.

"But remember what kind of boy I was," Mr. Render said to Claude. "No, you see, I was raised to do it right. This was my father's motto, 'do it right.' My mother embroidered it on a sampler for him one time and I still have that sampler." Mr. Render paused reverently, apparently thinking about the sampler. "I went home with my family and enrolled in Mrs. Rubenstein's school. I went to her and told her that I intended to become a dancer like Nijinsky, and I wanted her not only to teach me everything she knew but also to tell me everything she knew about him *and* his sister."

"What was that?" I called out eagerly.

"Not much. Not very much at all. It turned out that the woman had met Bronislava—that was the sister—once at a party in Paris when she was a student: her one claim to fame. She said she had been in the *corps* at the Paris Opéra but I doubt it. She had no technique whatever. She liked broad effects—simpering grace for women"—Mr. Render mocked this by repeating his *bourrée* imitation—"and big leaps for me. I say 'me' because I was the only boy she had ever gotten her hands on. I think if I hadn't been naturally strong and adaptable she would have ruined me in the first month. She had me leaping like a frog, on cold muscles. It was madness, but during the year before I graduated from high school I thought I was wonderful. I adored performing, even though that first recital I had to partner Catherine. Ugh!"

"What did your parents think?" Claude called out amid the laughs.

"Dance—ballie—is not an honorable profession for a man in America," Mr. Render pronounced. "The day will come when it will be, as it is in Europe and Russia. The day will come when a male dancer will be as respected and admired as a professional football player or baseball player."

Disbelieving laughter met this outlandish idea.

"No, I am perfectly serious. The day will come when your brothers and your boyfriends will be in class along with you, as boys are in Europe. Claude is a pioneer. You should all be very proud of Claude."

Everyone peered around at Claude, who stood looking savagely at his feet. Some people also glanced at Albert, skulking to the rear. "And Milly too," Mr. Render continued. We transferred our gaze to Mme LeBreton. There was a scattering of applause.

Then Mr. Render returned to his own life, and in the next half hour, while our lunch sat waiting on silver trays getting stone cold, told us about the terrible conflict with his distraught parents over his decision to go to London to try to join the Diaghilev troupe instead of going to college, then his years in London trying to get a toehold, as he put it, in the world of dance without being Russian or even French. He had to start over from scratch with another teacher, an old Russian lady. He got better fast, but then he began to grow bald. He told a funny story about losing a toupee on stage during a performance of *Les Noces* (the work, by the way, of Bronislava Nijinska, whom Mr. Render came to know rather well). He could not progress in the troupe, he said, because he was not Russian. He met people. He knew the great dancers of that time, whom he named; the great artists, the great musicians; he participated in the great premières that are in all the books, though he never got a leading role, he never had a great role made on him because he wasn't, well, he wasn't *Russian*. He moved to Monte Carlo with the troupe when it became the official ballet of the opera there; he toured Europe with the troupe again and again. He began to have his own ideas for "ballies" but Diaghilev would not pay attention to *him*. What was Nijinsky like, Claude called out. Oh Nijinsky was gone by this time, quite mad, locked up; never danced again, so sad. He, Render, in contrast, was admirably sane and healthy but growing increasingly angry at playing second fiddle—fifth or sixth fiddle, rather—to people like Massine and Lifar, especially Lifar. When Diaghilev died in 1929 (a sordid business) he, Render, boarded ship and came home, like an immigrant. He had with him some other disaffected dancers and a backer, Auguste Benet; they intended to start their own troupe and mount their own "ballies" and of course the rest was history. "But nothing since has equaled the spirit of those days in London," Mr. Render said. "They were so *interesting*. It was interesting to breathe the air. It has never been like that since. Perhaps," he finished up ominously, "it would be better to do like Nijinsky and go mad over it and then die while it was still so infernally interesting."

With this Mr. Render got up from his lounge chair, waving away our further questions with a lordly gesture. Our eyes followed him as he made his way through our midst (much as a great conductor threads his way through the orchestra after a bow) and went to the edge of the pool. There he removed the brown striped robe and flung it to the side of him and dived into the turquoise depths. He cut into the water so rapidly and so deftly that we all stared in dumb amazement at the point where he had disappeared and, when he surfaced at the shallow end, rubbing his eyes, we all laughed in appreciation; some of us even clapped.

***

I expect the pool party would have been very different if Mr. Render had not been there. For one thing, we might have done a little horseback riding after lunch instead of the things we in fact did, but Mr. Render had denounced that plan over dessert. Dessert, by the way, was towering hot fudge sundaes from the soda fountain.

"No horses!" Mr. Render had shouted, jumping up from his sundae to stalk around the cabana. "I don't want to hear anything about my dancers getting on horses. First we're *sore*," he said, spreading his little legs and toddling around comically, "then we're injured. 'Trigger rook a jump, Mr. Render, and threw me and broke my neck and now I can't dance!'" he said in falsetto. "Performance is in three weeks, dear people," he thundered. "There will be no horses. No roller skates. No pogo sticks. No hammocks! Once I had a dancer who rolled out of a hammock and broke her leg. No, no horses. You have to be very very careful with yourselves!

"Rest while you can. Pamper yourselves!" he commanded, taking to a chaise longue in his burnoose, looking distinctly drowsy. Taking her cue from him, Mrs. Merrick instructed us to change back into our clothes; then she took us up to the house for a sort of rest period. I was very pleased to be taken to the house. We went in the back, having climbed the hill and mounted a broad terrace, and I stood in a huge entrance hall that looked more like the lobby of a grand hotel than the rear of a private house, gawking like a tourist. Why, this rear hall had an elevator and paintings on the walls. There were mosaics on the floor and frescoes on the ceiling. The frescoes were so high I was not exactly sure what I was seeing, but I believe they were naked gods and goddesses.

We could do what we liked, so long as we followed Mr. Render's injunction to take care of ourselves, and Christabel would show us where everything was, Mrs. Merrick said, disappearing up some stairs; whereupon Christabel, our guide, ran into the little elevator and before I knew it most of the class was piling in pell-mell behind her and Christabel was clanging a golden gate across them and then all of them, packed and shouting, were ascending into the higher reaches of the house, their noise growing fainter and fainter, until finally nothing was left of them but some dangling ropes, which looked flimsy and sickeningly weak.

"I wonder what Mr. Render would say about most of the soloists riding in that elevator," I said to the people who were left behind, which turned out to be Nathan and Claude and, a little farther off, Cecilia.

"Did you want to go?" Claude said solicitously to Cecilia.

Cecilia shook her head and started strolling negligently down the hall. Claude rushed alongside her and took her arm in the manner of a cavalier. It was obvious to me that Claude wanted to be alone with Cecilia: here was a perfect opportunity, possibly his first. As he walked with her he matched his step to hers, just as he did when he was Little Boy Blue to her Little Bo-Peep, Robin Redbreast to her Jenny Wren, and all those other couples they had been in the past. Nathan did not perceive this desire for a *pas de deux*, or, if he did, he paid it no mind. He began to stroll down the hallway after them; so, quite naturally, did I.

"Where're those pictures Lyda was talking about?" Nathan shouted ahead to Claude and Cecilia in a companionable way, meanwhile peering at one of the pictures on the wall, an oil painting of a chrysanthemum. "Beldinsky's boids," he specified.

"The garden room," Cecilia said indifferently. "I can show y'all." So Cecilia had been here before! I had the idea that most of the girls who had clambered into the elevator had been here before, save Dorcas and Rachel.

Claude molded himself around Cecilia and suffered us to follow them. I felt sorry for Claude but it was hopeless, after all. It was obvious that he would never attain Cecilia: she was so very beautiful, and she was also in some other world than ours. Today she had seemed simply to go through the motions of the wonderful pool party. Coming over the lawn just then, for instance, she had simply walked, looking down at the grass rather than up at the house before us, which looked as grand as an ocean liner on the billowing sea. Now she just glided moodily along, her upper body in that pensive mode of a ballerina walking slowly across the stage, her hands pressed together at the wrists behind her, dragging one *pointe* and then the other behind her in graceful little jerks. Possibly this abstraction had something to do with her mother and Mr. Render (her father?); more probably she was thinking of Charlie Hill in Germany. I tried to imagine Charlie Hill in a state of military alert by the Rhine.

"God, the dough these people must have," Nathan said reverently as we passed from the hall through a dining room, a sitting room, each large enough to be a ballroom. The library here would have made an admirable wing at the Middleton Public Library.

Meanwhile I relayed to Nathan some things I had picked up about the estate during lunch. This was the real seat of the Merrick family: they called it the "old house." That house in town where Christabel's grandmother lived and where I had gone to the cocktail party was just the "new house." The old house had been built in the 1870s by Christabel's great-grandfather, General Edgerton T. Merrick, who had come to Middleton to start a new life after the Civil War. He had had the stones brought from Kentucky, where his family had flourished before that great debacle, and I believe certain parts of the interior, mantels and such, were also brought down from there. Christabel's grandfather inherited the house as a young man, sometime around the turn of the century, and his large family grew up there. He died about 1930, and when his eldest son, Buckingham Merrick, married Lyda Miller, the widowed mother gave the house to the young couple and had that new house built for herself in town. I thought that was awfully nice. I wondered whether my people in Ardis knew about this gracious transaction in the Merrick family. What a coup for Lyda Miller of Natchitoches, whose family had a bankrupt feed business, to marry into this family and enjoy the largess of a mansion that looked like a hotel or an ocean liner!

"They tell me there's a Blüthner in here," Nathan said, loping along after Claude and Cecilia.

"What's a Blootner?" I asked, looking among furniture and pictures and small pieces of sculpture, afraid Nathan would knock something over and break it.

"It's a piano, stupid," Nathan said genially, "a very fine piano. Lord I'd like to get my hands on a good piano. I'm so tired of Milly's piece a crap. "

The garden room was at the far end of the south wing of the house. This room too was very grand and earned its name by housing a forest of ferns and palms, some of them as big as trees. Long windows offered a view of the grounds to the rear of the house and I looked down to the back pool, which looked very secretive and private from this vantage point. Nathan found the piano he was looking for among the plants, also a whole wall of Mr. Beldinsky's birds. These added a hot, screaming tropical note to the otherwise cool and elegant room.

"Jesus those are weird boids," Nathan complained, going over to the Blüthner and beginning to play a transcription of Saint-Saëns' "Carnival of the Animals." It was the "Cuckoo" section, and Nathan chose to sing the part of the Cuckoo instead of playing it on the piano, perhaps by way of further comment on Mr. Beldinsky's work. I examined the birds myself, feeling very happy to be at the Merrick house with these older dancers, accompanied by Nathan. This might be very rewarding, I thought. It was certainly more interesting than the juvenilities of Christabel and the others. "Their eyes don't *look* at you, do they?" I observed, trying to interest these older people, particularly Cecilia, who had sunk into a white wicker chair the moment we entered the room, bothering with neither the birds nor the Blüthner. "Portraits' eyes usually follow you, but these have eyes that go different ways, don't they? Look at that cockatoo there. One eye goes this way, one eye goes that way—"

"Hell, I'm *glad* they don't look at me," Nathan said over his playing. "They look like they could put the hex on you."

"Picasso had eyes going in different directions," I said broadmindedly. "Just think, y'all, Mr. Render actually knew Picasso. I mean he *knows* Picasso. Isn't that incredible?"

"Did any of y'all *talk* to Render today? How is he feeling?" Claude said, dropping down into a chair next to Cecilia.

I sat down near them. "I don't think he's even thinking about us," I said sagely. "I think he's just enjoying being here."

"Old Jiff certainly knows how to enjoy himself," Nathan said, through some fronds.

"Just so we do well enough to please him," Claude broke out, making fists and pounding them into his spongy hair with sudden fury. "This playing around drives me wild! I feel like a mouse with a big cat after him batting him around with his paws. He goes away for a long time, suddenly he's back, but he doesn't *do* anything; he doesn't even say anything; he just plays with us and makes speeches about his life!"

"Claude!" Cecilia bothered to say.

"You're one of the worst, Cecilia," Claude said, turning to her. "You have the best chance of anybody of getting in NDT and you don't even care. Even *you've* been playing around in the water like you don't have a care in the world while *he*—he *and* she—get soused and talk about the old days. Doesn't anybody care about the future? This is so important! Our whole lives depend on this!"

"No, they really don't," Cecilia said slowly, brushing a tendril of nearly dry hair off her broad and flawless forehead. Swimming had washed Cecilia's makeup off but, though pale, she looked lovelier than ever. "Poor Claude, you're turning into a maniac."

"Isn't that what it *takes*?" he said, teeth bared. "Isn't that what old Render meant when he talked about Nijinsky, and himself? Those guys don't sit around being patient and reasonable!"

"Mr. Render seems very reasonable to me," I observed, earning a glare from Claude.

Nathan had left off playing; now he came over and sat down. "Look, Claude," Nathan said, "I know you're eager but it's like I was telling you before, relax! This is nothing to him. This is kid stuff. He'll take you if he said he would. He said he would, didn't he?"

"He said he *might,*" Claude said miserably.

"He will, he will. Frankly I think he'd take anybody who wanted to go half as bad as you do. I expect he'll ask Cecilia," he surmised, looking appreciatively up and down Cecilia, who was unconscious of this. "But the problem is, what there is to take you *to*. I told you, Claude, there's all that in-fighting going on. He looks real tired this time. I told you what he said about his board of directors. They make him dream about claws."

"Mama says Geoffrey's practically washed up," Cecilia said, clearly bored.

"She said that?" Claude shouted. "When did she say *that?*"

Cecilia shrugged.

"I wouldn't say that," Nathan said impartially. "I'm just saying there's a lot of in-fighting and there's someone just waiting to step into the master's shoes."

"Nils Lundgren," I mused.

"That's right!" Nathan said, looking at me with interest. "How'd you know about Lundgren?"

"I know a lot about the dancers," I said modestly, studying the fingernails on my left hand. Actually I wanted to gnaw these nails, this was so exciting, but I restrained myself as I reflected on the turtlenecked Dane who had danced Jesse James and who was undoubtedly one of those who could do a triple *tour en l'air* without visible effort. This is part of the reason Claude was so unhappy: he still could not do the triple every single time, and never could he do it without visible effort. I realize now that I had been using Nils Lundgren as an image of what it was Claude was straining after, and it was a new and very interesting idea to think of Geoffrey Render in contest with him too. I thought about how tall and slim this Lundgren character was, how much hair he had.

"It'd be just my luck to get up there in time for the revolution," Claude said bitterly. "Milly never said that to me," he went on, turning back to Cecilia. "About him being washed up. When did she say that? Was it recently?"

"Don't pump me, Claude, I can't *stand* that. Don't push on me!" Cecilia cried, rising. A deep frown now creased the flawless forehead. She jumped up and down a few times with her arms stiffened, as I had seen the angry Swanhilda do in *Coppélia*. "You're driving me crazy. being so frantic. I don't remember when Mama said that. She talks on and on. She talks all the time! Everybody talks all the time! I'm never by myself. Why can't I just be by myself?"

With this Cecilia ran duck-legged out of the garden room, brushing past ferns and causing a gentle shower of their ruffly leaves. Claude hurled himself out of his chair as if to follow her but hesitated, looking with infinite yearning after her, then threw himself into a second tour of Mr. Beldinsky's birds. They looked more normal now after these explosions of emotion: I think they were distraught birds.

"What's the matter with her?" Nathan said to me in a low voice.

"Love, I think," I reported quietly. "You didn't know her boyfriend, Charlie Hill, but he was taken into the Army in January and I think she still misses him."

"She'll forget him," Claude proclaimed feverishly from over by the flaming cockatoo. "She *will* forget him. It'll just take some time. She knows I'll wait."

"It may be a while, fella," Nathan said, loping back to the piano, where he began tumbling out roulades of Beethoven, his way, I think, of comforting Claude in his affliction.

***

The woods way in the distance beyond the house looked very beautiful, and after this conversation I walked out to explore these woods by myself for a little while. It may seem strange that I did this, but we had been given the run of the place, and by this time in the day I felt quite at home there. The question of my safety did not cross my mind in this place where everything was so clean and polished, where there wasn't a single leaf on the lawn, where the gravel was raked and the bushes were trimmed in pleasing symmetrical shapes. You could tell it wasn't like Ardis, where there are wild pigs in the woods.

So far the main effect of the party had been to get me entranced by Mr. Render again. He had become the frowning, hovering genie during his absence, but now I saw all the charm and interest of his personality again. He stirred up controversy, but didn't great men always? How happy he was! How well he knew how to live! I walked down a path through the Merricks' woods—sure enough, not tangled and messy like the ones behind my relatives' houses in Ardis but charming, even picturesque woods, thinking about Mr. Render. I imagined him having awakened from some beautiful dream in the cabana and wandered out alone onto the grounds and back into the woods, where I might come upon him at any moment, sitting at the foot of a tree, listening to a spring bird or watching a spring flower, getting ideas for his ballets. But really it did not matter to me whether Mr. Render was actually out in the woods or not: as I saw it that day, he pervaded the whole Merrick place, something like Pan.

I did not in fact find Mr. Render in my wanderings, but I did find a lake and the stables and even a little merry-go-round. I walked all the way back to the lake, which had a quaint little gazebo out in the middle of it; then I turned back toward the house. Some distance away I could hear the ruckus of a new Marco Polo game issuing from the back pool, where I found Mr. Render at the center of the party, cavorting around like a dolphin.

Later we played croquet and touch football. Near the end of the strenuous afternoon most of the class lay on the flat stretch of lawn directly behind the big gray house, panting and sweating freely. One by one we had dropped out of the touch football game, and I remember how cool and fresh the grass felt. It was unusual grass, probably very costly—fine, almost feathery grass that smelled wonderful and seemed to emit a little breeze. Claude and Albert and Hilary and Adelaide were still playing football on the lawn around us. Every now and then the football soared over, and one or the other of them pounded by. Now Hilary came running by, hair streaming like Atalanta's.

The party was almost over and we were just waiting around for a surprise, Mrs. Merrick had said, something in the line of refreshments. She and Mr. Render and Mme LeBreton were above us on the terrace, Nathan too (Nathan did not know how to play football, he said). They were sitting in white ironwork chairs and talking quietly over more drinks. They all looked fresh and tranquil. Mrs. Merrick now wore an elegant yellow slacks outfit, and Mr. Render had put on a new shirt with his shiny black pants, at least it was new to me. Before, he had always worn plaid flannel shirts, but this was a spring shirt made out of a light fabric with a sheen to it. It was a brilliant peacock blue and had palm trees on it.

Everybody on the lawn yelled as Claude caught a long pass from Hilary and bounded past a certain oak tree for a "touchdown." He celebrated this with a beautiful leap embellished by some neat *batterie*. I looked anxiously up at Mr. Render, who might think Claude would hurt himself in this athletic exuberance, but Mr. Render was gazing complacently at Claude, perhaps remembering his own football days in Toledo. Then the game was over and Claude flung himself down on the grass not too far from me; so did Albert. A powerful odor of sweat wafted across the cool grass.

"That was a good play you made a while ago. I really enjoyed it," Claude said to Albert, Claude's ferocious teeth flashing in the afternoon sun. He undoubtedly referred to a play in which Albert had forgotten himself and tackled Adelaide, bringing her down with a thud.

"Thanks," Albert said, lolling in the grass. He was no longer in his controversial bathing suit; he was in bulging Bermuda shorts. "I played a little football over in Biloxi before I started dancing. Of course I wouldn't want to play now. Too much chance of injury.

"Claude," Albert said urgently, after they had heaved a minute. "You know what they called me over at my school in Biloxi? You're not going to believe it."

"What?" Claude said lazily.

"They called me 'Stump'."

Claude gave Albert a fine stare.

"Old Render's amazing," Albert said dreamily. "I stayed down at the pool after lunch and talked to him a long time. I wanted to find out if he thought I'd ever be any good."

Claude propped himself up on one arm the better to study Albert. "And what did he say?"

"He said, we all begin at the beginning," Albert said. "We all begin at the beginning. Isn't that wonderful?"

"Very profound," Claude said, glittering his dark little eyes at Albert.

"I wish my mother could have heard old Render talking about his life out here today. She would have gotten a big kick out of it. She's always wanted to live in New York or London. She's an actress, you know. She's playing in *Dial M for Murder* right now at the Biloxi Little Theater."

"I thought you said your mother was a dental hygienist," Claude said.

"She *is* a dental hygienist during the day, to make a living, but she's *really* an actress. She knows all about the theater. I know it would have thrilled her to hear his stories, and find out how similar his life was to my life."

"And how's that?" Claude inquired.

"Stump," Albert said, with satisfaction. "Also, how I got started dancing by going up to Jackson to see NDT this fall and got hooked the minute Nils Lundgren came out on the stage. I knew right then that I was going to be a dancer, just like the old man said happened to him. I don't have a sister, I just have Mother, but other than that the story's the same. Of course I didn't try to train in my hometown—you can't get any decent dance instruction in Biloxi! It was a miracle Render came down here this year and I could get in St. Stephen's at midterm. Well, no, it wasn't a miracle. I deserved it, we worked to make it happen.

"Say, how'd you get started, Claude?" Albert inquired fraternally of Claude, who was smirking at the woods in the distance.

"Nothing so dramatic. Started taking lessons when I was eight, along with most of these girls," Claude said. "A real oddball."

"Naw, you're good," Albert said generously. "You're damn good. You're gonna make it. Me—I'm no good yet, but I'm gonna be good. You know, Mother and I have this idea," Albert said, checking around to see if anybody was listening. I looked away for an instant. "I'm gonna train like hell and next summer after graduation we're gonna go to New York. I'll audition for everybody. I probably won't be good enough for NDT but there's always a shortage of male dancers and surely I'll get work somewhere. Hell, I'm strong," he said, beating on his chest like a gorilla. "Mother's always wanted a shot at Broadway. She's sick of cleaning teeth."

They went on talking, Claude dealing very kindly, I thought, with Albert's overweening ambition. For my part, I just stared at Albert in amazement. I thought he was a grievous dancer, utterly without talent, but I couldn't help being impressed with his self-confidence. An artist needs self-confidence to get over the difficulties of being a beginner. I knew Mr. Render had had it back there in Toledo, I thought Claude had it now, and here Albert was with it. Of course in Albert it looked like lunacy rather than self-confidence, but possibly the very fact that he had it meant something positive in his case. And we did all begin at the beginning, that could not be denied.

It should also be pointed out that Albert was not the only one dreaming that day out at the Merricks': the place seemed to induce grandiose dreams.

"Look at those beautiful bodies," I heard Mr. Render muse not too long after this. He was looking, I imagine, at Melissa and Stephanie, who were wrestling, for some reason. "Think of the possibilities, with all that youthful energy. *Mother Goose* is only the beginning."

"Somebody's got to do the work, Geoffrey. Somebody's got to write the checks," said Mme LeBreton, who was never that dreamy, even here.

"All right, Milly," Mr. Render said agreeably. "My point is just that there's not a reason in the world Middleton can't have a real ballie company. I mean a genuine professional company. Once the theater is open you could have a season. Finance it like the New York companies do with a *Nutcracker* or some other seasonal ballie. You know, I've always wanted to do a ballie on Santa Claus. That's very American, you know, the tradition of Santa Claus. Perhaps I could make a Christmas ballie for you."

"You'd be a darling Santa Claus," Mrs. Merrick said affectionately.

"You're nuts if you think my school could put on a season," Madame said languidly.

"Not your school as it is today," Mr. Render said. "I'm thinking of what it could be, what it *will* be, with the support of incredible people like Lyda." I heard the sound of a kiss. "She is an angel. I mean that literally, kids," he said in louder, instructive tones meant for everybody down on the lawn. "That's our nickname in the theater for someone who underwrites a production and makes it all possible. You see, with angels like this there's no reason why Middleton can't have its own ballie company. What I'd really like to see is an academy down here to train children for ballie like they're trained in older countries—Russia, or France, England. Something more comprehensive than the NDT school. We'd give you little barbarians a well-rounded education in the arts. We'd form your minds as well as your bodies; we'd have our hands on you *all* the time, not just three or four times a week. We'd get them young, Milly, six or seven."

I looked at my classmates lying around me on the grass, lithe and hot and healthy. I did not know whether I liked Mr. Render calling us barbarians.

"I think we really *ought* to discuss a new school once this gala is over," Mrs. Merrick was saying. "Of course your little building is utterly charming, Milly, but Buck and I were talking about this the other night. There's just so much land out around the theater and that area to the south of town is really opening up. It's going to develop very fast in the next few years. Wouldn't it be delightful to have a ballet school out there? Something big and airy, with a country feel to it."

"Marvelous!" Mr. Render exclaimed. "Marvelous!"

I could just see the new ballet school out in the woods near the Merrick Theater: clean, open, up in the trees, "modern" like some of the houses in Collegetown were, mostly glass. I could hear a piano reverberating through its spaces—a fine piano, a Blüthner perhaps, with a fine pianist like Nathan playing it (no Mrs. Fister in the new school!)— and the thud-thud-thud of feet. But I didn't like to think of Madame's school moving away from Sycamore Street—why, it had always been at the head of our street; I couldn't imagine anything else up there! Mme LeBreton did not seem to care much for this line of talk either. She was silent as Mr. Render and Mrs. Merrick talked on about a ballet academy out in the piney woods.

I lay on the cool grass visualizing the new school, but instead of being in the woods, suddenly it was in a large field which seemed to be at a high altitude because the air was very thin and chill, like mountain air, and the grass had delicate little flowers growing in it, frosty pastel flowers of a kind never seen in these parts. The school was not just one building but a whole series of buildings strung together. They were white and had the festive air of tents, though I am sure they were built out of something more substantial than canvas, porcelain perhaps. The building stretched gaily across the field, with flags or pennants in bright colors flying from the roofs, blowing in a gentle wind. Snatches of music traveled on the wind too: Chopin and Bach, I believe, or Ravel.

"I wish somebody would take a picture of that cake," Mr. Render said loudly, making me jump. I had fallen asleep, I guess, and begun to dream. "Lyda, send someone for a camera. I want your picture beside this gorgeous cake."

Everyone got up off the grass and mounted the terrace and jostled around a table to see a huge pink cake, which glowed in the late afternoon sun. "To a Glorious *Mother Goose*" was written across the cake in rose-colored icing. Christabel danced around it, shouting over and over how it had a candle for every dancer in the production; then a maid lit the candles and we blew them out. After that we stood around gobbling down the delicious cake as if we were at a wedding reception, and Mr. Render licked his fingers. His pretty shirt looked more and more luminous the lower the sun got, as if it had neon properties.

21

This euphoria could not last, I thought, and sure enough ten days later the roof fell in—but I am getting ahead of the story. I was braced for the worst anyway; I think all of us were. Even during that swimming party (our sojourn in paradise!) I expect most of us remembered that any number of things could go wrong in the three weeks ahead. The theater was not finished, the costumes were not finished, and most importantly of all, the dances were not perfected, and they seemed to be waiting for us in a kind of limbo back in the studio, where before too long Mr. Render would pass judgment on our work of the last three months. It was very possible that he would take one look at our dancing, turn on his heel and march off, never to be seen in the South again.

This look was to come right away. The next day Mothers called everybody to come to the studio to run through *Mother Goose* for Geoffrey Render even though it was Sunday—he couldn't wait until Monday, it seemed. We assembled there at two o'clock in an awful state of dread. It was warmer than the day before, and the atmosphere in the studio was close and oppressive.

"Open those windows," Mr. Render sang out from the Mothers' Bench, where he sat with his hands on his knees, ready to watch. "No, don't turn on the air conditioner, Milly. You ought not to even have an air conditioner in here. It isn't good for the kids. Crank 'em wide.

"Forget I'm here," he said absurdly. "Just run through it like any other rehearsal."

Members of the advanced class looked at each other with an alarm which we imagined was greater than anybody else's alarm since we were the soloists. We were also distinguished from the hoi polloi by having colds of differing degrees of seriousness, having spent the previous day in and out of the Merricks' back pool. Stephanie and Dorcas sported awful coughs; Lola kept sneezing, leaving a web of phlegm on the front of her leotard. Mme LeBreton brought the huge and unwieldy group to order with her stick and soon (too soon!) *Mother Goose* began. Except for Nathan's playing and the thumps of feet, a terrible silence followed. Little Boy Blue bounded out, Little Bo-Peep floated around, the little sheep gathered and scattered, all in this terrible silence. At first Mme LeBreton murmured a few words of correction or encouragement, but before too long she was silent too. It became clear that this was a trial and that Mr. Render was a judge on the bench. Silence was apparently an essential part of this trial.

It lasted almost two hours without a break. We went straight through the ballet, with Mr. Render taking his parts of Humpty Dumpty and Old King Cole, still without commenting upon our dancing, as if this were a real performance. We did all the daytime dances and then all the nighttime dances ("Wee Willie Winkie" and "Hush-a-Bye") and then *my* big number, "Jack Be Nimble," and still he didn't say anything. We watched him anxiously when we could. When he wasn't dancing he was watching, in that alarming way he had, and after a time I saw that a kind of film came over his eyes with so much watching. Actually he had the expression on his face I had imagined he would wear sitting out in the woods, seeing birds or dryads or whatever: a kind of rapture of attention, which I observed but could not really enjoy at the time because I was so afraid he was gathering evidence of some awful crimes we were committing.

The penultimate number of *Mother Goose* was "Hey Diddle Diddle," a spirited *divertissement* featuring Christabel as the cat, Adelaide as the cow, Rachel as the dish, Dorcas as the spoon and me as the dog. After this, the rest of the cast surged onto the floor for the finale, which featured a reprise of Cecilia's and Claude's variations at the beginning as Little Bo-Peep and Little Boy Blue. I could see one or the other of them soaring above the heads of the dancers in front of me during the churning of this last huge ensemble: then we fell to the floor. We were supposed to go to bed at the end, you see. Mme LeBreton, as Mother Goose, circled among us, "putting us to bed" and even "tucking us in" in pantomime. Mrs. Fister, as the Old Woman, was the only one who did not fall to the floor. In fact, I observed that she was waiting by the light switch. It was well known to all of us that at the end of the finale the lights in the theater would go down, leaving only Mr. Beldinsky's luminous moon dangling stage right, and now good old Mrs. Fister, clearly having caught on to the fact that this run-through was supposed to simulate a performance, stood cannily by the light switch, ready to extinguish the fluorescent lights.

Nathan hit his last chord, giving it a throbbing tremolo to simulate an orchestra. I lay prone on the floor, heaving from the finale, among a hundred and fifty other bodies, also heaving. We had been instructed to lie there as if we were dead, without moving a muscle, and so we did. It was easy because we *were* nearly dead. Like a drowning person, I suffered a quick replay of my life, at least the last two hours of it, with everything that was wrong with the performance flashing vividly into my mind. The children going round the mulberry bush had run into each other three stanzas early! I had managed only twenty-two *écartés!* From the window I heard a lone bird scream; a car whizzed down Sycamore Street.

Frankly I was stiff with fear, waiting for the denunciation, but it didn't come and finally—it probably wasn't more than a minute but it seemed like a very long time—someone who had been at the party sneezed and broke the little spell and I looked up. Mr. Render was sitting stock still on the Mothers' Bench with his eyes closed and his hand on his heart, and, fortunately before I had time to worry about whether he was well, he opened his eyes and said, "Congratulations, people, on beautiful work. Congratulations, Milly," which brought all the dancers to their feet and made us cheer, just like at a pep rally.

"Well, Milly, the notation helped, didn't it?" I heard Mr. Render say later, when we were going through the ballet again, more slowly and with plenty of comments like a more ordinary rehearsal. "None of the little lapses and alterations I expected to see."

"It certainly did, Geoffrey," Mme LeBreton said brazenly. "It was invaluable."

***

Mme LeBreton was looking very tired these days, and after Mr. Render came back and satisfied himself that things were going well she stayed home a few days for what was described all around as a "well-deserved rest." Mrs. Merrick also absented herself from the studio after that Sunday trial, at which she had acquitted herself surprisingly well as the queen: she had problems at the theater, which wasn't quite finished even though the performance was only a dozen or so days away. She was having the most fearful struggles out there with villainous painters and electricians and carpenters. As a result, we were left in the exclusive charge of Mr. Render, which is something dancers all over the globe would envy, I thought. We had days and days of rehearsals with Mr. Render, which were exhausting but also fulfilling, and I mustn't forget to mention Nathan, whose playing (which had been sensitive from the first day he came to us) now fit around our movements like the tights around our legs.

In my mind, the sun rose and set on these sessions. I was compelled by law to attend school five days a week, but I was just a disembodied, absent-minded figure there (a sylphid or a wili) with my mind back at the studio. Nor was I the only one obsessed with *Mother Goose:* it seemed to me that the whole city was just as taken up with *Mother Goose* as I was. Mr. Beldinsky had designed a *Mother Goose* poster which was everywhere you looked, in every score window, on every wall.

Every morning when I came down to breakfast my father would be sitting at the kitchen table waiting to show me the latest photograph or feature story about the production in the newspaper. The *Chronicle* naturally gave a lot of space to the production and as a consequence advance ticket sales were brisk. Newspaper reporters and photographers prowled around the studio, which we pretended to find very objectionable, and I looked anxiously at the paper each morning to see if I was in it. I wanted to be in the paper, of course, but at the same time I rather dreaded publicity, like Claude. I did not have to worry: the photographers concentrated on Cecilia, who looked remarkably like Anna Pavlova in the blurry newspaper photographs, and of course Mr. Render. My father remarked that Mr. Matlock, his and Mother's law partner, thought Mr. Render looked like Napoleon. I found my picture just once: I was the blurred maid fighting off a bevy of speckled blackbirds in "Sing a Song of Sixpence," but still I looked eagerly at my father's face as I came in to breakfast every morning to see if I was famous.

***

Actually it happened the day the shoes arrived. That day, ten days before the performance, about twenty-five or thirty of us were just beginning to warm up for a rehearsal in our new rapid and casual way when a panel truck crunched into the parking lot, grinding gravel and sending up a cloud of dust.

"It's Mr. Bartlett!" Melissa screamed, craning to see out of a casement window. "Come on, y'all!"

Leaving Mr. Render standing in the middle of the floor with his hands on his hips and his mouth open, most of the dancers rushed pell-mell out of the studio, flapping the screen door violently and repeatedly. Out back, Mr. Bartlett was just unfastening the rear doors of the truck.

"Is it the shoes?" someone cried rapturously. "Is it the *shoes?*"

Mr. Bartlett flung the doors open dramatically and there were stacks and stacks and rows and rows of Capezio boxes, just like in the back room of his shop. I think he might have liked to give a little speech or somehow make a ceremony out of this, but some of the dancers, led by the incorrigible Christabel, pressed into the truck and started pulling out boxes. Soon everybody had boxes and girls were pulling shoes out of them—beautiful, gleaming toe shoes in all the colors of the spectrum, with the tissue paper flying around and about and finally floating down to the gravel.

"Girls! Girls!" Mr. Bartlett shouted ineffectually as he wrestled with Christabel for a silver shoe. "Put those back! Give them back! Listen to me!"

Later, when order was restored, the rehearsal proceeded as usual. I remember clearly that Mrs. Fister had come and Mr. Render was working with her on "There Was an Old Woman" while the rest of us took a break. They were out in center floor and Mr. Render was once again trying to get Mrs. Fister to act distressed, even overwhelmed, by her numerous children, which was very difficult because she was so pleased to be the center of attention like that and kept smiling and nodding all around. Anyway, things were going along in a jolly mode when I heard some smart little clicks, like the repeated firing of a cap pistol, and suddenly Mrs. Merrick was in the front studio, not waiting at the edge of the floor until Mr. Render finished the number as ordinary studio decorum demanded, but clicking her shiny little pumps right on across to his side, even though Mme LeBreton did not like street shoes on her linoleum. I was awfully glad today was one of the days Mme LeBreton was taking a well-deserved rest.

"What?" Mr. Render shouted when Mrs. Merrick had whispered something in his ear. He slapped himself on the head. "God in heaven!"

Nathan broke off playing and noisily pushed the piano bench back. "Is it Milly?" he asked.

"No, no," Mr. Render said distractedly. "It's not Milly. It's the theater. Lyda says the roof has fallen in."

Now Mrs. Fister looked as distressed and overwhelmed as even Stanislavsky could have wanted; so did we all. In fact, the rehearsal dissolved, and the crowd of dancers so lately plundering the panel truck and probably still excited by *that* now ran in all directions, gabbling at the top of their voices, like Chicken Little and her friends.

"Shut up!" Mr. Render shouted.

"It looks like it's been bombed," Mrs. Merrick said into the sudden silence in a low, thrilling voice. "Like some terrible thing that happened in Europe during the war. The foreman told me he heard a sound like pecans cracking and he looked up to see a beam come plunging down, then the whole roof.

Mr. Render put a supportive arm around Mrs. Merrick, who had never looked so tiny and frail. "What about the performance?" Claude called out in the silence.

Mrs. Merrick managed to answer. "Well, it will simply have to be postponed. We don't really know anything yet. I haven't been able to

reach the contractor. I *did* get Alfred—our attorney, you remember—
he's calling the architect in Houston. We'll sue everyone, of course."

Claude hurled himself into a corner to storm over this devastation
of his plans. Mr. Render, meanwhile, gave a philosophical shrug. "Keep
warm, people," he called out. "No, don't anybody sit down. And don't
leave. Practice something you're having trouble with. Find a spot.
Nathan, play something they can all use."

Feeling ghastly, I watched Mr. Render lead Mrs. Merrick to the
Mothers' Bench and sit down with her. I found my spot nearby, holding
on to the sill of the casement window to do some dazed *battements
tendus.*

"Well, is it a fatal flaw in the building? Is it kaput?" Mr. Render
inquired tenderly of Mrs. Merrick.

"It looks like it. Of course it's too early to say. It may be months
before it's fixed. When this hits me, really hits me, I'm going to be
hysterical. I haven't even told Buck yet. He's down in New Orleans.
Milly doesn't even know. I thought she would be here."

"I'll tell Milly. But she'll handle it well. She's an old trouper. *She*
knows you can't expect anything in the theater but the unexpected," Mr.
Render said majestically. "Let's not talk about postponement, though,
all right? Maybe this thing can be patched up—"

"It's the roof, Geoffrey, the entire roof. Just wait till you see it!"
Mrs. Merrick insisted.

"Yes, still, let's not talk about postponement. It simply isn't in the
cards a week away from performance."

The dancers, quite naturally, had begun to gabble again and Mrs.
Merrick looked irritated. "Maybe the children had better go home, under
the circumstances."

"I don't think so," Mr. Render said comfortably. "We aren't finished
with our rehearsal yet."

"But we *are* finished, for the time being," Mrs. Merrick said in a
higher voice, a wild glimmering of the projected hysteria in her eye. "I
don't think you understand yet."

"I don't think *you* understand, darling Lyda," Mr. Render said
affectionately. "I can't postpone! Just think for a moment. Tickets are

sold. The dancers are ready: I have them tuned just to the right pitch. There is a rhythm in these things that we just can't violate. Make the public wait, make these *children* wait, and *Mother Goose* will get stale, or rotten. No, it's simply not possible to postpone. We'll have to perform in another theater," he finished, shrugging, rubbing his nose with one negligent finger, looking out at his cast. "There's bound to be a stage somewhere in a town this size we can use.

"Geoffrey!" Mrs. Merrick said, drawing away from him and looking at him in horror, as if he had just sprouted horns and a tail and, inside his shiny little shoes, cloven hooves. "All of a sudden you seem unconscious of the fact that this is my gala première. You would not *be* here—*Mother Goose* would never have come into being except as the gala première for *my theater.* You must be losing your mind to think of putting it on in some other theater. Where do you think you're going to do it, at the *high school?"*

Mrs. Merrick gave a short laugh at this ridiculous proposition.

"Well, I don't know," Mr. Render said, ignoring her irony. "They have a good-sized gym."

"Gym?" Mrs. Merrick repeated, the wildness flaring higher.

"The thing is, my dear Lyda, I'm a busy man and I have solid commitments the rest of the spring and the summer, through the fall I believe. This is the only time for me."

"With all due respect, Geoffrey, if it came to that we could put on *Mother Goose* without your actual presence," she said, eyeing him critically and at a distance, as it were.

"No you couldn't," he returned, still genial, "not without my consent. It is very much *my* ballie. *I* made it."

"But it's *my* gala."

"It *was,* until your roof fell in. A roof like a pecan shell, well! Isn't it fortunate that it fell in *this* week instead of next week, with all of us in it, maybe even with an audience in it! Talk about lawsuits!"

"Did I tell you? A workman was hurt, and he may have been killed, I don't know. They were trying to dig him out when I left to come to you," Mrs. Merrick said, staring at Mr. Render as if she wished it had been he that was buried under the beams.

"Good God!" Mr. Render said, drawing back blankly.

"All right, just *be* stubborn, Geoffrey," Mrs. Merrick said finally, when they had uselessly gone back and forth over the matter of postponement again. "We'll talk this over later. With Milly too, of course. But you can't do a thing, you know, without the *funds* we discussed."

But after all was said Mr. Render would not call off the rehearsal, and soon Mrs. Merrick clicked out again. I saw the black limousine shoot backward out of the parking lot like a cannonball. Then, as unbelievable as it seems, Mr. Render went right on with the rehearsal as if nothing had happened, giving Mrs. Fister and the children funny little instructive speeches about their dances and quelling questions about the catastrophe, particularly those of the desperate Claude. Oh how I admired Mr. Render, his suavity, his wisdom, his unflappability: not for him running around and screaming "The sky is falling! The sky is falling!" His mind was taken over with the dance, his "ballie," which would exist come hell or high water, as they say over in Ardis. We moved through *Mother Goose* that afternoon with special reverence because of our new and perilous circumstances. Meanwhile, I could not help remembering how Mme LeBreton had said "Money, Geoffrey, don't forget money." She was a very practical woman, yet she was certainly a dedicated artist too. I was not at all sure, in my own mind, whose side she was going to take in the disagreement I had witnessed that afternoon.

***

That night I sat in the library at home with my parents, telling them about what had happened. It was very warm and the windows were open, their long white curtains blowing gently now and then, letting in the sounds of cars passing up and down Sycamore Street and the steadier hum of traffic up on Tates Parkway. I had the vague notion that this automotive stir was related to the catastrophe out at the theater site; I imagined the concerned parties dashing around Middleton from point to point to discuss the situation. I knew for a fact that telephone wires were humming since Dorcas had already called me twice. Naturally everyone was aboil: everything was changed, possibly everything was lost. I felt anxious in every nerve, like a child who has just heard, sometime around the middle of December, that there has been an avalanche or an earthquake up at the North Pole that has destroyed Santa's workshop, and, unless substitute arrangements can be worked out by Santa and Mrs. Claus (who aren't, by the way, exactly seeing eye to eye), there won't be any Christmas this year.

"Just fell in?" my father said after a short silence, rubbing a tooth with the stem of his pipe. We had talked about everything we knew or could guess about the situation, but he wanted to return to this central fact, which seemed so arbitrary and fortuitous and puzzling. "It must be faulty design. I've never heard of anything like that happening."

"Maybe they were hurrying to get it finished and left something out," my mother suggested.

"I thought there was a screw loose in that project," my father said drily. Mother sighed.

"Mrs. Merrick is going to be *so mad* if they go on without her," I said. "All that money"—

"Can they manage it without her, I wonder?" Mother said, with the zeal with which she always contemplated thrift. "The Mothers' Guild must have made a *fortune* at that bazaar last month."

"They're saying the Civic Auditorium is booked that night with some performance or other," I said after a while, passing on to another problem.

"That ole Melbert Dole from up around Dagbert," my father said slyly. "You remember that ole boy, Caroline? He can sure pick it!"

Mother looked haughty at the mention of Melbert Dole, who was a country singer from north Louisiana of some national repute at that time. My father cherished a certain liking for the kind of music called "country" but was not encouraged by my mother to cultivate it.

"I have no doubt Mrs. LeBreton and Geoffrey Render can get around Melbert Dole," Mother said archly. "But Lyda Merrick is another matter. Do you remember that ole girl Lyda Merrick? Lyda Miller, rather?" Mother said, sparring playfully. "From up around Natchitoches?"

"Pretty girl," Father said absently.

"Ambitious," Mother announced. "Didn't even graduate from State when Buck Merrick came along. She saw her chance and took it."

"Smart, though," my father cautioned.

"Yes, pretty! *And* smart!" Mother admitted. *"Still.* I want Meredith Louise to understand that she doesn't—"

"I don't like her!" I said fervently, in case my mother was about to say that fatal thing, that Mrs. Merrick didn't think like we did.

"I'll bet that contract has Geoffrey Render right around the neck," Mother said, pursuing her vision of Lyda Merrick's calculating character. "You know, Lawrence, it's possible she's devised a contract so they can't move a muscle without her."

"Naw, she's playin' with them *big* boys from New York, hon," my father said, dropping into their private Ardis talk for a spirited debate on the nature of the contract in the case. They loved this kind of talk; I often wondered if they talked like this all day at the office down Tates Parkway.

"There's got to be something in there about construction delays," Mother was saying when the telephone rang out in the kitchen. She got up to answer it. "There are always construction delays, hon. *Surely* the contract specifies that the production will take place in the new theater when it's completed."

"You know," my father said subversively while Mother was out of the room, "that Melbert Dole has a lot of fans in Middleton. A lot more than you'd think in a little city like this!"

In a few minutes Mother came back.

"Well, we'll get a look at that contract!" she said happily from the door, having paused there for the dramatic effect, very unusual for Mother. "That was Julianna James—president of the Mothers' Guild at the ballet school, Lawrence—and it seems there's a meeting at three tomorrow. The Merricks' lawyers want to call New York to talk with Geoffrey Render's lawyers, and Mrs. LeBreton needs representation too. The Guild wants us to represent her!"

"Call her Madame, Mother," I begged, even as I looked at her with new admiration, imagining for the first time that, in this unusual situation at least, she might actually be more useful than the regular Mothers, even those talented ones who had made all the cookies and crafts for the annual Spring Bazaar.

***

The next morning the *Chronicle* had a banner headline about the catastrophe: "THEATRE COLLAPSES: OPENING DELAYED."

"Haven't seen type this big since one a them Merrick rigs blew up in the field up there by Plain Dealing," my father remarked at the breakfast table.

"I wouldn't think it would be too good for business," Mother said, peering down through her glasses at the pictures of the ruined building, several of which showed Mrs. Merrick looking tragic in the rubble. "People will be afraid it's not safe, even after they fix it up."

That worker, by the way, was all right, having been extracted from this rubble after only an hour or two, then taken over to the Anderson Memorial Hospital where he was kept overnight for observation.

I had not been wanting to go to school the last few weeks, since they didn't dance there or talk about dancing, and my classmates and I did not meet there, not as dancers anyway. But this day I could not wait to get to school since that was the only way I could see people who felt like I did and even possibly find out about any developments that had taken place in the night, and in this way live through the time until the rehearsal at four-thirty. Clearly most of my classmates felt like I did: whenever any of us dancers spotted each other that day we let out cries of anguish and made for each other, cutting across all kinds of lines and boundaries, both literal and figurative, sometimes embracing and crying aloud. Claude and Hilary and I had one of these impassioned meetings in a hall midmorning (a threesome the likes of which had never been seen at school before, and not even over at the studio when life was more normal). At lunchtime I formed part of a gaggle of dancers gathered in the cafeteria. We blocked the window where people were trying to deposit their trays when they were finished with them and before long we were sent out by the teacher on duty down there, still hanging on to each other and wailing dramatically.

Nobody knew very much. The two people in the best position to know something, Christabel Merrick and Cecilia LeBreton, were no help at all, Christabel being off at her Catholic school, St. Anne of the Rocks, and Cecilia being off in some other world, I think. Cecilia wouldn't join in any of the anguished groups I've described and was even heard to say she "didn't give a flip" what happened to *Mother Goose,* that she hoped it was canceled. In this she disagreed with her mother. Oh yes, we did find out one important thing: Adelaide, who had driven Mr. Render over to the LeBretons' house to deliver the fell news the evening before, could report that Mme LeBreton was all for going ahead with *Mother Goose* without Mrs. Merrick or a cent of her money, and I confess this did not surprise me because I had seen for some time that Mme LeBreton hated Mrs. Merrick's elegant guts. But still, no one knew where justice lay in this tussle between Mr. Render's "ballie" and Mrs. Merrick's gala, or just what could happen without Mrs. Merrick footing the bill. Sometimes a very pleasant thing happened. Hilary James had naturally told everybody that her mother had hired my parents to represent the interest of the studio, and occasionally during these conferences throughout the long day the feverish participants would turn to me for the private legal angle. I had never had such cachet.

After the last bell rang at three o'clock I went out the side door of the school building, which put me on that big hill overlooking the parking lot. As they had done all day, other dancers gravitated to the same spot and I found myself talking with Lola and Claude and Dorcas, elbow to elbow, in an intensely friendly way.

"They're meeting now, aren't they?" Claude said, screwing up his sharp face in his anguish.

"Yes, they are," I said wisely, looking out over the parking lot to the gym. It seemed so long ago that we had gone in there, scared to death, for the audition! How cold it had been! Now it was very warm and a muggy wind was blowing; it threatened rain.

"Look, y'all. There go Hil and Steph with their lovers," Lola said sarcastically, pointing out the glossy heads of Hilary and Stephanie bobbing between two rows of parked cars. The yellow Pontiac was nosing toward them, but the top was up and I could not get a good look at the Merrick boys. "It makes me sick to see Hil and Steph suckin' up to the Merricks!" said Lola, who was a strong partisan of the Render-LeBreton forces.

"Somebody *has* to be nice to them. I don't know how we're going to have anything if we don't!" said Dorcas, the sycophant.

"Look, y'all," Lola said, gathering the three of us together to form a huddle, "why don't we hop in my car and ride out to the theater and take a look at it ourselves? I can't stand this waiting. What do you say?"

Lola was a cheerleader and used to inciting strong feelings and bold actions on the football field and the basketball court; perhaps this is why Claude and Dorcas and I (ill-matched band!) scooted down the steep hill, following her lead to her car, which was a Volkswagen of kelly green. How sporty I thought that was! Volkswagens were new and strange at that time, very "foreign" for Middleton, and thought to be hideous. I was impressed at being herded into this exotic vehicle by a girl who was a jaunty little cheerleader and also—make no mistake about it—one of the most outstanding members of the senior class. I was supposed to take the bus home, but I was sure my parents wouldn't mind my getting a ride with a senior and taking a detour out to the theater. It could be war, and this was like getting into a tiny little tank and taking a tour of inspection out to the front lines.

I was stuffed in the back seat with Claude, and Dorcas sat up front with Lola. Lola kicked on the motor, which sprang into rip-roaring life right below me; then she took off with a lurch, driving as if the theater were on fire and not just caved in. I perforce was sitting very near Claude in this hurtling roar. From my angle he was all shoulder and strange hair. Up close like this Claude's hair looked like a hunk of auburn-colored Spanish moss. He sat forward in the seat all the way out there, devoting himself to what we were going to see, as if it would somehow help him with his career.

As we turned off on the side road that led to the theater it started to rain, and in spite of the spring foliage the woods looked even drearier than the first time I had seen them. We weren't the only people to go out to the theater that day. Among the bulldozers and steam shovels, which seemed to be in exactly the same positions they were before, we saw a number of other cars, and when we scaled the hill we found ourselves in a small milling crowd. The outside of the structure didn't look too different from when I'd seen it in January (still blank, sacramental).

Inside it didn't look too different either, except that what had been the roof was now lying in a confused-looking rubble on and around whatever seats or other appointments had been put in place since that time. A number of people were swarming around in the wreckage. The theater looked something like a kicked anthill, in fact.

Claude and Lola and Dorcas and I stood in an unhappy knot observing all this.

"Well, you can kiss this place good-bye," Claude said. A drop of water ran down his cheek but I am not saying that the sight of the theater made Claude cry: it could very well have been a drop of rain that had fallen upon him through the jagged hole in its roof from the sorry gray sky.

***

I kneeled on the sofa in the library and peered down at the street, waiting for Mother and Daddy to get home from that meeting. They had not come by five, or five-fifteen, nor yet five-thirty. They had never still been away from home at this hour and at five-thirty I told Lucille, who was clumping around in a disgruntled way, that she could go home.

"They gon' get mad?" she asked.

"No, Lucille," I said. "They'd want you to go on home, I'm sure."

Everything was topsy-turvy, as if there had been an earthquake. Lola had roared us back to town and dropped everybody off at home in time to change for the rehearsal at four-thirty. I did this, but when I got to the studio it was dark and empty (bringing to mind the lines from "Old Mother Hubbard," "But when she got there, / The cupboard was bare") and, like some other dancers who showed up, I turned around and went on back home to wait for news.

Thirty or forty cars must have gone up or down Sycamore Street during that time. I recognized some of these. The Cadillacs of both Rachel and Dorcas went toward the studio, then away from it; I thought I saw the yellow Pontiac, though that might have been some other speeder. At long last the family Chevrolet eased down the street from the direction of Tates Parkway and the studio and turned for the climb up the driveway. I scampered out the back door and met it at the top, waving wildly.

"What happened? What happened?" I cried, jumping up and down.

"It's a long story," Mother said, getting out of the car stiffly, as if she were returning from a long journey.

"Looks like the performance is on for Saturday a week at the Civic," my father imparted, "but it was a knock-down-drag-out."

It took me some time to find out what had happened. For one thing, when we got inside, Mother was very distressed to find out that Lucille had gone and "had left that child alone," "that child" being me; she wanted to discuss this, since it seemed to bring to light a streak of carelessness in Lucille's character hitherto unsuspected. For another, my mother was so tired and agitated by the long meeting that she had trouble "thinking about supper," yet resisted my father's idea of going up to Ricciarelli's, an Italian restaurant we liked up on Tates Parkway, since that was what we did on special occasions like birthdays and this was just a weeknight. But at last we decided to go up to Ricciarelli's and I was sent up to my room to change clothes.

In the restaurant they finally told me that there had been an awful fight resulting in a rift between the Merricks, on one side, and Mr. Render and Mme LeBreton on the other. Mrs. Merrick had led off with evidence that the roof had fallen in not because of any major structural fault but because of some minor mechanical flaw, easily correctible, a loose screw maybe, as my father had facetiously suggested, or maybe the want of a nail, which caused the loss of the horse's shoe and the horse and the battle and the kingdom in the nursery rhyme. This little mechanical flaw, whatever it was, had similarly enormous consequences—the toe shoes, the ballet, the gala première, and the world-famous choreographer—all lost, just like that. Mrs. Merrick insisted that the theater could be repaired quickly and opened by June first. My mother said Geoffrey Render laughed at this. Even if the theater could be opened by June first, he had contended with reckless belligerence, that was far too late for *Mother Goose*. He talked, to continue the wartime metaphor, as if *Mother Goose* were cannon that had been transported with difficulty and rolled into place and loaded, and were now ready to fire, *now*. If they weren't fired, he seemed to suggest, they just might explode. The legal wrangle had been fierce.

My mother and father reminisced over the breadsticks you ate while waiting for your spaghetti and meatballs at Ricciarelli's about the long and closely written contract which had everything to say about who was going to do what by which date. The joint work of Alfred Wellesley, the Merricks' lawyer, and whoever was the NDT lawyer in New York (both of whom must have been deeply suspicious by nature), this contract not only had Mr. Render by the neck but also Mrs. Merrick, who was obliged to pay Mr. Render the staggering sum of twenty-five thousand dollars for his work, and Mme LeBreton who, as Ballet Mistress, was bound to perpetuate that work just exactly as Mr. Render wanted or submit quietly to being sacked. It required Mr. Render to produce a work that was "original" but which also was acceptable to its sponsor (Mrs. Merrick) and the representative of its performers (Mme LeBreton). In fact, it sounded as if the only one whose dissatisfaction had no legal outlet in that contract was Colette the cat, and it might be that she was mentioned somewhere in the fine print.

But Mr. Render, who must have been party to hundreds of contracts like this in his time, was right about the main thing. It was his "ballie" all right: the NDT lawyer had made sure that Mr. Render retained exclusive performance rights, although it was certainly to be assumed that he would graciously allow the LeBreton School of Ballet to perform it again, that he would possibly even make them a gift of it. On the other hand, Mrs. Merrick was right when she claimed it was her "gala première," if he wanted to be paid, that is, since she was not obliged to pay him until the performance actually took place; and sure enough her lawyer had inserted a clause about construction delays. This contract got several heated readings, according to my parents' account of the meeting. "It was *priceless,*" my mother said with tears in her melancholy eyes, signifying how funny something was. "We'd looked at that contract three or four times and then we noticed that Geoffrey Render hadn't signed it."

"You noticed, Caroline," my father said, watching her proudly.

"I thought Lyda Merrick'd have a hissy fit. It was *priceless.* Course that didn't really alter anything. Mr. Render's been acting on the contract all this time, so it didn't make a lick a difference whether he had signed it or not, but for a while she *thought* it did!'"

"Did he forget to sign it?" I asked, admiring this irregularity.

"I have an idea he never signs those things," my father said philosophically. "Keeps his options open. *I* have an idea he dud'n like to be tied down."

"Then come to find out Lyda Merrick hasn't *paid* anybody. Course she wasn't strictly obliged to pay anybody until the thing was over, but I gather people are complaining about it," Mother said primly. "There were some pretty angry letters from New York people. And poor Mr. Bartlett, and the sewing lady. I feel sorry for the sewing lady."

"But it all boils down to enforcement," my father said. Our spaghetti had come, and we shook Parmesan cheese all over it and started expertly winding it on forks and spoons. "The man is supposed to present the ballet in the Merrick Theater when it's finished, whenever that is. That's clear. But how are you going to *make* him? He *refused*."

"You wouldn't have believed it, Meredith. Lyda Merrick said 'You have to present it in my theater' or something like that and Mr. Render turned around and said 'I can't. I have pneumonia!' It was priceless," my mother said.

"Ha! Ha!" I said, imagining his blank and regal stare. "Well tell me, how did y'all get the Civic Auditorium? Didn't that Melbert Dole have it?"

"Your daddy talked to Melbert Dole's lawyer," Mother said, without using the inverted quotation marks for Melbert Dole's name anymore. "It's going to work out just fine. Turns out he's been sick with some kind of kidney thing and really wanted to cancel. So they were glad to bow out and let the ballet have the Civic. They were *so* nice. I wish the *Chronicle* could give him a nice write-up, but I doubt they will."

"You know who that lawyer was?" my father said to me. "Ole Sam Allison, from Ardis. Do you remember the Allisons?"

"Of course I do. April Ann Allison is *my* age," I declared.

"You know, Lawrence," Mother said, "I have to admit, now that it's all over, I was surprised Lyda Merrick didn't say anything to either one of us. She's *bound* to remember *one* of us. Or the name 'Jackson.' She didn't say pea turkey!"

"She was preoccupied, Caroline," my father said. "She was dead set on gettin' 'em to behave like she wanted 'em to."

"All those Millers are like that," Mother said, pursing her lips. "You remember her cousin Lucy, the one that went to Hollywood?"

"Pretty gal," my father mused.

"Well," Mother said dismissively, "it's settled. I think it's settled best for the girls. I didn't like the idea of Meredith Louise standing around first on one foot and then the other waiting for the Merricks to get that building finished. This has been plenty enough distraction from schoolwork as it is, and I for one'll be glad when it's over."

"I can't believe it's so soon," I said, suddenly nauseated and not hungry for spaghetti at all.

After we had eaten and were waiting for our little slab of spumoni, Mother, who had seemed to enjoy recounting the meeting, underwent a change of mood. I have said that she and my father never discussed important things in front of me, and now she seemed distressed, all of a sudden, that they had been violating this rule. I expect there was also concern in her mind about professional ethics. She looked at me sternly.

"Now Meredith Louise, I don't want you going and telling all this to the children at school. It's none of their business. Mrs. LeBreton wouldn't want you children knowing what happened at the meeting."

"What *about* Mme LeBreton?" I asked recklessly. "How did *she* react?"

"Lawrence, tell Meredith not to say anything at school," Mother complained to Daddy.

"Meredith, don't say anything at school," Daddy said.

"Where is Mr. Render going to stay?" I asked, struck all of a sudden by the fact that Mr. Render had been staying out in paradise but surely had been expelled from there by now. "He was staying out at the Merricks', but he can't stay *there.*"

"I guess he'll have to stay somewhere *else,* dear," my mother said absently, looking for the waiter with the spumoni.

"Aw tell her, Caroline," my father said. "Her classmates'll know right away. There's nothing really strange about it. It doesn't necessarily mean a thing. *I* didn't think a thing about it."

"For heaven's sake, where is he staying?" I cried out.

"He's staying at Mrs. LeBreton's now," my mother said portentously. "He went straight from Lyda Merrick's house to Mrs. LeBreton's house. He's staying *there* now."

"Oh," I said noncommittally, "that's nice," associating this transferral with the automotive hubbub I had noticed the night before. "That's sweet of Madame," I said with great innocence, meanwhile thinking dangerous thoughts about love affairs and possible paternity. This removal put Mr. Render and Mme LeBreton under one roof for the first time, together with the girl who might well be their daughter. This made them seem like a real little family in my mind, much like my own little family: something like the three bears.

"I don't know what Meredith Louise is going to *think* about all this," my mother broke out suddenly, as if she had read my mind. She flung her red and white checked napkin up on the table like a flag at the Indianapolis 500. "All these comings and goings, all this irresponsibility!" Mother raved quietly. "It was all I could do to keep from screaming in there this afternoon. I simply couldn't believe it. Lyda Merrick trying to run everything and hurting people's feelings like that. Telling Mildred LeBreton she'd build her *own* school and run her out of business, and telling Mr. Render he was a 'has-been.' Then *those* two people acting so silly and behaving like children telling her how useless and bossy *she* was, *they* not having seen to the contract, just like children, I declare. Completely irresponsible. Then," Mother whispered, "this business of Mr. Render living out at the Merricks' and now living at the LeBretons' little house," Mother said, giving the word "living" a lurid emphasis. "I worry about Meredith Louise thinking all this is all right!"

"I don't think it's all right!" I protested, but feebly, since I knew things had gone too far and nothing I could say would forestall what was coming next. I braced myself.

"I've been worried about Meredith Louise being so involved in this kind of thing run by people like Lyda Merrick and even Mrs. LeBreton. I *like* Mrs. LeBreton, I even like Mr. Render," she said largely, "but when you get right down to it they just don't *think* like we do."

"There, there, hon, take it easy," my father said, patting Mother's hand. She was trembling like Marie Taglioni. "You're just worn out. Come on, let's get you home."

"You did a mighty fine job this afternoon," he said as he gallantly pulled out her chair and escorted her out of Ricciarelli's. I trotted along behind them, my stomach twirling with Italian food and all of the private things I had heard.

22

The first rehearsal of *Mother Goose* down at the Civic Auditorium with the orchestra took place three days later, and it did not go well. In fact, that day it seemed to me as if before the quarrel with the Merrick people the personnel of *Mother Goose* had all been sailing grandly along in a luxurious ocean liner, its portholes shining with light and its flags rippling; but now, after the quarrel, we had been dumped overboard into the very cold, dark sea, in a small, possibly unseaworthy dinghy in which we bobbed perilously while watching the great ship steam on without us. Mrs. Merrick managed to put a good public face on this act of inhumanity: within a day or two of the savage meeting, the *Chronicle* carried another picture of Mrs. Merrick standing in elegant regret among the rubble in the aisles of the Merrick Theater and an article that quoted her as saying she would devote all of her time in the coming months to the repair and completion of the theater for the community of Middleton, as if she intended to go over there every day and toil alongside the workmen. The article also quoted her as saying that Mme Mildred LeBreton and Geoffrey Render had graciously consented to honor promises made to the public of Middleton and present *Mother Goose* on schedule (you saw them dancing and her, meanwhile, lugging bricks and timbers). I must say it was well done: she made it sound as if we had elected to jump overboard into that dinghy and actually enjoyed bobbing in it.

We weren't as bereft as I had thought we would be, though. I had assumed that Mrs. Merrick would take Christabel with her, and probably also Hilary and Stephanie, who so lionized the Merricks; I had worried a good deal about this since it would deprive the cast not only of its Queen but also its "Little Girl with the Curl" and the Baby in "Hush-a-Bye," its "Curly Locks" and its multipurpose Horse, and one member of the Trio so central to a variety of scenes. What a frantic reshuffling of roles this would bring about! As one person was elevated to a new role and another raised to take her place the effects would be felt all through the hierarchy of the cast, down unto the Townspeople and the Beggars. But this did not happen: the day after the rift Christabel appeared at the studio with a bright and playful air, as if nothing had happened. I imagine that if her mother had tried to withdraw her from the production, Christabel had pitched some kind of fit and Mrs. Merrick, surely tired from that legal row, just sighed and gave in. Likewise Hilary and Stephanie appeared at the studio as if nothing had happened. In fact, they were delivered there by the yellow Pontiac, which I found very curious but did not worry myself about. I knew I had no hope of understanding Hilary and Stephanie, or Christabel, most certainly not Wendell and Wexler Merrick: I knew they didn't think like we did!

As it turned out, the only change in the cast was the Queen. I had thought that Mme LeBreton herself might assume the Queen's role since the Queen danced only twice ("Sing a Song of Sixpence" and "The Tarts") and did not have to appear on the stage at the same time as *Mother Goose*; also because there would be a sort of justice in Mme LeBreton's becoming Queen after Mrs. Merrick had abdicated in that rude way. Instead, though, Mrs. Farfel showed up the day after the rupture. Mrs. Farfel! One of Madame's off-brand rivals as a teacher of dance, the teacher who produced the dancers who had fat thighs and wore purple leotards, and who now swelled the ranks of the Townspeople, playing common women. I was very surprised when Mrs. Farfel turned up. I do not know why she was asked—one doesn't question the composition of the trembling crowd in the lifeboat, one just prays and hangs on— but she certainly was not an asset to the cast, except possibly insofar as she soothed Mme LeBreton's soul by offering the greatest possible contrast in appearance and manner to the villainess Lyda Merrick. But people were worried about more serious things than Mrs. Farfel's sudden and puzzling accession. They were depressed about having to go back down to the Civic Auditorium to perform, also about how we were going to pay for everything. It was going to cost a fortune, my mother said. Even as my parents and I had mulled over the situation at Ricciarelli's, the Mothers' Guild was meeting to decide how to pay for Mother Goose. Actually the situation was exactly as it had been before: no one had been paid a cent, but now that our ship had gone out, so to speak, our situation looked desperate. For one thing, while Mr. Render and Mrs. Oleander and Mr. Bartlett and Mr. Beldinsky had all been reasonably content to wait for their money, the production was now, in these final hours, confronted with less gentlemanly workers who most decidedly would not be this patient. I speak of the musicians in the orchestra, who were already hired for several full rehearsals and the performance, also the stagehands. The musicians and the stagehands were members of notoriously bold unions which demanded full payment after each session. Even Mrs. James, President of the Guild and Mother *extraordinaire*, was cowed by this and conferred desperately with my parents, who advised that the Guild try to get a large loan from a bank at once. Miraculously, they did this within twenty-four hours: Mr. Martin, Melissa's father and the president of the First Middleton Bank and Trust, agreed to a loan of the princely sum of ten thousand dollars. Even more miraculously, the Mothers had potholders shaped like tutus and wooden basket purses with a pirouetting Mother Goose on the lid in Middleton's bookstores and specialty shops within a mere two or three days. The mothers surpassed themselves this time.

But it was bleak down at the auditorium on Saturday morning, even I had to admit that. Before, I had defended the place against the scorn of my classmates, at least in my own mind. I have said how I saw a certain antique charm in the red plush and velvet and the gold ormolu, but this had long since been eclipsed in my mind by the projected glories of the new Merrick Theater, and it was when I first arrived at nine o'clock, entering the auditorium from the rear as the audience does, that I took the measure of the place and thought of that business about the dinghy and the ocean liner. All the house lights were on and the main floor was empty of the folding chairs which constituted its usual amateurish

"Orchestra" and "Orchestra Circle"; a janitorial crew dry-mopped its bald expanse. Ahead, the stage was exposed to everyone's view and innocent of scenery. It was strewn with ladders and boxes; ropes dangled down behind it with that distressingly weak aspect of those ropes which dangled from the elevator out at the Merricks', had I cared to think of *them*. The way things looked that morning we might as well have been preparing to perform in an old circus tent in the middle of a pasture or the beat-up old gymnasium of a country school. The place looked like a gymnasium with that shiny floor and the windows with frosty glass way up there beyond the topmost balconies, which looked like rude bleachers.

Mr. Render and Mme LeBreton stood out in the middle of the main floor right under the chandelier talking with a gray-haired man I took for Dr. Viner, the old music professor up at the college who was to conduct the venal musicians. The chandelier, which I had thought so scintillating the night NDT performed, looked tawdry in the morning light, I observed gloomily. Now I would have thought that Mme LeBreton and Mr. Render would be awfully depressed at their miserable surroundings, but there they were, laughing with Dr. Viner, and I thought at the time that they were the kind of people who would sing in a lifeboat and work at cheering up the other passengers, not just sit there in dull despair. Or, I reflected less kindly, maybe this was what my mother meant by their being like children, laughing like this after a terrible quarrel which left them adrift in a sea of financial risk. In any case, they stood with Dr. Viner much as they used to stand with Mrs. Merrick in happier days, in an amiable trio, smoking cigarettes, even though the Civic Auditorium was full of "No Smoking" signs, and laughing at jokes I couldn't hear.

Dancers were running around everywhere, helter-skelter, much as they had before the audition, and making noise of similar thunderousness. Getting closer to Mme LeBreton and Mr. Render on the crowded floor, I decided they were less like children than my idea of parents of a large family who *like* children a great deal. Like such parents, they seemed remarkably unconscious of the hubbub around them. The musicians were down in the orchestra pit, beginning the disturbing cacophony of tuning up; and a team of stagehands, led by the silvery Mr. Beldinsky, carted scenery and props around on the floor and up on the stage, shouting and sometimes even swearing. Mothers were everywhere this morning; there were even some fathers. Backstage, where I went to take off my street clothes and do my barre, more stagehands, dancers, and parents converged, bumping into each other and fussing. Everyone was mighty put out by the theater. Depressed, I did my warm-up holding on to Humpty Dumpty's wall, which lay at a forlorn angle against a brick wall.

"All right! All right!" Mr. Render shouted at last into this havoc, banging Mme LeBreton's stick on the shiny floor. His high sweet voice reverberated through the auditorium as if it were a very large public bathroom. "Let's get under way here. There are some problems with scenery—we'll just have to be patient with Mr. Beldinsky and his crew. Particularly about the bridge. They're going to use milk cartons, people. One of the little last-minute changes. We're going to have to be awfully careful not to knock them down too soon. And they'll be testing the fly system so don't be surprised if somebody comes zooming across the stage. It's not a bird or a plane, it's Mr. Beldinsky."

Everyone tittered nervously at this joke, impressed, I am sure, with Mr. Render's good cheer in the face of our disaster, the way, you might say, he simply rowed forward, as if it were the movement that counted and not the quality of the vessel.

"So ignore the stage crew—jump over 'em, if you have to, and try to watch the conductor. This is Dr. Viner, kids, our conductor. You already know Professor Viner, I'm sure, from the college."

Dr. Viner, who looked venerable and had just the leonine hair I thought a conductor should have, smiled and bowed politely several times all around. As he mounted a small podium and brought his orchestra of some fifty musicians to the ready the spectators found seats and creaked into them, and dancers like myself who did not appear until several numbers into the program drew in toward the stage and clustered around Mr. Render and Mme LeBreton to see what would happen.

We listened apprehensively to random tunings—the zigzag of a violin, the slice of a clarinet, the swath of a trombone—and finally they drew together in a concentrated buzz on the pitch of "A." This

"A," sustained by Dr. Viner a good minute, lightened the mood in the auditorium. I forgot the dinghy for the moment and thought instead of an airplane. I had flown in an airplane once and this is how it had sounded going down the runway before it lifted off into the wild blue yonder. This was a great moment in the year of *Mother Goose,* I thought: we had a theater (even if it was the wrong theater, the old and ridiculed theater) and we had an *orchestra.* I remembered what a change it had made to have Nathan playing the piano instead of Mrs. Fister, and now we were progressing from the piano (which is a stark and solitary instrument, no matter how well it is played) to a full orchestra. It was a new epoch in the life of *Mother Goose,* all right, and we were all a little thrilled by the urgent, searching "A" vibrating throughout the auditorium. I smiled at a blackbird, I remember; she smiled back at me.

I have not yet said that *Mother Goose* opened with the overture and the mazurka of Delibes's *Coppélia*—the quintessential ballet music. It begins with the tones of French horns played gently, as if from afar, in a melody which seems to announce the dawn. Gaining momentum with the entrance of the violins, this melody swirls suddenly (here the curtain rises on *Coppélia*) into a heart-lifting mazurka punctuated by throbbing bass drum and crashing cymbals—a thrilling oom-pah-pah that is ballet at its most dashing. I am sure it is not necessary to say that Mr. Render's choreography interpreted this music to perfection. Little Boy Blue (Claude) is discovered "under the haystack, fast asleep" in the opening bars—*Mother Goose's* curtain rises sooner than *Coppélia's*—he awakes, stretches, rises to his feet in a slow spiral of a *pirouette,* and then, drawing a small golden cornet from his tunic, summons his sheep from the meadow and his cow from the corn, then leaps with the explosive music into a bravura solo full of dazzling leaps and great sweeping turns.

Clearly Mr. Render had conceived a curtain-raiser to exploit both Delibes' and Claude's gifts to the full. But, regrettably, at the rehearsal that Saturday this did not come off in the stirring way intended by Mr. Render. Dr. Viner raised his baton, thereby shutting down that preparatory buzzing, and gave the downbeat for the overture to *Coppélia.* The French horns, instead of gently intoning the opening melody, blatted it proudly, while the violins manfully sawed away beneath them. Dr. Viner leaned into the orchestra, making the frantic gestures of a handsome but cumbersome bird trying to get off the ground, but these did no good.

"No no no no," Mr. Render shouted across the floor. "More softly! *Piano.* Claude, more slowly. Like a flower opening, please."

The orchestra began again. This time they played more softly, all right, but the French horns gurgled and cracked, while the violins raced ahead. After several attempts at the opening, with Claude patiently corkscrewing upward on the stage, the orchestra lurched into the mazurka, where again the tempo was wrong or the players were too incompetent to deal with the music. Again and again Mr. Render toddled across the floor and stopped Dr. Viner, gesticulating at the musicians and then doggedly returning to his post mid-floor with Madame. Nathan, who had arrived sometime during this disheartening opening, stood there too, stooped and brooding over the music.

"Be patient, why don't you?" Madame croaked after the fourth such halt in Cecilia's Little Bo-Peep variations. "This *is* their first rehearsal."

"It's not the Philharmonic, Maestro," Nathan said from Mr. Render's other side. "It's just a pick-up band."

"I *know* what rehearsal it is and who they are," Mr. Render retorted, thrilling all of us who hung around him hoping he would do something dramatic about the terrible orchestra. "I'm just wondering what in hell they'll do with Ravel when they can't play *Delibes.* "

It took one hour to get away from the first three dances in the meadow and into the house where I first appeared with Old Mother Hubbard, although on this day there *was* no meadow and there was no house, only Mr. Beldinsky and his assistants toiling over their components. I went backstage somewhere during the torturous progress of "Three Blind Mice" and observed Mr. Beldinsky drilling holes in a large piece of scenery. I recognized his helper: he was one of the college boys who had come to the audition in December, the one with the clean-cut features who wore a crewneck sweater and blue jeans and white tennis shoes. His name seemed to be "Bruce," and Bruce and Mr. Beldinsky were working with grim dedication, Mr. Beldinsky, usually so colorless, almost flushed with his efforts.

"Try fitting *that* on *this,* Bruce," Mr. Beldinsky said with a ragged sigh.

Once on stage for my first solo as the dog in "Old Mother Hubbard," I had a better view of Mr. Render's marches forward to correct and denounce the orchestra and Dr. Viner, who he was calling "Viner" by now. It was really rather discomfiting, even though he hardly glanced at me. In fact, most of the dancers, realizing that Mr. Render was much more concerned about wrong notes than wrong steps, saved themselves and merely walked through their dances; likewise, I just walked through mine. (Mrs. Fister, the Old Mother Hubbard, walked through hers too, but then she always walked through hers.) Mr. Render had a lot to object to. My dog *divertissement* was supposed to be animated by a waltz from *Les Sylphides,* but not as this orchestra played it! "No, Viner, that won't do!" Mr. Render shouted, coming forward for the umpteenth time. "Too slow! And there isn't any *blood* in it. The dog has to bound around, don't you see. You've got to make it *pump* for the dog!"

Mr. Render grew more and more agitated as the morning wore on. In addition to the awful musicians he also had to deal with the problems presented by the decrepit theater. The questionable fly system was tested and pronounced "creaky" by Bruce, "risky" by Beldinsky, but Madame, Adelaide and even Mrs. Fister, all three anxious to soothe Mr. Render, insisted on going through with the flying portions of their roles; in fact, they sounded as if they could hardly wait to risk their lives flying out over the stage. Then, the lighting system proved to be terrible, nothing at all like Robert Neville from the college's theater department had expected to have to work with "out at the Merrick." Mr. Neville worked all morning with wildly dramatic sweeps and spots in a spectrum of violent gels, appearing every so often to shout and wave his arms angrily at Mr. Render. And then there were the predictable inconveniences and irritations backstage: people hated the dressing rooms, which Lola said were like cells in a mental hospital, though how she could know that I couldn't say; and as usual they hated the animal life there. Twice a dancer ran through the corridors and into the wings screaming about a mouse.

Then also, even a director not bothered by questions of dancing had to be vexed by some of *our* dancers. Mr. Render's patience was almost gone by the moment when Albert Wasserman as Jack struggled through the shoulder-sit with Melissa, teetering visibly, meanwhile miming his ascent of the hill. *"Hold* her, man, get a hold of her *somewhere,"* Mr. Render shouted, which made Albert flush and sweat and the orchestra break into rude laughter. Then there was Mrs. Farfel, who was a homely woman with hair that was obviously dyed black, a long bumpy nose, and lips painted to resemble a bow. This morning she wore a clinging nylon dress and clumsy black shoes rather than practice clothes. I had an opportunity to watch Mrs. Farfel and Mr. Render work together in "Sing a Song of Sixpence," where, it will be remembered, I became the maid after Alma evaporated. By this time Mr. Render had appeared as Old King Cole, and it was not lost on me that he did *not* walk through his part but danced "full out." (start new para?) Consequently I *chasséed* down my clothesline with intense energy. The music was an orchestration of the well-known tune for this nursery rhyme by a composer friend of Mr. Render who had also done treatments of "Baa-Baa Black Sheep" and "Three Blind Mice" and it was apparently easier for this so-called orchestra than Delibes or Chopin. Mr. Render thus turned his attention to the stage, where he had the task of teaching Mrs. Farfel what Lyda Merrick had done. I had considered the Queen role as non-dancing and so it was: Mrs. Merrick's great contribution had been her smooth golden beauty, which turned out to be no small thing. When this Mrs. Farfel ate bread and honey there was so much to *look* at on her—the funny mouth, the long nose, the shoes, which looked like something Minnie Mouse would wear—that the effect was entirely different. I heard laughter from the wings and of course the pit.

"Why couldn't that woman dress right?" Mme LeBreton said out of the side of her mouth to Nathan during the next number, "The Tarts," when I was once again out front. "The old bag looks like she thinks she's doing us a favor."

"She looks like the tart," Nathan said supportively.

After a period of struggling against Mrs. Farfel, who made a baleful queen, Mr. Render returned to his struggle with the orchestra. He was right about Ravel. By my last solo, "Jack Be Nimble," the music for which was the glorious *valse noble* from *Adelaide*, Dr. Viner was flailing helplessly and the orchestra had, as Burns would say, "gang aft aglay." Mr. Render was rigid with rage. With the last splayed, wavery chord of the finale, with all us dancers, remember, lying out on the floor, tucked into bed, Mr. Render shouted, at last, "All right, all right. Break. Break for an hour. Lunchtime." It was two-thirty.

The stage lights came on. Mr. Render was among us, right beside Mother Goose. "Oh Jesus, Milly," Mr. Render said wearily. "I knew they were going to be bad, but not *this* bad. Nathan my boy, give me some of that stuff in your canteen," he said over to Nathan, who loomed in the wings, joking with some girls. Mr. Render took a long and thoughtful swig from Nathan's flask. He wiped his mouth and hitched up his black pants.

"Why don't we use records, Geoffrey?" Mme LeBreton said solicitously. She took his arm and began to walk him off the stage. They proceeded to talk as if they were alone although a group of us followed along behind them, like a swarm of bees. "Wouldn't that be the most practical thing to do? It's what we've done in the past at recitals. It works just fine. The acoustics in this old barn are so bad you probably couldn't tell the difference."

"I won't have it, Milly," Mr. Render said petulantly. "I won't have my ballie stripped to nothing. It's very damn near naked now. I will not have these children dancing to a phonograph. It's a humiliation. She'll exult."

"So what?"

"Besides, the publicity promised an orchestra. Tickets are sold."

"And the contract, of course," Madame said, expressing the very thing that, as a junior Jackson, I had on my mind. "We *do* have a contract with these musicians."

"So we do," Mr. Render said indifferently. Suddenly he stopped cold. I was conscious at this moment of all the sad commotion in the auditorium: the hot dancers clothing themselves, disgraced musicians sheathing their instruments, stage crew shoving their fragmented properties around. Mr. Render, who had seemed old and sad to me, as if he were about to call for his pipe and bowl and, instead of fiddlers, some slippers of defeat, now seemed to swell with a new idea.

"I'm an idiot," he said with a strange exuberance, striking himself on the forehead. "Milly, I've got an idea. But first, is this Viner your uncle or anything?"

"No—"

"Your father-in-law, perhaps?"

"No—"

"Your landlord?"

"No, Geoffrey, what in—"

"Nathan!" Mr. Render boomed. We all craned around, looking for Nathan, who was across the stage, still in the wings, with his head tilted way back to drain the last drops out of his flask. "Nathan," Mr. Render called, "I'm going to sack Viner. You're always saying you want to conduct. Well, I'm going to give you a chance. It's not Carnegie of course, it's not even the State Theater. It's what you'd call an out-of-town opening." Mr. Render laughed. "I want you to take those men, Nathan, and teach them to play this ballie," Mr. Render continued in tones that I am sure penetrated every cranny of the old Civic Auditorium, even unto the mouseholes. I could not see him but I believe Dr. Viner was still down in the orchestra pit and learned of his dismissal in this way. "I don't care how you do it and I don't want to know anything about it. But if you can do it by next Saturday, Nathan, why—it'll launch your career!"

23

After lunch (hamburgers brought in by the Mothers), the rehearsal had gone from bad to worse. Nathan had taken over as conductor of the rowdy musicians, Dr. Viner having departed with frigid dignity, and although he obviously exerted himself to the maximum the "orchestra" still blatted and scraped, and Mr. Render continued to run down to the front of the auditorium to rant and rave at them. Mr. Beldinsky had hammered and sawed on a contrivance something like a lazy Susan to rotate the Humpty Dumpty wall (this was to substitute for the putative rotating stage), but although he had worked himself up to the high color of an Indian, he had not been able to make it work without Bruce out on the stage, in full view of the audience—giving it a good push. Mr. Neville had continued to flash the stage with lights made lurid by a set of antiquated and unsatisfactory gels, about which he shouted and swore from the lighting booth out into the black void of the auditorium. Later, Mrs. Oleander had shown up with some half-finished costumes and tried to conduct fittings in a dressing room, but she was very sick with an ear infection and coughed all over everybody and Mme LeBreton, frazzled now, had had to send her home. Meanwhile, dancers had walked through their parts, then huddled disconsolately in the wings, or gathered in the "green room," a ratty chamber which was actually the color of corroded iron, to lament the doomed production.

The next day, after our usual Sunday dinner of pot roast, I went up to my room and threw myself on the window seat. It was a sunny spring day, but I hardly noticed this, being too preoccupied with thoughts of the fiasco down at the dark old auditorium. I lay there for some time, looking out of the window into the bright green pointy leaves of the sweet gum tree. There was nothing to see except, after a while, the Indian family from down the street passing by. They were exotics, even in this neighborhood: an engineering professor, his wife, who wore saris and had a red dot on her forehead, and their four little children, two of them still babes in arms. They seemed to be out for a walk. The two children who could walk kept darting into the street and the mother and father kept having to snatch them back while continuing to hold the babies. This grappling was a particular problem for the mother, whose sari threatened to unwind. They took a long time to go by because they went from side to side as much as they went forward. But I did not pay too much attention to the laborious progress of the Indian family: I had to worry about the so-called orchestra, which Nathan was going to rehearse up at the college starting about now (one o'clock), the so-called costumes, which were still mostly ragged flaps, my *écartés,* which were a shambles, oh, a whole list of things! *Mother Goose* was only six days away. I envied the Indian family, just walking up Sycamore Street in the shade without a care in the world beyond preserving the lives of its children.

When the telephone rang downstairs and Mother called me, saying Mme LeBreton wanted me to come over to her house, my heart turned over, as they say; I thought everything was lost. "Is it going to be canceled?" I asked desperately into the phone, having reached it in two or three *grands jetés.*

"No no no," answered Adelaide, who was over at Mme LeBreton's doing the calling for her. "Don't be silly. Geoffrey is making ice cream and he and Milly thought it would be a nice occasion for a get-together. I'm calling just our class. Come on over. Come as you are, Milly says."

Mother stood near the phone in the kitchen, hugging herself and frowning. "What *is* it, Meredith Louise? Surely not another rehearsal! I was *so* counting on your resting today. You're *so* tired. You've got circles," she said, peering at my eyes.

"It's not a rehearsal, it's an ice cream party!" I said, running out of the kitchen, leaving my mother frowning in the kitchen, worrying, I know, about my going over to Mme LeBreton's house, where Geoffrey Render was "living" for the present and where they didn't "think like we do." "Can you drop me at Mme LeBreton's?" I asked my father as I sprinted through the library, where he was reading the Sunday paper.

I got dressed so rapidly and got my father on the road so soon that we passed the Indian family, still toiling up to the head of Sycamore Street. All the way over to Inglenook, where Mme LeBreton lived, I was frantic about the possibility of cancellation. Everyone wanted the show to go on—well, almost everyone—but it could be that enough was enough. Mr. Render and Mme LeBreton were no longer young: it might be that they just couldn't take this pressure, and the debt, and the trouble. That was it! *Mother Goose* was *so much trouble:* they had to wonder whether it was worth it! I'll die if it's canceled! I wanted to scream, but I knew my father would be alarmed at such hysteria and probably turn the car around and take me back home where Mother would require me to go to bed.

Rachel Mintz came to the door of Mme LeBreton's house. "Is it canceled?" I asked urgently. "Tell the truth."

Rachel took a little dancing step backward. "Canceled? Of course not. Come on back. Mr. Render's making ice cream. It's the best ice cream in the world."

I really did not believe what Rachel and Adelaide had said about ice cream. I thought "ice cream" was some sort of ruse to get us over to Mme LeBreton's so they could tell us *Mother Goose* was canceled (like sinister figures in cruising cars offer little children "candy"). And so, after following Rachel through Madame's little house, I was rather astonished to step out the back door and see that in fact ice cream was being made. Mr. Render was in Madame's back yard toiling over a big old ice cream freezer, turning the handle and talking to the small bunch of people gathered around him back there.

"Welcome, Jack," Mr. Render said to me gaily, pumping the handle. "You're just in time. It's almost ready now. You're in for a treat, you know, if they didn't tell you. This is the best ice cream in the world."

Startled by this preoccupation with ice cream, even a little upset by it, I looked around. Not too many people were there: Madame, of course, wearing her sunhat and sunglasses (this back yard had no trees and the day was almost hot without shade) and that same raspberry caftan she had worn out at the Merricks' the day of the pool party. This back yard certainly had nothing in common with the Merricks', I thought. Mr. Render was wrestling the ice cream freezer on a small uncovered flagstone patio with long blades of grass sprouting up between the flagstones. Beyond that was a small lawn that obviously hadn't been cut since the previous summer and sported a heavy growth of weeds and onion flowers. This unkempt patch was surrounded by hedges which waved at an awkward and somehow unwholesome height and prevented any view of neighboring gardens. I couldn't help longing for the velvet lawns and topiary of the Merrick place.

Also tromping around the little patio and even out into the yard, though you got black seeds from the weeds on your legs by doing this, were some of the dancers from our class and a few essential Mothers: Mrs. Mintz was there with Rachel, and Mrs. James was there without Hilary. (Hilary and Stephanie had "gone riding," Dorcas said, rolling her eyes.) So Dorcas was there, also Melissa and Lola; and Adelaide, of course. I was surprised to see Christabel there, after the feud; but she was gamboling about near Cecilia, who sat on one of the few things to sit on in that back yard, an old plastic ottoman that Christabel either tried to squeeze on beside her, claiming it was her "tuffet," or sat right by so that Cecilia could fool with her hair. Claude was there too, stalking around in the weeds.

When I got there Mrs. James was booming forth the information that one-half of the tickets were sold and reflecting that this was either very encouraging or very discouraging, depending on the way you looked at it, like the proverbial pitcher half full of water. Mrs. Mintz wanted to discuss another printing of the *Mother Goose* poster. Mrs. James brought up the problems they were already running into with the printing of the programs.

"I got the recipe for this ice cream at a little *pension* in the south of France," Mr. Render sang out in the middle of this. He said it as though in answer to a question, though I had not heard anyone ask one, and of course all other talk ceased. "I hadn't even planned to stop there! I

had been visiting friends in the country and I planned to drive on back
to Paris but I had some car trouble and so I had to stop in a little town.
Can't remember the name of it. It had a garage, thank God, and I left
the car there and went to a *pension* they told me about. Well, it turned
out to be one of those wonderful little places they have in France, a
beautifully decorated little place, neat as a pin. The owner was the chef
and his wife was the housekeeper and"—here Mr. Render let go of the
crank of the ice cream freezer so he could kiss his fingertips—"I passed
one of the best nights of my life there. Dinner," he said, cranking faster,
"was a beautiful meal. *Coq au vin,* I think, and the tiniest little peas I've
ever seen, and fresh bread and fresh butter and more beautiful food than
I've ever seen in one place. Finally it came time for dessert. 'Oh but no,'
I said, '*mais non,* I couldn't eat another thing,' but Monsieur Duvall—
that was the chef's name—Monsieur Duvall said, 'You have room. I
have made a *glace*—ice cream. You will have room for this ice cream. It
is the best ice cream in the world.'

"What could I say?" Mr. Render asked, straightening up and
holding his arms out in a helpless-looking second position, showing
his belly. "M. Duvall brought the dish of ice cream out. I tasted it, and
it was *delicious.* The best ice cream I'd ever had in my whole life. It
was caramel, but not like any caramel ice cream *I'd* ever had before.
Well, I knew I had to have the recipe, but I didn't know how to go
about getting it. You know how these Frenchmen are, how proud, how
jealous. But do you know, he was wonderful about it. I just came out
and asked him for the recipe and he said, 'What time are you leaving?'
I said, in the morning. What time? Oh, no particular time, I said. Well
come down to the kitchen about nine o'clock and I'll show you how
to make it!"

"That's because you're so famous, Geoffrey," Mme LeBreton said,
swishing by in the caftan. "He wouldn't have done that for any of *us.*"

"Nonsense, Milly. He didn't know me from Adam. He just liked to
be appreciated."

The ice cream was ready, and no one could talk about anything else
because we had to get chairs to sit on and bowls and spoons to eat the
ice cream with. There were some folding chairs in what Mme LeBreton

rather optimistically termed the "potting shed," and I followed Claude in there to bring them out.

"What's going on?" I asked Claude urgently inside the shoddy shed. "He was *furious* last night and now he's going on and on about ice cream!"

"Damned if I know," Claude said, pulling recklessly at the rubber-tipped leg of a folding chair held fast in a daunting pile of junk. "Maybe he's crazy, I don't know. Maybe they're drunk again."

With some trouble we extricated a few chairs and after a time everybody was situated in Madame's little backyard with bowls of the legendary ice cream. It was, of course, delicious, particularly when you were tired and hot and anxious. For a while all you could hear was the click of spoons against bowls and the buzzing of some insects swarming out of those hedges. This ice cream was infinitely better than that insipid store-bought stuff that had come out of the ice cream bar in the cabana of the back pool out at the Merricks', I thought loyally; why, it was even better than my mother's snow ice cream.

Mme LeBreton did not fool with the ice cream: she had been having one of her Manhattans when I got there, and continued having them, and soon Mr. Render, sated with ice cream, joined her in this. After everyone else was finished with ice cream (this meant three or four bowls in the case of some especially capacious feeders like Mrs. James and Claude), there were some renewals of the murmurings about *Mother Goose*— together with the dronings of the insects I heard the sibilant words "costumes" and "dressing rooms"—but once again Mr. Render began to speak. Everyone else, even the Mothers, automatically fell silent and listened. We were all drowsy from the warm sun and cold ice cream.

"It tickles me to hear the kids complain about the auditorium," he said, to no one in particular. "NDT's theater isn't a bit better than that."

"They're spoiled rotten, of course," Madame said languidly.

"They need to go on the road a few months," he said in an offhand way. "I was thinking about the old days and what it was like to go into a town and find out what kind of theater they had. Or what kind of stage, rather. There was rarely a real theater. I had forgotten how that feels, after so many years in New York."

"You toured this fall!" Madame protested. "You played that very auditorium this fall!"

"Oh that," Mr. Render scoffed. *"That* wasn't touring, not like the old days. The advance men take all the adventure out of touring now. I don't have a thing to do with the arrangements when we tour. Nils does practically everything! I was hardly there, Milly. They just trotted me out when it was time."

After brooding on this a moment Mr. Render suddenly smiled and looked quite happy. "Do you remember, *do* you remember the picture of Anna Pavlova on the side of the bus?" Then Mr. Render told us how Mme LeBreton, or Milly Frobish as she was, had decorated the side of the Ballet Benet tour bus, while Mme LeBreton pretended to be embarrassed and affronted by the recollection.

"In 1933 or 1934, I'm not exactly sure when, Milly here had the idea of painting a picture of Anna Pavlova on the side of the bus, a sort of publicity stunt," Mr. Render recalled with zest. "You kids *do* know who Anna Pavlova was, don't you?" he stopped to inquire.

"Sure! Yes!" some people said sleepily.

"Of course Anna was dead by then, poor darling—she had died sometime in 1931—but I didn't think we ought to use her picture on our bus. I thought it would give the impression that she was in the troupe, or had been in the troupe at one time, or at least had taught some of us, and this wasn't the case."

"No one would have thought that, stupid," Mme LeBreton murmured, sounding ready to start arguing about it even now.

"But she persuaded me," Mr. Render said, ignoring her. "She was such a pretty thing I couldn't tell her no for long. And I had to admit Anna made a fine symbol for a touring company. She was a tourer without equal, kids. She went everywhere. I believe she went to every town on the globe. I saw her twenty or thirty times without even going out of my way to see her—she came to *you* in those days. Most of the places our little outfit went she had been. She was the only ballie dancer most people had ever heard of. Now, *that's* fame," he said instructively. "No other dancer's ever approached it. Especially not now, when ballie's gotten so hoity-toity. I guess I thought," Mr. Render said, getting back to the main point, "I guess I thought a picture of Anna might pep up the troupe more than drum up business. This was in '34, maybe, '35. We were just about out of gas by then."

"See, it *was* a good idea," Mme LeBreton murmured.

"We were real pioneers," Mr. Render said, a gleam in his eye as he recalled the bus. "Of course we weren't the first dancers to cross the country. There had been others, as far back as the eighteen hundreds, but they were mainly soloists, like Anna, where we were a regular little troupe. Much as I disliked the old goat, I was trying to do the same kind of thing in America as Diaghilev had done in Europe. I'd never have admitted it. I wasn't alone in this, of course: other people who had learned from Diaghilev had come over too and struck out like we did. Scads of Russians, of course. Forever Russians! But we were all pioneers, going out into the wilderness with ballie!"

"People looked at us like we were from Mars when we pulled up in some of those towns," Mme LeBreton remembered. "We'd stop and get out on the main street—there was always a main street and they all looked alike—and the people on the street would stop and stare at us exactly like we were little green people stepping off a spaceship."

"Well, more like we were the circus," Mr. Render said. "As I remember it, you thought a picture of Anna Pavlova would solve this problem. They'd know what we were and what we were doing there. Before I knew it she was out there painting Anna Pavlova up on the side of the bus! God, I'll never forget that picture of Anna Pavlova! Part of it looked wonderful—Milly did her in the swan costume, of course, and she got the position just right—little hands *croisés,* little foot pointed. The only trouble was she couldn't get the face and hair," he said, smiling. "The face looked like a man's and the hair looked like a coonskin cap instead of a bun, and the more you tried to doctor it up the more it looked like Daniel Boone!"

"What do you expect, with house paint and a brush three inches wide," Mme LeBreton said pugnaciously.

After this Mr. Render and Mme LeBreton talked some more about touring, recalling the long bus rides, the bad food, the miserable hotels, the injuries, the illnesses, the bedbugs, and the fleas. Mr. Render told about a time when he had influenza but performed anyway, throwing up in a wastebasket in the wings between numbers. Mme LeBreton remembered a time a flat threatened to topple over and she stood in front of it, shoring it up and praying for the final chord. Of course it sounded wonderful the way they talked about it, and everybody listened raptly, except for Cecilia, who toyed with Christabel's hair and looked out beyond the hedges, then got up and went inside the house right in the middle of a particularly funny story about a performance in Oklahoma one time when the theater or hall was struck by lightning. How rude! I thought. I suddenly felt very hostile toward the beautiful, negligent Cecilia: Milly Frobish might have continued on that bus having such adventures if it had not been for Cecilia. I was unclear on the details but I had a strong association in my mind between the end of Milly Frobish's career and the beginning of Cecilia. Cecilia seemed to have taken the place of the career; or it had been poured into Cecilia by some means, and now she embodied it, but without even seeming to care. It was maddening! I saw Claude turn and watch Cecilia wander away; then he watched the back door a long time after she went inside while everybody else laughed about the thunderbolt that blew the fuses in Oklahoma, so long ago.

That bus! We all talked happily about the Ballet Benet bus with Milly Frobish's artwork on the side as the ice cream party finally broke up late in the afternoon. I could practically see the embattled bus, emblazoned with a dancing Daniel Boone, crawling this way and that, the length and breadth of America. At this time I did not have a very clear idea of America's state of development in the 1930s, my only knowledge having come from my parents' laconic observations on the desperate conditions which ruled Ardis during the years of the Great Depression; and so I imagined a horrifyingly poor America, tangled and dusty with poverty (in many ways not unlike this forlorn "garden"), with that bus inching through it, bringing the energy, the fantasy, the joy of Mr. Render's "ballie" to those suspicious and hostile natives whether they wanted it or not. How I wished Mme LeBreton could have been able to stay on that bus! I wanted to be on that bus myself, with toe shoes and costumes and a beloved, someone like Mr. Render who would tell me I was a "pretty thing," and do whatever I wanted, and hold my hand. Such misery as they had on that bus in their rides across America must have been a wonderful thing to make them forget, even for a little while, the catastrophes of *Mother Goose.*

BOOK FIVE

MOTHER GOOSE

24

Through most of the following week Mr. Render continued to display that genial philosophical attitude that allowed him to apostrophize caramel ice cream and rhapsodize on the trials of the past at the same time as we were lumbering through the final stages of the first production of *Mother Goose,* though this attitude was sorely tried, very sorely, on Wednesday night, the occasion of our next rehearsal down at the Civic Auditorium.

This was three days after the garden party. I should say that these three days had been extraordinarily busy. We were either over at the studio or down at the auditorium every minute we were not at home asleep or at school; we were either dancing or standing by anxiously for news on all the contingencies Mr. Render handled so well—Mrs. Oleander's ear, Mr. Beldinsky's wall, Nathan's orchestra. Now, *that* was a worrisome subject. Nathan appeared at some afternoon sessions, where he played the piano as wonderfully as ever, but his face was white and he rushed away without saying a word to anyone. He had even lost the arch and ironic look that I had thought was part of his physiognomy. He looked, in fact, as though the person dearest to him, his mother, perhaps, was in a local hospital and he had to get back to the bedside to hold the nearly lifeless hand extending from under the oxygen tent. This is not far from what he was doing: we were given to understand that his "pick-up band" spent every evening in frantic rehearsal at the music building of the college. There was a comforting rumor too that this so-called orchestra was going to get a transfusion in the form of certain instrumentalists from New York, to be flown down to Middleton at Mr. Render's expense. All *this* Mr. Render took very well, reaching up to pat the wide-eyed Nathan on the shoulder from time to time, saying, "You'll do fine, my boy. You'll do splendidly."

On Wednesday night the company of *Mother Goose* was down at the Civic Auditorium running through the ballet for the last time before the dress rehearsal, which was to be on Thursday. Now this dress rehearsal was two days before the performance instead of one day because, while *Mother Goose* had ousted Melbert Dole from the Civic Auditorium without any real problem, it had hit an obstacle that could not be dislodged. It so happened that Roundelay, the freshman dancing club at Middleton High, was holding its Spring Cotillion at the Civic Auditorium on Friday night, and that could not be changed! As a result, our dress rehearsal would be Thursday, even though as of Wednesday Mrs. Oleander, who was " porely," as she put it, had not yet finished the costumes, and, even more disturbing, even though the animal masks had not yet arrived from Dallas. All *these* things Mr. Render took very well, however, padding lightly around the Civic Auditorium on Wednesday night, watching and correcting and encouraging, not even rattled by the fact that Nathan was off at the college with his orchestra in the belief that they were not fit to play in public yet, so that Mrs. Fister had to play the piano. It was horrible how the acoustics of the big old auditorium gave such awful scope to Mrs. Fister's jouncy approximations of the music.

What I am talking about—that which sorely tried Mr. Render— happened, or, I should say, became known, shortly after the "Three Wise Men of Gotham" number. Now while Mr. Beldinsky and his minions had still not adjusted all of the sets and properties to our reduced circumstances, they did have a fully completed, good-looking backdrop to simulate the seaside town from which the three men—the Trio of Melissa, Stephanie and Lola—"went to sea in a bowl." There had been some talk of a real "sea" in a plastic tank out at the Merrick Theater but no one deigned to miss this, and the backdrop had lately been hoisted to general admiration. Being free at the moment, I went out to the front of the house to observe its effect, finding a seat in the lower balcony, where I was charmed and cheered by the sight of the Trio doing its jolly knockabout dance. They "capsized" and flailed comically; then, back on "dry land," a crowd of beggars in leotards thronged to the stage ("Hark hark the dogs do bark, / The beggars are coming to town").

As it happened, Mr. Render was standing in the aisle next to the balcony where I went to sit, looking across the auditorium at his ballet on the bright stage. During the time of "Three Wise Men of Gotham" and then "Hark Hark" I became more interested in watching Mr. Render than what was going on down on the stage, for the paradoxical reason that he gave the impression that there was nothing in this world so fascinating as what was going on down on the stage. He gazed intently at the stage, hugging himself, bobbing and weaving as the Trio, then the beggars leaped and twirled.

Since the lower balcony where I was sitting was enclosed by a small wall with a rail, I could see only Mr. Render's head, for the most part in profile, and his upper torso. He looked disembodied then, just by the accident of our physical situation, and perhaps this reinforced my impression of his fanatical absorption in the dance on the stage. I envied his complete abandon: it was as if he himself were not even there at that moment, but somewhere else, and I had the distinct impression that while he knew down to the last detail what was really happening on the stage he also saw something far more wonderful than I did, something that came from some unassailable place in his mind. But just then, as I was watching Mr. Render's transported head, it was joined by Claude's head. This was very startling: Mr. Render's head was nearly bald, mostly eyes; Claude's head billowed with rolling auburn curls and, as he spoke some words I could not hear, his desperate mouth looked like it was hinged way back in his head, like a wolf's.

Claude delivered his news to Mr. Render who did not, I remember, even flick his eyes from the stage. I believe Claude must have delivered it twice: he darted at Mr. Render's ear twice, then withdrew, leaving Mr. Render looking with what appeared to be the intensest pleasure at Hilary entering the stage with great flopping *pas de chevals* for "Banbury Cross." By this time I had sprung out of my seat and rushed out of the lower balcony, past the impervious Mr. Render, out into the hall and after Claude, who was bounding away.

"Claude! Claude!" I cried. "What *is* it? What's happened?"

Claude paused in his headlong rush down the empty hall, his face "working," as they say, under the pressure of some extreme emotion. "It's Cecilia," he managed to say. "She has collapsed."

"Is she hurt or what?"

"Hurt," he repeated with a snort, as if it would be wonderful if she were only hurt. "She's—she's going to have a baby."

"Oh my gosh," I said slowly, appalled at the awful news, wanting to fall down on my knees and cover my head at the shock and the shame, but forcing myself to behave maturely. I took Claude's arm and we began to walk down the hall together, around to the door backstage. "Did you tell Mr. Render?"

"I told him, but I don't think he heard me."

"Oh my gosh…"

"I guess this is the end," Claude cried despairingly in the resonant hall. "She's ill. She fainted. She can't stand up now, much less dance. It's all over for *Mother Goose.* No one could ever take her place. It's all over for *me.* I can't go on without her. Oh Meredith," he moaned, stopping and taking me by the shoulder, "I always believed we'd end up together," he said, meaning Cecilia and himself. "I always thought she'd come around to *me* in the end, no matter what. But now she's gone and done *this.* There isn't anything worse she could have done, except die."

"She'll probably wish she had died," I murmured, faint myself from the pain of Claude's grip on my shoulders. His thumbs seemed to be working some pressure point. But finally he released me, and we walked on around the hall toward the catastrophe backstage, while the black Middleton sky pressed itself against the old windowpanes, some of them broken, high in the wall.

***

We found Cecilia lying wanly on a narrow iron bed in her dressing room. Mme LeBreton sat on the edge of the bed bathing Cecilia's lovely domed brow with a wet washcloth. Cecilia was very pale, and her mother had turned the ghastly color of what in those days (when less attention was given to the feelings of people of other, darker races) was called the "flesh" Crayola.

"I thought I could make it through Saturday night, y'all," Cecilia explained in her little-girl voice to a large and variegated audience of dancers and stagehands.

"He is not coming *right* now," Claude announced sternly as we entered the tense room. "He wants to finish the act, and I have to dance Georgy now," he finished, exiting backward like a courtier and slamming the door.

I joined the growing crowd around Cecilia, who was lying in state. Even at this moment of high emotion, I thought of "Snow White," where the dwarfs gather mournfully around the maiden they believe to be dead. This group of onlookers (many of whom were the little dancers who were the beggars or wives, the horsemen or flowers) was not really mournful, though, but alarmed and respectful, and of course admiring. At first I was startled by this: I have said how I felt at that time about someone being "pregnant" and how I had worried about this stigma appearing upon Cecilia. Now it had happened: Claude had said she was having a baby and here she lay, not even denying it; and her mother wasn't even shrieking aloud. Poor doomed *Mother Goose:* it had survived a roof falling in, it had survived the loss of its financial backing, it could probably survive a pitiful orchestra, but surely it couldn't survive the pregnancy of its prima ballerina. Nothing could long survive *pregnancy,* as I understood it.

Madame stroked Cecilia's head absently. Once she murmured, "Don't try to think, now, angel. Just rest."

Information was not given out in any systematic way during those first few minutes. Out on the stage, not far away, "Georgy Porgy" and then "Jack and Jill" were being pounded out; meanwhile the backstage chaos I have described continued around us. They were working on the sets even now, and the crash of hammers and rasping of saws never stopped. I managed to learn from an obliging flower, meanwhile, that Cecilia had fainted dead away while drinking a Coke in the hall and that when she had been brought around she confessed that she was Mrs. Charlie Hill and was expecting a baby in six months. The flower explained that they had "gone to Arkansas" in January, by which she meant, as I already knew from other scandals at Middleton High School, that they had crossed over the state line to Arkansas to be married because there you only have to be sixteen to marry instead of the eighteen you have to be in the state of Louisiana, perhaps because of the laxer social customs among the hillbillies in the Ozarks, who constitute a lower social class than is to be found just about anywhere in Louisiana, I believe. This news cast a legitimating glow over the situation which began to look "maternal" instead of just wicked, and I too began to beam proudly at the little mother. At the same time, of course, I doubted that Cecilia had really gone to Arkansas, but even the retrospective intention to go to Arkansas lightened the air and permitted the purifying glow. There was no real mystery why this union, whether illicit or otherwise, had been kept secret. Middleton High School frowned on married students, and it expelled pregnant girls. Naturally (and I think the littlest beggar knew this at once without having it explained to her), naturally Cecilia would not want to lose Charlie Hill to Germany and then get booted out of school. Cecilia lay there with the sainted air of a young girl determined to have her education.

"I *think* I can dance, y'all," Cecilia said, straining to lift her head.

"You'll do no such thing," Mme LeBreton said with a flare of the nostrils. "You're not strong. We won't take any chances."

I had noticed before that Mme LeBreton acted very fine in emergencies, and now, in a situation which seemed to me just about the worst possible emergency—except maybe a fire in this rickety old theater that killed the dancers and razed all of the sets and costumes—she looked exalted. The bad news spread among the dancers and probably made its way out to the house (much like a fire) soon afterward; and while the alarm grew and the crowd around the bed in the small dressing room swelled, the LeBreton women remained amazingly calm. It occurred to me that Mme LeBreton might have been the heroine of many a dressing-room catastrophe. Certainly she had never before struck me as so complete a veteran.

Her rescuers had wrapped Cecilia up in a white sheet. Perhaps my impression of her would have been different if she had been wearing her Mrs. Peter costume, that brief and disreputable piece of red clinging lingerie, but she was swathed in this sheet and looking as if she were dead, or about to be. She looked like an angel, really, which was quite appropriate because she was in fact dead to the production, like that other "angel" Lyda Merrick. We all knew we had lost our prima ballerina. Mme LeBreton seemed to accept this fact with astounding ease. She lit up a cigarette, remarking once, hoarsely, "Well, you can always teach." But she also glanced repeatedly at the door of the palpitating room; it opened and shut countless times during the ten or fifteen long minutes it took the stomping herd out on the stage to get through "Georgy Porgy" and "Jack and Jill." "Jack and Jill" stretched out much longer than it ought to, Albert's fault no doubt. All this time we waited for the end of the act, when Mr. Render would come through that door. Cecilia waited like a moribund Snow White; her mother attended her valiantly, and Hilary, I noticed with interest, Hilary most particularly waited too. She had recently performed "Banbury Cross" and now she walked around the room, as well as she could in this crowd, with hands on hips, looking down at the floor, her face flaming with the heat of performance and eyes alight, wild almost, with what I realized to be the hope that Cecilia's roles would be hers. I observed a hand of Hilary's to twitch, a toe to point, as if she were going over the roles in her mind as she paced.

The door opened once again and Mr. Render stood there. At once the nervous throng froze into a rigid tableau with Cecilia and Mme LeBreton at its center. The only evidence of life in the room was a ferocious odor of perspiration. Cecilia kept her eyes closed in a delicate way but Mme LeBreton raised hers boldly to Mr. Render. "What's this I hear!" he said grandly, standing impressively at the door for another moment before sweeping in through the crowd toward the piteous display of Cecilia's body.

"Cecilia!" he shouted, waggling the dead girl's shoulder.

"She's— She's—" Mme LeBreton began bravely, but could not continue.

"Claude has told me all about that. Now let's have a look," Mr. Render said with the vigorous cheer of a doctor. "Cecilia my dear, how far gone are you?"

"Far gone?" she queried, eyelashes fluttering open. "How do you mean?"

Far gone? I wondered indignantly. Why, she's almost *dead.*

"I mean, how many months are you into your state of motherhood?"

"Oh, three," she said, smiling very slightly and turning one of the shades of her mother's leotards, vermilion, I think.

"Cecilia is married, Geoffrey," Mme LeBreton put in. This did not attract Mr. Render's attention.

"You've seen a doctor?"

"No. I didn't want to worry anyone."

"With these results," Mr. Render said quickly, with a sniff; then, with that single criticism out of the way, he went on to what concerned him. "Do you feel like you can get up? Get up, why don't you, and see if you feel dizzy."

"Geoffrey you *aren't* proposing that the child dance," Mme LeBreton bawled.

"There there, that's fine," he said, supporting Cecilia, who teetered away from her iron deathbed with a glassy smile. "Rachel, call your father to come take a look at her, would you?" he tossed back over his shoulder as he proceeded with Cecilia out of the room and you knew as well as you knew your name, out to the stage, leaving everyone, Mme LeBreton and Hilary in particular, in openmouthed shock.

"I don't think my father knows how to *do* babies," I heard Rachel murmur, troubled, as we trailed after them, craning our necks to see.

***

I cannot imagine a more vivid demonstration of the proposition put forward by Mme LeBreton that day, so long ago, on which we first learned the shocking idea of *Mother Goose* that ballet came first for Geoffrey Render, before everything, what anybody thought or what anybody felt. For the rehearsal went on, *not,* certainly, as though nothing had happened, but it went on, nevertheless, where I would have thought that under such circumstances it would have silently packed up its paraphernalia and skulked into the night. Soon Act Two was under way and we were dancing to the crazed and jerky music of Mrs.

Fister. Seeming to defy nature and every canon of good sense, Cecilia danced Mrs. Peter in "Peter Peter Pumpkin Eater," looking vacant and otherworldly, but, still, able to dance. Everyone hovered anxiously in the wings, hands pressed to mouths. It distressed me to watch Cecilia: having by this time of that year almost completed my high school biology course, I knew enough about human reproduction to be able to visualize the fertilized egg clinging for dear life to the wall of her uterus as she so nimbly performed the lunges and leaps which dramatized Mrs. Peter's determination to be free, and I cringed every time she landed on the stage. Of course I anxiously watched Claude too: poor old Claude, acting feckless and deprived as Peter Peter Pumpkin Eater, his interpretation of that role no doubt heightened by this latest heartbreak.

Mr. Render's character dances as the King dominated the first half of Act Two, however: more proof, if further proof was needed, that ballet could flood his consciousness and drive away any other thought or care. He was jolly Old King Cole, calling for his pipe, his bowl, and his fiddlers three; then he was the canny and calculating king counting out his money; next he was a revengeful king who beat, "full sore," the knave who stole his queen's tarts; and in the course of the dances he partnered Mrs. Farfel as if she were a woman of the highest distinction instead of an old hag. Indeed he performed as if he were in a gala performance at the finest theater in New York City instead of a sadly shaken rehearsal at the Civic Auditorium in Middleton, Louisiana, where there had lately been a disturbance equal in effect to a wide rift in the earth.

And he did all this in spite of a stormy quarrel with Mme LeBreton which began during "Peter, Peter" while Claude, Cecilia, and the fertilized egg had performed out in a wandering spot of orange light. At that time Mme LeBreton and Geoffrey Render had stood shoulder to shoulder in the wings watching this and exchanging remarks out of the sides of their mouths, while I hunkered nearby.

"Of *course* I didn't know anything about it. I knew, of course, she thought she was awfully in love with the boy," Mme LeBreton said.

"She has been well until tonight?" Mr. Render said, examining Cecilia, now doing a tortuous backbend out of Claude's clutching arms.

"Off eggs in the morning, now that I think about it."

"Couldn't you have *watched* her, just this little time?"

Mme LeBreton stiffened; this was visible even in the wings, in the penumbra of the orange spot. I imagined that I saw her thin and matted hair bristle.

"This is *madness,* having her flip all over a stage when she's feeling so faint. She'll miscarry."

"I do hope so," Mr. Render said distractedly. *"Why* will you women get pregnant?"

"Don't you know?" Mme LeBreton said dangerously, shifting her stance.

"I'm so tired of this," he went on stolidly, aggrieved. He continued to look at his ballet on the stage, but in a different way from the way he had looked at it from the balcony a little while before. That had only been about a half hour ago but it seemed like an epoch! As I saw it, he was aggrieved not because of Cecilia's plight, nor because of his old friend Milly's antagonism, but rather because he could not smile upon this embodiment of his work in the same fine unblinking oblivion as he had enjoyed back then: he had to frown and think and consider things while he watched. "This happens all the time in my company," he went on peevishly. "A girl falls out in rehearsal. Usually a dress rehearsal, but sometimes even a performance. The first thing she says is 'I didn't want to be any trouble,' while everybody scurries around, either trying to get her back on her feet or, if she's too far gone, trying to replace her. She is pregnant, naturally."

"How inconsiderate of her," said Madame.

"But we've arrived at a rule of thumb. I let girls dance until they show. That's about five months for a girl built like Cecilia. There's not a reason in the world why Cecilia cannot dance this performance, provided nothing is drastically wrong."

He can't be her father; at least he can't think he's her father, I thought, heart pounding, as Mme LeBreton said, "Have you asked her? I didn't hear you ask *her."*

"The thing is," Mr. Render said, turning to Mme LeBreton as "Peter Peter" was coming to a close, extending one foot in preparation for going on stage for his series of royal appearances, "I had every intention of taking her back with me to New York. She's too old of course but she has a special quality and I am sure there is work for her in the *corps.* That face! And a lovely body too if this doesn't ruin it. You see this is an awful disappointment to me, Milly. I think I've found someone, and then they're suddenly impossible. It's too cruel. It reminds me of you!"

With which remark Mr. Render leapt onto the stage, smiling, with an arm sprung upward in a gesture designed I am sure to thrill the upper balconies and set them cheering before he ever danced a step. Then he proceeded to dance, as I have already described, just as if he were performing for crowned heads, or at least very special and sophisticated heads in New York City. I believe everyone was powerfully affected by this example of professionalism and sought to emulate it. Somehow, perhaps, the show would go on.

As I warmed up to do my climactic solo as Jack, then the taxing ensemble of "Hey Diddle Diddle," people were buzzing about how Madame and Cecilia had disappeared together and were now closeted in the same dressing room as before, and how Dr. Mintz had arrived at the Civic Auditorium not too long after this and joined them in there. Later, after his kingly stint, Mr. Render also went into the dressing room. This meant that during the second, darker half of Act Two, that portion lit by moonlight, there were no adult directors of our exertions at all, only Mrs. Fister flailing on her piano down in the pit. During this time I felt uncertain, untended, even abandoned, most acutely during "There Was an Old Woman" and also "Old Woman, Old Woman" when Mrs. Fister left her piano and came up to the stage to clomp through her parts. Then there was no music at all, just the sound of feet, which sounded eerie, like ghost cattle at midnight. During these interludes, I could hear the sounds of voices coming from that dressing room backstage, particularly the barking voice of Dr. Mintz, but also the other voices rising higher and staying up in this alarming crescendo longer than seemed possible, outside of grand opera.

***

I have found this out about scandals: people out in the world—as opposed to people like my mother and father who were actually retired from the world, though I did not recognize it at the time—anyway, worldly people are never really upset by shocking things and in fact appear to enjoy them. Cecilia's pregnancy made her friends act very superior and smug for a while: I am thinking about Lola and Hilary and Melissa and Stephanie, even Adelaide. Right away, Adelaide assumed a proprietary air over Cecilia, as if she were going to serve as midwife at the delivery of the baby and then as its governess. I do not think anyone believed that Cecilia and Charlie Hill had really "gone to Arkansas," but that did not matter: it was a case of love bursting the bonds. Even at fourteen it seemed reasonable to me that certain girls gifted with beautiful flesh could not last out the full four years at high school, an institution devoted for the most part to the development of the brain: several other Aphrodites in Cecilia's class, then other such girls in every succeeding class down to my own, turned up pregnant and "married" in the same equivocal manner as Cecilia. This happened again in the four years of college, on a higher plateau. Confusing my myths, I had a vague image of these girls as Daphnes running toward the goal of graduation, in high school or college, but, overcome by love, the love for which their natures destined them, turning into rooted trees, which is to say married women, proto-Mothers, before they could reach that goal. Cecilia was clearly one of these Aphrodite-Daphnes, more beautiful than anyone else, more desirable, more likely to fall by the wayside, where she would no doubt flourish and bloom while the rest of us went running wearily on.

But at this point Cecilia was in a puzzling transitional stage, with her limbs just beginning to be transformed into the leafy laurel branches; and the lively question during the remainder of that shock-filled rehearsal was whether she would dance. The upraised but indistinct voices in that dressing room no doubt debated this, without announcing a decision to the general public. Next day we learned that Cecilia *would* dance. She was absent from school, but this was not because she was collapsed and in the hospital or anything like that but because she was at home, resting for the dress rehearsal. I saw her at home, in my mind's eye, sitting in a chiffon negligee among piles of bright-colored cushions, her hair loosened and floating around her, the leaves just beginning to sprout from her strong white shoulders.

***

In our family if a girl had gotten "secretly married" in the ambiguous way Cecilia had and turned up pregnant (though these things are one and the same: no one, so far as I know, was ever "secretly married" without being pregnant), such a girl would be the cause of much pity and terror. The pity would come in not so much for the wayward girl as for her mother, who would presumably be "crushed," the terror in the appraisal and reappraisal of the methods by which that mother had raised her, hereby shown to be fallacious. I knew this from discussions I had overheard among the mothers in my family, I mean the mothers in the Jackson and Meredith families in Ardis and its environs, who took cases of this kind as a personal warning, and, hearing of them, would draw their daughters in even closer to their breasts, meanwhile looking anxiously around for other wild and marauding boys.

I knew I must tell my parents about Cecilia so that they would not hear about the matter from more reckless lips. "The most interesting thing has happened," I said candidly at the breakfast table the morning after the disturbed rehearsal. "Cecilia LeBreton married Charlie Hill before he went into the Army and they didn't tell anyone." I did not mention anything about a baby right at first in the hope that my mother would take this as a platonic gesture on Cecilia's part, something patriotic, by way of cheering up the troops.

My father rustled the *Chronicle* he was reading and Mother cracked her coffee cup into its saucer.

"Married?" she said. "She married secretly?"

"So it seems," I said. "They announced it last night at the rehearsal. Everybody's real excited about it. It was very romantic, they say. She wanted to marry Charlie because she thought he might get killed in Germany."

"Lawrence, did you hear that?" Mother said anxiously, leaning over to rattle his paper. "Mrs. LeBreton's daughter married, secretly." She eyed me. "Will the daughter finish school?"

"Of course, of *course*," I said with warmth. "Graduation is only seven weeks away!"

"It must be *killing* her mother," Mother said with a soft moan. "Poor Mrs. LeBreton. This big production, I hear her health isn't too good, and now this. She just lost her husband a year ago. Why, she must be *crushed!"*

25

We don't even have all our costumes, I thought in despair as I gathered my books together for school. Before leaving I went over to my closet and looked forlornly at the two costumes hanging there: the red- and white-striped satin Jack Be Nimble jumpsuit and the rusty brown fake fur dog suit. How gay they looked! I had never had anything that looked so festive, not even my tutus for the two recitals I had been in, not even my Lark tutu. Neither satin nor fur was a material familiar to our house, where cotton and seersucker and, in winter, wool held sway, and where in a few years polyester would be welcomed in all seasons because of its no-nonsense upkeep. I rubbed these costumes affectionately and prayed that my other costume, the peasant maid's dress, would somehow get finished, that all the unfinished costumes would get finished. Most especially, I prayed that the masks would turn up. The Mothers had been calling Dallas every day about the masks and, like the costumes, they were "almost finished" or even "on the way." We'd been giving the people in Dallas the benefit of the doubt, but here it was, the day of the dress rehearsal!

I suddenly remembered something: I had forgotten to darn the toes of my new toe shoes! I snatched them from their boxes—there were three pairs, in rich, unexpected colors (scarlet, rust, periwinkle)—and caressed the bright, smooth satin. They were "professional"-style toe shoes instead of student-style, which means that they had slick satin toes instead of the usual ground-gripping doeskin. It was my job to slash this satin and then darn it the way professionals, like the doe-eyed, ladderchested NDT women, do practically every day of their professional lives; but I had kept postponing this mutilation so as to prolong my enjoyment of the sight and the feel of these smooth and risky satin toes. Now, though, I had to stuff the shoes back in their boxes and grab my books and run down the stairs; I'd have to darn them after school. Marie Taglioni was sitting in the doorway to the library as I came clattering down the stairs, but she ran off and hid under the couch. There was another job: I had to catch Marie and take her down to the auditorium to be in the St. Ives number. And poor Marie was still so timid. That might prove to be the greatest difficulty of all.

It was a beautiful morning, still damp from what must have been a hard rain during the night but sunny, with a breeze. I toiled up Sycamore Street, afraid of missing the bus and having to wait fifteen minutes for the next one, which would make me late for school, and worrying about all the things I had to worry about—Marie, the shoes, the costumes, Cecilia, everything!—neglecting, I am afraid, the pleasures of the fresh spring morning as I labored up the street, which seemed as steep as the side of a mountain.

Just as I dragged myself around the big curve of Sycamore Street, I saw Mrs. Oleander's bulbous old Plymouth turn into the parking lot of the studio, and coming right behind it (exactly as cars nose along after each other in a funeral procession) Mme LeBreton's maroon Lincoln. The Lincoln had two people in it, and the other was Mr. Render. Another car was already in the lot. This third car held Mrs. Mintz, and as I drew near I saw these adults get out of the cars and start opening back doors and trunks. Oh, this was a reassuring sight! Mrs. Oleander's Plymouth was stuffed with costumes and Mrs. Mintz's Cadillac was loaded with big cardboard cartons which must surely contain the masks.

"Hello!" I called out tentatively, trying to see what they all had, not forgetting to look at Mme LeBreton to see if she was "crushed." "Wrecked," maybe: she had on those unflattering pedal pushers and looked as if she hadn't slept at all, except that her hair was both flattened and pushed up in the back, like the hair of someone who has lain in bed for days.

"Well, Meredith," she said. "Have you come to help again? I expect we could use a hand right now if you have a few minutes."

"She could also try on her mask," said Mrs. Mintz, who was trying to wrest a large carton out of the back seat of her car. "I'm scared to death they won't fit the girls and then what do we do?"

"I have a costume for her too," Mrs. Oleander droned. "I don't know whether it'll fit her right acrost the chest. It's been so long since I measured her and girls her age is swellin' all the time. You kin hardly keep up with 'em."

"Don't worry, Mrs. Oleander, I'm the same," I said as I extracted five or six costumes from her car, where several dozen costumes were hanging from a string stretched "acrost" the back seat. Holding them high, I stumbled blindly over the rocks of the parking lot and stood half-smothered by them while Mme LeBreton fiddled with the key in the lock of the back door.

"Good morning, Colette my love," she said rapturously when she and the rest of us, burdened like pack animals, got in. The cat rubbed her ankles, then my ankles, everybody's ankles as we found places for these last trappings of *Mother Goose.*

"There's nothing like a studio in the morning," Mr. Render said from under the load of costumes he was carrying, then sighed deeply. "It's like an old abandoned house, or a graveyard. You expect to see grass growing in the corners."

"That's idiotic, Geoffrey," Madame said firmly. "Quit talking nonsense and put those costumes in the back studio. You can hang them on the barres or the doors. People will be coming by all day to get them. Then put the boxes of masks in the front. I want the children to try them on and do some steps: it worries me whether they can *see* out of the damn things. Meredith, honey, trot out and get some more costumes. Geoffrey, help Annette with those boxes. I've got to feed Colette."

"Madame, is Cecilia all right?" I took time to ask.

"Certainly, honey," Mme LeBreton said robustly. "She's fine. She was asleep when we left her, and she will be in good shape for tonight and Saturday. Mr. Render and I are bushed," she said, be ginning to rub an eyelid with a forefinger in a thoroughgoing, searching way, making the eyeball move around. *"We* just about stayed up all night. But listen, there's nothing for you kids to worry about. Tell the kids today at school,

Meredith. Tell everybody Cecilia is feeling well and *can* dance. And
Mrs. Oleander has just about finished the costumes and the masks were
at the bus station this morning, and everything is going to be all right."

"Even the orchestra?"

"Well! The orchestra!" Mme LeBreton said with a snort. "Hell, I
can only promise so much! That's Nathan's problem. Poor devil!"

But Cecilia was "fine": that made me feel better. So did the
costumes that I helped bring in, which were so vibrantly colorful they
looked as if they could dance by themselves. Poor Mrs. Oleander, on
the other hand, looked all limp and washed out from her illness, and I
had the absurd thought that she had poured most of the life in her into
these brisk and shiny costumes. She did not have a little tow-headed
daughter with her that morning: of course it was almost time for the
Middleton public schools to convene; but I had another absurd notion,
that all four or possibly five of them had perished in the final fracas of
costume-making, and that their lank, thin bodies were stacked around
their mother's sewing room among the parti-colored scraps.

"They're kinda shipshod," Mrs. Oleander said as we hooked the
hangers holding the costumes over the barres in the back studio. Handing
me my peasant costume for "Sing a Song of Sixpence," she said, "I just
tacked some a them layers a crinoline under that dress, hon. Be careful
careful when you put it own.

"Mr. Render! Mr. Render!" she called wanly. "I run up Humpty
Dumpty at four this mornin'. I need you to come try it own. I cain't
move them seams out another friction of an inch, though. There iddn
but a quarter inch in there now. Sure hope they don't come asunder own
stage."

Mr. Render said "All right, Ophelia" in a resigned sort of way and
began to unbutton his shirt—this was a bright red sport shirt much
like the one he had worn to the pool party out at the Merricks', only
without any palm trees on it—and I believe he would have undressed
right there in front of me and Mrs. Mintz, not to mention Mme LeBreton
and Mrs. Oleander, had Mme LeBreton not nudged him hard and hissed
out, "Really, Geoffrey, the *child,*" which stopped him and caused him
to go into the bathroom to change. I believe this potential immodesty of

his came from living the kind of public life he must have lived—I had thought before that he was probably never alone like ordinary people. I also thought, later, that this helped explain the thing that happened next.

***

I was thrilled with my peasant costume, which I hugged to my breast as I helped Mrs. Oleander and listened to her talk. It had a white blouse with a drawstring neck, a black lace-up bodice, and a full skirt of polished cotton in periwinkle blue. Actually, it looked remarkably like the dress Hilary wore so often except that it had much more of a romantic fairy-tale quality (it was, after all, a full-fledged costume, not a mere street dress): its sleeves were puffier, its skirt fuller; and under this skirt were ten or twelve petticoats of stiff bristling net, just when petticoats were in fashion at Middleton High School too, although these petticoats had so much more of a romantic antebellum quality than those petticoats which the most fashionable girls wore to school, even those of Danna Masters and her sister Evelyn. It was exciting to have this feminine costume to wear, no matter how much I liked the dog and Jack, and it crossed my mind that I would not have had the opportunity to wear it had it not been for the weaknesses of Alma Doyle, the married girl, the late, unlamented ballet student who was now, I supposed, a full-fledged tree.

I was less excited about my dog mask, a fierce and hot-looking property which before long I had extracted from a big cardboard carton in the front studio. I also pulled out masks for sheep and mice and flowers and such individual masks as Adelaide's cow and Dorcas's spider.

"Milly dear, I've simply got to go," Mrs. Mintz said, rattling her car keys.

"Run on, Annette," Mme LeBreton said. "I can't thank you enough for picking up the masks. Both of you have been wonderful. I can't think what we would have done without Ralph last night."

Mrs. Mintz did not say anything to this reference to Dr. Mintz's obstetrical services the night before but only pressed Mme LeBreton's hands. I observed this with interest: Mrs. Mintz looked tragic, as visitors to a funeral home do in conversation with the bereaved, and I got the idea from the way she looked that she and Dr. Mintz took a really dim view of "secret marriages," possibly even dimmer than my parents'. Mme LeBreton looked tragic too for the few seconds that Mrs. Mintz pressed her hands, but this passed and I do not think the expression came naturally to her.

"Now, Meredith," Madame said cheerfully when Mrs. Mintz had gone. "Group those masks, will you? If you could separate the different animals. And look inside for the little tag with the size. Put the smaller ones in front, maybe. You can put 'em on newspapers. Aren't there some newspapers in the back somewhere?"

There must have been a hundred animal masks in those boxes. I got the newspapers from the back, spread them out down the length of the front studio on the far side over by the barre, then began the task of categorizing the masks, even though I knew this would make me even later for school. What was I missing? Homeroom, with Dorcas whining behind me, biology. I'd had plenty of biology lately! Here in the studio, I seemed to be doing my duty, even "facing facts" in a vague but valiant way. Frankly, I found the masks a rather depressing business: this was the underside of *Mother Goose,* the bizarre, even perverse aspect of it that had made it controversial in its beginnings. The masks were well made, but they had big staring eyes and fearful-looking teeth. I thought of the day *Mother Goose* was announced and how I first learned of it from Hilary and her mother, leaving here in tears. I was seeing them again, rounding the back corner of the studio on that frigid January day, with Hilary crying as if she had just been frightened by one of these masks, when Mr. Render bounded into the front studio where Mme LeBreton and I were working. He was now wearing his Humpty Dumpty costume, which was a white blouse and black overalls, both of wet-looking satin. He went to a mirror, looked at himself approvingly and tossed off a *pirouette six.*

"Geoffrey, you do look like an egg," Mme LeBreton observed. After his display of virtuosity Mr. Render seemed melancholy again. Now he sat down on the Mothers' Bench, sighing disconsolately and fingering the floppy white satin bow of his blouse.

"This is a fine studio, Milly," he said. "So peaceful. I was hoping for some peace and quiet down here. I couldn't wait to get away from the company, and that eternal wrangling. I've been playing tug-of-war with Nils Lundgren for a couple of years now and I think it's finally worn me out."

"Nonsense, Geoffrey," Mme LeBreton said beside me, with her head down in a box. "You just haven't had any sleep."

"You know I was thinking for a while of retiring down here. Right away, I mean. Letting Lyda build me a school."

"That octopus?" Madame shouted, popping out of the box. "You'd actually put yourself in the tentacles of that octopus?"

"I've dealt with bigger octopi than Lyda, Milly," he said carelessly, getting up from the Mothers' Bench and wandering over to the casement windows. He tried to crank open a window. "Why, in New York Lyda would just be a tiny octopus, a little pet turtle. I could have handled her."

"If you had done that," Mme LeBreton said, and I thought she was going to say "we would have become rivals, and enemies," but she did not, surprisingly, say that but instead said, "you would have broken Claude's heart. I believe it is just about broken now, with Cecilia married like this, but not entirely broken because he still believes that he will be going to New York, under your protection."

"Oh, he wouldn't be the first boy not to go to New York. It wouldn't kill him," Mr. Render mused, wrestling with the crank.

"I think it would," Madame averred, and I silently agreed.

"Maybe it would," Mr. Render said casually, finally getting the window to open and peering outside into the warm morning. The good fresh air came in, and I could see a million motes of dust in the sunbeams coming through that window when I glanced around. "No, Milly darling, I was hoping for some peace and quiet down here. A chance to make a ballie like I used to, from scratch, with new, young people. I even had a new theater to look forward to, lots of money even. I knew you and I had a little misunderstanding to patch up, but that took care of itself quickly enough, didn't it? Then the old familiar things started coming up. Jealousies and ambitions, people pushing and shoving and trying to get on top."

"Was I trouble, Geoffrey? Was I?" Madame asked rather pitifully.

"Not you, darling. Not you. We lost our theater, then our money, then our orchestra was a disaster, but we still had our little dancers," he went on mournfully, "our pure, fresh little dancers. That's heaven, Milly," he said, beginning to stride around the center floor. He had not put his shoes back on when he had changed into his Humpty Dumpty suit and now he was just wearing socks; this striding, then, was soundless and looked very graceful. He rolled around rather than walked, like an egg. "Just heaven, to have those eager little bodies to work with. Then your daughter, my best material, gets herself pregnant. Oh God, I hope she can pull it off Saturday night. Just one performance, God, just Saturday!"

"She wants to," Madame said humbly.

"My God! How many times has this happened to me, Milly? I find a girl who has quality and presence. I work with her. *Just* when I have made something on her she does this. Do you know what this reminds me of?"

During this increasingly impassioned monologue I had been scuffling around on the floor, on my knees, categorizing the masks. At this moment I was facing the great mirror which runs the length of the front studio. My head jerked up in alarm and I met my own eyes, wide with horror. Oh God, I thought, with a sinking feeling, as if I were in the dinghy and saw a wall of water, high as a mountain, bearing down upon it, *now* is when they talk about having Cecilia.

"It reminds me of Miss Orchid, Milly. Do you remember Miss Orchid?"

Knowing nothing of Miss Orchid, I looked around in the mirror for Mme LeBreton. She stood behind me somewhere, her hands on her flaring hips, but I could not see her face in the mirror. She did not say whether or not she remembered Miss Orchid.

"I've thought of Miss Orchid more than once since I met Cecilia. Since I saw her, I should say. I saw her at least once before, that time in the elevator, but you know that! No, she doesn't *look* like Miss Orchid, but she reminds me of her in many ways. Both of them were beauties. Of course Cecilia had more talent, but Miss Orchid could mimic talent. Yes, she could," Mr. Render said with a reminiscent smile.

"Cecilia's not dead, you know," Madame said haughtily. "I hope Miss Orchid is, though."

Not noticing the dangerous irony in these remarks Mr. Render murmured, "No, no, not to my knowledge. But of course you remember her, here is her picture," he said from the Mothers' Bench, where he began studying the gallery that memorialized Mme LeBreton's professional past, and of course his own. "I'd actually forgotten about this picture with the both of us and Miss Orchid. I wonder where that was taken?"

"Shut up, Geoffrey!" Mme LeBreton burst out. "Don't rattle on like that about Viola Orchid! I remember her every day. Don't compare that trollop to my daughter Cecilia!"

"Hardly a trollop, just because of a baby, now," he said tolerantly.

"Baby! What baby? *Your* baby?" Madame shouted.

"Milly! Milly! Of course not my baby," he said soothingly, while I writhed about on the newspapers in an agony of embarrassment. Not for the first time Mme LeBreton and Mr. Render seemed to have totally forgotten my presence.

"I knew there would be a baby!" my teacher cried out hysterically. "That's what she wanted! She was after you from the very first, Geoffrey! She wanted to get you to marry her any way she could, and that of course is one of the ways."

"Milly, what are we talking about?" Mr. Render said, rubbing a hand across his shiny head. "I think I'm lost."

"What are *you* talking about? What's this *baby?*" Mme LeBreton cried, exactly as I would have expected her to cry out as Cecilia lay swathed in otherworldly glory on the narrow iron bed down at the auditorium. Here was the kind of maternal hysteria I had been schooled to expect!

Mr. Render turned and took the picture to which he had alluded earlier off the wall. Looking troubled, he said, "Well now, I suppose it was after you left us that Viola Orchid announced she was pregnant. It happened a lot like last night: she fainted during a performance. Made an awful uproar. Tore up the evening. When she came to, she told us that she was secretly married to a trumpet player she had met in Oklahoma somewhere. She left the company after that."

"That baby wasn't yours, Geoffrey?"

"No, goddamn it, it wasn't, Milly. For God's sake! Jesus Christ! It's coming back to me now. I had forgotten, by some sweet mercy, how jealous you were of that child—Miss Orchid, I mean. You were so crazy on that point I tried to forget it, and as you can see I succeeded. You were a tiger on that point!"

Riveted, I watched Mme LeBreton in the mirror. She was still standing center floor; then she started pacing, not unlike a tiger. "I didn't know about the trumpet player," she said testily. "I don't think I believe in the trumpet player."

"Well hell, then," Mr. Render said jauntily in his Humpty Dumpty suit, "don't believe in the trumpet player! That's just what she told me. There's always a trumpet player or a bus driver or a—"

"—automobile mechanic," Madame interjected, referring to her "son-in-law."

"Or even a plate glass manufacturer," Mr. Render tacked on triumphantly. "You ran off with a plate glass manufacturer, right before the première of *Night Birds*. But you weren't pregnant, were you, Milly? I didn't like to ask."

"Of course not! Girls are not all alike, Geoffrey. I know you think they are."

"History seems to suggest it," he said moodily. "Then why did you marry that man? It couldn't have been love."

"Why not? He was a fine man, a kind man, and I miss him. Besides, Geoffrey, I was sick of the life. I think those five years of touring killed me, it's just taken this long to do it. I could not take wandering around anymore without some place that was mine.

"Mine," she repeated; her studio rang with it.

"That was just freedom, Milly," Mr. Render said lightly. "You just couldn't take freedom. What you should have done is stayed on and married me. Then we could have gone to New York together." This, I believe, was intended as a pleasant gallantry on Mr. Render's part, but it was not taken as such by Mme LeBreton, who had been inflamed by the things he had been saying so easily and who now went across the studio, took the picture which Mr. Render was fondly studying, and threw it to the floor, where it landed with a crack, face down, spewing glass across the well-worn but immaculate gray surface. Then she reached across him for another of the pictures in her gallery to throw, or so it seemed;

he reached up to restrain her, and they remained locked together a few moments like this, as if they were about to dance.

"I asked you to marry me, you terrible old goat, and you laughed!" she said, heaving.

"No, no, that couldn't be. That couldn't have happened."

"But it did happen. In the bus. Don't you remember?"

"No, no, I don't remember."

"Of course you remember. Behind that church. I think," she said, huffing, "you must be teasing me."

"No, I wouldn't, Milly. Not now. I do not remember!"

"The night Maxwell LeBreton proposed to me for the last time I came to you and told you about it. I told you I wouldn't marry him if you would marry me. And then, my dear one, you laughed."

"I couldn't have, Milly."

"You could. Because you were in love with her. If she hadn't come out of nowhere and ruined things I think you would have married me, like I wanted."

"I could not marry, right then," he said, standing back, dropping her arm. "I *had* to stay free, then. And now, when I don't want to stay free any longer, everyone is gone. It was my being free you hated, Milly. I think you still hate it!"

"Free," that provocative word, made Mme LeBreton dive at the pictures again. This time Mr. Render did not try to restrain her.

"There *was* an awful fight in the bus that night," Mr. Render mused in his high sweet voice above the crashing of pictures. "I do remember the fight, Milly," he said somewhat pedantically, "I just don't remember all the details of the discussion. I remember how furious you were. You know, you helped me when I did a ballie later on Prometheus: I used some of your moves for the Furies. But I do swear, darling," he said, raising his voice to be heard over the noise, "I cannot remember your proposing to me. You were such a pretty thing then. I hardly see how I could have turned you down."

Wishing to die or at least become invisible, I crouched over the masks. Mme LeBreton continued to hurl pictures for a while, and Mr. Render continued to stand apart and think, in a startled sort of way. It was this scene I thought of, a decade or so later, when certain minority groups rioted in the major cities to draw attention to the injustices they had suffered and the white majority, while deploring this form of protest, did in fact stop and really think about the injustices for the first time. Oh Lord, deliver me, I prayed during this earlier riot.

Soon Mrs. Oleander came into the front studio and looked around her a moment before stepping daintily across the floor, strewn with shards, in her nurse's oxfords. "Just go on and *have* a go-to-pieces, Miz LeBreton," she said impassively. "It'll do you a world a good. Many's the time I've pitched some dishes at Otto and it makes you feel a dang sight better."

Mme LeBreton stopped the throwing and hitched up her pedal pushers with dignity, pushing back her hair with the back of her hand.

"I know what it is about them masks now," Mrs. Oleander allowed, standing out to the side of the glass shards and looking down on the grisly row of masks. She had her hands on her hips and her little paunch stuck out. "They remind me a that Bateson boy. Did y'all have time to get a glimpse a Meredith in her dog mask while y'all was talkin' just then? Why, she looked like Claude Bateson does ever day of the week. I always thought there was somethin' peculiar about that boy and now I relize it's that he looks like he's wearin' one a them masks, 'cept he never takes his *off*. I'm gonna have nightmares about them masks. I swear to goodness," she said, looking around her, "it looks like there's been some kind a war. I bet it looked like this over in Korear."

I was an hour late to school that morning. As I waited, racked and shaken, for the bus at the corner of Sycamore Street and Tates Parkway, then boarded the bus and rode to school (guiltily averting my eyes from the offices of Wilson, Matlock, Jackson and Jackson), I was haunted by that other bus, the touring bus with the picture of Anna Pavlova on the side. I was imagining the collapse of Milly Frobish's professional life in a country town, someplace like Ardis. I saw the church in Ardis, the simple white frame church with the cotton fields stretching beyond it, all the way to the horizon. It was easy to draw the Ballet Benet bus up to the rear door of this church building and see the young Milly Frobish and the young Geoffrey Render (the people in the pictures) quarreling like tigers inside it. In fact, in time I began to think that this quarrel had actually taken place in Ardis, and that Milly Frobish and Geoffrey Render actually parted company there, to go on and become Mme LeBreton and *the* Geoffrey Render, Artistic Director and famous choreographer, just as so many other people had had to leave there to become themselves.

***

That afternoon as I darned my toe shoes (such laborious work, allowing plenty of time to brood), I went over and over this scene in my mind. I would have to adjust my ideas about Mr. Render and Mme LeBreton, I said to myself; I would have to separate the fact from the fiction. I could keep the bus but I would have to throw out the baby, by which I mean Cecilia, who, despite everything I'd thought about nutcrackers and sugar plum fairies, really had nothing to do with Mme LeBreton's drama—I almost called it "tragedy," thinking about that craggy old face. I'd gotten used to thinking about Cecilia as very possibly the daughter of Geoffrey Render (this had given her a wonderful aura); but now I'd have to see her as a more ordinary girl.

I was still shaken by what I had witnessed in the studio. It had been open war all right ("Korear"!), and I had been right on the front line, with shells whizzing past my ears. When it was over I had been surrounded by broken glass, as if there had been heavy bombing. We always seemed to be in rubble.

Frowning over my darning, I faced an awful prospect. I saw my parents and me in the family Chevrolet, loaded down with my costumes and shoes and my dog mask, with me clutching Marie, riding down Captain Frick Street toward the auditorium for the dress rehearsal but not seeing the auditorium standing at the head of the broad street, just a pile of rubble with maybe a little smoke rising from it and also, way up in the sky, a goose ascending with Mme LeBreton on it, or possibly Mr. Render, none of us being able to tell for sure which one it was.

When my parents and I really drove down to the Civic Auditorium that evening for the dress rehearsal, me in the back seat, clutching onto Marie Taglioni in the midst of the costumes, I was afraid to look down Captain Frick Street for the Civic Auditorium because I was pretty sure by this time that it wasn't there. I was fairly certain it had been devastated by all the adult passions let loose on the land—jealousy, lust, greed, possibly even gluttony. So I kept my eyes closed, trembling, I think as much as the timid Marie (who, sure enough, had been extricated from under the couch with great difficulty). My father, who always drove slowly, slowed the car even more.

"Not *here,* Lawrence," my mother said. "Can't you get closer? Look, I'm sure there are some places in that lot right by the stage door."

Well, I thought, hope flaring, Mother wouldn't be talking about parking places beside a heap of rubble, and I opened my eyes, seeing the two calm heads riding in the front seat and, beyond them, the ornate old Civic, looking like a picture in a book of architectural curiosities. Marie howled pitifully, and I loosened my grip on her ribs.

26

I didn't really breathe right, though, until the opening bars of the overture from *Coppélia,* when Claude "awoke" from his "sleep" and turned, rising for his solo like a phoenix from the ashes. I was still awfully churned up by the argument, and then there was the havoc of unloading the car and getting installed in a dressing room, which I shared with eight other dancers and the cats, then getting into the first costume and applying makeup. This is the first time we had all been in the costumes at the same time and they were fantastic—you could hardly tell who anybody was since they were all some whimsical new character (an animal, more likely than not, with a strange mask). I am glad to say the masks looked more benign now that they were attached to bodies. Everybody scampered around backstage acting very silly in the masks; Mme LeBreton, Mother Goose rather, failed entirely to corral us with her staff.

The costumes began to come apart as soon as the dancers did so much as a *plié,* but the big worry before the dress rehearsal was the music. When the orchestra started concentrating on the "A," it seemed that everybody stopped what they were doing and came to stand breathlessly in the wings. The ancient red velvet curtain at the outer edge of the stage shuddered. On our side of it, Claude, looking almost handsome with everybody else in animal masks, lay "fast asleep" in his blue velvet tunic under a haystack. Mr. Beldinsky and Bruce were toiling over the haystack, making some last-minute adjustments on it. The orchestra stopped the "A"; we knew that Nathan must be raising his baton. "But-uh-but-uh-but-uh-but-uh but-uh-but-uh": there was a portentous kettledrum roll; then the sweet and moody French horns, which were miraculously steady, sounding like the dawn (very much as they were supposed to); then the swirling, swelling strings which grew even louder while the velvet curtain labored upward by means of a softly screaming pulley to reveal the sleeping Claude, who rose from his sleeping position, as I say, like a phoenix from the ashes. "Oh God!" someone moaned, signifying our joy and our disbelief that the orchestra was actually playing the music. We hugged each other and danced around the wings as Claude hurled himself about on the stage: Nathan had done it; somehow he was "playing" the musicians of the orchestra just as he had played the broken-down piano at the studio. They sounded brilliant: they sparkled with cymbals, they throbbed with drums. They had that wonderful beat of Nathan's: after the hugging and the dancing around we stood in the wings, swaying involuntarily like wildflowers in the wind as Nathan's musicians played *Coppélia.* When they did not sound brilliant (and they did not, sometimes) they still sounded regular and very gay, like a heartbeat during moments of high excitement.

The orchestra set an allegro pace for the dress rehearsal. It also seemed to set the standard of performance. In his first solo Claude did the triple *tour en l'air* that had given him so much trouble and landed *agenouillement,* on his knee, without pulverizing it. Following his lead, almost all of the dancers performed the difficult things Mr. Render had asked them to do with hardly a misstep. Though pale, Cecilia danced charmingly. The scene in the meadow faded rapidly into the scene inside the humble cottage where, while Mr. Beldinsky hammered on a windowsill, Curly Locks and the Three Blind Mice and Little Jenny Wren (Cecilia again, looking very realistic piled up in bed as an invalid) and the other colorful characters did *their* intricate dances with celerity. I know I had never been so wild and rollicksome as Mother Hubbard's dog, notwithstanding the hot mask.

I got so caught up in the flying dress rehearsal that I almost forgot I had to go back and superintend the cats for the St. Ives number, which led off the third portion of Act One that takes place on the road to the "town." "Oh gosh, the cats!" I said out loud, shouldering through the crowd of dancers in the wings watching Christabel portray so convincingly the bratty girl with the curl in the middle of her forehead, and running down the hall toward the dressing room where the cats were. As I ran I worried that the cats had escaped from the dressing room, or that they were in a terrible fight and had torn each other's fur off—cats don't have long memories, you know, and when we had arrived there a while ago Marie had not seemed to recognize Colette, her mother, much less "Carlotta Grisi," "Lucille Grahn" and "Fanny Ellsler," who had been produced by their new owners for the occasion and who were renamed Jet, Muffin and Stripie, I believe. Marie has probably had a heart attack, or turned completely white, I thought nervously, dodging Albert, who was turning out of the male dressing room in his Jack (of "Jack and Jill") costume, looking pretty white himself. When I heard screams and shouts coming from the end of the hall I ran faster, careening around the dressing-room door to see a small crowd of dancers over in the corner, which was pulsating with their screams. These were mainly the little girls who were going to dance the seven wives coming from St. Ives; they were dressed as peasant women and had kerchiefs on their little heads.

"What *is* it? Tell me what's happened," I demanded, with the authority of a dancer much more advanced than they were.

They did not speak but just looked around, rolling their eyes superstitiously like peasants confronted with the unknown, and silently parted. What I saw then was Colette and her kittens gathered around the corpse of a mouse, which did not seem to have any head.

"Marie!" I shouted uselessly. "Oh, Marie! How could you?"

Marie looked up at me from the disgusting feast. She had blood on her white whiskers and a peculiar expression of fulfillment.

***

When I try to think what I observed that night between Mr. Render and Mme LeBreton I cannot remember anything much. Mainly they were in different places: Mr. Render out in front, keeping things rolling, Mme LeBreton backstage, trying to repair the damage incurred to the sets and costumes at that fast pace. Of course everybody was too busy to think, but I did think about one thing as I watched Cecilia performing her various variations: she wasn't all that beautiful; maybe Evelyn Masters was right. It seemed to me that everybody else was glamorized, you might even say augmented, by their costumes that night, but Cecilia was somehow diminished. I looked at her closely with her heavy stage makeup on—of course Cecilia did not have to wear a mask—and for the first time thought I saw a resemblance to Maxwell LeBreton (was it the nose, or somewhere around the mouth?).

Anyway, I did not have much time for speculation at the dress rehearsal. Soon the cats were on, and I stood fondly in the wings watching the seven wives trudge across the stage lugging their burlap sacks, with the placid little heads of Colette and her four kittens sticking out of them. (They were two cats short, you'll notice: two wives had stuffed cats, but no one cared—the real cats had set the tone!) The real cats did very well during this number, perhaps because they were full of mouse; they did not even try to climb out of the sacks. The other numbers on the road went well too, and the valiant company got through "Hark Hark" and "Banbury Cross" and "Georgy Porgy" and "Jack and Jill" without any disturbing incidents, in happy contrast to the night before, when all this stretch of dances had been sadly disrupted by Cecilia's egg.

Naturally there were some mechanical problems at the dress rehearsal with sets and costumes. Mr. Beldinsky never stopped hammering. Bruce had worked up some guy-wire contraption to rotate Humpty Dumpty's wall from the wings, but people kept tripping over it and pulling it apart, and twice somebody bumped into the milk cartons which made up London Bridge and they all fell down, way long before they were supposed to, and everybody had to help pick them up. Poor Mrs. Oleander never stopped "tacking," as she called the process of repairing all the sleeves that ripped out and all the seams that "come asunder" in the costumes that were in fact all too "shipshod." There was also frantic concern over the muslin costumes like Hilary's Curly Locks and Christabel's Horrid Girl. They "wiltered," Mrs. Oleander wailed, "plum wiltered," under the pressure of the torrid lights and the sweat; they'd have to be washed and starched before Saturday and no one was sure whether such fragile costumes could survive laundering.

But these were details. After an "intermission" filled with hammering and tacking, Act Two went on in the colorful, rapid way of Act One.

We had the garden scene, where Mr. Render took the stage as the King, and Mrs. Farfel was the Queen (and not too bad, either, if you stopped expecting her to look like Mrs. Merrick and just saw her as a comic kind of monarch). Then came the final nighttime portion, heralded by Wee Willie Winkie and climaxed, if I may say so, by myself as Jack Be Nimble, followed by Dotty Winkle as the candle doing *fouettés.* I did all twenty-four *écartés* in perfect time with Nathan's orchestra. After this there was a small rip in the "crouch" of my jumpsuit, though I didn't tell Mrs. Oleander, preferring to take care of this intimate repair myself, at home.

During this last part of the dress rehearsal we all united in worry over the fly system, which of course was the chief mechanical problem at the auditorium. I couldn't help thinking of the midway of the state fair they have in Middleton every year, where a lot of the rides like the Ferris wheel and the rocket are old and dangerous looking. I thought of the determinedly hilarious expressions on the faces of those who insist on going on those rusty old rides and also of the horrified expressions on the faces of their friends or relations who stay behind in the swirls of noisome dust on the midway as we observed Mme LeBreton, Mrs. Fister and Adelaide being attached, each in her turn, to the ancient devices of the fly system at the Civic Auditorium. Each flew out across the stage, causing the audience of Mothers and fathers out in front to gasp delightedly, the cadres of dancers in the wings to cower and moan. But everything turned out all right. I never saw a gruesome accident at the fairgrounds, and I didn't see one that night at the Civic Auditorium either, or the night of the performance. The three women who rode the fly system were probably as safe as Colette and her kittens swinging along in their burlap sacks.

"This is *so* disorganized, isn't it?" Dorcas complained after the finale, when Mr. Render was up on the stage trying to arrange the order of the bows and curtain calls with Mme LeBreton. "They could have done this months ago."

"Oh I don't know," I said, peering over scores of faces, only some of them human, to see whether Mme LeBreton and Mr. Render looked friendly toward each other at all.

"I think *we* ought to bow before the Townspeople," she said.

"Look, there's Nathan!" I said. Nathan was coming out on the stage. He and Mr. Render were embracing, though whether this was part of the curtain call scheme I didn't know.

"Well I've *had* it," Dorcas went on, although we were not supposed to be talking: we were in various piquant positions and we had big stage smiles on our faces. All this time the parents and other people out in the house were applauding doggedly. "I'm quitting. I'm not taking next year. I have a test in American History tomorrow and I haven't even read the book! Everybody's quitting," she said out of the corner of her mouth. "Are you going to quit?"

"Of *course* not, Dorcas," I said out of the side of *my* mouth which was smiling broadly. "This is no time to think about that! Shut up!" I said, though these things are hard to say without moving your lips. The applause was light since there weren't too many people out there, but it was sustained. Claude took bows, and Cecilia too. Nathan took another bow and Mr. Render stood by, clapping. What a job Nathan had done! I wanted to clap for him too! Of course we didn't know (since Nathan and the orchestra had worked in such complete seclusion) how he had done it—how he had purged the earlier "orchestra" of its worst players and made the rest play so well, nor did we know which of the musicians had been brought in from New York (surely some violinists, though, surely the entire French horn section!). Anyway, Nathan had performed a musical miracle. Now he was embracing Claude, who looked wrung out but still manly in his blue tunic, and at the time I had the idea that they were more gratified by the way the rehearsal had gone than anybody else there on that crowded stage. It seemed to point the way to brilliant careers for both of them.

27

I think, looking back on it, that I danced like a real dancer at that dress rehearsal just about the only time in my life: I mean danced hard, without thinking about it—barreling over the falls with complete abandon, without a cry of any kind. I did not realize this at the time: I just knew that the dress rehearsal had been very exciting and that the interval between it and the performance on Saturday night was horribly dull. Saturday was particularly dull because I didn't have anything to do. I couldn't go anywhere because Mother said I looked exhausted and had to stay home to rest.

What Mother really said was that I looked "hollow-eyed"—this was the Ardis expression for "fatigued," pronounced "holl-eyed"—and I had to admit that she was right when I looked in my mirror and saw dark circles under my eyes and a haggard kind of expression in them I had never had before. Actually I was not displeased by this: I referred to the picture of Tamara Genovese stuck in the frame of my dressing table mirror and saw that I looked more like that urbane figure than I would have thought possible when I put it there. I looked older, I thought, and my hair had grown so long that my ballet knot was quite respectable now. Of course I would never attain that Mediterranean languor, but I studied my face with new hope, having nothing else to do while I waited.

Saturday morning I passed some time reading the *Chronicle*. I wore a somewhat bitter and mocking smile while doing this, since the *Chronicle* had almost nothing in it about the cataclysmic event called *Mother Goose*. That is the way it had been ever since the severance of the ties between the studio and the Merricks ten days before, and it made the paper look very trivial in my eyes, with all its articles on remote national affairs and paltry local events. There was one local event of some interest, however: the Roundelay Spring Cotillion, which had taken place the night before down at the auditorium. Now, *this* caught my attention since it had been in the Civic. It took place where our audience would sit, near our scenery! The event had had a Civil War motif, the boys dressing as Confederate officers, the girls as Southern belles. Decorations had transformed the auditorium into a "gracious plantation," the paper said, going on to describe the plaster of Paris columns and the four hundred rosebushes in antique wooden buckets (four hundred!). There were several pictures of laughing Roundelay members in their antebellum regalia, but none of our dancers, as it happened.

It did not surprise me that Dorcas called while I was reading about the Roundelay dance since she always called the morning after these functions for the purpose of complaining about them.

"I'm so tired, Meredith," she said. "I'm dead on my feet."

"How're they going to get all that stuff out of the auditorium by tonight?" I said. "All those rosebushes?"

"Don't talk to me about rosebushes," Dorcas said histrionically. "They gave me an awful allergy.

"Oh gosh," Dorcas said then, like it was an afterthought. "I have to tell you. Guess who came?"

"Who?" I asked, slouching on a stool in the kitchen, feeling awfully bored.

"Wendell and Wexler came, and they're so handsome, Meredith! Somebody was saying they're going to be in a movie somebody's going to be making around Coushatta. Some producer their daddy knows. But listen, guess who else came."

"John Wayne."

"No, no," said the humorless Dorcas. "Christabel. Christabel came!"

"Oh?" I said, sitting up straighter. "How could *she* come? She's only in the seventh grade."

"Crashed," said Dorcas. "She came in with Mark Brownfield. You wouldn't believe what she came as. You don't know, do you?"

"How could I know?" I cried from the innocent seclusion of my house on Sycamore Street. "Tell me, would you?"

"Well, her appearance was kinda brief. They came in late, then somebody's father took them right out because she came as Topsy. You know, Topsy from *The King and I.*"

"Uncle Tom's Cabin," I corrected absently.

"She had on an old cotton dress like a slave and she had blacked her face and her hair. She looked just like a Nigra. So did Mark. He looked just like a Nigra too."

"Lordy mercy," I said faintly. "How come Mrs. Merrick let Christabel do a thing like that?"

"Hilary said Mr. and Mrs. Merrick are out of town and so they didn't know. They left Christabel with the maids," Dorcas said, "but Christabel does anything she wants to, *as* we know. Hilary said she and Steph and them were going out to the Merricks' after the Cotillion and have a swimming party. Can you believe? They're getting *so wild,* Meredith. It's really awful the things they do. Mama said she thought maybe I ought to *quit* Roundelay."

"Maybe so, Dorcas, maybe so," I said, though I was thinking of something else entirely. I was thinking how shocking it was that life was going on in Middleton that had nothing whatever to do with *Mother Goose.* I was not particularly shocked at the gothic events of the Roundelay Spring Cotillion or what might have taken place out at the Merrick place afterward; I was mainly shocked that some girls had the mind to bother with that other kind of dance these days.

***

In the spring my room was like a treehouse or an aerie, the leafy branches of the sweet gum tree came so close to the windows; and later that day I retreated up there to pass the time leafing through my collection of souvenir programs for the thousandth time. But as the afternoon wore on I stopped feeling bored and began feeling very nervous about the performance. I have always suffered from stage fright, and that day I had the worst case of my life as I thought of all the things to be frightened about. I thought about my solos, which in many ways were too hard for me, and about the prospect of doing them in front of a whole auditorium full of people. Then, paradoxically, I started worrying that nobody would come. We had worked so long, and it was possible that no one would come to see the results. There was that ominous silence about *Mother Goose* in the *Chronicle*. It had carried only a tiny advertisement on the movie page no bigger than the small box which said what was playing today at the movie theater up by the college, which was all the Mothers could afford. I knew Mme LeBreton and Mr. Render weren't worried about whether there would be an audience—the performance itself was the thing in their eyes— but now I seemed to see things from a different point of view. Up in my room, all alone, I began to feel as if I could see all of Middleton from my window if I should walk over there and peer through the trees, possibly even the whole north half of the state. In this view the studio and its concerns—even Mr. Render, who came from New York City, way up over the horizon—looked very small, while the Merricks, whose voice the *Chronicle* was, were seen as the most prominent features of the topography. They were represented, in fact by innumerable oil derricks as well as by the small pumping machines you see between Middleton and Ardis that look like grasshoppers working humbly and obsessively to further the Merrick interests. In a city which put a high valuation on civic duty, the Merricks were without question the most dutiful and the most prominent, while Mme LeBreton and Mr. Render were, in contrast (let's face it!), Bohemians, persons of frivolous and possibly bizarre interests, whose "business" was the play of children, and who lived mysteriously tangled and irregular lives. My face flamed up for Cecilia.

For a while, I saw the venture of *Mother Goose* with the steady, responsible gaze of the upstanding citizen. It looked wild, foolish and more than a little seedy. On Thursday night at the dress rehearsal Mrs. James had announced that three-quarters of the tickets had been sold, but now it struck me that those tickets had been bought in the spirit of civic duty for which Middleton was so justly noted. Kind and thoughtful readers of the prize-winning *Chronicle* had bought those tickets much as a gentleman or lady who comes to the door of a fine Middleton home consents to buy cookies from the shining little Middleton Girl Scout. Just as that gentleman or lady will most probably not eat the cookies himself or herself, but will instead save them to offer a little grandchild or nephew, these ticket buyers probably had no intention of actually coming to the performance. Even if they had, they would surely change their sober and responsible minds once they realized that the performance was no longer supported and sanctioned by the Merricks, that it was now an unsponsored, unsanctioned performance, what you might call a rogue performance, just as they would not buy cookies from little girls who had been expelled from their Middleton public school and now lived among gypsies camped in the piney woods somewhere out of town.

Fortunately such broodings were interrupted late that afternoon by another telephone call. When my mother called me from downstairs my first thought was the usual one, that those in charge were notifying me that *Mother Goose* was being canceled, this time because of the city's disapproval.

"Hello," I said stoically.

"Hi, Meredith, it's Alma." It took me a few seconds to remember who Alma was. "Oh *Alma!*" I cried. "How *are* you?"

"Oh fine. I'm great."

"Are you long distance?" I asked, because her voice was so faint.

"Oh no, I'm right here at home. I just wanted to wish you luck or whatever you're supposed to wish. I think you're supposed to say 'break a leg', but I can't bring myself to say that. I sure don't want y'all to break any legs."

"Well I appreciate that, I really do. Are you *coming?*" I inquired urgently.

"Of course. I wouldn't miss it for anything in the world. Tom is bringing me," she said with pride.

"Tom," I mused. "And Tom doesn't even like ballet," I said, to show that I remembered Tom. The truth is I didn't even remember Alma all that well. It seemed like years since I had seen her and I couldn't summon up an image of her face, just its olive sheen.

"He likes it better now, after he got involved in the production."

"What? How?" I cried.

"You didn't know? It was a behind-the-scenes sort of thing. Tom helped Mme LeBreton get a loan at the bank after the Merricks pulled out."

"Gee!" I said, recalling that Melissa Martin's father was also said to have done this.

"Well," Alma added conscientiously, "he didn't *really* help y'all. Y'all'd undoubtably have got the money anyway, but Tom drew up the papers. He got a promotion, you know: he's an assistant manager now," she said, as if I should have read it in the paper. Possibly I should have: the *Chronicle* did carry a lot of stories on promotions in the banks and businesses of Middleton, which was a very progressive city.

"You know I kind of hated to quit. I've missed y'all a lot."

"And we've missed you," I said warmly, lying of course, since as far as I knew no one had noticed Alma's disappearance. Besides, I had been very glad to get her part as the maid in "Sing a Song of Sixpence."

"I guess you know why I quit!" she said gaily.

Actually I thought she had quit because she could not stand the pace of daily rehearsals. If pressed, I would have to apply some more biology knowledge acquired that year in school, Darwin's theory of natural selection: the strong and the fit survived the grueling obstacle course toward this climactic day, while the punier students fell by the wayside. And in Alma's case there was also the factor of the husband Tom, who liked clean laundry, good meals and basketball more than ballet. I saw this "Tom" better than I could see Alma: a tall, athletic person, the kind of fellow people call a "guy," or even a "good guy," with a blond crew cut; a stalwart, gum-chewing philistine whom Alma lubriciously worshipped.

"I'm *pregnant*," Alma announced joyfully. "We're going to have a baby in November. November seventh, the doctor says!"

"That's great," I said with an enthusiasm I did not feel. *Now* I could see Alma, pale but shiny, on a narrow iron hospital bed in a winding sheet.

"I *had* to quit when I found out," she gushed. "My doctor insisted. I'd been having some trouble and he said I would probably have a miscarriage if I kept on taking."

"Oh dear," I said supportively. I thought of the vulnerable egg again and how it might be ripped away by the dance; the word "miscarriage," of which I did not have a very clear understanding, made me think of a baby carriage holding the long-awaited offspring of Tom and Alma, flying out over the edge of a cliff.

"You know Cecilia's pregnant too," I confided, glad to have, at my age, something to contribute to this very grown-up gynecological conversation.

"No!" Alma exclaimed, clearly ready to rejoice.

"Yes," I said happily, giving the account intended for the public since Alma was no longer one of us, "she married Charlie Hill in January before he went into the Army but she didn't tell anyone. Now they're expecting."

"I knew she would marry soon," Alma said.

Alma was appalled that Cecilia was dancing that night and I enjoyed this, as it reinforced the idea that we performers were the fittest, having survived so much during this year, having endured so many calamities, both civic and personal. According to Alma, Mme LeBreton's spunkiness in mounting *Mother Goose* against all the odds was legend throughout the community. My chest swelled with pride as I talked with Alma: instead of being ragtag gypsies, outcasts, exiles, we were outlaw heroes, like Robin Hood and his merry band of men, perhaps.

After a light supper that evening I had a few more minutes in my room before it was time to load the car and go down to the auditorium. It was beginning to get dark, and the cool breeze that had blown into my room through the trees was growing chilly. I went to close the windows but stopped, caught by one of my favorite sounds, which I call "car horns at dusk" and which signals the coming of the night and all its excitements. This was just traffic up on Tates Parkway, but that evening it sounded to me as if it were all of Middleton, bumper to bumper, impatient to get downtown to the Civic Auditorium to see *Mother Goose*.

Oh, I thought with a pang, "gala" fit this festive sound of car horns at dusk, and for just a moment, before I closed the windows, I wished the urgent line of cars were making its way out to the Merrick Theater. There, at the end of the line, out in the woods, we would have had a real "gala," searchlights playing over the sacred theater and down on the people alighting from their cars at the foot of the hill. I saw a long black limousine slipping into place there and Mrs. Merrick stepping regally out of it, wearing a diamond tiara which refracted the powerful beams of the sportive searchlights.

28

The performance that night was not anything like I expected, the main thing being that dancing turned out to play such a small part in it. When we got to the auditorium everybody was backstage examining the programs, which like everything else about *Mother Goose* got finished only at the last possible minute. They *were* remarkable programs— every bit as thick and glossy as the programs NDT had sold back in October—and they did require a lot of study because they contained a myriad of candid photographs of classes and rehearsals none of us had seen before, and of course we had to look for ourselves. Then we had to check for our names. Someone sharp-eyed noticed that "Albrecht Anselm" was listed to dance Jack of "Jack and Jill" and the Knave in "The Tarts," which was either a monstrous typographical error or proof that Albert Wasserman had taken a stage name, for God's sake. Someone else noticed that the costumes had been "executed" by one "Madame Oleander" and this too provoked boisterous laughter.

"Who sold all these ads?" I asked Rachel Mintz. "There must be a thousand ads in this program."

"The Mothers," Rachel said indignantly. "Why, they've done so much they've just about killed themselves. And now they're going to usher, too!"

"I know, even *my* mother's an usher," I said.

"*My* mother's selling orangeade at intermission," Rachel said.

In fact, Mothers were everywhere, doing everything. Back in the old days, Mme LeBreton wouldn't let Mothers backstage at the recitals, just as she kept them out of the studio most of the time. But now, Mothers were a large component of the growing crowd backstage: they were running around at will with their hands on everything and everybody. It was not hard to imagine more Mothers out in the house industriously dividing up the programs (my own dignified mother right along with them!) and setting up the orangeade concession. Later on in college, when I read about Marie Antoinette and the ladies of her court playing at being milkmaids at Versailles, I thought of the lacquered and bejeweled Mothers out in the golden smoky halls of the Civic Auditorium during the intermission of *Mother Goose,* counting out change for twenty-five-cent cups of orangeade.

I was holding Marie, and finally when I couldn't hold her any longer (she suffered from this hubbub) I took her back to the dressing room, where I donned my dog suit and my makeup. I had some trouble with this. I would not have said I was nervous, at this point: I might have thought I was just jostled in the confusion of the dressing room when my eyeliner kept going jagged and my false eyelashes kept getting stuck somewhere up near my eyebrows, where they looked like those caterpillars that bother us in the spring. But I finally finished and, with my mask tucked under my arm, went on out to the stage with the vague idea of carrying out my duty to find some kind of ersatz barre and warm up.

But attention out there had shifted from the program to the audience. There was an agitated little crowd stage left, down by the curtain. At its nucleus were Lola and Stephanie, who were already in their costumes as two of the Three Blind Mice but who, rather ironically, I thought, could see with more than ordinary acuity because they had a small but apparently quite powerful telescope which they were wiggling around in a hole in the ancient velvet of the curtain.

"There's the Colonel!" Lola cried, twisting on the telescope to refine the vision.

"The Colonel!" everyone repeated, crowding up closer to the curtain. I had the fleeting idea that Lola, by means of that little instrument, was peering out into the Roundelay ball where the Confederates were dancing. I could even hear sabers rattling until I realized that the sound

I was hearing must be metal folding chairs being scraped by the people making their way through the rows of the Civic Auditorium's crude, removable "Orchestra Circle" and "Orchestra."

"God, there's my math teacher," Lola moaned.

"That's our neighbor across the street," Stephanie said, having seized the telescope. " And there's Mary Alice and Dixie and Matt! Matt came, y'all!"

"Matt came! Matt came!" chanted the crowd.

"Reverend Fowler," Lola announced, like a butler.

I certainly needn't have worried about nobody coming, I thought, feeling sick at my stomach. Lola and Stephanie went on with their relentless identifications, finding friends, relatives, and a number of public figures who were known to all of us cowering behind the curtain—the rector of the Episcopal Church, the mayor, a newscaster from one of the television stations, and the milkman whose route was in Gilbert Oaks. Lola thought she saw our representative to the United States Congress, but Stephanie disputed this.

"Hey, there's Paul!" Lola bawled. "He really came!"

"Paul?" I said, pushing forward through the crowd, some primordial nerve struck by this name. *"Paul? Paul who?"*

"Oh, Paul Wheeless," Lola tossed back, already poking the spyglass around in the hole for the next sighting.

"Paul Wheeless!" I said faintly, falling away from the spyhole. "That's not possible! It can't be Paul Wheeless," I said to someone in a sheep suit. I broke into a cold sweat, flabbergasted by this completely unexpected collision between my life at the studio and my life at school.

Well, there wasn't actually much to my life at school these days: I hardly thought about it. My mind reeling, I tried to think of the last time I had seen Paul Wheeless. Lordy mercy I couldn't even picture his face. But I had seen it just the day before, I was able to recall: I had seen him in the hall at school. I had handed him a draft of some proposed new rules for the code of student conduct, which was work I had done for that committee I was on in that other life. I had just dashed it off between numbers as I sat crumpled in the corner of the studio at a rehearsal, but he had not seemed to detect this haste, at least not in that first glance, and

I remembered that he had thanked me in a very gentlemanly way. Now I almost swooned, remembering the compliment to my industry. It hit me hard: Paul Wheeless was out there!—and here I was, dizzy in a dog suit.

Mme LeBreton came out on the stage and tried to sort things out with her stick, but I was hardly conscious of what was happening in the last hectic minutes before curtain time. I do know that the chief Mother, Mrs. James, came hallooing through the wings with Mrs. Elmira Schuster, the stout woman who for many years had written reviews of Middleton cultural events for the *Chronicle* under the name of "Clara Vere." I was too distracted to think much about this surprising attention to *Mother Goose* by the *Chronicle*. A commotion was made over Mrs. Schuster. Mr. Render appeared out of nowhere, dressed in his King costume. Clearly an old hand at this, he kissed Miss Vere's hand and, looking regal in his cape and crown, walked her around the chaos with an arm around her shoulder.

One more thing happened before the curtain went up. As if "Clara Vere" the *Chronicle* employee had been a lowly forerunner, a vague foreshadowing of the real thing, Mrs. Merrick herself entered the auditorium, along with her family. I did not go to the curtain to see this last great spotting for myself, but many did. It caused a number of sarcastic exclamations ("The nerve!" "The gall!" "Fine thing!") but not, I remember, from Hilary, who ran over and seized the spyglass and stayed at the hole with it as if she were glued there, the better to see Wendell or Wexler, I forget which one it was she was so in love with.

"I can't believe your mama came," someone said nervily to Christabel, who had come out into the fracas of dancers and scenery fluffing up her Horrid Little Girl dress.

"She wouldn't miss it for the world!" Christabel said, lynxeyed and smiling. Everybody just stared at Christabel, so lately Topsy on the other side of that curtain. Before this, I don't think any of us had appreciated just how horrid Christabel could be.

***

Our performance of *Mother Goose* went by in a kind of golden flash. But my mind was less on the ballet than on its audience, which by all indications was the entire city of Middleton. Of course once the curtain went up and the performance started, we could not see any individuals out there in the house, and the audience became an entity which took on a personality of its own. Happily this was a jolly personality, which expressed itself in long laughter and ready applause.

Lord, I was nervous. I spent the early part of Act One trembling in the wings. I was not the *most* nervous dancer in the wings: one of the little sheep waiting to go on threw up right by my feet and Dorcas, well, Dorcas was back in the bathroom having diarrhea of such velocity (as she told me later) that she very nearly missed her entrance as Miss Muffet's spider. But, broadly speaking, I was among the nervous ones and *not* one of those who seemed to enjoy this final crisis and even come into their own in it. Among these were the nerveless exhibitionists like Hilary and Lola and of course Christabel, but also more nearly normal people like Stephanie and Rachel, and any number of the smaller kids. With their makeup and costumes on, their smiles got so big you thought their jaws would break and their eyes lit up with a supernatural light when they moved out of the dark wings and onto the bright stage. Fortunately, since they were the stars of the show, both Claude and Cecilia were in this category. And I do not have to say that Mr. Render was like this with his bold, commanding smile, his uplifted arm; Mme LeBreton too threw herself into her dancing and her duties of supervision backstage like the seasoned old trouper she was.

Almost everything worked. Claude did his triple *tour en l'air* as Little Boy Blue with an offhandedness that made it seem as if he had been tossing them off all his life. Cecilia, though up close she looked a little green around the nostrils, did her dangerous leaps and lunges without that calamity called a miscarriage. The other soloists and the ensembles danced with vigor and aplomb. The costumes mostly held together, although "Madame Oleander" lurked in the wings with pins in her mouth and a threaded needle in her hand, waiting for seams to burst, and the orchestra held together too, sounding, I thought, as good as a record would have because they got most of the notes, also because they didn't stop every whipstitch, as we had been used to having them do, but sailed right on at a grand pace. The scenery usually worked right,

Humpty Dumpty's wall revolving after Bruce prodded it from the wings with a white tennis shoe. The lights played on all this effectively, if a bit luridly; and, most importantly, the fly system hauled Mme LeBreton, Mrs. Fister and the bovine Adelaide across the sky with no loss of life or limb. In fact, all of Mr. Render's theatrical tricks came off. Near the end, I was very gratified at the audience response to my twenty-four *écartés,* and little Dotty Winkle as Little Nanny Etticoat did her thirty-two *fouettés*—his canniest trick, I guess, out of all the tricks—to a roar of voices.

Not everything went right, of course. Actually, with all the mechanical perils like the rickety fly system and the teetering London Bridge to worry about, I forgot to worry about the dances. I watched without much anxiety as Albert ("Albrecht," rather) and Melissa started "Jack and Jill." This was the last number of Act One and a lot of us crowded into the wings to watch it. Albrecht took Melissa's hand and they began their progress up the "hill" (a *papier mâché* incline which, from up close like this, looked like an obstacle you'd find at a miniature golf place). He padded, his giant buttocks roiling in his tights, and Melissa, glassy-eyed with concentration, did her *piqué* turns around him. I do remember worrying that the toes of her toe shoes, which were darned like mine, would catch in the rough *papier-mâché* and that *she* would fall down first and spoil the storyline, but this did not happen: Melissa twirled competently around Albrecht as he labored up the "hill." Then Albrecht turned to Melissa and, with a set and dogged expression on his face and an audible "chuff, chuff," took hold of her and hoisted her up on his shoulder. As in the early days she missed his shoulder, going over it and landing on the stage like a hundred-pound sack of flour. The audience, which had a large maternal element in its jolly personality, said "Ooooh!" then laughed and applauded wildly as the curtain came down.

In the short interval before the curtain rose again for the bows Melissa kicked Albrecht smartly on the shin so that when the audience next saw him he was doubled over in pain. I do not know what the audience thought about these irregularities but it seemed to accept them joyfully as part of the fun. Nor do I know what Mr. Render or Mme LeBreton thought:

the performance was not like any of the rehearsals and nothing had any consequences, suddenly, but what the audience thought.

Another thing that caused some trouble was the cats. They did their part well enough in "St. Ives" and the audience seemed thrilled to have live cats on stage (they just "lapped it up," as my uncles in Ardis would say). After this I am afraid that in the heat of performance we rather neglected the cats, however. One of the wives and I had put them in their dressing room where once again they had dishes of food and water and a litter box and also probably a plethora of mice and the kinds of insects that inhabit dirty old buildings, but someone must have opened the door. During Act Two, just as Mr. Render-Old King Cole was miming his request for his fiddlers three, one of the kittens wandered out on stage. This too the audience lapped up. People kept finding the cats asleep in costumes or shoe boxes. "Lucille Grahn," who was more feisty than the others, hid behind the curtains which constituted the "wings" and pounced on several dancers, also Mrs. Oleander, who had a little fit, screaming "That thang lurped at me!" over and over until Mme LeBreton threatened to gag her. Most regrettably, one of the cats, possibly this same Lucille Grahn, got disoriented and mistook the resin box in the wings for the litter box. Hilary discovered this as she was stamping around in it before her solo as the horse in "This Is the Way the Lady Rides," and, in a very unladylike way, shouted coarsely, "God y'all, there's shit in the resin box," but not loudly enough, I think, to be heard in the Orchestra Circle.

***

But the evening was a triumph in spite of these things. Before long we were doing the throbbing finale, then falling to the floor to be tucked into bed by Mother Goose with the milk cartons of London Bridge rumbling noisily about us. Always before it had been hard to lie prone after the finale, as still as if we had been shot dead, but that night it was easy on account of the applause which seemed to roll over us and press us into place. What a gorgeous sound applause has!

Then the applause swelled dramatically, and I couldn't resist turning my head just enough to be able to see Mme LeBreton and Mr. Render taking the first bows. They stood hand in hand, and, in the instant I saw them, were busy looking at each other in the enraptured, adoring way partners in the dance look at each other when they're taking their bows. Nobody would suspect they had had such a terrible fight only the day before yesterday. Why, they looked like lovers, and I remember thinking at the time that they would probably get married now—though that certainly didn't follow from what I had witnessed at the studio; it just seemed inevitable all of a sudden from the way they stood bowing together under the hot lights. Mme LeBreton took deep curtsies, rather, and Mr. Render kissed her hand and devoured her with his eyes. They were obviously a couple that was bound together by something very strong: at the very least, a love for the dance. Clearly they loved the dance! And how Middleton loved them! A few times during the year I wouldn't have been surprised if Middleton had spat upon Mme LeBreton and Mr. Render, or run them out of town—they certainly didn't belong here!—but now Middleton was on its feet, cheering them. Somehow they were important in their passions; it was only proper that Middleton should exalt them.

But soon we were up and taking our bows, and Nathan and Mr. Beldinsky and even "Madame Oleander" came out, and then the flowers started: bouquets brought from the wings, then wild, random floral tributes flung from the house, with the applause and the cheers continuing all the while.

***

Afterward, so many people crowded backstage to congratulate us on the performance that I didn't have the opportunity to change out of my dog suit, though I was very hot in it; I just had to stand there shaking hand after hand and accepting congratulations on the performance. This was even more rigorous than climbing the stairs at Middleton High School saying "Hi!" "Hi!" "Hi!" because I was shaking hands with everybody (thinking every second, though, of Paul Wheeless, who was somewhere in that crowd and might come up to me next). So many people came back, in fact, that it seemed like some kind of dream where everybody you know or have ever known in the past files by to see you—a dream about your own funeral, for instance—and I had the impression that people were lined up all the way back around the smoky horseshoe corridor of the Civic Auditorium, waiting to get backstage and pay their respects. In a haze I saw all manner of friends and acquaintances: my old piano teacher, a group of girls I used to play with in the fifth and sixth grades, even the Indian couple from down the street. (The man introduced himself to me as Dr. Azziza and said he had often seen me riding my "leetle red biseekle" while his wife, wearing a sari and looking more like an exotic member of the cast than a member of the audience, just smiled mysteriously.) The Masters came back. I hugged Danna, and Mr. Masters kissed my hand with Mrs. Masters standing by, saying, "It was grand, Meredith, simply *grand."*

The Masters passed on to other dancers who were classmates of Danna and Evelyn—Rachel, Lola, Adelaide, oh, everybody was backstage still in costume receiving people, and I realized that we had instinctively formed a receiving line. Middleton has a lot of receptions for one thing and another—weddings, graduations, debuts—and later when I was involved in some of these things I thought about what it was like backstage after the performance of *Mother Goose* when the cast "received" Middleton. Of course the people in the audience were much more varied than a guest list at a reception. The most surprising evidence of this to me was the appearance of a carload of my relatives from Ardis. They hadn't told us they were coming, and my parents brought them back, my mother in an intense state of mock indignation.

"Look who's here, Meredith Louise," she said, exhibiting Uncle James and Aunt Lucy and some other folks from Ardis. "Why, I might not even have *seen* 'em if I hadn't been an usher." Uncle James, who would be taller than anyone else in the crush even without his Stetson on, looked around him with a wry glare.

"We didn't want to put y'all out any," my Aunt Lucy said. She was a small woman who was only three or four years older than my mother but who looked at least ten years older, possibly because of her crimped, old-timey hairdo rather like Madame Oleander's. She was a little plump, too, and in the black speckled dress she had on she looked like a little country hen.

"Well that's ridiculous," my mother said, as if offended, although I knew she admired, even expected, this kind of scrupulosity in her relatives. "You've got to stay over. We've got *worlds* of room at the house."

"Nope," my Uncle James said with cheerful obstinacy, looking out over the heads of everyone, smacking his lips. "I've got to milk at five. I'd have to be on the road by three. I don't expect you'd like to make my coffee at two-thirty, would you, Caroline? I don't expect Caroline would like that, would she?" he said, seeking corroboration from his wife and the other folks from Ardis, who knew that my mother was a lady lawyer and not a regular housewife.

"Naw, we just come over to see Meredith Louise do her pie-roots. She did a mighty fine job. Last time I saw anybody jump as high as Meredith Louise was when the Cates boy put the firecrackers under that old hound dawg the Cateses had and that dawg went about fourteen feet up'n th'air," Uncle James said, in a humorous drawl.

I smiled and blushed because this was a very high compliment, from him, and for a few moments my parents and my aunts and uncles continued to jest in this vein. Then they began to argue about whether the Ardis people would stop by our house before the drive back home, which was apparently inevitable. Our house was "way out of the way," being so far down Tates Parkway as to be almost across town; on the other hand, it wouldn't take more than forty-five minutes to drive back to Ardis, since the highway that goes from Middleton to Ardis and then on across Texas would be empty at this hour except for a few trucks. Just thinking about that stretch of cotton fields and oil fields (which would be dark except for the red lights of the radio towers about half way) made you feel sleepy, so my mother was insisting that they come to the house for a pot of coffee.

During this badinage the crowd was thinning very quickly the way crowds do after a performance, as if the auditorium were going to sink, or turn into a pumpkin, and suddenly I caught sight of Mr. Render and Mme LeBreton, standing over by the Old Woman's giant shoe-house still, like me, in their sweaty costumes. They looked worn out, but I didn't have time to think anymore about *them,* being too shocked at who was with them: none other than the Merricks!

"Look, Mother!" I said, nudging our side's lawyer, but she was too busy carrying on with Uncle James and Aunt Lucy.

I stared unbelievingly at Lyda and Buckingham Merrick, and old Mrs. Merrick *(not* Wendell and Wexler, however, who I guess had already roared off into the night with Hilary and Stephanie, if they had come at all). Why, Mr. and Mrs. Merrick had been reported as being out of town only the night before, and it seemed to me it would have been the decent thing for them to stay out of town during the brave and independent performance of *Mother Goose,* but here they were, lingering afterward with Mr. Render and Mme LeBreton as if they were family! I could not hear what they were saying because of the wrangle among the Merediths and Jacksons taking place around me, and sometimes even my view of them was blocked by pieces of scenery being trucked out by Bruce and the others, but they appeared to be talking very amiably, as if there had never been a "knock-down-drag-out." Possibly this was because the sweet little old dried-up mother was there (Mrs. Merrick the elder): she had the air of being protected and sequestered and was looking around brightly as if she didn't get out very much, and it is possible that having the cocktail party at her house the previous fall was a nice memory for her that they didn't want to spoil with the sordid details of the breakdown of the alliance that came out of it (just as they wouldn't tell a sweet little old lady of that advanced age if a favorite nephew died or got a divorce, or anything that Wendell and Wexler did). Or, on the other hand, possibly Mme LeBreton and Mr. Render and Lyda Merrick did not feel any rancor anymore, or had made up their quarrel in meetings I did not know anything about.

In any case, they stood talking in what looked like fonder accord than that among my family, which hadn't had any breeches or quarrels so far as I knew on account of that mysterious affinity that comes from "thinking" alike. Well, perhaps Mr. Render and Mme LeBreton and the Merricks thought alike too, when all was said and done. Just then Christabel ran up, still in her cat suit from "Hey Diddle Diddle," and hugged Mr. Render passionately, kissing him on the cheek and making him laugh one of his long laughs. This reminded me how when Mr. Render first came to Middleton and stayed out at the Merricks' Christabel had been "in love" with him, as grown-ups say, and had carried off his wineglasses and hidden them in her room, refusing to give them back. As I watched Christabel now I thought at first that she was throwing herself at Mr. Render because she loved him so much and wanted him to take her with him when he left, which had to be soon, but then I realized that this was not the hug of someone who was "in love." Christabel's eyes were wide open, for one thing, and I saw that hugging Mr. Render in her cat suit was just Christabel's latest adventure, the next stunt after Topsy, and not by any means would it be the last.

I was not the only one who had noticed this group. Suddenly I became aware that my Aunt Lucy was debating with my mother about whether she, my aunt, should go over and speak to Lyda Merrick, who had been her classmate Lyda Miller at the branch of the state university in Barston. My mother was trying to encourage her to do it if she wanted to, while Aunt Lucy, who seemed to regard this as an unpleasant but unavoidable duty, hung back because she doubted Lyda Miller would ever remember *her*. But suddenly Aunt Lucy broke out of our group and quick-stepped over to their group. My heart stopped, I think, as I witnessed what I thought of, even then, as the most incongruous juxtaposition I had seen that night, even more incongruous than the pastor of the First Baptist Church shaking hands with Claude in his Little Boy Blue costume, or Mr. Oleander kissing the cheek of Mrs. James. I suppose my Aunt Lucy and Lyda Merrick started out much the same way, one in Ardis, the other in Natchitoches, but they certainly had ended up in different places, if appearances count for anything. Lyda Merrick had on a blue-gray silk suit that looked like it came from Paris or at least New York, and her hair was in that smooth golden chignon; my Aunt Lucy, on the other hand, had on a black print rayon dress that she wore to the Ardis Methodist Church (a Sunday-go-to meetin' dress, as they'd jokingly say there), and *her* hair, which was brown and short, had a home permanent in it so that it looked like chicken feathers. Now, I do not want to create the impression that Aunt Lucy was an ignorant country person, because like my other relatives in Ardis Aunt Lucy drove over to Middleton often and (by means of the *Chronicle)* knew as much about what was going on in town as the people who lived there. Nor do I want to give the impression that I thought she was what they call a hick and was ashamed of her, because this was not at all the case. I am simply saying that here was a moment when one of my people from Ardis took it into her head to go over and talk to the Queen of Middleton, thus leaping the distance between the two farthermost points on my private conceptual map of the area, and that there was an open and undeniable contrast between them of country simplicity and urban glamour, plain enough for anybody to see.

"I don't think Lyda'll remember Lucy," Mother said to me in a melancholy voice, observing their convergence.

But I guess she did. After giving my Aunt Lucy a blank but gracious look, Mrs. Merrick did some pretty exclaiming and the two women hugged each other.

"Meredith!" someone was calling as I watched this. "Meredith! I was looking all over for you. You did great!"

I turned to see Alma Doyle with her arms thrown out to hug me. She had on a black suit and a little black hat with a veil through which her eyes and face were shining. I believe I would have known she was pregnant from this first sight of her even if she had not already told me. Unlike Cecilia, who might look more ordinary to me now but who did not look particularly pregnant, Alma looked manifestly maternal now, you might even say matronly, even though her stomach still looked flat under the little straight skirt of the suit. Alma hugged me hard, flattening my face against the little veil over her face, which felt both sharp and slippery, like fishing line; then she pushed me away to get a full view of me in my costume.

She still held on to me with one hand while looking me over, though, and with the other she brought forward a slight, dark-haired man in a suit of a bold and wrong-headed plaid. "Meredith, this is my Tom," she said joyfully.

"Tom" nodded stiffly. "That's not Tom!" I almost said, since I was so startled not to see the tall blond athlete with the crew cut (the "guy"). The real Tom was small and wore glasses; even worse, his complexion showed the traces of acne and his hair was already thinning on top.

"Meredith was my very best friend at the studio, honey," Alma was saying. "Can't she jump well? We always said she was a wonderful jumper."

Tom looked at me coldly, as if I were responsible for a burned dinner or some other domestic inconvenience. In defiance of this I said, "Why don't you come back and take, Alma? We miss you!"

Alma took a step back, giving me a merry and incredulous look from behind the veil. "With the Baby? That's not possible! I won't have a minute with the Baby! Of course if it's a little girl *she* can take in a few years. But Tom wants a little boy. Tom," Alma asserted proudly, "wants five boys, enough for a basketball team."

Jerky old Tom, I thought, as Alma pressed me to come see the baby after it was born, just as if we had been the closest of friends. But when I said good-bye to her it was with the sure knowledge that I would never see her again. It was over! I think it hit me for the first time that *Mother Goose* was over when I said good-bye to poor old Alma and watched her walk away with jerky old Tom. "I'd better run get my costumes," I said to Mother, who seemed to have come to some understanding with our relatives from Ardis since the group was now shifting and surging in a way that signaled departure, and my father and Uncle James were rattling their car keys in their pockets.

"Don't you need me to help?" Mother called out after me as I ran through the few people left backstage and the remaining pieces of scenery, feeling sad. Suddenly I was filled with a kind of blankness, unable to imagine what life would be like now. Everything would scatter to the four winds; it would be a long, long time before all these people and all these things—all these different forces—could be brought together in one place again. I felt desolate, like Humpty Dumpty after the fall.

I believe I had forgotten about Paul Wheeless when I got to the corridor where my dressing room was and, going down it, glanced into another dressing room and saw Paul Wheeless actually standing there, with two Mothers and two little dancers in flower costumes loading him up with the paraphernalia of the performance. He did not, I believe, see me. Lordy mercy! I thought, uttering the Ardis oath, starting to run down the hall, forgetting all about that desolation. I raced to a mirror in my dressing room, where I peered frantically at my face. Could I change clothes? He had looked almost fully loaded so *no;* besides, I looked pretty cute in the dog suit, I decided after a quick *plié* to get a full-length view. I'd have to hurry! I snatched up my other two costumes and the other toe shoes and looked desperately around for Marie, who proved to be asleep under a wad of tissue paper, then ran back into the hall, dovetailing neatly into the little procession made by the group with Paul Wheeless in it, which was going down the hall. Why, one of those little girls must be Paul Wheeless's little sister! Was it possible that his little sister "took" from Mme LeBreton without my knowing it? Of course it was possible: all nicely brought up little girls in Middleton took ballet from Mme LeBreton at one time or another.

Here followed some nerve-wracking moments as Paul Wheeless's family and that other little dancer's family and *my* family, including the Ardis contingent, got themselves organized and moving toward the stage door. To my horror, Paul Wheeless's people moved faster than my people, who were talking more, and some of them went out of the door first, but then some of mine went out of it, and I saw that Paul was holding the door for them. It was a very heavy fire door, with one of those clunking bars across it to open it, and because he was so polite Paul Wheeless got stuck there holding it open for the whole herd of people (his *and* mine) until—oh, glory—*I* passed through, managing somehow to say hello.

"Well hi, Meredith," he said as we stepped together into the cool night air. "I looked for you earlier! Congratulations on your dancing. You were really good."

"Thanks," I said, ravished.

"Why, was that your kitten?" he said, looking at Marie, whom I must have been half-strangling. "The cats were really cute!"

"You know I didn't even know you *took* dancing," said Paul, who was wearing a suit and looked very manly in the night. "You should have told me! I would never have asked you to do those rules the other day."

"It was nothing," I said honestly.

"That's amazing," he said, looking down at me very intently. "You must've been working yourself to death these last few months. I know at *our* house all we've heard about is *Mother Goose* from Mary Alice. She hasn't been able to think about anything else. But *you,*" he said, "you do so much at school!"

The families were now fanned out from the auditorium, going toward their cars in the parking lot which lay across a little private street. We started walking across the street, and Paul Wheeless took the elbow of my dog suit in a gentlemanly way to protect me from injury by traffic, even though there wasn't any.

"Oh a lot of us have been doing it—Cecilia, Lola, Claude," I said with modesty.

He shook his head. "They're not *real* workers. I'm talking about the people who really shoulder the load at Middleton. I was talking to Anne Markham about you at intermission a while ago. She was telling me about all the work you've done on the *Merrymaker* this year."

"Really?" I said dreamily, smitten in the face by the coolness of the night air. I had not realized how extremely hot and stuffy it had been inside the auditorium.

"You'll be staff next year. I guess you saw those *Merrymaker* people here tonight. Anne's writing it up."

"Yes, yes, I think I did," I said, since I thought I had seen everyone in the whole city. I was going out of my head a little, I think, talking to Paul Wheeless like this out in the night. I was ready to describe how Middleton had mixed itself all up together this evening, and how his being there was arguably the wildest ingredient in this peculiar mix, wilder even than my relatives from Ardis, but then I saw that my parents were at the Chevrolet. My mother's head stuck up above the roof; she was looking for me.

"I'm glad I saw you—I've been meaning to talk to you," Paul said. "You know Student Council elections are coming up soon, and I've been looking for a really dependable freshman to help me with my campaign for president. Do you think it's possible you'd have time? We'd have to meet and plan strategy, organize poster parties, design handbills—"

"Oh *yes,*" I said passionately.

"Great," said Paul. "I hoped you'd say that. I might as well tell you we were saying how likely it is you'll be nominated for a Student Council office next year. I hope you'll have time."

"Oh!" I cried. "Oh I'm sure I will," I said, the stars reeling in the sky. I backed slowly away from Paul Wheeless toward my car. "Anyway, I don't think I'll be taking ballet next year," I said without thinking, blushing in surprise.

***

There was a cast party following the performance that night at Mme LeBreton's studio, but there was no question of our stopping there because the folks from Ardis had agreed to come by our house for just a minute. But even if they had not, I do not think I could have gotten my parents to stop. We already had a good idea what this party was going to be like: backstage, Nathan Feldman and the New York musicians—in particular a disorderly French horn player and an equally rough percussionist— had been celebrating the success of the evening's music by guzzling champagne out of Dixie cups and even shaking up the champagne in the bottle and squirting each other with it. It was plain to me that the people at the party weren't going to think like we did and that it would be better to head on down Sycamore Street and go home. Anyway, by the time we passed the studio that night I had practically forgotten about the cast party, my mind being taken up with the wonder of walking with Paul Wheeless, and I only barely noticed that the little studio was ablaze with light and pulsating with music from the record player or possibly from instruments in the hands of the wild New Yorkers. I could hardly wait to get my relatives on the road to Ardis and go up to my room and think about Paul Wheeless. I also had to think about what I had told him—about not taking ballet anymore, I mean. I had astonished myself, saying that: I had never even thought that before, much less said it; it had just popped out of me from somewhere. Even so, I knew that it was true and that whatever was happening back there at the studio, and whatever would happen in the future, would have to happen without me.

***

Curiously enough, for many years what I remembered about the night we performed *Mother Goose* was not the dancing but the people I saw backstage after the performance was finished; then of course I remembered going out the stage door with Paul Wheeless, when—I see, looking back on it—I seemed to turn a corner in my life and go in a different direction. It happened all of a sudden: I was going one way as hard as I could, then I simply turned and went another way. But a good number of the people who took part in *Mother Goose* continued in the same direction: I think of Claude, who became a leading dancer with NDT, where he is still going strong in roles calling for ferocity; and Nathan, of course, who is in that elite of conductors who have multiple jobs and spend half the time in a jet going from one great orchestra to another; and most of the dancers, who did not stay dancers but went on to become Mothers of other little dancers, which counts for something. I think of Cecilia, the Daphne-Aphrodite who continued on her destined course of being someone's beloved, in the process of which she would also be a wife and mother, possibly even a Mother; and Hilary and Stephanie, who were Daphne-Aphrodites too—indeed, Daphnes with a yellow Pontiac to speed them on their way.

Of course not everyone was set on a straight and triumphant course that night. I am thinking of Albert Wasserman—the "Albrecht Anselm" that was. As my mother and father and Marie and I drove away from the auditorium I saw him walking down the sidewalk of Captain Frick Street. I hardly noticed him at the time, being so preoccupied with everything that had just happened to me, but later, as I sat on my window seat by the open window in my room, in the dark, I spared a thought or two for poor Albert. There were some strange aspects to his solitary flight from the auditorium. Where was that mother of his, the actress-dental hygienist? Come to think of it, I hadn't seen her at the dress rehearsal or the performance, times when *any* mother—even my mother!—would be in anxious attendance. Why, I had even seen Claude's mother (a surprisingly normal-looking individual, as it turned out). And where were Albert's costumes? Everybody else came out of the auditorium burdened with costumes while he strode down the street in the dim light of the streetlights empty-handed.

Albert Wasserman walked into a well-deserved oblivion, as far as I know, but through the years I have heard about most of the other people who took part in that night. Mr. Render and Mme LeBreton did not in fact get married. The truth of the matter being that Mme LeBreton was very ill at the time and did not have long to live. But Mr. Render did come back to Middleton, in time, and his Middleton Dance Theatre, which is based in a fine new studio on the site of Madame's old place and performs regularly at the Merrick Theater, is a bustling little regional company today. His *Mother Goose* is a favorite all over the country, not just in Middleton. But the things I heard or read about Mme LeBreton or Mr. Render after that time have never seemed as real to me as the events of that year I have been telling about, and I always think of them as they were the night of the first performance of *Mother Goose*. I have the clearest picture of how they looked when it was over and they were taking their first bows: I guess they could not really have looked this way, but I remember them as two giant figures, dark against the hot light of the footlights, almost monumental; that is to say, far away, immutable, inscrutable, and permanent, as adults always seem to the very young.

Made in the USA
Columbia, SC
16 June 2019